"Forgive me, Madame ... stallions and dancing Gypsies ... frighten you ... what does, if I may ask?"

Wild, untamed men. Men who exude virility and strength.
When she didn't answer directly, the viscount raised a brow. "Do *I* frighten you?"

Phoebe felt in danger of falling into those eyes, of becoming completely lost in them. She could imagine women all over England melted inside with just a look from him. "You? *No!*" she said with a smile that hid her melting. "Oh no! Not in the least ..." She paused and peered at him. "Unless I *should* be frightened of you?"

⸙

USA Today bestselling author Julia London creates a world of daring passions and dangerous loyalties in her wonderful Desperate Debutantes novels.

"A charming Regency twist on the story of *Beauty and the Beast.*"
—*Publishers Weekly* on *The Perils of Pursuing a Prince*

"Witty, spicy, and funny ... will have readers lining up for the sequels."
—*Library Journal* on *The Hazards of Hunting a Duke*

The Dangers of Deceiving a Viscount
is also available as an eBook

The Dangers of Deceiving a Viscount

The DANGERS of DECEIVING a VISCOUNT

JULIA LONDON

POCKET BOOKS

New York   London   Toronto   Sydney

Pocket Books
A Division of Simon & Schuster, Inc.
1230 Avenue of the Americas
New York, NY 10020

This Pocket Books trade paperback edition January 2010

POCKET and colophon are registered trademarks of Simon & Schuster, Inc.

For information about special discounts for bulk purchases, please contact Simon & Schuster Special Sales at 1-866-506-1949 or business@simonandschuster.com.

The Simon & Schuster Speakers Bureau can bring authors to your live event. For more information or to book an event contact the Simon & Schuster Speakers Bureau at 1-866-248-3049 or visit our website at www.simonspeakers.com.

Manufactured in the United States of America

10 9 8 7 6 5 4 3 2 1

ISBN 978-1-4391-8718-0
ISBN 978-1-4165-5290-1 (ebook)

For my mother, who taught me to dream.
For my father, who taught me to go for it.
For my steps, for supporting me
as if I were one of their own.

The DANGERS of DECEIVING a VISCOUNT

Prologue

―――∞∞∞―――

1822

Wiliam Darby, Viscount Summerfield, Baron Ivers, rode the last mile to Wentworth Hall full bore. The letter from his father's secretary was in his breast pocket, stained red by the sands of the Egyptian desert, smelling of salt from the passage across the Mediterranean, and tattered at the folds from Will's frequent reading of it.

The earl has suffered a terrible fit of apoplexy that has left him paralyzed. You are needed at home, sir.

In the six years since Will had left Wentworth Hall to take his grand tour of Europe—a tour his father had urged a restless young man of two and twenty to take before duty and responsibility claimed him—he'd received many letters from his father. In the first letters, the earl had exulted in the sights Will had seen and the adventures he'd experienced, as related weekly in a letter home. The tour was supposed to have lasted two years, but Will had gone on to India instead of coming home as expected, and his father's letters had changed in tone. While the earl still enjoyed the tales of Will's travels, he often reminded his son of his responsibility to his family and as the future Earl of Bedford, and asked him to come home.

Will always wrote that he would, and truly, he always meant to come home. But invariably he'd meet a fellow traveler who would feed his wanderlust with a tale of the Himalayas or searching for treasure in the oases of Africa, and Will would be off again.

In the last two years, his father's letters had cajoled and pleaded with Will to come home and marry as he ought, to provide an heir before it was too late, before the earl was gone. His father professed a longing to hold his grandchild in his arms. Will was confident he would fulfill that wish, but he believed there was ample time for marrying and fathering children.

Then had come the last letter from Mr. Carsdale, the earl's secretary. It was delivered to Will in a Bedouin tent by his loyal manservant, Addison, who had been with him since his eighteenth year and had traveled the world with him regardless of whether he liked it or not. Addison had come from Cairo on a Bedouin train and was wearing a *kaffiyeh* wrapped around his head, his clothing and eyes red from the stinging sand. When Will read the letter, the words seemed to sag on the vellum under the weight of what they related.

He'd left Egypt at once, of course. He'd taken the arduous Bedouin route to the sea, and had booked passage on a ship that sailed through a stormy sea and the Straits of Gibraltar, which had almost cost him his life when the clipper was shipwrecked. It had taken him three months to reach England's shores. Another week was spent purchasing a horse and arranging to have his things and Addison sent to Wentworth Hall, and yet another week riding across the rain-soaked English countryside.

At last, Will and Fergus—the Welsh pony he'd acquired—were riding up the lane to the majestic hall that had housed his ancestors for centuries. The sight of the mansion warmed his heart. It was built in the shape of an H, and stood four stories high. Ivy covered the corners, and row upon row of six-foot paned windows looked out across the woodlands, the deer park, and the fields where the estate's sheep and cattle grazed.

He reined to a hard stop in the drive, surprised and unsettled that no footman or groom hurried to attend him. Will flung himself off Fergus, shoved his cloak over his shoulder, and reached for the letter. Clutching it in his gloved hand, he vaulted up the steps to the double-door entry, flung them open, and strode inside.

The foyer was empty. *Completely* empty—devoid of furniture and accoutrements. The only things left were the very large paintings of mythical scenes that filled an entire wall. Will walked on, vaulting up the stairs to the family rooms on the first floor. But as he reached the first-floor landing, he stopped, unable to comprehend what he was seeing. A broken chair was lying on its side. Papers were strewn across the carpet as if they'd been scattered by wind. A large black area in the carpet appeared to be the result of a burn, and the candles in their wall sconces had been left too long, the wax having melted onto the silk wall coverings and the carpet beneath them.

Stunned, Will moved on, pausing to look in every room and finding them in the same condition. The rooms smelled musty, as if they had not been aired in months. The sitting room was strewn with trash and books and, inexplicably, ladies' shoes. In the grand salon, furniture had been shoved up against the walls and it looked as if a game of lawn bowling had been interrupted, with balls scattered across the floor and a porcelain vase lying in pieces.

He reached the library last. In that room, books were out of their shelves and stacked in various configurations; a thick layer of dust on the floor was marked with foot traffic.

Will turned slowly in a circle, taking it all in, trying to make sense of it. As he turned toward the hearth, where a mound of blankets had been piled, he caught sight of a figure rising from the chaise longue. It was a young woman whom he'd obviously awakened. She stood up, blinking at him. Her gown was too small for her lanky frame and it looked rather old. Her hair was pinned awkwardly to the back of her head, and her blue eyes were the only spots of color in her pale face. But something struck him as familiar, and Will squinted at her. *"Alice?"*

The woman did not respond, but he was certain it was his sister standing before him. She had been eleven years of age when he'd left home, a little wisp of a girl who'd followed him about and peppered him with endless questions or begged him to take her riding or to play with her in the garden.

"Who's there?" a hoarse male voice demanded, piercing the silence.

It appeared that what Will had believed to be a pile of blankets was actually another person. That person came up on his elbows, knocking over an empty glass when he did, and blinked in Will's direction.

"I think it is our brother," Alice said uncertainly, staring curiously at Will.

"Who?" the young man asked, pushing himself up and struggling to his feet. It was no easy task. His shirt-tail was hanging to his knees, his trousers were covered

in dust, and the rest of his clothing was in the pile of blankets, for all Will knew. His hair was standing on end and he had the scraggly growth of an unshaved beard.

"Joshua," Will said, looking at his brother, the sibling who was closest to his own age, who'd been only fourteen when he'd left. "Do you not know me?"

"Will! What are you doing here?" Joshua demanded, peering closely at him. "Who sent for you?"

"Did you not receive my letters?" Will said, moving cautiously forward. "Where is everyone? Where are the servants?"

With a snort and a flick of his wrist, Joshua said, "Gone. They've not been paid in ages. Only Farley and Cook remain."

"And Jacobs, the footman who tends Father," Alice offered, still eyeing Will curiously. She stood self-consciously, her arms folded tightly about her. "Are you to stay here?"

"You won't want to remain here, I assure you," Joshua said. He took an unsteady step and knocked over a bottle of amber liquid that spread across the floorboards and into the blankets where he had been sleeping. Neither he nor Alice seemed to notice it.

This was wrong. This was terribly, horribly wrong. "Where is Father?" Will asked in a sudden panic.

"Father? Where is he ever?" Joshua asked. "In his suite, of course."

Will dared not ask after his two youngest siblings, Roger and Jane. He just turned and strode from the library, his footfall matching the rhythm of his rapidly beating heart. As he hurried to the master suite, his crime became clearer. *He'd stayed away too long.*

Will rapped hard on the door of the master suite, and was reaching for the handle when the door suddenly opened. An enormous bear of a man dressed in shirt-sleeves and waistcoat peered suspiciously at Will. "Who are you, then?"

"I am Summerfield, the earl's son. Where is my father?"

The man's eyes widened, but he opened the door and bowed his head at the same time. "Just there, milord," he said, pointing.

Will swept past him. The room smelled of ointments and smoke; the drapes had been pulled shut, save one window, which provided only dim light. Yet it was enough light to see his father in the shadows. "*Dear God*," he muttered in horror.

His father was seated in a wheelchair. A lap rug had been draped across his legs, and his hands, bent with apparent uselessness, were folded together in his lap. His head lolled unnaturally to one side.

But as Will drew near, the Earl of Bedford lifted his gaze, and in those wet gray eyes Will saw the light of recognition shimmer.

"Papa," Will said. The earl moved his lips strangely, but no sound came forth, and Will realized he could not speak. Grief dealt him a crushing blow. With the letter still clutched in his hand, he fell to his knees and pressed his cheek against his father's bony knees. He'd stayed away too long and any apology he could make was not enough.

It would never be enough.

One

In the back room of the smart Bond Street boutique, Mrs. Ramsey's Haute Couture Dress Shoppe, Lady Phoebe Fairchild stood among dozens of gowns made of China silk, velvet, satin, and muslin, gaping in disbelief as Mrs. Ramsey calmly explained that her reputation, the future of her dress shop, and indeed her livelihood depended on Phoebe's ability to deliver gowns.

When the tall and cadaverously thin woman had finished, Phoebe was dumbstruck. No words would come, no coherent thought, no stinging retort.

"If you are unable to do as I ask, Lady Phoebe," Mrs. Ramsey said, "I shall have no choice but to expose you to the entire *ton*."

Phoebe gasped. "Madam, what you are suggesting is *blackmail*!"

Mrs. Ramsey smiled, her lips all but disappearing behind tiny teeth. "*Blackmail* is a harsh word. *Charlatan*, *imposter* . . . now *there* are two words that are not harsh enough . . . *Madame Dupree*." She cocked one brow high above the other, letting the words fill the air around them.

Phoebe could not think. She felt entirely incapable of it. The business of making gowns—the very thing Mrs. Ramsey had threatened to expose—was a plan Phoebe had hatched with her sister Ava and her cousin Greer two years ago. It was a plan that had been born out of desperation after the untimely death of Phoebe and Ava's mother, Lady Downey. Their stepfather, Lord Downey, had commandeered their inheritance and had made it plain he would marry them to the first men to offer. The three of them had quickly determined they needed money to put in motion *their* plan for avoiding such a fate. Ava had determined to marry well, Greer had gone in search of an inheritance, and Phoebe . . . well, Phoebe had talent with a needle. It was the only thing she had to offer.

She'd always been talented with a needle, and made a hobby of making gowns for the three of them, or enhancing the ones they bought in exclusive Bond Street shops such as this one. The spring her mother had died, Phoebe had latched onto an idea. What if she took the gowns from her late mother's closet and refashioned them into lovely ball gowns to be sold? Ava and Greer had agreed—it would bring in some sorely needed money.

There was only one small problem: to enter the business of making gowns would give the appearance to the rest of the *ton* that they were desperate—which, obviously, they were. But the *ton* would flee from desperate debutantes and their prospects would be reduced to nothing.

So they had invented a reclusive *modiste*—Madame Dupree—and had introduced Madame Dupree's work to Mrs. Ramsey. They claimed the French *modiste* was in much demand in Paris, but, tragically, had been made lame and disfigured in a carriage accident, and therefore could not and *would* not go out in society. Phoebe had very graciously offered to act as the liaison between Mrs. Ramsey and Madame Dupree. If Mrs. Ramsey would provide her customers' precise measurements, Madame Dupree would make gowns that would delight them and be highly praised by the ladies of the *ton*.

It seemed the perfect ruse, and, indeed, to Phoebe's way of thinking, it had worked very well for two years.

Until today.

Until today, Phoebe had no inkling that Mrs. Ramsey suspected she was Madame Dupree. Apparently, the shopkeeper had suspected it for some time, for when Phoebe delivered two gowns that afternoon, Mrs. Ramsey had locked the door of her shop and then asked Phoebe if she could arrange a meeting with Madame Dupree.

That was the moment Phoebe had felt the first curl of doom in her belly. "Oh, I'm very sorry, Mrs. Ramsey. I'm afraid that's not possible," she'd said as congenially as she could.

"After all this time?" Mrs. Ramsey asked haughtily. "Surely she trusts me by now, Lady Phoebe. I have a very lucrative proposition for her—and she certainly seems to accept *you* readily enough. Why do you suppose that is?"

Phoebe had been so flustered she did not respond. She could not recall a time Mrs. Ramsey had been anything but courteous—but now the woman folded her bone-thin arms over her woefully flat chest, narrowed her eyes beneath a row of tiny pin curls, and said, "I know perfectly well what you are about and I am fully prepared to tell the world of your scandal."

"What *I* am about?" Phoebe echoed with a desperate laugh as the sense of doom coiled tighter. "I assure you, I am about nothing other than delivering the two gowns you commissioned from Madame Dupree."

"And where, precisely, does Madame Dupree buy the fabric needed for the gowns she makes? Or do you do that for this poor disfigured woman as well?"

It had gone from bad to worse. Phoebe was woefully bad at lying and stumbled through her every response until Mrs. Ramsey had cut her off with an ultimatum: either Phoebe take on the account she had just established with a Lord Summerfield of Bedfordshire for an unheard-of number of gowns and other articles of clothing or Mrs. Ramsey would expose Phoebe's deceit to the world.

It seemed this Lord Summerfield—a name that Phoebe had never heard before—was the son of the ailing Earl of Bedford. He'd recently returned from abroad and discovered his sisters had not been properly presented to society. Toward that end, he'd ordered new wardrobes for them both. He was prepared to pay a premium to have them done by late autumn: two thousand pounds.

Two thousand pounds.

Mrs. Ramsey practically drooled with glee when she reported the agreed-upon sum and made it quite clear she would not lose it merely because Phoebe had invented Madame Dupree and was the one who was *really* behind the gowns all the women of the *ton* suddenly could not do without. Mrs. Ramsey had already promised Lord Summerfield that she would send Madame Dupree to Wentworth Hall in a fortnight to make the clothing she could not readily provide from her shop. Her only problem being, of course, that Madame Dupree did not exist.

Nevertheless, Phoebe insisted she would *not* hie herself off to Bedfordshire as a servant to anyone.

"Indeed?" Mrs. Ramsey drawled. "I do not think your esteemed family would appreciate such a scandal at this point in their political lives—do you, Lady Phoebe?"

Phoebe gasped. Mrs. Ramsey was referring, of course, to the very thing Ava and Greer had feared most when they had tried to convince Phoebe to stop making the gowns this past Season. As they were both married now, and to very wealthy men at that, they no longer needed the money Phoebe's clandestine sartorial occupation brought her. *Particularly* not now that their lord husbands, Middleton and Radnor, had been moved by their wives' work with the Ladies' Beneficent Society, a charitable organization that endeavored to help women who had landed in the poorhouse. Middleton and Radnor had drafted and proposed reforms that would give women who were forced to earn their livings some basic and decent rights. But opponents of the reforms saw such measures as opening the door to other untenable actions, such as woman suffrage and, God forbid, *temperance.*

A scandalous exposure of Phoebe's deceit would bode ill for her brothers-in-law, and might cause the derailment of reforms they were trying to steer through Parliament.

"You wouldn't!" Phoebe cried. "You are a woman in trade, Mrs. Ramsey! You stand to gain a great deal from their reforms!"

"Yet I stand to gain *two thousand pounds* with Lord Summerfield's commission," she snapped. "That is a year's receipts!"

Phoebe scarcely recognized Mrs. Ramsey at that moment. She was the devil, and Phoebe could all but see the tiny horns sticking out of her wretched pin curls.

* * *

Phoebe had recently left her stepfather's house to live with her sister, Ava, in the much larger and grander Middleton House. After a restless night through which she could see no way out of her predicament, she dragged herself to Ava's dressing room. Ava, now the Marchioness of Middleton, was there with her nine-month-old son, Jonathan. So was Phoebe's cousin Greer, the new Lady Radnor and Princess of Powys. She was cooing over her godchild.

Both women took one look at the dark circles under Phoebe's eyes, the crooked buttoning of her gown, and knew something was very wrong.

The three of them sat on the floor in a tight circle with Jonathan at the center crawling over them and gurgling as Phoebe told them the awful truth.

"You poor darling!" Greer cried when Phoebe had finished. "That wretched woman won't get away with this treachery! You mustn't worry, Phoebe, we will think our way through this!"

The Last Unmarried Daughter of the Late Lady Downey—Phoebe was convinced the entire *ton* thought of her in exactly that way—rather doubted that.

"I knew it was a dangerous game you were playing!" Ava moaned. "Really, Phoebe, you live in fantasy without considering the consequences of fantasy becoming reality! *Now* what are we to do?" Ava asked, pausing to kiss the bottom of Jonathan's foot. "It will be a horrible scandal! There are those in the *ton* just waiting for something like this to happen! And if it does, even Lord Stanhope won't have you."

"What?" Phoebe cried. "Is that all you care about?" She bent over, scooping up Jonathan onto her lap and burying her face in his neck. "I've told you a dozen times, Ava, I don't *want* to marry Stanhope."

"Yes, but it is my duty as your sister and your

friend to help you find a match, and I take that duty very seriously!"

"It is scarcely *your* duty, and really, Ava, you might as well face the fact that when a woman has been out an astonishing *four* Seasons without gaining an offer, to continue to pursue one only makes her situation worse."

"*Four!*" Greer exclaimed. "Has it really been as many as that?"

"Four," Ava said, wiggling four manicured fingers at Greer. "In her first Season out, she was the youngest of three unmarried Fairchilds and therefore, third in line to be considered," she said, bending one finger. "In her second Season, Mama died and we were in mourning, weren't we? There was no money for her to enter society in the third Season—"

"Not to mention the scandal *you* created by pursuing the marquis," Phoebe reminded her.

"Yes, the scandal," Ava said airily, and bent the third finger. "And in the fourth, Greer followed my scandalous path and returned to London married to the elusive Prince of Powys, much to everyone's great surprise, and I had my confinement and gave birth to my darling, sweet boy." She smiled lovingly at her child.

"That *is* four," Greer said, nodding thoughtfully. "Astonishing. Thank goodness Stanhope is expected to offer."

"Why? Because I am so desperately close to being put on the shelf?" Phoebe huffed. "I say again, I will not accept a match with Stanhope, and please do not try and persuade me with the fact he is one of Middleton's dearest friends, for he is also destitute and in search of a fortune. Not a marriage." She gave a kiss to Jonathan's cheek. He grabbed her earring and pulled. "*Ouch, ouch,*" she said, handing Jonathan to Greer so that she might extract her earring from his chubby fist.

"What do you expect?" Ava demanded. "How can we possibly arrange a *marriage* for you when you are so reluctant to be out in society?"

"That is simply not true!" Phoebe insisted, although she knew her sister was right. She did not care for London society. Never had. When they were girls at Bingley Hall, Phoebe had been content with her painting and drawing and her first sartorial creations, reticules (dozens of them, all haphazardly sewn and poorly beaded, but her mother had carried each one proudly), than going on the round of social calls that Ava and Greer found so delightful.

Granted, her first Season out had been very exciting, but Phoebe now found the routine of it tiresome. All of the so-called gentlemen bachelors seemed to believe that by virtue of merely *being* bachelors she must find them quite desirable, and they leered at her more often than not. If she paid the slightest attention to any one of them, rumors spread quicker than the plague that Lady Phoebe Fairchild desired a match with that particular gentleman.

Moreover, the older she became—two and twenty now—the more it seemed as if the conversations at social events with people she scarcely knew were entirely too vapid, and she could not abide sitting in overdone salons along with dozens of unmarried debutantes who all shared the singularly uninspired goal of gaining an offer of marriage. She felt root-bound in a society she did not care for, like some old bush whose limbs had become entangled with the others around it and could not be extracted.

"You are so difficult!" Ava said. "You are uncommonly beautiful, *far* more beautiful than me—look at your lovely pale blond hair. Mine is a common shade. And your eyes, such an unusual color of blue, while mine are very plain. And you are more handsome than Greer with all that Welsh blood in her—"

"I beg your pardon!" Greer said, putting a hand to her inky black hair.

"You are handsome, Greer," Ava said impatiently, "but Phoebe has always been considered the handsomest of us all. Really, I should think if only she would go out into society with a cheerful disposition, she would gain a half dozen offers instantly!"

"Thank you, Ava. I had no idea I was so handsome, yet so morbid."

"You know very well what I mean."

"I do not. But really, whether or not I am in society has little to do with Mrs. Ramsey's threats."

"She's right," Greer said as Jonathan began to babble. She handed him back to his beaming mother. "But what can Mrs. Ramsey do, in truth? Very little if you ask me."

"Oh, I think she could do quite a lot," Phoebe said morosely. "She stands to gain two thousand pounds and is *quite* determined to fulfill Summerfield's order, no matter the cost to me."

"Who *is* Lord Summerfield?" Greer asked. "I've not heard of him."

Phoebe shrugged. "I know only from Mrs. Ramsey that he lives in Bedfordshire at a place called Wentworth Hall. The family rarely leaves the country for town and his sisters have not been presented to any society."

"Does she truly expect Lady Phoebe Fairchild to go to this . . . this *country* place as Madame Dupree and make *clothes* like a common seamstress?" Ava cried.

"She does indeed," Phoebe said solemnly.

"What a vile, *wretched* woman!" Greer added angrily. She was vile, all right.

The more they talked, the more the three of them grew convinced there was no way to refuse Mrs. Ramsey without irreparable harm to Phoebe's reputation and Radnor's and Middleton's Parliamentary work on behalf of poor women. The consequences were powerful instigators.

But how could she manage to meet Mrs. Ramsey's demands and maintain her secret? Phoebe wondered.

At the very least, she had to keep her true identity a secret—nothing could make her predicament worse. After much discussion, the three women felt more confident about Phoebe's ability to assume a false identity in Bedfordshire. As the Parliamentary season had closed, everyone was leaving the heat of London for the cooler breezes in the country, and wouldn't return to London until late autumn, when Parliament would reconvene for a short session.

Further, they determined no one among their group of acquaintances hailed from or would be in Bedfordshire. They believed there were only three people in that county who might possibly know Phoebe, and actually, Phoebe had never been formally introduced to any of them.

The first was the elderly Earl of Huntingdon, who, by all accounts, was too infirm to receive callers. The Russell family lived in Woburn Abbey, but they were in France for the summer. And finally, there was the infamous Lady Holland, whose parties in London were legendary. She had a house in Bedfordshire, but Ava had learned from Lady Purnam—their mother's lifelong friend and a general busybody—that Lady Holland would be in Eastbourne until the Little Season began in the autumn.

There was really very little danger of Phoebe's encountering anyone she knew in that sleepy little corner of England. That left the real hurdle—Phoebe's identity.

"A widow," Ava insisted.

"How did her husband die?" Greer asked.

"I hardly know," Ava said with a shrug as she rocked Jonathan in her arms. "How do men typically die? A fall from a horse or some such thing."

"I scarcely believe scores of men are falling to their deaths from their saddles," Greer said drily. "Perhaps a wasting illness. That is sufficient to keep the questions to a minimum." The three of them wrinkled their noses.

"All right, then—where am I from?" Phoebe asked.

"The moors, north of Newcastle," Greer said instantly. "No one *ever* hails from there. It's practically uninhabitable."

"And you mustn't be too dreamy, Phoebe," Ava warned her sternly. "You know how bird-witted you can be with your head in the clouds."

"I beg your pardon, I am not *bird-witted*," Phoebe protested.

"Yes, but you have a tendency to let daydreams cloud your common sense."

"That is ridiculous! I do no such thing!"

"You *do* have a rather vivid imagination," Greer said kindly. "You must have a care that you do not allow it to run away from you. You must concentrate on your work and your disguise if this ruse is to work."

Phoebe clucked her tongue. "Honestly, with the number of gowns Mrs. Ramsey expects me to make in a *very* short time, there will hardly be time for sleep, much less daydreaming—or even talk, for that matter. What could possibly go wrong?"

Two

T he fabrics Phoebe would need to make the gowns were sent ahead by cart and mule on a very warm Friday, when the smell of sewage settled on London like a dirty blanket. The following Monday, Phoebe departed at dawn, wedged into a public coach between a thickset man who continually dabbed at the tiny rivulets of perspiration that erupted at his temple and a woman whose head kept tipping onto Phoebe's shoulder as she nodded off. But sleep seemed impossible to Phoebe, given the heat and the uncomfortable traveling conditions.

This was not what she'd imagined. She had pictured herself riding in a carriage alone with the tools of her trade around her, a mysterious and exotic savior on her way to transform some poor young women with her gowns. They would look up to her in reverence for making it possible for them to enter society and dazzle all those around them. They would be swept up into romance and social intrigue by virtue of their good looks and exquisite clothing, and Madame Dupree would be satisfied with a charitable act well done.

Certainly she had not envisioned such cramped quarters or doleful traveling companions.

After twelve excruciating hours, Phoebe arrived in Greenhill, a picturesque village of thatch-roofed, whitewashed cottages, a central green, and a high street splashed with the colors of summer flowers planted in window boxes. The air smelled of sweet jasmine—it was a lovely, idyllic place, the very sort of place in which Phoebe had often dreamed of living. Her spirits were immeasurably improved—now she could imagine herself tending the flowers that grew outside of her cottage every morning, after which she would paint or read or sew—whatever her heart desired. Ava and Greer would come from London, and they would . . . No. Not a cottage, she would need something larger. And at least one servant, for Phoebe was hopeless in the kitchen.

Nevertheless, she was blessedly happy to be put out of the coach in that quaint little village. Her instructions were to wait for a carriage from Wentworth Hall.

Stiff and sore from the long drive, Phoebe put a hand to her back and bent backward.

"Madame Dupree?"

She whirled around to look at the top of a man's head. He was small and impeccably dressed, and as he swept his hat off his head he revealed a pair of unusually pointed ears. "I am delighted to make your acquaintance, madam. I am Mr. Addison, sent from Wentworth Hall to fetch you." He bowed so low that Phoebe could see the perfectly round bald spot at the crown of his head. "I beg your pardon that my French is less than adequate, but may I say, *Enchanté, madame.*"

"Oh, thank you," Phoebe answered in English—she hadn't imagined anyone speaking French to her until this moment. "But I am English, sir." Mr. Addison looked surprised. "My husband was French."

"Ah. Very good, madam," Mr. Addison said, inclining his head. "If you will follow me, the wagon is just here."

Wagon?

He gestured to the trunk she'd brought; a young man picked it up and settled it on his shoulder and winked at Phoebe.

"This way," Mr. Addison said, and walked briskly around the corner.

Phoebe quickly followed him.

The two men settled her on the wagon's bench between them. On the drive to Wentworth Hall, Mr. Addison took great pains to point out some of the landmarks. Phoebe thought it beautiful countryside, particularly in the fading light of the day. A blaze of yellow rape, a flowered fodder, blanketed the fields outside the village. At a distance, sheep and cattle dotted the hills, and as they moved toward the woodlands, Mr. Addison pointed out a herd of seven or eight horses grazing near the ruin of an old crofter's cottage. As the coach neared, the horses loped away.

"Wild horses," Mr. Addison said. "You might see them about the hall from time to time, but if you draw too close, they will bolt. No one has been able to corral them since they moved into the area to foal."

Wild horses! She could think of nothing more thrilling or exotic! And they were beautiful, too—red and brown, with white socks, their bodies sleek and tall. Her mission was definitely becoming more appealing. *Madame Phoebe Dupree, maker of fine clothing and tamer of wild horses.*

The wagon rolled on, through stands of Scotch pines mixed with oaks, their roots covered with delicate, lavender wildflowers, their boughs more than thirty feet above Phoebe's head. The wagon rumbled over an old stone bridge, past a ruin of some sort, and then up, winding around a hilltop. When they crested the hill, Wentworth Hall came into view, and Phoebe sat up with a start, taking it in.

Oh, but it was grand. It stood four stories high with a dozen or more chimneys, situated in a lush, green dale. They rounded a corner, passing through a stone gate and by a stone gatehouse, and up the road to a circular drive built around a large fountain and green where two peacocks pecked the grass for grubs. In the distance was a stone gazebo next to a small lake on which several swans glided.

It was beautiful, an idyllic picture that belonged in a painting in some grand drawing room. It reminded Phoebe of Bingley Hall, where she'd spent the happiest moments of her childhood. She had long harbored a secret hope that she might one day live again in the country. She imagined children—she wanted squads of children—and pets and various wooded paths to explore and astonishing vistas to sketch and paint.

"The Darbys have resided at Wentworth Hall for more than two hundred years. It was built in the late sixteenth century for the first Earl of Bedford," Addison told her. "He was a favorite of Queen Elizabeth."

"It is quite impressive."

"His lordship is in the process of making several great improvements," Mr. Addison said proudly. "When he has finished the renovation of the house, there will be none grander in these parts."

Phoebe's imagination began to soar—she was mistress of this grand house, standing at the door to greet her guests as they arrived, wearing a gown with crystal beading, which naturally matched the beading of her shoes. She would host lovely gatherings with music and games and suppers on the terrace. She assumed there was a terrace. All grand houses had terraces.

The wagon rolled to a halt on the drive in front of the mansion. Mr. Addison stepped down first, grabbed a box under the bench and set it on the ground, then helped Phoebe down as two footmen opened the pair of doors at the entrance and hurried down. Once she was on terra firma, the wagon rumbled on, kicking up a great cloud of dust. Phoebe coughed and waved the dust from her face.

"This way, Madame Dupree," Mr. Addison said.

Phoebe looked up at the house. She expected the interior to be full of fine paintings, French furniture, and Belgian carpets. Yes, she would very much enjoy her time here. She would be inspired to create beautiful gowns in such serene surroundings.

She followed Mr. Addison, but as he started up the wide stone steps to the entrance, they were both brought to an abrupt halt by a horrific, bloodcurdling cry. A moment later, a young woman rushed out the door, her golden hair flowing loosely down her back, her day gown stained at the knees and lap. "I shall have your head, Roger!" she shouted. "I shall pike it at the gate! Will! *Will!*" she shrieked as she fled past Phoebe down the steps.

Shocked, Phoebe watched the girl dart recklessly into the path of a rider who was fast approaching. The rider reigned up sharply to avoid hitting her, cursing as he wheeled his horse about.

"Will! You must come!" the girl pleaded, oblivious to the calamity she'd just avoided.

The rider glanced to his right; Phoebe met his hazel green, sloe-eyed gaze for the briefest of moments before he looked again at the girl. Phoebe had never seen a man sit a horse quite like he did. He dismounted with smooth agility and strode to the girl, clamped a massive gloved hand on her shoulder, and said something only she could hear.

The girl turned and looked at Phoebe. "I beg your pardon, mu'um."

At a loss as to what to do or say, Phoebe curtsied.

The man put his arm around the girl and strode forward, bringing her along, pausing on the step where

Phoebe stood. He was tall, over six feet, and his figure was muscular and athletic. He squeezed the girl's shoulder and sent her hurrying inside, then looked at Addison. "Have the post brought up to my rooms."

"Yes, sir. If I may, milord, may I introduce the seamstress, Madame Dupree?"

His gaze slid over Phoebe; she noticed his eyes were more green than brown and flecked with gold—colors that reminded her of autumn. He was dressed in fine clothing—a riding coat that fit his form tightly and to perfection, a neckcloth that was tucked neatly into an embroidered waistcoat, and Wellingtons polished to a high sheen. He was not wearing a hat, and his golden hair had been streaked white by the sun. His clean-shaven face was tanned. He was dressed like most men, but there was something about him that was unlike any other man she had ever met, in London or elsewhere.

This man made Phoebe catch her breath in her throat—she felt an energy about him that seemed to swell around her. He was robustly masculine and completely untamed.

She tried hard not to gape at him like a silly child, but found it impossible to avert her gaze from him.

He nodded. "How do you do." He turned away, toward his horse, without waiting for a response.

"Actually, my lord," Phoebe said, "I am a *modiste*."

Beside her, Addison jerked a wide-eyed gaze to her as the tips of his ears began to redden.

Summerfield turned slowly and looked over his shoulder at her. "I beg your pardon?"

Phoebe smiled sunnily. "I am a *modiste*. A seamstress sews. A *modiste* designs the article of clothing." He cocked a brow. Phoebe could feel a bit of a flush in her cheeks. "It's a French word."

Summerfield turned completely around. He looked a little surprised. "Thank you for pointing that out," he said, in a voice rich and deep and with a slight accent Phoebe could not quite place. "I was not aware."

"I wouldn't expect you to be, really," Phoebe said breezily. "It's a word used exclusively in relation to women."

"Ah," he said, and looked her over once more. "Welcome to Wentworth Hall, Madame Dupree. Addison will show you to your rooms." He shifted his gaze to Addison, then turned around again, strode impatiently to his mount, and swung up.

As he wheeled his horse around, Phoebe could see a recklessness in the set of his broad shoulders and the grip of his thighs against the horse. He set the horse to a gallop and rode around the corner of the house at much too fast a pace.

Addison cleared his throat; Phoebe realized she'd been staring after Summerfield and blushed. "This way, if you please," he said, and led her into the house.

Into chaos.

The renovations Addison had spoken of were in full swing. Scaffolding in the foyer drew her eye up, to where the ceiling was being painted. Great swaths of cloth covered the marble floor. Addison introduced Phoebe to the butler, Mr. Farley, who briskly showed Phoebe up to her quarters. As they climbed three flights of stairs, the sound of sawing and hammering was heard on every floor, and a fine layer of dust covered everything.

Somewhere in all that noise, Phoebe heard a door slam and the sound of raised voices.

Mr. Farley obviously heard it, too, for he quickened his step and seemed to speak louder as he pointed out various things about the house and urged her to mind her step as they stepped over tools and buckets and moved around furniture pushed to the center of the corridor to allow work to be done on water-stained walls.

"The renovations have been completed on the east wing, where the family resides," Farley explained as they slid by a ladder. "The renovations on the west wing should be completed early next year."

They reached the last stairway, which was considerably narrower than the others. Phoebe gathered that the rooms on the top floor were reserved for servants, whose number she would be among for the next six to eight weeks.

At the top of the stairs, a row of closed doors stretched out from the right. There were only two on the left. Farley took a key from his pocket and opened the first door and held it for her.

As Phoebe walked into the room, her heart sank with disappointment. It was hardly the sort of accommodation she had imagined would be made available for a French *modiste*. It was a small bedchamber with a single bed in one corner, a faded counterpane neatly placed on it. There was a hearth, a chest of drawers, and a small vanity. The paint was peeling from the walls; the floors were wooden and scuffed.

"And the workroom," Farley said, walking to an interior door. It opened onto an adjoining room.

Her workroom was covered in a thick layer of dust that suggested it had not been used in some time. Several pieces of broken furniture lay around the room. The fabrics and dressmaking tools Mrs. Ramsey had sent ahead had been tossed haphazardly into a corner. At least someone had had the presence of mind to put down a canvas cloth to keep them from the filthy floor. As in the other room, paint was peeling from the walls and a large water stain marked the plain ceiling.

But the room was at the end of the wing and at the front of the house, and on three walls were pairs of six-foot windows. Phoebe moved through the debris to look out the windows. She grazed her hand against the casing and leaned forward. The views below the windows were of lush greenery and vivid gardens, and, Phoebe noted, the front drive.

"Mrs. Turner, the housekeeper, will deliver you a bucket with water and lye, as well as rags and mops, on the morrow," Farley informed her.

"Oh?" Phoebe said, her brow wrinkling in confusion. "Do you mean . . . ?"

"A footman will be along shortly to start a fire in the hearth," Farley continued, clearly meaning precisely what Phoebe feared—she was expected to clean these rooms herself. He nodded politely. "If there is nothing else?"

"No, thank you," she said, a bit rattled.

He bowed and left her to her rooms. Phoebe stood there a moment. She closed her eyes and imagined a famous *modiste* in a wonderfully appointed work-room. With a sigh, she opened her eyes, removed her gloves, and tossed them along with her bonnet and reticule onto a broken chair. She looked around at the mess. It would take quite a lot of work to make the room functional, she thought, and apparently, she would have to do it herself. It seemed she would have to reimagine her fantasy somewhat.

Phoebe idly walked to the windows facing west and looked out over the sublime landscape in the day's fading light. There were rolling green lawns, extensive gardens, and a deer park beyond. She smiled, shifting her gaze to the lawn just below, and imagined the feel of the cool grass beneath her bare feet.

As she gazed at the lawn, two figures emerged from the house. One was an elderly man with thinning white hair, seated in a wheelchair. His body was covered by a lap rug, and his hands were folded neatly on top of it. The person who rolled him out to the middle of the lawn was Summerfield—she recognized his riding coat.

They paused near the fountain, and the two men watched the sun sink into the woods until the light faded and Phoebe could no longer see them.

Three

No one thought to bring Phoebe any supper, and as she was entirely unaccustomed to foraging on her own, she retired early and hungry.

She was jarred awake sometime later by the sound of raised voices rising up to her through the flue. She sat up with a start and stared into the darkness, straining to hear. There were at least two men involved in the argument, and a woman was crying.

The arguing shocked her. She lowered herself and pulled the coverlet up under her chin, folded her pillow around her head to block out the sound of the voices, and tried to sleep.

But it was impossible—the arguing continued until

the morning hours, and it felt as if she'd hardly slept at all when she was startled awake by the sound of hammering. At the first heavy *thud,* she shot up with a gasp, and then groaned when she realized what it was.

She felt very cross as she washed and dressed. It was so early the night mist had not even lifted from the ground. Who could be working at such an ungodly hour? Phoebe could only guess how long it would be before someone brought her lye and water. Or a bit of food, for heaven's sake.

Perhaps she could walk around the grounds. She liked to walk—it cleared her head. Once she began to work, the Lord only knew when she might have another opportunity.

Phoebe picked up her shawl and strode from the room.

No one seemed to be about save a footman delivering coal upstairs. She stepped outside, gathered her shawl about her, and began to walk in the direction she had seen the viscount ride yesterday, around the corner of the house. The path diverged at one point—it looked as if it led to the stables on her left, but on her right the path went through a huge wrought-iron gate and into the most extensive parterres she had ever seen.

She moved slowly, the train of her pale yellow morning gown pulling with the weight of the dew on her hem. The path led to another gate, beyond which was a lawn. There was not a sound, not even the smallest breeze. Phoebe detected the scent of water and fish and moved in that direction.

The abrupt and disembodied snort of a horse frightened her out of her wits—it sounded as if it was almost on top of her. Phoebe stilled instantly, catching her breath to listen, to discern where it was. It was a moment before her eyes could focus in the mist, but she saw horses moving like ghosts just ahead of her.

Phoebe slowly released her breath but remained perfectly still as she watched them, listening to the sound of grass crunching between their teeth. The heat of their bodies was dissipating the mist around them, and she recognized the sleek bodies of the wild horses she'd seen yesterday. They were magnificent creatures, large and beautiful and astoundingly graceful. They grazed across the path ahead of her, unhurried in their movements.

As a child, Phoebe had been an excellent rider. She rarely had the opportunity now, but she still felt a strong affinity for the animals and had an undeniable urge to touch these horses. Her heart pounding with excitement, she carefully moved forward. She envisioned herself riding across a summer meadow on the back of the largest horse—the same horse that suddenly lifted its head and pricked its ears in Phoebe's direction, lifting its nose to sniff the air. He knew she was there—perhaps he could even see her—but he was hardly concerned with her presence and lowered his head to the grass again.

Phoebe took another, deliberate step forward. Two of the horses moved away. But the big, rusty-coated horse remained, obviously content with his breakfast and unafraid of her. She wanted to touch his silken mane, to stroke his long neck and nose, and impulsively held out her hand.

The horse ignored her, and, in fact, turned slightly so that he would not see her.

She moved again, but something caught her eye. She turned her head slightly and saw Summerfield standing only yards from her. He instantly lifted a finger to his lips, signaling her to be silent as he nodded at the horse.

Phoebe nodded. He motioned her to remain where

she was, and shifted his gaze to the horse, watching him closely as he moved fluidly to where Phoebe stood and silently moved to stand behind her.

How Phoebe managed not to make a sound was nothing short of miraculous, because she could feel the man at her back, standing inappropriately and deliciously close to her. She could feel the lapels of his coat against her shoulder blades, his leg against her skirt. His body was twice the breadth of hers, twice as hard as hers.

A charge ran through her and she shivered uncontrollably; Summerfield cupped her elbow as if to steady her, and then slid his bare palm down her arm, to her wrist, and wrapped his fingers around it. He slowly lifted her arm out, palm up.

Phoebe tried to draw a breath without gasping with delight and pleasure at the touch of his hand. Her arm was on fire, her skin sizzling where his hand held her arm aloft. But then he slipped something into her palm and curled her fingers over it. Phoebe's pulse leapt and he felt it, for he slipped his other arm around her waist, holding her steady against his chest.

Oh God, dear *God*, she could feel every solid inch of him, his warm breath on her ear, and the blood rushing through her veins. She glanced down at the arm that held her—his hands were big and there was a curious mark on the side of his wrist, a thick black line that curved out of his cuff and in again.

Still holding her hand, Summerfield nudged her forward and stepped with her, almost as if they were dancing.

The big red horse lifted his head and fixed one large, unblinking eye on Phoebe. She held that beast's gaze, her courage emboldened by Summerfield's iron grip on her.

The horse turned his head partially toward her and Phoebe felt a surge of excitement that shortened her breath. The horse's nostrils flared and his eye shifted to her palm. Phoebe quickly uncovered the thing in her hand, too riveted by the horse to look at what she held. Summerfield gently nudged her forward again.

The horse turned about fully then, eyeing them both, and with a shake of his head and a toss of his mane, he stepped forward. Summerfield's arm tightened around her waist, pulling her more tightly to him, and Phoebe honestly didn't know which excited her more—that this man who smelled of soap and leather and musk was holding her tightly or that the enormous, feral horse was walking toward her.

She inadvertently shrank back when the horse reached her, but Summerfield held her steady as the beast stuck his nose in Phoebe's palm and drew what she saw were dates between his teeth. Perhaps it was the tickle of his teeth against her palm, or the giddy feeling of being held so recklessly by Summerfield, but Phoebe had to bite back a laugh. The horse sucked the dates into his mouth, then pushed his nose against her palm again, seeking more. She struggled to keep from gasping with exhilaration, but when the horse lifted its head and put his nose to her face, she thought she would die with the laughter bottled up inside her.

She reared back, but Summerfield stood behind her like a stone wall, holding her firmly to him with the strength of what felt like ten men as the horse's snout passed just in front of her face, flaring and contracting, then snorting again, spraying her shoulder.

It thrilled her beyond compare. But Summerfield obviously mistook her silent laughter for fear. He caressed her arm soothingly as he reached for the horse with the other. Unfortunately, the horse was not in the mood to be touched today, and jerked his head away from Summerfield's hand and gracefully trotted away, past the two horses of the herd that were still grazing. The two smaller horses started after the red, and the three of them began to lope along the edge of the lake, disappearing into the mist.

Still, Summerfield did not release her. "Please forgive my familiarity," he said low in her ear. "I only meant to keep you from harm." He dropped his hand from her and, regrettably, stepped away, creating a draft at Phoebe's back as he moved in front of her.

But he took one look at her exuberant smile, heard the small laugh of pleasure that escaped her, and suddenly smiled, too—a brilliantly warm smile of surprise that ended in a pair of dimples in his cheeks and small lines of laughter fanning out from his hazel green eyes. "I beg your pardon—when I felt you tremble, I assumed it was fear, not laughter."

"I am not so easily frightened," Phoebe said with gay abandon, remembering that she was Madame Dupree. "Very little frightens me, actually," she continued recklessly, embracing her new identity. "With the exception of Gypsies sometimes. I'm never certain if they are thieves or merely dancers. But certainly a *horse* does not frighten me."

"Oh?" he said, his smile full of amusement. "You are as fearless as that?"

"Mmm." She glanced around Summerfield to where the horse had stood. "He is *beautiful*," she said reverently.

"He is," Summerfield said as his gaze curiously wandered the length of her. "Forgive me, Madame Dupree, but if wild stallions and dancing Gypsies do not frighten you, what does, if I may ask?"

Wild, untamed men. Men who exude virility and strength.

When she didn't answer directly, he lifted his gaze to hers. "Do *I* frighten you?"

Phoebe felt in danger of falling into those eyes, of becoming completely lost in them. She could imagine that women all over England melted inside when he merely looked at them. "You? *No!*" she said with a smile that hid her melting. "Oh no! Not in the least . . ." She paused and peered at him. "Unless . . . I *should* be frightened of you?"

One corner of his mouth tipped up in a wolfishly lazy smile. "I suppose that depends on what a beautiful young woman such as you might find frightening in a man."

God help her, he was flirting with her. She felt a silly flutter in her belly and her chest, felt her palms grow damp.

He seemed to sense what his smile did to her, for his smile deepened, his lips dark against his golden skin. "You remind me of my sisters," he said casually. "I think nothing frightens them, either—with the notable exception of thieving Gypsies, naturally." His gaze flicked over the length of her. "Perhaps you should be about the business of clothing them. Do you know the way back to the house?"

"I— Yes," she said, nodding. "Yes, of course."

"Very good." He smiled, touched his hand to his forehead, and she caught sight of that curious curving black line on his wrist. He strode away from her, taking the path the horses had taken, his gait strong and long and sure.

Phoebe watched him, holding her shawl tightly about her and memorizing the swing of his arms and the cadence of his gait. When he had disappeared, she sighed with girlish longing.

"Oh *dear*, Madame Dupree," she muttered to herself, and reluctantly turned back toward the house.

A few hours later, Will met his childhood friend, Henry Ellison, in Greenhill. When Will had returned from abroad, he'd felt almost like a visitor in a foreign land— nothing was as he remembered it, and what he did remember fit him ill, like a poorly tailored coat. But Henry had sought him out, had been genuinely glad to see him after all those years. Henry had grown an inch or two, and what once had been a thick head of brown hair was now thinning. But his blue eyes and effervescent smile were very much the same, and he had insisted on helping Will reacquaint himself with the English gentry. He was Will's one true friend.

Henry was in high spirits when they met at the public house for a pint of ale. He'd returned just days ago from London, where he'd been spending quite a lot of time as of late. There was a woman there who had captured his fancy completely and he seemed only slightly bothered that she was a married woman. But then Henry had never been particularly discriminating about women, and frankly, neither had Will.

When Will handed two shillings to the serving girl, Henry squinted at the tattoo that peeked out from the cuff of his shirt. "Been showing that around, have you?" he asked before sipping from his tankard.

"What?" Will asked, glancing at his hand. "This?" He pointed to the tattoo.

"Yes, *that*. You've managed to scandalize my dear mother with it."

"How so?" Will asked, since he'd not seen Henry's mother since the last time he attended church services— a month or more ago, to be exact.

Henry leaned across the table. "Lord Summerfield,

haven't you the slightest sense that the entire county is talking about your tattoo?" he whispered loudly. "Apparently, you rolled up a sleeve to help a poor man in need of wheel repair on his wagon, and now everyone is quite titillated by the little bit of that serpent that peeks out from your sleeve."

Will shoved his sleeve up a bit and looked at the symbol. The night he'd done it, he'd been a guest in the palace of an Indian prince. His hair had been so long he'd worn it bound at the nape with a leather tie, and he'd donned the *dhoti kurta,* the long garments Indian gentlemen wore. During the course of the evening, he'd partaken of the *hookah* pipe the prince had offered him, and sometime after that—the details were a bit hazy—he'd taken the tattoo that was offered.

"That serpent curls around the ancient Hindu symbol for peace and prosperity," he said, looking at the tattoo on his wrist. He lifted his gaze to Henry. "It is a form of art."

"It is a form of the devil," Henry said cheerfully. "Or at least Mrs. MacDonald, the vicar's wife, would have my mother believe."

"The *devil*?"

"The devil. But you may trust that I stood in defense of you." Henry winked and took another swill of his ale.

"What do you mean, stood in defense of me?" Will asked, frowning.

"When the ladies started speaking ill of you," Henry said blithely. "My mother's friends. They were in her drawing room discussing some sort of ecclesiastical event—I'm not entirely certain *what* event, really, as I find such topics tiresome and tend not to listen—but when the subject of your wrist was raised, and the ladies began to toss words like *heathen* about, I simply had to step in."

"And what did you say?"

Henry brought his tankard down with a clap. "What do you think I said, my good friend? I told them that you are indeed a heathen!" he said, and laughed.

Will smiled.

"What was I to say, then? All that talk of your spiritual journey you've subjected me to—you had me fearing for my very soul!"

"My talk of a spiritual journey is the last thing your soul should fear," Will said with a wry smile. "I should think your soul has far more to fear in your illicit affair with Mrs. Montaine."

"Have a care!" Henry whispered hotly, and glanced around the crowded, noisy public room to see if anyone had overheard. When he was satisfied they had not, he grinned at Will. "Come now, Summerfield. You really must allow me to introduce you to her sister—"

"I think not," Will said, and tossed back the rest of his ale. "I've enough to keep me occupied with my brothers and sisters. Speaking of which, I'd best be home. The good Lord only knows what havoc they have wrought this afternoon."

"Oh, for God's sake, have another pint. If they haven't harmed anyone, you might afford it."

Will stayed, but he felt rather uncomfortable. He supposed he really didn't know how to fit in with the country life any longer. He'd been gone too long, experienced too much of the world to simply pick up where he'd left off.

Ever since he'd stepped into Wentworth Hall after his six-year absence, he'd felt much like a duck out of water. He was, inescapably, a changed man. He just wasn't certain what, exactly, he'd changed into.

Four

After introducing Phoebe to the kitchen and a hot meal, Mr. Addison informed her that Ladies Alice and Jane were presently visiting their elderly cousin in Leicestershire and would not return until two days hence, so Phoebe should feel free to use the opportunity to clean and organize her workroom.

"Isn't there anyone to help me?" she'd asked bleakly.

Addison had seemed taken aback by her question. "To scrub the floor?" he asked, as if he couldn't conceive of her needing help for such a dreadful task.

"Oh, very well," Phoebe had said, a little petulantly. "I suppose there is a first time for everything."

She scrubbed the floors, swept the cobwebs from the corners of the ceiling, and washed the windows. She found a footman, Billy, who was more than happy to move the broken furniture from the room. And from Farley, the butler, Phoebe managed to extract a long worktable and three chairs.

The work was physically taxing—she'd no idea how hard servants worked until now. She was so exhausted that she rarely left the pair of rooms she had been given except to dine and to walk in the early morning. And each morning, she saw the wild horses, but try as she might to get close to them, they always shied away from her.

She thought of Summerfield often. She couldn't seem to get him out of her mind. The delicious feel of him pressed against her and his lack of concern for propriety were incredibly intriguing. She thought of his handsome face, his arresting eyes, his broad hands, and that curious black line at his wrist. She'd never been so captivated by a man—and Lord knew she had been captivated by more than one at various points in her life: a footman when she was twelve; Mr. Frank Byers, the vicar's son, who'd bought a commission in the army; and Lord Lithgow, whom she had admired from afar, as he was, unfortunately, happily married.

But Summerfield had seized her imagination like no one ever had, which led her to think of him in more intimate terms.

At work in her rooms at the top of the house, Phoebe could see the comings and goings at Wentworth Hall, and there was quite a lot of coming and going. In addition to Summerfield—who would ride out, hatless, bent over the neck of his mount as if he were in a race—Phoebe saw two more men. Because both of them were similar in build and had the same golden hair as Summerfield, she assumed they were related. On one occasion, she heard arguing and walked to the window to see Summerfield calmly standing in the drive with hands on his hips as one of the other men railed about something that had him greatly agitated.

There was quite a lot of arguing in this house, she'd noticed. She could hardly keep away from it—she heard it through the flue and from the servants she had begun to befriend.

Mrs. Turner, Wentworth's housekeeper, was a jolly woman. She arrived at Phoebe's room on the afternoon of her first day at the hall with Frieda, a chambermaid, in tow. Frieda, Mrs. Turner explained, was to help Phoebe with the sewing and whatnot. Frieda smiled meekly and curtsied awkwardly. She looked to be about the same age as Phoebe. Her hair, a grayish brown, peeked out from beneath her worn cap, and she wore a black gown, as did all the chambermaids. Her eyes, however, were large and almond shaped, richly brown, and very expressive.

When Mrs. Turner left, Frieda instantly relaxed. "God blind me!" she swore, taking one of the chairs without being asked. "I thought she meant to punish me with all this talk of needles. I don't care for needlework in the least, I'll have ye know."

"Oh?" Phoebe said, uncertain what to say to that.

"*Oooh*, quite lovely," Frieda said, eyeing the bolts of fabric Phoebe had stacked neatly on a small console table. "All for the brats, are they? Ye might nick a little for us, eh?"

Phoebe gasped.

Surprised, Frieda laughed and clucked her tongue. "You've never kept a bit back for yourself? They must pay a decent wage to you in London, then, by the look of your fancy clothing."

Phoebe looked down at the gown she'd made herself. It was the color of the golden wheat that grew at Broderick Abbey, the Marquis of Middleton's county seat. "I've certainly not kept anything for myself! And there will be no *nicking* of anything," she said sternly, forgetting, for a moment, that she was not a lady in this house.

"All right, all right," Frieda said congenially. "You hail from London, then?" she continued as she stretched her legs in front of her, propping them on another chair. "I've been to London, I have," she said, and began to recite everything she'd ever heard of London, most of it confirmed in the one visit she had made with her father. When Phoebe did finally induce Frieda to pick up a broom—by slapping the girl's feet from the chair—Frieda swept efficiently as she rattled on about a footman named Charles with whom she was apparently smitten—and intimately familiar.

Phoebe was shocked and riveted by Frieda's chatter. She'd never heard a woman speak so freely of her personal and physical relations with a man. Even Ava, who had never been shy about her body, blushed and stammered when she hinted about her physical relationship with her husband.

Not Frieda—the girl talked as if she had known a variety of men in the biblical way.

Fortunately, Mrs. Turner returned the second day to lend a hand with the cleaning—which prompted Frieda to be a bit more helpful and less talkative. Mrs. Turner, however, chatted freely about the happenings at the hall. Phoebe liked the rotund Mrs. Turner very much. She had a cheerful spirit and kind manner about her, and from her Phoebe learned that Summerfield had been gone from home for more than six years in pursuit of a variety of daring activities.

"What sort?" Phoebe asked.

"Oh, to hear Mr. Addison tell it, all that a body might do," Mrs. Turner said. "Climbing the Himlains, for one."

"The Himlains . . . do you mean the Himalayan *mountains*?"

"Aye, that's it. And he sailed around the Mediterranean on a merchant ship, just like my grandfather done. The ship wrecked, too, you know. He almost drowned. But his lordship saved a dozen sailors if he saved one. Addison told me all about it."

Phoebe gaped at Mrs. Turner.

"Oh! And the dromedaries!" Mrs. Turner continued. "They rode dromedaries through the Egyptian desert with all the heathens there, all just to see some ancient ruins or some such." She snorted. "As if we've not enough ruins here to gaze at. But it was in India that he received the mark of the beast."

"The *what*?" Phoebe asked, spellbound.

Mrs. Turner glanced at her. "Haven't seen it, eh?" She pointed to her wrist. "It's just here. Addison says it is a marking from India. It was an *awful* thing to have done, if you ask me. Seems almost sacrilegious."

"Goodness and mercy," Frieda exclaimed.

It didn't seem sacrilegious to Phoebe. It seemed beautiful. She stared at Mrs. Turner as her mind's eye filled with images of Summerfield hanging from a mountaintop, or at the helm of a ship, sailing through dangerous seas while monstrous waves and howling winds tossed and turned the ship about and then pulling sailors from the water.

"His lordship has a devilish curiosity," Mrs. Turner said. "He would have gone to China next had the old earl not taken a bad turn when he did."

"You've been at Wentworth for a time, eh?" Frieda asked.

"More years than I'd like to admit," Mrs. Turner said jovially. "Save the year there were no servants. I came back just as soon as his lordship asked, though, for I was brought on as a chambermaid, just like you, Frieda." She paused in the scrubbing of the window sash. "That was such a lovely time, when his lordship was a boy and his mother was alive. But when he grew older, he became quite restless, as young men are wont to do. The old earl sent him on his way, told him to have done with it, and come home when he had." She stared wistfully out the window. "He came home, all right—a changed man, to my way of thinking. He's not like us now."

"How do you mean?" Phoebe asked. "Like who?"

"Like country people," Mrs. Turner said. "But I mean nothing by it. Just that he has different sensibilities, that's all. He holes up in his room with his things from his travels, and he wears that awful necklace beneath his neckcloth."

"Perhaps he still has a bit of wanderlust in him," Frieda said. "But what a *handsome* man Lord Summerfield grew to be, eh? Handsome as the devil."

"Handsome and possessing a fortune that makes him the most desired bachelor this county has seen in a century," Mrs. Turner said, to which she and Frieda laughed. "On my honor, I've not seen so many callers in all my years at Wentworth Hall as I've seen since Summerfield's return. I cannot imagine there are so many unmarried young ladies in all of England as there are in Bedfordshire at present. And they seem not to care a lick that he's a heathen."

"Why should they?" Frieda said with a snort. "The man's fortune is grand enough that they might forgive a mark or two."

The two women burst into laughter again.

"How will that poor man *ever* choose a wife among them?" Mrs. Turner asked as she returned to the window sash. "And he will choose, do not doubt me. It is the old earl's dying wish to see him married."

"Farley said he won't marry until the renovations are done and Lady Alice and Lady Jane are married off, for he fears they would frighten a new wife unto death," Frieda offered.

"Ach, those two!" Mrs. Turner said with a cluck of her tongue. "And the boys! What trouble they bring to this family! Mr. Joshua Darby is too old to be cavorting about as he does, if you ask me."

"That one is a bad seed. Did you hear that he refused to pay his debt after a game of cards?" Frieda whispered.

"They argue terribly," Mrs. Turner said with a sigh. "Lord Summerfield is trying to make Joshua into a gentleman, but..." She glanced at Phoebe and suddenly straightened. "Frieda," Mrs. Turner said sternly. "Madame Dupree has not had the pleasure of meeting any of them yet, and it won't do to speak ill of them."

"Very well," Frieda said cheerfully. "We'll content ourselves by merely thinking it," she said, and laughed when Mrs. Turner frowned at her.

It was too late—Phoebe's mind was already reeling.

Five

———

Her workroom cleaned and organized, Phoebe was putting together the wire forms she would use to model the sisters' figures one morning, when Addison informed her that Lady Alice and Lady Jane would be presented to her at three o'clock.

In preparation, Phoebe laid out samples of all the fabrics that had been sent up from London when she heard an awful commotion in the hall—a sudden outburst of shrieking and pounding that made Phoebe believe someone was actually being harmed. She rushed out into the hall, and there, in the narrow hallway, the young woman she'd seen her first day here was hitting— *hitting!*—a young man who was wailing like a child.

Phoebe rushed forward and grabbed the young woman's arm before she could slap him again. "Stop it!" she cried. "What in heaven's name are you doing? *Stop* that before you hurt him!"

"She cannot hurt me!" the young man huffed angrily as he darted out of the young woman's reach. "Papa shall hear of this, Jane! Mark me!" he bellowed as he ran down the corridor and disappeared down the stairs.

"Oh yes, run to Papa! What shall he do strapped in his chair, then?" she shouted after him as he raced away. She looked at Phoebe with eyes filled with tears and jerked her arm from Phoebe's grasp. "I *hate* wretched Roger, I swear I do," she whimpered.

"Lady Jane or Lady Alice?"

"Jane."

"And wretched Roger?"

"My brother! He has no right to go into my things!"

"Of course not. But neither have you any right to hit him."

"And what business is it of yours if she did?" a third voice asked.

Phoebe turned toward the sound of the woman's voice. She could be none other than Alice—she looked so much like Jane, only taller and more slender than her younger sister. Her gown was too short for her lanky frame, and, like Jane's gown, its style was dated.

With her arms folded defensively, Alice walked toward Phoebe. "You're merely the seamstress, are you not?" she asked coolly as she halted before Phoebe. "You have no right to speak to my sister in such a manner. I could have you dismissed for it."

Thankfully, Addison appeared at the top of the stairs before Alice could say more.

"Aha, Lady Alice, you have come after all!" he said

cheerfully. "And here is Lady Jane, too." He smiled, but Phoebe noticed that his smile did not quite reach his eyes. "I beg your pardon, Madame Dupree. His lordship desired to make the formal introductions, but he is receiving callers."

"Mr. and Mrs. Frederick," Alice said with a roll of her eyes. "If they think their Elizabeth has the *slightest* chance of marrying my brother, they are sadly mistaken."

"That will be for his lordship to decide," Addison said briskly, and gestured to the workroom. "Shall we?"

Alice sighed as if she were being asked to mount the gallows, and walked with great deliberation into the room. Jane straightened her gown and followed her sister.

Addison's smile faded a little as he noticed Jane's torn sleeve and mussed hair. "Oh *dear*, Lady Jane! What has happened?"

"Nothing!" she exclaimed, wide-eyed. "Why should you think anything has happened?" she asked as she swept past him and into the room.

Addison looked at Phoebe; Phoebe shook her head. He clamped his mouth shut and marched into the room, the tips of his ears blazing red.

Once inside, however, he did try to put a bright face on it. He introduced them all, and before she fell gracelessly onto a chair, Lady Alice Summerfield inquired of Phoebe, "Aren't you to curtsy?"

She was not going to care for Alice, that much was plain, but Phoebe forced herself to curtsy.

"Lady Alice and Lady Jane are preparing for their coming-out," Addison said with false cheer. "Lady Alice is eighteen years old, and Lady Jane will be seventeen in two months' time."

"Both excellent ages for a debut," Phoebe remarked.

"How would *you* possibly know?" Alice asked coldly. "Did *you* come out?"

"Lady Dupree makes gowns for debutantes, Alice," Jane said pertly. With dark gold hair and green eyes, Jane was smaller and prettier than her sister. Or perhaps she only seemed prettier because she smiled.

"That hardly makes her an expert," Alice said petulantly.

"Lady Alice," Addison said, smiling tremulously at Phoebe, "his lordship expressly bade you to be cooperative."

"Oh, his lordship, his *lordship*!" she exclaimed angrily. "He bids me constantly!"

"You mustn't pay her any mind," Jane said with a sigh. "She is in a snit because she—"

"*Hush,* Jane," her sister snapped.

"I *won't* hush. I have just as much right to speak to Lady Dupree as you."

"*Madame* Dupree, you silly child."

"*Madame* is the same as *Lady* in English," Jane retorted.

"It is *not* the same, it is *vastly* different, which is why you will never make a match, Jane, for you are so silly!"

"Ladies!" Mr. Addison exclaimed, his eyes wide with horror now, his ears cherry red. "I beg of you, please!"

Alice pressed her lips together, but she shifted a cold gaze to Phoebe, taking in her gown and her hair.

"I am certain Madame Dupree is eager to be about her work," Addison said, and glanced nervously at Phoebe. "His lordship would like to know if there is anything you might require in order to do your work here?"

"He has been very kind to make Frieda available to me, sir."

"Very good," he said, already backing toward the door. "If there is nothing else?" He'd already stepped through the door. Phoebe could hardly fault him—but the moment he was gone, she felt outnumbered.

She looked uneasily at her charges. Alice was sprawled in a chair like a beggar. Jane was twisting a lock of hair around her finger like a little girl. How could the daughters of an earl possibly be so ill-suited for society?

"Shall we get on with it, Madame Dupree?" Alice drawled. "I have better things to occupy my time than being fitted."

"Heavens, Alice, you are always so cross!" Jane said with a huff. "It's as if you blame Madame Dupree for keeping you from Mr. Hughes."

Alice instantly colored. "*Hush*, Jane!"

"Why don't we take some measurements?" Phoebe tried.

"I *won't* hush," Jane said haughtily, ignoring Phoebe and glaring at her sister. "Alice is in love with Mr. Hughes," she said in a singsong voice. "But he is the son of a blacksmith and Will says that he is not the sort of match the daughter of an earl should expect to make, particularly before she has been presented to society."

"I swear I shall throttle you, Jane!" Alice cried. "It is hardly a servant's concern!"

Jane laughed derisively. "All the other servants know it—why shouldn't this one?"

"Which of you would like to be first?" Phoebe asked, holding up the string she would use to measure them, feeling a bit like a piece of furniture.

"At least there is a gentleman who finds me worthy of his consideration," Alice snapped. "Unlike you, who have never had a gentleman so much as *look* in your direction—"

"That is not true!" Jane said fiercely.

"What do you like in a gown, Lady Alice?" Phoebe asked, stepping in between them.

Her question seemed to startle Alice. She jerked her gaze to Phoebe and looked at her as if she were mad. "Nothing!"

"That certainly gives me quite a lot to work with. Do you prefer silks? Brocades? Perhaps velvet?"

"Isn't that *your* task?"

"You are absolutely right. Shall we measure you?"

"Do you *mind*, Madame Dupree?" Alice snapped. "I am speaking to Jane!"

"You weren't speaking, you were shouting," Jane said. "Just as you shouted at Will for telling you that you cannot see that horrible smithy before he banished us to Cousin Mathilde's house in Leicestershire—"

Alice gasped. "How dare you, you horrible, willful, spoiled brat!"

"All right, that is quite enough!" Phoebe cried, looking at both of them. "On my word, I have never seen two ladies behave so abominably! This is neither the time nor the place for your silly arguments, so Lady Alice, please do stand so that I may take your measurements."

Alice gasped again and gaped at Phoebe. "How *dare* you speak to me thus?" she demanded as she came to her feet. "How *dare* you?"

"It is clearly time *someone* spoke to you," Phoebe muttered. "Hold your arms out like this," she said, demonstrating. She would not be cowed by Alice's supercilious behavior, particularly if it meant prolonging this interview one moment past what was absolutely necessary. Complete censure in London seemed preferable to enduring such childish bickering.

"You must think very highly of yourself, Madame

Dupree," Alice spat as she flung her arms wide, "to presume to speak to *me*, the earl's oldest daughter, in such condescending fashion!"

Phoebe ignored her, and quickly measured her arms before turning around and putting the string to a yardstick. "Now the waist," she said briskly.

"My brother will certainly hear of your impudence," Alice said as Phoebe wrapped the string around her waist. "I shouldn't be surprised if he dismissed you at *once*."

Good *Lord*. What hell was this? "Then I shall owe him a debt of thanks," she said as she went down on her knees and measured Alice's length. "I never imagined I'd be forced to endure such childish behavior!"

Apparently, Alice feared she might thank Summerfield for her dismissal, for she didn't say anything as Phoebe finished measuring her, and Jane laughed.

By the time Phoebe had taken both sets of measurements and forced the two young women to look at the fabrics instead of argue, she had learned that Alice was desperately in love with Roland Hughes, that the bane of Jane's existence was her brother Roger, and that their other brother, Joshua, was a source of constant trouble for the earl and Summerfield.

They had just begun to argue over the fabrics for their first formal gowns when there was a knock at the door. Phoebe eagerly looked up, hoping it was Addison or Farley come to fetch them—but it was Summerfield, and she felt an uncharacteristic flush heat her face. She was not a new debutante or inexperienced in the presence of men, but she suddenly felt as if she were.

"*Will!*" Jane cried happily, running to him. Alice turned away from him.

Summerfield kissed Jane's cheek and walked over

to the table to have a look at the bolts of fabric on the table.

He glanced at Phoebe and gave her a bit of a smile. "I hope you don't mind the intrusion, Madame Dupree. I had hoped to introduce you to my sisters myself, but I was unavoidably detained."

"Are you going to offer for Miss Frederick?" Jane asked brightly. "Alice says you won't."

"Alice says many things," he said, looking pointedly at the older girl, who pretended to study a silk. "And you should not ask such things, Jane."

He was dressed impeccably, Phoebe noted, which should hardly have surprised her, having noticed in her short time here how meticulous Addison was about his own clothing. Summerfield's attire was cut with a perfection she envied. The brown coat fit his shoulders flawlessly, as did the waistcoat that tapered into his trim waist. And the black trousers that fit him like a glove were cut *exceptionally* well.

So well that the heat in her face deepened as she recalled the feel of him—*all* of him—at her back.

He lifted a white silk and felt it between his fingers; Phoebe caught sight of what Mrs. Turner had called the mark of the beast. He was, if Mrs. Turner was to be believed, a wolf in sheep's clothing.

Why did that titillate her so?

"Quite nice," he said absently.

"I chose the white for a ball gown," Jane said. "Lady Dupree said it would go well with my hair."

"Ah," he said, and glanced at Phoebe again.

Lord, those *eyes*. A woman could be in serious danger if she held his gaze; Phoebe averted her eyes to the fabrics.

"Which did you choose, Alice?" Summerfield asked.

"I hardly care," she said petulantly. "Let the seam-stress decide."

"She chose the lavender silk," Phoebe said, and lifted it up for him to see.

He looked at the fabric, then at Alice, and smiled so fondly at his sister that even Phoebe felt a little tug in her chest. "An excellent choice. She will be beautiful."

There was an instant change in Alice. Not so much as a smile, oh no—the girl was determined *not* to smile—but her shoulders seemed to square a little and her expression seemed much less sour.

Summerfield walked around the table to Alice's side. He cupped her face in his big hand and kissed the top of her head. "When you are through here, Alice, I should like a word with you in Father's library."

"I suppose Cousin Mathilde sent a letter reporting our behavior?" she asked caustically.

"No. But I shall inquire of Cousin Mathilde straight-away."

Jane groaned, but Alice looked away with a bit of a smirk.

"When you are done," he said again, and glanced at Phoebe over the top of Alice's head. "Thank you, Ma-dame Dupree. I will leave you to your work." And with that, he left the room.

Both Alice and Jane waited until they could no lon-ger hear his footfall. "What have you done, you witch?" Jane hissed at her sister.

"Nothing at all," Alice said, prompting another round of arguing.

It took several minutes to entice them to leave, and when they had gone, Phoebe put her back to the door and took several deep breaths.

She very much would have liked to pull every hair

from Mrs. Ramsey's head for this. It was going to be a very hot summer with those two.

At that very same moment in Greenhill, several women had gathered for afternoon tea to celebrate the arrival of Miss Rebecca Callinghorn's Scottish cousin, Lady Amanda Waters, to the county.

Lady Amanda was said to be seeking the warmer climate of Bedfordshire, but Miss Caroline Fitzherbert knew that she had come to join the ranks of those young ladies vying for a marriage proposal from the viscount. Anyone who said otherwise was a liar or a fool. There wasn't a woman in this room who wasn't actively pursuing a match for a daughter or a niece or herself.

And as if to prove her point, the conversation inevitably turned to Lord Summerfield. Of course it did—there was hardly anything else worth mentioning in this backwater county.

There was some speculation as to who would win Summerfield's hand, but Lady Kealing brought it to a halt by being very haughty.

"My Bertha will not be among those eligible," she said with a sniff. "There's something a bit off about him, if you ask me."

"Martha, really," Caroline's mother said. Unlike Lady Kealing, her mother was quite keen to see a match with her daughter. "I shall never understand why a bit of a mark on the man's wrist should cause such consternation. It hardly says anything about his character at all."

"Indeed it does, Lucy!" Lady Kealing protested. "And besides, it is not just that ghastly mark. My husband saw him one night standing in an open field where the wild horses often graze, just staring up at the moon—he knew it was him by the color and length of his hair. Imagine, a grown man standing in the middle of a field and staring up at the moon without as much as a dog to keep him company!"

Miss Callinghorn and Lady Amanda exchanged alarmed looks.

"Is it a crime to look at the moon?" Caroline's mother demanded.

"Of course not, Lucy," Lady Kealing said with a withering look for her. "But you must admit it is odd. And with that mark on his wrist . . . Well," she continued, straightening her back. "I should not like *my* daughter to marry a heathen."

Caroline's mother bristled. She shifted in her seat and put down her teacup a little too forcefully. "I scarcely think a *heathen* would have saved all those sailors from drowning," she said crossly. "Or be so good to the poor earl. He's taken quite good care of him."

"Indeed he has," Mrs. Frederick opined. "We had Summerfield for supper one night, and he was very kind to my girls. Very polite." She cocked her head and frowned a bit. "But he did bring a peculiar sort of liquor to share with Mr. Frederick that made him quite ill. I cannot recall the name, but he said it came from the Orient."

"I am not surprised. He's not attended church services in weeks," Lady Kealing said darkly, and sipped her tea.

Stupid woman, Caroline thought. He was the best bachelor this county had seen in ages. Who could fault him for Mr. Frederick's weak constitution? Who could claim that his refusal to sit through another of the vicar's exceedingly tedious sermons was a mark against him? She thought him rather clever for it, actually.

"Speaking of church services," Mrs. MacDonald interjected shyly, "my husband has asked me to pass along some news I hope you will all welcome. . . ."

As she proceeded to go on and on about some church matter, Caroline looked at Bertha. She suspected the real reason her mother would not throw her name into the melee was because the girl was far too plain to attract the eye of a man like Summerfield.

No, a man like Summerfield required someone far more comely and clever, and Caroline knew precisely who it should be.

Six

After a long and busy day, Phoebe retired again that night to the muffled sounds of arguing floating up from the flue.

The next morning, exasperated at having been awakened at dawn once again by hammering, Phoebe was up and dressed. She had no fear that either Alice or Jane would be roused before noon—Frieda said they slept until one or two o'clock every day.

She tried to work, but it was impossible—the hammering annoyed her no end. By late morning, she was feeling out of sorts and left the house with her sketchbook under one arm. She paused in the massive foyer to rearrange freshly cut hothouse flowers that were rather tragically stuffed into a vase, and then went out into the morning.

Phoebe lifted the hem of her skirts and marched around the house and through the gardens and toward the lake, to a stone gazebo that had been erected, she suspected, to house small orchestras in the summer. She sat on a stone bench attached to the wall and began to sketch the line of firs that formed part of the walkway to the lake, thinking of a lavender gown for Alice.

As her eye moved down the line of firs, she spied, much to her private delight, Lord Summerfield at the lake's edge.

The feral horses were there.

Summerfield had his back to her, and was standing perfectly still. He was wearing buckskins tucked into a pair of Hessians, and a lawn shirt tucked into the buckskins. He had left off a waistcoat or coat, and by his foot was a hat, tossed carelessly aside.

Phoebe shifted around on the bench to have a better look. His shoulders were broader and stronger than she remembered, his back tapered into powerful hips and thighs. She imagined one of those thighs between her legs and released a quiet sigh of longing before turning the page of her sketchbook. She began to try to capture the image of Summerfield and the horse.

The large red stallion, standing a few yards away from the rest of the herd, ignored Summerfield as he nibbled a fresh patch of grass. Summerfield slowly raised his arm, palm up, and took a step toward the horses. Two of the horses standing nearby shied. But not the red, oh no—he did not even lift his head. Summerfield took another deliberate step, and another, until his hand was just below the horse's nose. After what seemed hours instead of moments, the horse finally lifted his head and touched his nose to Summerfield's hand.

Phoebe gasped softly as Summerfield stepped closer, his free hand going to the horse's mane and neck, stroking it carefully as the horse chewed whatever offering he'd brought him. It was magical—it was almost as if

Summerfield and the horse had formed an acquaintance.

And then, as if sensing the acquaintance, another of the wild horses came forward to sniff the viscount. A pregnant mare followed that one. Phoebe was mesmerized by the scene playing out before her—the man standing amid those wild beasts, befriending them so easily. But when a flock of birds suddenly rose from the trees, it startled the herd and the horses cantered away, disappearing over a rise in the land. Summerfield watched the horses until he could no longer see them, then stooped down and picked up his hat and walked away, through a path that led into the woods.

Only then did Phoebe look at her sketch of him standing before the horses. She quickly filled in the morning shadows and trees. It was a very rough sketch, but it captured the magic of . . . of his physique. The sketch would make a fine painting—the wild man taming the wild horse. Actually, Phoebe could imagine him taming any number of things. Children. Dragons. *Women* . . .

She closed her eyes and imagined him stroking her hair as he had stroked the horse's mane. The image warmed her, made her feel strangely full. She often had such thoughts—more times than she supposed was decent. But she felt like something was building in her, something tall and massive from which it felt she could easily fall. Into what, she didn't know, but she had a feeling it was something tantalizingly dangerous.

With a sigh, she opened her eyes, shut the book, and started back to the house.

When Phoebe walked through the main entrance, the sound of female voices reached her, and she noticed that someone had moved the flowers. As a pair of carpenters was hard at work near the main stairwell, Phoebe chose a different path to avoid disturbing them and encountering the women. That path led her down a corridor she had not yet seen.

This corridor had obviously been renovated. The paint on the walls was fresh, the carpet new. She walked by an open door. The room inside—a salon, by the look of it—had just been painted, too, judging by the smell of turpentine. But it was the color that caught Phoebe's eye, and she frowned slightly, pausing to duck her head inside. The paint was the color of pewter, which she thought rather too dull in a room that received very little sun. It was too cold and uninviting for a receiving salon. As no one was within, Phoebe stepped across the threshold to have a look.

Oh no. Oh *dear.* The furniture had been placed awkwardly about the room, a table there, an ottoman here, and two overstuffed chairs shoved side by side against a wall. With her foot, Phoebe pushed the ottoman away from its place by the door. Then she moved the table near the ottoman, and followed that by pushing the two chairs into a grouping. She was considering the placement of a side cart when she heard footsteps behind her and quickly snatched up her sketchbook and whirled around.

At the threshold was one of the Darby brothers she had seen from her view in the workroom. He was her age, perhaps a bit younger. He was dressed in a coat of black superfine, with his hair cut short and curled around his face, as was the current fashion. He was a handsome man—but not as handsome as his older brother.

He smiled darkly when he saw her. "What have we here?" he asked, wandering insouciantly into the room as he boldly took her in.

His manner made her tense; she knew his expression, had seen it directed at her many times in her life, and it made her feel exposed.

"My, my," he said, his gaze lingering on her bosom. "Who is this woman, this beauty, wandering about Wentworth Hall when the other ladies gather like a gaggle around my brother? You are not known to me," he said, raising his tobacco brown gaze to hers.

"I beg your pardon, sir," Phoebe said with a curtsy. "I am Madame Dupree. I have been retained as a *modiste*—"

"A *what*?"

"A dressmaker."

He frowned a little at that. "*You're* the seamstress? I thought seamstresses were little old women with bowed backs and gray hair," he said as his gaze dipped to her bosom again.

Phoebe gathered her shawl and held it just below her throat to block his view of her flesh.

"Where is your husband, Madame Dupree?" he asked brazenly, looking up, peering at her. "Has he no care for you? He should not allow his beauty to be sent off alone. Where is he?"

The young man was sorely lacking in etiquette—a gentleman would never question her so boldly. "I am widowed," she said simply.

"A widow, eh?" He smirked. "A widow is a man's dream, they say, for she does not require marriage or a fee for her favors."

Phoebe blanched, appalled.

But the younger Darby chuckled and pointed at her sketchbook. "If you are a seamstress, what are you doing here?"

"Ah . . ." She glanced around. "Just admiring things."

"Admiring what? Are you a thief, seamstress?"

"Certainly not!" Phoebe exclaimed. "I was looking at the furniture."

"Why?" he asked as he strolled in a circle around her.

Phoebe debated what to say, and finding nothing plausible, she finally admitted the truth. "It was poorly arranged."

He gave a bark of surprised laughter. "I beg your pardon?"

Phoebe lifted her chin. "It is not very inviting, in truth."

He laughed again. "You are a curious thing, are you not? What have you got there?"

Phoebe glanced at her book. "My . . . my sketchbook."

"A sketchbook?" he said, his smile going deeper. "And what have you sketched, Widow Dupree? Let's have a look," he said, holding out his hand.

She instantly moved the sketchbook out of his reach. "I beg your pardon, sir, but I would rather not."

"I hardly care if you would or would not," he said easily, gesturing for her to give him the book.

"It is private."

His gaze turned dark with anger. "You do not *refuse* me, madam. I am the son of the Earl of Bedford, and *you* are a servant in my house. You will do as you are told if you want to retain your employment. Now let me have a look."

She was shocked to be treated so rudely, but moreover, she was furious. "No, sir," she said politely but firmly, even though her heart was racing. "I prefer not—"

With a growl, he suddenly grabbed it from her hand.

"Stop that!" she cried, lurching for it. "That belongs to me!"

The young man opened it. And grinned with delight. "Well then, I should—"

Whatever he might have said was lost—Phoebe was jostled when Lord Summerfield suddenly surged past her and clamped his hand down on her sketchbook. She hadn't heard him come into the room, and apparently, neither had his brother. Summerfield was taller than his brother, broader and thicker, and glared down at the younger man with a murderous gaze. "Joshua," he said through clenched teeth, "the lady does not want to share her sketches." He yanked the book from Joshua's hands. "Please do apologize."

"She is not a *lady*, she is a seamstress, and she is rather suspiciously lurking about the room—"

"*Joshua.*"

Summerfield's commanding voice had the desired effect. Joshua shifted his blazing gaze from the viscount to Phoebe. "I beg your pardon," he said curtly.

The viscount stepped aside. "Now go."

Glaring at his brother, Joshua strode forward, pushing past Phoebe as he quit the room.

When he had gone, Summerfield closed the sketchbook without looking at it—thanks to the slew of promises Phoebe had just made to God in exchange for his not looking—and handed it to her.

"My sincerest apology for my brother's abominable behavior," he said tightly.

Phoebe nodded. "Thank you for retrieving my book," she said, and held it tightly to her chest for a moment.

He said nothing, but his gaze was intent on hers. His scrutiny made her feel awkward. Yet he was not looking at her in the same manner men generally looked at her. There was no lust in his expression. Just curiosity.

"I beg your pardon," Phoebe stammered nervously. "I was indeed lurking where I ought not to have been, but I noticed—" She winced, dismayed by her lack of decorum.

He glanced around. "Noticed what?" he asked.

"Nothing at all," she said, clutching the sketchbook tighter.

"There is something," he contradicted her, and looked at her questioningly.

Phoebe glanced heavenward a moment, then sighed. She'd been a fool to wander where she should not have been. "It is the color, my lord."

"The *color*?" It was clear he did not understand.

"The thing is," Phoebe said, relaxing a little, "the room does not receive a lot of sun, and the gray color will make it seem cold."

He glanced at the walls.

"And . . . the furniture is a bit . . ."

He shot a look at her; Phoebe hesitated. "A bit . . . ?" he prompted her.

"Scarce. A rug, perhaps," she said, sweeping her hand to the floor. "And a divan."

Summerfield looked at the furniture she had rear-ranged.

While he looked at the furniture as if he'd only just noticed it, Phoebe looked at him. He'd changed out of his buckskins and lawn shirt, and into attire more appropriate for a viscount. But his neckcloth, she noticed, was hastily tied and hung crookedly. His shirt cuffs were bunched beneath the sleeves of his coat, as if he'd just thrown it on. The curious black mark on his wrist, which she had glimpsed the morning he'd helped her to feed the horses, was even more visible, and she could see it was a tail that curled up the inside of his arm.

He was not a fastidious man, and the effect was rather stirring—Phoebe could very well imagine him scaling mountains and sailing the high seas. Good God, she could hardly look at him without that blasted heat rising in her cheeks. But how could she help herself? He had the most striking hazel eyes she had ever seen, and his mouth . . .

He suddenly looked at her and caught her staring at him.

She blinked. "I should . . . go," she blurted. "Thank you," she added. But as she began to walk away, she clumsily dropped her sketchbook. It hit the table and fell open on the carpet. With a gasp, she instantly went down on her haunches to retrieve it. Unfortunately, Summerfield was faster, picking it up before she could reach it.

Phoebe's heart started to race. "How clumsy of me! Thank you," she added, extending her hand for the book.

But Summerfield was intent on closing it. He turned the book over in his palm to do just that, and her sketch caught his eye. He paused. One dark golden brow rose high above the other as he looked at it.

There it was, then. Phoebe wanted to die. Preferably in a manner that was fiery and completely engulfing, but she'd settle for the earth simply opening and gobbling her whole.

When Summerfield glanced up, his eyes were shining with amusement.

"Ah . . . you were standing down there," she said, gesturing vaguely to the window, "and I . . . *ahem* . . . I was walking. And you were there," she said again.

God help her, she sounded absolutely ridiculous. Her voice trailed off; she was at a loss for words. She could only imagine what he must think of her, now that he'd discovered her nursing a childish infatuation. She was hardly the sophisticated *modiste* he had hired and she sighed in exasperation.

Summerfield smiled a little. "The likenesses of the

horses are done admirably well," he said as he closed the book. "But I confess, I am not familiar with my image from that particular vantage point so I cannot say whether it is a fitting likeness or not."

"It is . . . it is an *excellent* likeness," she muttered.

His smile widened a little. "Are you often in the habit of sketching unsuspecting subjects?"

She took the book and looked up at his laughing hazel green eyes. "Actually, in spite of its being a particularly rude habit, the answer is yes."

Summerfield laughed.

Why wouldn't the earth open up and suck her down into Hades *now*? What a cabbagehead she'd suddenly become! "If you will excuse me, my lord, I should like to go and bury myself in a very large hole."

He grinned, but Phoebe had already started moving, practically sprinting, from sheer mortification. She did not, however, make it very far, for Farley suddenly appeared in the doorway with three women on his heels, all of them craning their necks to see inside.

"Ah, there you are, Summerfield!" one of them called, waving her hand and pushing past Farley.

"Mrs. Remington. Mrs. Donnelly. Mrs. MacDonald. Please do come in," Summerfield said. "I beg your pardon for being late to your tour—I had a rather urgent matter to attend to," he said.

Feeding wild horses, Phoebe thought. She stepped out of the way, and bowed her head as the three women sailed into the room. She intended to go right out and on to her work, but Farley stood just at the threshold, blocking any hope of an unnoticed exit.

"You are too kind to let us tour the hall," the woman Phoebe thought was Mrs. Remington said. "What you've done to it is . . . is . . . Well. Words fail me," she said with a smile.

"Thank you."

"And *this* room!" she added cheerfully. "Rather remarkable, isn't it?"

"Rather remarkable in how poorly it was done," one of the other women added.

Phoebe swallowed a gasp.

"I beg your pardon?" Summerfield said, his brow furrowing with confusion as he, too, looked around the room.

"Oh, I mean no disrespect, my lord! I am certain it will be as charming as the other rooms when you have refinished," the woman said brightly. "But the color is atrocious. And the drapes!" She shook her head.

The drapes were indeed awful, Phoebe had to agree.

"Rather reminds one of what might be worn to a funeral dirge," the third one said, and the women laughed.

Standing behind them, Phoebe put her hand over her mouth in shock. They didn't realize the room had already been redone—but all they had to do was take one look at Summerfield's face to know it. He looked quite disconcerted as he stared at the drapes.

"Summerfield, really! It will all be put to rights once you've put your magic touch to it!" Mrs. Remington avowed when at last she noticed his pained expression.

"I beg your pardon, madam, but I *have* put my 'magic touch' to it. I oversaw the decoration of this room myself."

That remark sucked the air right out of the room. The three women gaped at him. The room was suddenly so quiet, Phoebe could hear one woman's rapid breathing.

"It's . . . it's beautiful," Mrs. Remington said, trying desperately to recover. "Quite extraordinary, really. Is it perhaps the style in Egypt?" she asked, her facial expression full of hope.

"No," Summerfield said, and calmly clasped his hands behind his back, forcing a smile. "It's rather warm here, wouldn't you agree? I suggest we repair to the terrace. Farley? The lemonade, if you please. And if you would be so good as to show the ladies to the terrace, I shall be along momentarily."

"Yes, my lord. Ladies?" Farley said, gesturing toward the door.

The three of them floated out, each of them gamely trying to compliment something on their way.

When they had left, Summerfield looked at Phoebe.

She drew a deep breath. "I . . . I was just going," she said, and turned toward the door.

"One moment, if you please."

She winced, then turned around. "My lord?"

"What color?" he asked, gesturing to the walls.

She looked around the room. "A buttery yellow."

"Thank you," he said, and turned to study the walls as Phoebe quietly fled.

Seven

Phoebe had a rather stern talk with herself that afternoon. She was to put the terribly alluring Lord Summerfield from her mind before she made a complete cake of herself.

And she tried to do just that for several days.

Unfortunately, Frieda made it impossible. The girl was constantly at the window reporting on the steady stream of callers. It seemed the household rumors were true—there was no shortage of anxious mothers and weary fathers vying for Summerfield's attentions. When Frieda wasn't reporting on who was calling, or that Summerfield and his brothers had ridden off, dressed properly, "to have a look at the ladies," her brown eyes glittered and her slender hands flew across the fabrics she sewed as she talked incessantly about Charles, who had taken certain liberties with her recently that an ebullient Frieda was not the least bit shy to share.

Such visual images of intimacy between a man and woman only made Phoebe think of Summerfield more.

Unfortunately for Frieda, however, once she had given Charles such liberties, he wasn't quite as keen to court her.

"Why is it," she asked as she squinted at a seam she was stitching, "that a man will behave in such a bloody ill way? I gave him a poke as he wanted! Oh, I know better, I swear I do, but you know how it is, eh?" she asked Phoebe in all seriousness. "Sometimes a lass is made helpless when a lad touches her in the right way, ain't she?"

Phoebe did not answer and, in fact, hid behind the wire dress form where she was pinning a dress for Alice. What she knew about such touching was woefully little.

If Frieda wasn't nattering on, Alice and Jane were in the room arguing. Not a day passed that they didn't come to the workroom to engage in some ridiculous debate about fabrics and styles. Phoebe was eager to be done with the two young women—she'd never met more unruly and wildly inappropriate young women in her life. They were beasts! There was not a kinder thing that could be said of them.

Yet in spite of her inappropriate thoughts of Summerfield, and Frieda's distracting chatter, and the constant need to mediate between the two sisters, who seemed to have nothing better to do than interfere with her work, Phoebe made some significant progress in the first week.

But on the seventh day, all her hard work began to unravel.

It began when Mrs. Turner apologetically informed Phoebe that Frieda was needed elsewhere that afternoon. She also informed Phoebe that Summerfield had just that morning decreed a supper party would be held at Wentworth Hall in a week or so to honor the Remingtons, a landed family with two bachelor sons. "He is very hopeful for the girls' prospects," Mrs. Turner said with a wince that suggested she was not quite as hopeful.

Neither was Phoebe.

An hour later, both Alice and Jane burst into Phoebe's workroom.

"Madame Dupree!" Jane cried. "I *must* have the green gown completed before week's end!"

"For God's sake, Jane!" Alice snapped, shoving her sister out of her way like a common ruffian. "I am the oldest!" She jerked her gaze to Phoebe. "You shall finish *my* gown, the lavender one, and the shawl you said you would make to go with it."

"I was here *first*, Alice!" Jane shouted, shoving her sister back.

"Stop that, both of you!" Phoebe insisted. "I haven't even begun the evening gowns! I cannot possibly finish them in time, so might I suggest that you—"

"But you can finish one, and it shall be mine!" Alice snapped.

With a shriek, Jane hit her sister. Phoebe was instantly between them, holding her arms out to keep them from one another's throats. "I will not finish a *single* gown until you behave like ladies!"

"What *gall* you have to tell us how to behave!" Alice said angrily.

"Mark me, ladies, it will hardly matter *what* you are wearing if you behave like street ruffians! No man shall want you, no man shall offer, nor will either of you *deserve* an offer!"

Jane cried out, Alice looked absolutely shocked, and poor Frieda—Phoebe thought she might faint dead away.

But Alice quickly regained her composure. "I beg your *pardon*?" she seethed, turning on Phoebe. "Oh, I shall *delight* in having your position, you stupid chit! You will not work again in this county, I assure you!"

"You may trust that I will not," Phoebe shot back. "Lady Alice, forgive me for saying so, but you have a tendency to behave in a manner that makes you *quite* unattractive—"

"Dear God, you have lost your *mind*!" Alice shrieked. Behind her, a wide-eyed Frieda furiously nodded her agreement that Phoebe *had* lost her mind.

"I am only attempting to be honest in order to *help* you—"

"I think you had best pack your trunk, Madame Dupree," Alice said in a ragged voice, and flounced from the room.

Phoebe sighed and looked at Jane. Jane was rooted to the floor, her bottom lip trembling, her eyes filled with tears. "Lady Jane—"

"No!" Jane said with a quick and violent shake of

her head. "You are *very* foolish! You act above yourself and you are but a servant in this house! I hope Will tosses you out as you deserve!" she cried, and whirled about, running after her sister.

Phoebe threw down the fabric she was still holding, exasperated.

"Oh, Phoebe!" Frieda said fearfully. "He'll turn you out, he will!"

"I hardly care if he does, Frieda! Those two young women have crawled out from beneath a rock, and I shouldn't care if they are properly clothed or not! Never in my life have I met more ill-mannered people!"

Her breath was coming in angry spurts. How could she possibly have convinced herself this ruse would work? Honestly, at the moment, she hardly cared. She would rather be exposed to the entire *ton* than endure another moment of Alice or Jane Darby.

"His lordship sent Charlie's brother off for much less," Frieda said tearfully. "Oh *Lord*, where will you go?"

"I hardly know or care," Phoebe said imperiously. "Wherever I go shall be more peaceful than this house can ever hope to be!" And with that, she marched into the adjoining room to pack her things.

When a grim-faced Farley came for her later, Phoebe was dressed in her best traveling gown and her trunk was packed.

Farley paused at her door, glanced quickly over his shoulder, and then whispered, "What *happened*?"

"What happened, Mr. Farley, is that those two young ladies are the most ill-mannered, boorish, *despicable*—"

"Yes, yes, of course," Mr. Farley said hurriedly, stealing another glimpse over his shoulder as if he expected them to pounce on him at any moment—not an entirely unfounded fear—"but did you *do* something to one of them? Strike one's face, perhaps? Kick a shin?"

Phoebe blinked. "Of *course* not! Did they claim that I did? *No*, Mr. Farley! I merely tried to stop them from hitting one another like the little barbarians they clearly are!"

"Yes, I am well aware, Madame Dupree . . . yet all that sobbing and you didn't even strike them?" he asked again, clearly perplexed. But he quickly shook his head. "Never mind that now. His lordship would see you at once."

"Excellent, for I should like a word with *him* before I leave," Phoebe said sternly, and swept up her bonnet as she sailed through the door.

She marched down the hallway, practically running down the stairs ahead of Farley. He caught her at the second-floor landing with a hand to her arm. "At least allow me to tell you where you might *find* his lordship," he suggested.

Right. Phoebe gestured impatiently for Mr. Farley to lead the way. He led her to the ground floor of the east wing. At a pair of smooth mahogany doors, he paused and glanced at Phoebe. "A word of advice, madam. Let him do the talking. He seems to chat himself around to a fair disposition."

"Thank you," she said, but she had no intention of putting herself at Summerfield's mercy.

Farley rapped lightly, opened one of the doors, stepped inside, and announced, "Madame Dupree, my lord."

Phoebe did not wait for his summons. Her head high, she swept past Farley and stepped onto a thick wool rug in a richly—yet oddly—appointed study. Summerfield was seated behind his desk and hastily rose when he saw her.

"Please do not bother yourself, my lord," Phoebe said proudly. "I will not give you any trouble, but I cannot, in good conscience, leave here without telling you that even if your sisters are dressed in the finest clothing your money can *possibly* purchase, they will not receive offers, for they have the manners of a pair of *apes*."

Summerfield's eyes widened with surprise. He put a hand on his waist. "*Apes?*" he repeated incredulously.

"I do beg your pardon, but I cannot possibly put it more kindly than that," Phoebe said. "They argue constantly, they push and shove like street ruffians, and they are *churlish*."

"Aha," he said, as if that explained everything.

"Please do not look at me like that," she said, unable to read his expression. Where she expected anger, indignation, he almost looked . . . *amused*. "I only tell you this to save you quite a lot of pain, my lord. If you put those two young women into society without some lessons in propriety and etiquette, you and they will become the laughingstocks of this county," she said, sweeping her arm wide.

"As bad as that?" he asked with a bit of a wince.

"I fear even *worse*," Phoebe exclaimed dramatically, and carelessly dropped her bonnet onto a chair. "I pray you never take them to London, for they'd be devoured by the *ton*," she said fearlessly as Summerfield moved around his desk and perched his hip on the corner of it, his arms folded across his chest. "You cannot possibly know the things that are said about untoward ladies *there*, sir—"

"Madame Dupree—" he started, but Phoebe was too agitated to stop now.

"Oh, you may save your breath, my lord," she said, waving a hand at him as she began to pace. "I am well aware that *my* actions have been just as reprehensible, and I realize the irony of speaking to you of your sisters' behavior when, in fact, *I* have behaved just as abominably. I should be quite disappointed if you do not dismiss me at once. Therefore, I have taken the liberty of packing my things." She paused and unthinkingly picked up a wooden carving of a squat and naked man, and quickly set it down. Behind the oil lamp.

"Madam—"

"Really, I am still shaking at my loss of composure," she said, thrusting her hand out for him to observe the shaking before clasping her hands together, horrified that they were, indeed, still shaking. "I am quite prepared to suffer the consequences. I have said enough. The fabric, of course, belongs to you, and I have left it in the workroom you were so kind to make available to me. I am certain Mrs. Ramsey can arrange for another *modiste* as soon as is humanly possible. There you are. I am ready to depart."

She stood with her hands clasped at her waist, her chin high. She was, at least, dignified at her lowest moment. She rather imagined she seemed like Joan of Arc just now, facing her unavoidable and tragic fate. So why didn't he dismiss her?

Summerfield stood up and walked toward her.

Phoebe, not understanding his intent—and thinking it potentially sinister, given her assessment of his sisters—stepped back. "I *am* dreadfully sorry for saying what I did to your sisters, but I have never been so *willfully* pushed, and I have indeed been pushed, for I have a sister who can be very imperious and a cousin who can be rather demanding, and I assure you, I am not so easily offended."

"I rather suspect you are not," he said, and put his hand on hers, which she held tightly clasped before her.

The touch of his hand sent an unexpected shiver through her. "Oh, I am not," she said loudly. "It takes quite a lot to unhinge *me*, my lord—"

"Madame Dupree," he said calmly, "might I please have your leave to speak?"

Phoebe blinked. She looked at his hand, large and brown, on her two smaller ones, and felt a strange pressure in her chest. It was astounding, really, that a man could seem so gracious and gentle, but at the same time exude the energy and strength of a beast. His energy dwarfed her.

She didn't want to hear what he would say, didn't want to hear his deep voice dismiss her, didn't want to hear a man as exotic and intriguing as he remind her what a complete cake she had managed to become in his presence. Yet with his hand on hers, she could scarcely think, and nodded mutely.

Summerfield took her hand—or pried it free, actually—and when he had it, he put it on his arm and covered it securely. He tugged her into moving, and led her to a seat on a silk-covered settee that seemed a little out of place in this very masculine study.

When he had seen her into a seat, he flipped the tails of his coat, sat directly opposite her in an armchair, and said, "Frankly, Madame Dupree, I must say straight-away—"

"—*Here we are*," she muttered beneath her breath, expecting to hear his condemnation.

"—that I have no intention of dismissing you."

Phoebe caught her breath—for a moment.

She leaned forward, peering at him. "I beg your pardon, but have you heard a word I've uttered, my lord? You should dismiss me at once!"

"Perhaps I should," he said with a lopsided smile, "but I am not prepared to do so at the moment."

"Oh good *Lord,*" she murmured in exasperation.

"Now, while I do *not* share your assessment that my sisters behave as apes, I will concede that they can be rather difficult. Given the circumstances, I believe you did what any decent person might have done."

Phoebe looked at him suspiciously. "You do?"

"If you can delay dismissing yourself from my employ, I should like to tell you something about my sisters."

She was helpless to refuse him; his eyes held her mesmerized, made her long to remain in this study with him until she'd lost her last shred of dignity. She absently ran her finger along the seam of the seat cushion. "Very well. If you must."

"*Thank* you," he said. "My mother died in the course of giving birth to Jane, and my sisters have never had the benefit of a mother's love or guidance. I think that has been rather difficult for them."

That certainly gave Phoebe pause. Her own mother had been taken from her when she was nineteen and she missed her counsel and guidance dreadfully.

"There was a governess, of course, but she was perhaps not suitable for teaching all the things they should know about society and decorum." Summerfield looked at Phoebe pointedly. "It is true that my sisters have not been properly trained for their roles in society."

That was a statement of the painfully obvious kind if ever Phoebe had heard one.

"Frankly, I was unaware of their predicament until only very recently. I am a bit older than my siblings, the nearest being seven years my junior, and I have been abroad these last few years. When I left, my father was in good health and in full control of my siblings and the estate."

As he spoke, some emotion that looked like grief—raw, hardened grief—flitted across his features.

"In the time I was abroad, my father fell into exceptionally ill health. He suffered an apoplexy and lost control of his kingdom, so to speak. His illness rendered him unable to speak or to move. There were no provisions made for the handling of the estate, except those left to me by virtue of being his heir. By the time I arrived home, it was too late. The estate had fallen into disrepair and my siblings were living on precious few resources. Now, my father rarely leaves his room and I fear his time on this earth is not long."

"Oh no," Phoebe said, facing him fully now. "How awful for you. I . . . I understand how difficult it is, for I lost my mother only three years past."

He nodded solemnly. "Thank you, for it is indeed very difficult. But my point, Madame Dupree, is that my siblings were left to rear themselves at a critical time in their young lives. Unfortunately, they did not do as well as one might have hoped—I fear they have made quite a reputation for themselves. If I am to believe my father's secretary, they are fairly despised in Bedfordshire."

"*Oh,*" Phoebe whispered.

Summerfield suddenly stood up and clasped his hands behind his back. "I am endeavoring to change all that, Madame Dupree. I am determined to see my sisters properly presented and married, and my brothers transformed into upstanding gentlemen. I know my sisters are difficult, but I hope that you will take their tragic circumstances into consideration when working with them. They desperately need the clothing only you can provide."

"But . . ." She wanted to please him, but the prospect of working another moment with his sisters was too horrible to contemplate. "I fear I don't know how to help them," she said.

"I suggest you show them the deference that is their due, but do not stand down from them."

Show those two hoydens deference? Phoebe shook her head. "Forgive me, but I am very ill-suited to this charge. That is, I came to work, and I cannot complete my work if they treat me, and each other, so rudely."

"Agreed," he said. "I have warned them both that they will be dealt with harshly if they behave so badly again. You need only tell me if they do."

Still, Phoebe hesitated. She suspected that it hardly mattered how he threatened those two little beasts; they would do as they pleased.

But Summerfield saw her hesitation and leaned forward, bending over her, forcing her to look up at him. He captured her with a soft, imploring look. "You will help me, won't you, Madame Dupree?" he asked, and smoothly, gracefully went down on his haunches before her. "There are some needs a woman has that I understand all too well," he said low, his gaze languidly drifting from her mouth to her bosom. "Yet there are other needs for which I am quite helpless." He looked up, into her eyes. "I need all the help you can give me. Please."

Oh, how *shamelessly* he seduced her! Phoebe couldn't help her smile. She was no naïve young debutante to be charmed into doing his bidding—yet this was one time a man's charming manner was having the desired effect.

She sighed, irritated by her weakness, and leaned back, away from his compelling energy. "Very well, my lord. I shall *try*."

He smiled fully, and it reverberated throughout her

body. "*Splendid.* Now, as to the supper party for the Remingtons next week. I trust you will have two new gowns completed for Alice and Jane, will you not?"

"What? *No,* my lord! I can't *possibly*—"

"I am certain you can," he said, rising to his feet and offering his hand to help her up.

"It is impossible," Phoebe insisted as she took his hand. But when she came to her feet, she was standing toe to toe with him, the top of her head even with his chin. He did not let go of her hand, forcing Phoebe to tilt her head back to see his face.

"Not impossible in the least, I am confident," he said with a sultry smile. "But it *is* impossible for Alice and Jane to miss an opportunity to be presented at their very best."

"I cannot, my lord," Phoebe said firmly, trying to pull her hand free. "The maid who was helping me has been taken away. As it stands, I must work round the clock to complete *two* gowns suitable for an evening engagement."

His eyes focused on her mouth and stirred something deep inside her. "*Two* gowns, Madame Dupree. I will accept nothing less, and Mrs. Ramsey has assured me you will do as I wish."

She jerked her hand free of his. "I shall do what I can, but I cannot give my word."

He chuckled low in his throat, looked at the Spencer coat she wore primly fastened, and touched the button just below her throat. "*Two* gowns, Madame Dupree." His gaze was practically simmering.

Phoebe wished she were free of the Spencer. She wished she could just *breathe.* "Well, then. I will ask for your leave, my lord, so that I may clamber to fulfill your command at this very *moment.*"

He smiled. "I rather thought you'd see the necessity. You may have my leave. Good afternoon, madam."

"It is practically evening," she said, and brushed past him, passing so closely that in any other circumstance, it might have seemed forward.

Phoebe forgot her bonnet, forgot everything but his hazel eyes and the ridiculously imprudent sense of relief washing over her that she wasn't leaving Wentworth Hall after all.

The seamstress intrigued him.

Will watched her go, his eyes drinking her in. Oh yes, she intrigued him, enticed him—she was an oasis in the middle of a social desert. He'd noticed the soft curves of her body the morning he had introduced her to the feral herd. With her hair hanging in one long, curly tail over her shoulder, her skin free of cosmetics, he'd thought then it was rare for a woman to possess such natural beauty. She was alluring. So alluring, in fact, that he'd felt a stirring of lust, a familiar tightening in his groin for a beautiful woman.

But he hadn't noticed until perhaps this very afternoon how stunning Madame Dupree truly was. Perhaps it was the wild curl of her hair, the color of cornsilk, and the way it was scarcely contained in her prim little coif. Or perhaps it was the delicate blush of her cheeks when he'd touched the button of her coat. Or the largest and most unusual blue-green eyes he'd ever seen in his life.

And perhaps it was that she did not treat him with dripping deference the way most people did, but with a confidence and self-assurance he had not seen in another woman since his return to England.

Frankly, he thought it interesting such a woman was working as a seamstress. She was a graceful, elegant beauty men would long to touch. Will would have thought some wealthy gentleman would have snatched her up, either as a wife or a mistress, and surrounded her with beauty and comfort.

He walked to the window and looked out at the sloping green hills of the estate.

The fact that she was working as a seamstress under *his* roof was something of a blessing at a point in time when he desperately needed one.

The truth was that Will had not understood how difficult it would be to slip back into genteel living after his life abroad. Things moved exceedingly slow in the English countryside, and, moreover, he found the decorum required of his position in society stifling. He was not the same man he'd been when he'd left Wentworth Hall all those years ago. His experiences had opened a whole other universe to him, one brimming with new ideas and opportunities. That universe had narrowed considerably since his return.

Here, he felt as if he'd been shipwrecked on a provincial island, and even though he was surrounded by people, he felt mightily alone. He longed to move, to do something that made his blood race.

He longed to make love to a woman. He *craved* it.

Will fingered the small blue Egyptian scarab he wore around his neck, the charm that was supposed to help him rise above the needs of the flesh to a higher plane.

He'd worked hard to live up to the expectations of his rank since returning to Wentworth Hall. His duty to his father and his title was to marry and produce heirs, to keep his cock in his trousers and avoid scandal, and he took that responsibility seriously. Father had seen to it that Will had been allowed to experience life. Now he would fulfill his father's wish and find a potential mate in the seemingly endless supply of unmarried young women in Bedfordshire, court her properly, marry her, and give his father the grandchild he'd dreamed of holding.

That duty was taking much longer than Will might have guessed. He'd not understood how difficult it would be to find a woman he could actually envision as his wife. He'd not been with a woman since he'd left Cairo, had no hope of finding a woman to bed who was not a harlot in this corner of England, and he was feeling the need with increasing urgency every day.

That need had grown very strong in the course of his interview with Madame Dupree. As she'd gone on about his daft sisters, he'd watched her pace, her hands flailing in her pique, and he'd imagined her with eyes half closed, her succulent lips parted, her lovely body nude beneath him as he thrust into her—

A knock on the door interrupted his thoughts; it was Addison with his gloves and cloak. Will would be joining Henry Ellison to dine at the home of Bernard Fortenberry, who had three unmarried daughters.

He tucked the scarab beneath his shirt. "How do I look, Addison?" he asked, presenting himself to his manservant's inspection. Addison maintained that the mark of a true gentleman was his fastidious dress—another skill Will had forgotten how to apply properly in his years of living in buckskins and lawn shirts.

Addison frowned slightly and reached up to his collar, straightening his neckcloth. "There we are, milord. Splendid, as always."

Will smiled and fit a hand into a glove. "By the bye, what can you tell me of Madame Dupree?"

Addison gave him a quick look before turning his

attention to the cloak. "Widowed, milord. Her husband was French. She is English."

He'd guessed as much. "Family?"

"She's mentioned a sister and a cousin who live on the moors north of Alnwick. No one else."

"The *moors*?" He found that curious. The North Country was sparsely populated and rather harsh in climate—Madame Dupree seemed too refined for it. "How long widowed?" he asked as he allowed Addison to hold up his cloak.

"I wouldn't rightly know, sir, but she is out of her widow's weeds. That would suggest two years or more. Shall I make the usual inquiries?"

Will's gaze flicked over Addison. "Indeed you should," he said. He fastened the clasp of his cloak at his throat, but he felt a slight flush in his chest. A young woman out of her widow's weeds might be as eager for a man's touch as a man would be to give it. "And sooner rather than later."

"Yes, milord," Addison said.

Honestly, Will hadn't felt this cheerful in several months. He smiled at Addison. "Don't wait up for me. I am certain Mr. Fortenberry will keep me as long as is possible with his talk of the accomplishments of his daughters, and I rather suspect that afterward Henry will know of a gaming table somewhere."

"Of course," Addison said. He picked up Madame Dupree's forgotten bonnet. "Leave it," Will said, stopping him. "I shall return it to her."

The tips of Addison's ears pinkened. "I shall put it here for safekeeping," he said, and placed it carefully on a shelf near the door, then bowed low as Will swept out, destined for another tedious evening of chatting up young women who hadn't seen as much of Bedfordshire as he'd seen of the world.

Eight

Since Summerfield had decreed Phoebe would create and finish two evening gowns in time for the supper party, she worked from the moment she arose until she fell exhausted into her bed. But in three days' time she managed to finish the design and cut two gowns, and in spite of the frequent interruptions of Alice and Jane, she and Frieda had begun the hard work of sewing the pieces together.

But there was no time for embroidering them, so Phoebe resorted to making little rosettes to adorn Alice's gown. She stayed up half of one night making them, and was up again at dawn, sewing them along the hem.

She had no time for herself and dressed simply in a very plain gown, her hair braided and hanging down her back.

Mrs. Turner brought a hard-boiled egg and some hot chocolate for her. "You'll waste to nothing if you don't eat," she'd chided her, but Phoebe had yet to touch it.

When she heard a knock at her door sometime after eleven o'clock that morning, she assumed it was Frieda. "Come!" she called, and heard the door open. "Ah, Frieda, I am so glad you have come. My fingers are numb and I've got four more of these bloody rosettes to attach." She sat back on her heels and looked at her handiwork. Rather nice, actually.

When Frieda didn't answer, she leaned to her right to peer around the dress.

Good Lord, it was Summerfield! With a gasp of

surprise, Phoebe came awkwardly to her feet—but her feet had gone numb from sitting as she was, and she stumbled a bit. She quickly righted herself, dusted her knees, and tried vainly to smooth the wild bits of hair that had fallen from her braid. "I beg your pardon, my lord, I did not expect you," she said anxiously, removing the long apron into which she'd stuck pins and needles and tossing it onto a chair.

"I have come to return your bonnet," he said, and held out the bonnet she had forgotten three days ago. "You left it behind in the study."

"Oh. Thank you." How curious, she thought, that he would bring it to her instead of sending it with a servant. She started forward, but Summerfield suddenly moved deeper into the room, toward Jane's gown, which was, at present, draped across the table.

He cocked his head thoughtfully. "Which of my sisters will wear it?" he asked.

"Jane . . . I hope," Phoebe said with a quick glance heavenward. Yesterday, Jane had complained of the gown's pale green color, even though Phoebe assured her it complemented her complexion very well.

Summerfield studied it a moment longer before turning back to Phoebe. His eyes flicked over her but seemed to linger on her lips. He held out the bonnet to her. "Your bonnet."

"Thank you," Phoebe said, and smiled self-consciously as she reached for the satin ribbons of her bonnet. "You are too kind." She gave the ribbons a slight tug.

But Summerfield suddenly clenched the back of the bonnet in his hand and wouldn't let go. His gaze drifted to the bodice of her gown. "Have you another name, Madame Dupree?"

She could feel the blood leave her face almost instantly, and she experienced a sick, sinking feeling of having been caught at her foolish game. How could he possibly know? *Mrs. Ramsey, of course!* That wretched woman had told him!

He waited for an answer.

"What do you mean?" she asked carefully, scrutinizing him for any sign that he might know who she was.

He smiled with surprise. "I mean only that 'Madame Dupree' seems so . . . formal. I thought perhaps there was another name by which I might address you."

Phoebe tugged again at the bonnet, but he held fast. "Do you mean a . . . a *given* name?" she asked suspiciously.

His smile widened. "Are you always so contrary? A *name*, Madame Dupree. A given name, a nickname . . . a name by which your sister might call you."

"Phoebe."

"*Phoebe*," he said, and nodded. "It suits you."

What suited her was some distance between them. She was standing so close she could count the whiskers in his sideburns, could feel the heat of his body. She tugged at the bonnet again, but he stubbornly held on, his lips curved in a cocky, wicked smile.

"I confess, Phoebe, it is difficult to appreciate your work without seeing it on a feminine form."

His eyes, Phoebe noticed, had turned a very warm green. She gripped the ribbons of the bonnet and gave it a harder tug. "Lady Alice's dress is on a feminine form just behind you, sir."

"That is not the dress I care to see," he said, and stepped closer to her.

"All right," Phoebe said. "If you will just give me my *bonnet*, my lord," she said, pulling hard, "I shall fetch Lady Jane and you may see the gown on her."

"Not Jane," he said, clearly enjoying their little tug-of-war. "*You*."

Phoebe almost let go. "But . . . but that gown is made to fit Lady Jane. Not me."

"You seem similar in size to me," he said, his gaze boldly wandering over her body.

"I assure you we are not, my lord. There are *many* differences."

"You are undoubtedly the most obstinate servant to ever inhabit Wentworth Hall. You are close enough in size and I assure you, *Phoebe*, that I will appreciate that gown on you far more than I can ever hope to appreciate it on my sister Jane. Do please don the thing so that I may judge its suitability."

Phoebe froze as fingers of indignation crawled up her spine. "*Suitability?*" she said, almost choking on the word. "It is made in the fashion of the latest styles from London—"

"I hardly care." He shifted closer, smiling down at her in a way that made her feel like she was slowly roasting on the inside, and said softly, "I want to see you in that gown. Put it on." He spoke like a man who was accustomed to ordering people about.

Phoebe glanced at the gown.

"*Now.*"

As accustomed as he was to issuing orders, Phoebe was unaccustomed to receiving them. "And if I don't?" she asked boldly.

Summerfield cocked a brow. "Perhaps you want me to put it on you."

Oh *Lord*! The suggestion made her heart leap. "You wouldn't."

He shrugged a little. "I've done worse."

Her heart leapt again.

"You will put it on if you value your position here," he added.

A million retorts skated through her mind—so many

that she momentarily forgot she was a servant in this house, that she had no choice but to obey him. She forcibly swallowed down the words on the tip of her tongue and looked again at the gown.

Summerfield let go of the bonnet and stepped aside so that she could pick it up. Phoebe tossed the bonnet onto the table, and with a heated look for Summerfield, she snatched up the gown and went to the thin silk privacy screen one of the footmen had brought up yesterday and stepped behind it. She could hear him moving about the room as she unbuttoned her gown with shaking hands, slipped out of it, and laid it across a chair.

He paused somewhere nearby and asked, "From where do you hail, Phoebe?"

"Lon— Ah . . . Northumberland," she responded, distracted.

"Any particular village?"

Phoebe paused and stared at the screen. A *village*? Blast Greer for her silly idea of the moors—Phoebe was hard-pressed at the moment to name one village in all of England! She squeezed her eyes shut and tried to remember the atlas she, Greer, and Ava had studied when they had concocted her false identity. "Berwick-upon-Tweed," she said brightly as that name suddenly came to her.

"Berwick-upon-Tweed?" He sounded surprised. "Then your father was a . . . a fisherman, I suppose?"

Lord, a fisherman? Phoebe grabbed up Jane's gown and pulled it over her head. "I . . . I scarcely remember him at all." That was really rather close to the truth— her father had died when she was only seven years of age.

She buttoned the gown as best she could, but couldn't reach the buttons in the middle of her back.

It wouldn't matter if she could, for her bosom was larger than Jane's—substantially larger, by the look of it—and she doubted she could fit a button into its hole with a lever.

"Are you dressed?"

That question startled her because he was now standing just on the other side of the screen. "Ah . . ." She dropped her arms and looked down. The décolletage was far too tight for her—she was practically spilling out of the gown.

"Are you coming out, Madame Dupree?"

"It doesn't fit," she said, studying the décolletage of the gown. "Jane is smaller than I am."

"Allow me to see it—"

"It really doesn't *fit*—"

"Are you indecent?"

"No! But I really must—" She cried out with alarm when he suddenly pushed the screen aside, propped one arm on top of it, and brazenly studied her figure in the gown.

"My lord!" she cried in protest. "I beg your pardon!"

Summerfield ignored her. His gaze was devouring her, taking in every inch of her in that pale green gown. With a nod of approval, he finally stepped aside, motioning her forward.

Phoebe didn't move.

"Come, come," he said impatiently, gesturing for her to step forward.

With one hand holding the gown together at her back, she marched forward and came to a halt in the middle of the workroom.

"*Yes,*" he murmured, and walked a slow circle around her, taking in the gown from every conceivable angle while Phoebe's face burned. When he at last moved around to stand before her, he looked into her eyes. "Beautiful," he said. "A diamond of the first water."

He was not referring to the gown. Phoebe could feel the pressure of him again, his masculine energy filling the room, pressing down on her chest, making it difficult to breathe.

"But I think there is one improvement that can be made when Jane wears it," he added silkily.

"This gown is perfectly made," she said, lifting her chin. "What could possibly be improved?"

"The bodice." He casually touched his finger to the skin of her breast, just above the bias of the gown's neckline, and traced a slow, tantalizing line across her flesh. "It is too low."

His touch made her feverish, but there was one thing Phoebe knew with all certainty—the décolletage of the gown was *perfect*. "It will fit Lady Jane properly, I assure you."

He gave her a lopsided smile. "It is too *low*," he said again, and brushed his knuckles across the swell of her breasts. "When a man sees a beautiful woman in a gown cut as low as this, his eye is drawn to her flesh, and he is overcome with the urge to touch her." He repeated his caress over her breasts again, but his eyes remained locked on hers. "That will not do for Jane."

Phoebe's skin was sizzling and the pressure on her was unbearable. His touch was unlike anything she'd ever known—it branded her, left an indelible mark. She imagined his brown hand against the pale skin of her bare breast, his mouth on her nipple. Such thoughts normally would have disconcerted her, but for some inexplicable reason, they emboldened her— or rather, emboldened Madame Dupree, who had nothing to lose. Phoebe knew instinctively that if she did not stand up to his seduction, he would devour her like a confection.

She smiled warily. "If a man is so overcome by the sight of skin, then I'd wager that man is not a gentleman and will not be in your sister's company."

Summerfield gave her a roguish grin and casually stroked her flesh once more before fingering a curl of her hair at her sternum. "And what of your company? I'd wager you know that a gentleman is diffident with women . . . but that a man knows how to satisfy her. I suspect you have not forgotten the difference between a man and a gentleman in your bed."

All right, then, *no* man had ever spoken to her so boldly, and certainly no man had ever caused something to fire so deep inside her and spread its damp heat to her arms and legs. It felt as if a part of her, deeply submerged, had broken off and was rising to the surface, a piece of unbridled desire bobbing about, seeking its way out.

Still, Phoebe held her ground. "Do you think you are the only man to speak so suggestively, my lord? That I am ignorant of the many ways a man might attempt to seduce me? Do you think I will tremble and wilt to your will?"

"Quite the contrary. I think you will blossom."

A white-hot shiver shot through her. "A blossom picked from the vine will dry up and blow away with the slightest wind once it has seen its glory."

He cocked a brow and smiled. "Not," he said, "if it is properly tended."

The abrupt sound of the door opening caused her heart to leap in her chest, and she instantly lurched backward, away from Summerfield. She heard Frieda's gasp of surprise, and then, "I beg your pardon, my lord!"

For a moment, Phoebe feared she would collapse of sheer mortification. As it was, she could scarcely make herself look at the girl.

But when she did, Frieda was gaping at the two of them.

Summerfield merely smiled. "It's quite all right, Frieda." His hot gaze raked over Phoebe once more before he turned from her and walked to the door. "Madame Dupree needs your assistance."

"Yes, sir," Frieda said, dipping a curtsy.

Summerfield walked past Frieda without looking back.

The moment he'd left the workroom, Phoebe whirled around and stepped behind the screen. Frieda shut the door behind Summerfield and ran to the screen. She pushed it aside and gaped at Phoebe, bright-eyed and smiling broadly. "What in *heaven*?" she squealed.

"Just . . . just put it on the table," Phoebe said irritably as she handed Jane's gown to her. "And whatever you may think, it was not *my* choosing to don it."

"No, of course not," Frieda said with a snort. She took the gown from Phoebe and held it up to her own body, admiring it in a mirror. "Would that he'd look at *me* like that. Makes a lass want to fall on her back and cock her heels to the ceiling, eh? You're awful pretty," she added thoughtfully. "Pretty as a picture. I'm not the least surprised he's taken a shine to you." She put Jane's gown onto the table and smoothed it out. "But I daresay Lady Jane would be fit for Bedlam if she knew you'd worn her gown. I'd have a care, were I you."

Phoebe thought better advice had never been spoken.

Nine

The strange pressure Summerfield had caused in her did not abate; Phoebe felt tense and tingly and on the brink of a breathtaking madness long after he'd gone.

Summerfield was no different from dozens of other gentlemen she'd met, yet she'd never been so drawn to a man as she was to him. Granted, she'd rarely been as direct with a man as she had been with Summerfield—it was not a luxury she could afford.

Lord Stanhope, her brother-in-law's dear friend, had made her laugh one night over whist, for he was delightfully charming when he was of a mind, and the very next morning, Ava had, rather indiscreetly, blurted that she and Middleton thought Phoebe and Stanhope would make an excellent match.

As a result, Phoebe avoided flirtations with gentlemen. And when Lord Stanhope or any other gentleman looked at her with hunger in his eyes, it made her feel queasy. But when *Summerfield* looked at her like that, it was almost as if she could feel the waves of his desire breaking on her, that feeling of sand giving way beneath her feet, as if she were in danger of being swept away by it.

She was extremely titillated by this odd twist of fate that allowed her to be blissfully free and whoever she wanted to be. No one here would try and make a match for her on the strength of a mere laugh. For the few weeks she resided at Wentworth Hall, her entire life was a work of fiction. She was free to enter the fantasy of being the widowed Madame Dupree, to possess that fantasy, body and soul.

And when she finished making the gowns, Madame Dupree and the fantasy would simply cease to exist. The French *modiste* would either return to France or die. Tragically, of course, in some awful accident—perhaps a carriage sliding off a bridge into the Thames at high tide and then sinking to the bottom, trapping Madame Dupree . . .

Well.

She could determine the exact circumstances later, and in the meantime, Lady Phoebe Fairchild would return to London in the autumn, to all the strictures of society and rules of decorum that had governed her life for as long as she could remember.

The very idea of becoming Madame Dupree in body and spirit put a smile on her face. And then a frown. That she even contemplated such a thing surprised her on some level. Where was her moral compass? What sort of woman dreamt of an affair with a man who was not her husband? Then again, what sort of woman denied herself the pleasures other women seemed to take for granted? And for heaven's sake, she wasn't thinking of *bedding* him—that had entirely too many consequences, even in her disguise. But a bit of heated flirting? Oh yes, she'd like that very much.

Phoebe wondered what her mother might say if she knew her thoughts. Her mother had always adored parties and flirting and social events where lots of ladies and gentlemen gathered. Even at Bingley Hall, her mother had been very much in love with Phoebe's father, but she had enjoyed the attention of other men.

Phoebe recalled an afternoon when her mother allowed her, Ava, and Greer to dress in some of her finer things for play. They wore her hats and her shoes and her jewelry over silky gowns that her mother had to belt up so that they could walk. Around and around the grand salon they had gone, following Mamma, pretending to be ladies out in society.

"You must never *appear* to pursue a gentleman's interest, darlings," Mamma had gaily instructed them, leading them about the room. "For gentlemen like to think *they* are the ones in pursuit. So you must let the poor things believe it, even if it is not the least bit true."

"But how do we make them believe it?" Ava had asked with a frown of concentration.

"My love, they will believe it if you merely smile at them," she'd laughed. "Here, watch me." She took a few steps, then paused to smile saucily over her shoulder before she continued her walk. She stopped a few feet away and whirled around. "There, do you see?" she asked. "If you smile at them as I have just smiled at you, they will follow you like puppies."

"But are they to follow like puppies *all* the time?" This from Greer, who had an insatiable need to understand the rules of engagement in all aspects of life.

"If you smile like your mother has just done," a male voice said low, "they will follow until they catch you, and when they catch you, they will eat you."

The four of them whirled about. To the girls' delight, their father had entered the room, was standing just at the threshold, leaning against the door frame, his arms folded as he watched them parade about like geese.

To this day, Phoebe could remember the way her mother's face lit up when she saw him standing there. "Darling, why ever do you say such things? You will give them nightmares!" she'd said as she glided across the room to plant a kiss on his lips.

"And *you* will teach them to tease a man mercilessly," he said with a smile as he touched the tip of her nose with his knuckle.

Mamma had laughed. "They are *girls,* Robert. I am not teaching them anything they weren't born already knowing," she'd said with a wink. When she turned away from him, she was still beaming, and Phoebe would never forget how tenderly her father had looked upon her mother.

She wanted that look of tenderness. She wanted a husband who adored her as her father had adored her mother.

Phoebe awoke early to the sound of birds chirping outside her window, and thoughts of Summerfield still crowding her mind. She began her work early, hoping to push those thoughts away in favor of practical considerations.

When Frieda arrived at the workroom at half past ten, she informed Phoebe that Alice and Jane had not risen from their beds in spite of promising to do so, and therefore the fittings would be after luncheon.

With a groan, Phoebe left Frieda to do the finishing work on Jane's gown, picked up her sketchbook, and went outside to design more gowns.

The day was warm; Phoebe was glad for the cover of the gazebo. She sketched two gowns for Alice that she hoped would offset her dour expression, and was interrupted by the sound of riders moving fast and hard. When she looked behind her, she saw Summerfield and his brother Roger racing up the wide lawn from the fields.

They were literally racing, their horses neck and neck. Summerfield's horse was taller and stronger than the one Roger rode, but Roger's seemed more sure-footed. As they rode down the lawn, the horses kicked up big clumps of grass; Summerfield suddenly veered right. Roger shouted; Summerfield led his horse to leap over a hedgerow, sending up a spray of water on the other side as the horse landed near the lake.

With a gasp, Phoebe jumped to her feet and twisted around, watching in awe as Summerfield and his horse swam diagonally across the corner of the lake while Roger and his horse raced around the hedgerow and a stand of trees.

By the time Summerfield had emerged from the lake, his clothing soaked, the horse dripping, he had two lengths on Roger as he disappeared around the side of the stables.

Phoebe sat down on the bench and stared into space. That was extraordinarily and utterly *fearless*.

It was an hour or more before Phoebe made her way back to the house, going in through the gates that led through the parterres. Every day she took a different path, for the gardens were large and exquisite. She paused to study a hedge of yew that had been trimmed in the shape of a dragon, a smile of pleasure curving her lips. But as she followed the curve of the dragon's tail in the path, she stumbled upon a man in a wheelchair.

The earl.

Several feet away stood a rather large footman, who was speaking to someone Phoebe could not see.

The earl sat with his head at an odd angle, but he was looking directly at her. "Good afternoon," she said, curtsying.

The earl lifted a single finger at the same moment the footman noticed her. The conversation he was engaged in ceased as he turned toward Phoebe.

"I beg your pardon," she said instantly, and moved, intending to leave.

"Madame Dupree?" Summerfield stepped around the hedge. His hat was under one arm, and he was still carrying his riding crop. His clothing was soaked through, all the way up to his chest.

"My lord, I do beg your pardon. I was not aware."

"Of course not. Come," he said jovially. "Please forgive my state of dress—I was engaged in a bit of a race this morning."

"Yes . . . I saw."

"Did you?" he asked, obviously pleased that she had. "Roger is still in the stables. He threatens not to come out until I admit I cheated."

"*Did* you cheat?" she asked, drawing a startled look from the footman.

But Summerfield laughed. "Hardly. The bet was only to be the first to reach the stables. There were no rules that determined how. Do you think I should not have swum across the lake, madam?"

"It seemed a bit careless," she admitted with a smile.

The footman's eyes widened even more.

"Sometimes one finds immeasurable joy in being careless," Summerfield said with a wink as he strolled forward. "Please allow me to introduce my father, the Earl of Bedford," he said, and put a hand on the elderly man's shoulder.

The earl's head had not moved, but Phoebe believed he was seeing her very clearly. She curtsied again. "How do you do, my lord?"

"Father, this is Madame Dupree. She has come into our service to fashion proper clothing for Alice and Jane." He glanced at Phoebe again, his regard warm. "It is good she has come."

Those words whispered through her, making her smile broadly.

"I have decided to host a house party over a fortnight,

culminating in a ball, and I can trust that in Madame Dupree's capable hands Alice and Jane will be turned out suitably." He shifted his gaze to Phoebe. "The guests will begin to arrive at the end of next month. Any later than that and we shall lose some of our most eligible young bachelors to London and the Little Season, I fear."

"But a month is hardly enough time to finish all the gowns you have commissioned."

"I am certain you will be successful," he said politely but firmly.

He was being completely unreasonable. Just because he thought she was a servant gave him no right to be so unreasonable. Phoebe forced a serene smile. "I can't imagine how you might be *certain*, my lord, given that you've never *made* a gown."

The footman's mouth fell open.

Summerfield, however, smiled with surprise. "I am *certain*, Madame Dupree, because you are an extraordinarily gifted woman."

Well. There *was* that. She glanced at the earl, who was still looking at her with bright blue eyes. Phoebe smiled, too flustered to speak.

"On the morrow, Madame Dupree, I should like you to accompany my sisters into Greenhill. They have impressed upon me the need for sundries that only a woman can help them purchase."

And she *certainly* had better things to do than lead Alice and Jane about a store stocked with unmentionables if she was to finish all the gowns, but Phoebe could only nod, her mind still racing through all that must be done to have the girls outfitted by the end of next month, and the fact that he'd called her extraordinarily gifted.

"Speak to Addison before you go and he will see to it that you have sufficient—"

"My lord!"

A man Phoebe had never seen before was rushing toward them, his eyes on Summerfield, oblivious to the rest of them.

"Mr. Carsdale?" Summerfield said, clearly surprised. "What the devil is the matter?"

"I beg your pardon, my lord," he said breathlessly, "but there has been a spot of trouble this morning."

"What sort of trouble?"

The man glanced warily at Phoebe. "Joshua," he said quietly.

Summerfield's fingers, she noted, curled even more tightly around his riding crop. "Join me in my dressing room while I change," he said, and looked at his father. "You mustn't worry," he said with a reassuring squeeze of the old man's shoulder. He instantly started for the house, the stranger hurrying to keep up with his long stride.

Phoebe glanced at the earl, then at the footman. "May I help you in some way?"

"No, mu'um," the big man said. "His lordship and I do quite nicely together, eh, milord?" he asked, and deftly tilted the earl's chair back a little, wheeled the earl about, and began to push him at a leisurely pace through the parterres.

Ten

It was beyond Will's ability to understand what drove Joshua to seek to destroy his reputation, his family's reputation, and indeed, his own life.

"I am uncertain how much was at stake," Mr. Carsdale, his father's secretary, said, speaking low so that Addison would not overhear—but Addison was hovering nearby, and Will was certain he hadn't missed a single word. "The injured gentleman and his companions have taken your brother in hand and are riding for Wentworth Hall at this very moment to seek satisfaction from you."

Bloody hell. Will turned to the mirror to tie his neckcloth and thought of his father, who was unable to speak or to write, but was capable of understanding everything completely—particularly that Joshua had cheated in a high-stakes poker game. *Fool. Careless, stupid fool.*

When his father heard of this—and he would, for Will could not keep anything so dire from him—he would not be able to bear it. It hurt Will monstrously that he could not seem to set everyone and everything to rights. More than anything, he wanted to assure his father that he'd not come home too late, that the Darbys would persevere as a family, maintaining respectability and social standing. But day after day, something happened to knock him flat, to make him think the family would never recover.

And now Joshua had been caught cheating. *Cheating!* It was inconceivable, despicable—his brother, raised in privilege and afforded an excellent education, was no better than a common thief.

"What do these gentlemen want, other than Joshua's neck in a noose?" Will asked, his calm belying his anger.

"Their winnings restored, I'd imagine, my lord."

At least they had a price. "How much, do you suppose?"

"Fifty pounds should suffice."

Will resisted the urge to choke on the exorbitant sum and finished tying his neckcloth. Addison appeared behind him, holding up a clean coat. Will slipped into it, adjusted the sleeves of his shirt. These delicate situations made him chafe. In Egypt, in India he would have handled this quite differently—consented to a public lashing or some such thing. It was certainly no less than Joshua deserved. But here he must tread lightly, speak and act with the utmost decorum, or he would only make a bad situation worse. "Well, then, Mr. Carsdale," he said calmly, "shall we repair to the salon to meet this calamity head-on?"

A half hour later, the men arrived with Joshua in their midst, his brother looking defiant as he strode ahead of them into the earl's study behind Farley. Will knew only one of the men, Mr. Aimes, a brash young man who was known to have a temper.

Will stood at the hearth, one arm on the mantel. "Gentlemen," he said casually, and shifted a cold gaze to Joshua.

"My Lord Summerfield, it is with great regret that I must inform you your brother is accused of cheating at a gentlemen's game of cards," Mr. Aimes said, dispensing with any greeting.

"That is a highly contemptible accusation, sir," Will said calmly. "I hope you are prepared to prove it."

"We are witnesses, my lord," another gentleman said, inclining his head. "Mr. James, at your service. I observed Mr. Summerfield marking a card."

"As did I, my lord," the third man said. "I am Sir Phillip of Batencourt. When I examined the deck of cards, I discovered several of them had been marked."

Will glanced at his brother. "Did you mark cards, Joshua?"

Joshua snorted. "Is this a court? Do you expect me to incriminate myself?"

"I expect you to deny it," Will said evenly. But his heart was racing.

Joshua shrugged and fell lazily onto a chair, one leg crossed over the other. His hair was mussed, his collar crooked. He had all the markings of a man who had been out all night, and his defiance and indifference were outrageous.

"What do you want of me?" Will forced himself to inquire of Mr. Aimes.

"Satisfaction, my lord."

"Do you suggest I second my brother in a duel?" he asked flippantly, but it certainly brought Joshua's head up; he looked anxiously from Will to Mr. Aimes.

"I had hoped to avoid such a tragedy, but if you refuse to make good on your brother's cheating, then I shall have no recourse but to demand such satisfaction as that."

Will looked at Joshua from the corner of his eye and shrugged. "It is an accepted remedy to such a crime," he said idly.

Mr. Aimes looked startled. "It . . . it is a last resort, my lord. Surely there is something short of that to which we might agree."

"Very well," Will said, and tried to hide his disgust as he walked to a French secretary and opened the panel, withdrawing a ledger. "Perhaps," he said as he dipped a pen in ink and quickly wrote a bank note for fifty pounds, "this might be something short of that." He sprinkled a little sand on it, then waved the bank draft dry before turning to Mr. Aimes. "I thank you for bringing my brother's behavior to my attention," Will said crisply. "If that is satisfactory, I assure you he will be dealt with in the harshest and most appropriate manner."

Mr. Aimes glanced up, surprised by the amount. "I think this will suffice."

"You have done my ailing father a great kindness by bringing Joshua home and allowing us to address it," Will said. "You have my word that our family will deal with this incident in a most discreet manner, and, I should hope, you will extend my generous father the same courtesy."

Mr. Aimes took Will's measure for a moment before extending his hand. "You have my word."

"Thank you," Will said. "Farley, see them out, will you?" he asked the unobtrusive butler.

He waited until the men had left and Farley had shut the door behind them before looking at Joshua. Joshua avoided his gaze and stood. "Well, then, if that is done—"

Will caught his arm. He heard Joshua's sigh, saw the unrepentant look on his face, and Will could not help himself. He hit his brother square in the jaw, knocking him flat on his arse. Joshua cried out and put a hand to his mouth, saw the blood on his fingers from a cut on his lip. A murderous look washed over his face; he scrambled up and lunged at Will, his arms swinging.

But Will was larger and stronger than his brother, and grabbed his arms, pushing him back, toppling him over a chair. They rolled across the floor, arms flailing at one another until Will pinned Joshua to the floor. He glared at his brother, his jaw clenched, as Joshua tried vainly to kick him off.

"*Why?*" Will demanded, and let go, coming to his feet to tower over Joshua. "How could you dishonor your father so?"

Joshua came unsteadily to his feet and shrugged. "I do not care to lose."

Rage exploded red hot in Will. "What in God's name is the matter with you, Joshua? Do you mean to see yourself *hanged*?"

"You'd like that, wouldn't you?" Joshua spat.

Will surged toward his brother, his instinct to put his hands around his throat. Joshua tried to escape, but Will caught him and threw him up against the wall, knocking over a small gueridon with a marble top. He held Joshua there, their faces only an inch or so apart. "If you disgrace this family again, I swear I shall hang you myself. You are a dishonor to your father, to your sisters, to your name!" he said angrily. "I confess I cannot fathom what has you so bent on destruction, but you are well on the path of seeing it done, sir!"

"What do you care?" Joshua shouted, and shoved with all his might, knocking him back a step or two. Glaring at Will, he straightened his coat and said, with great vehemence, "My life is no concern of yours, Summerfield! We were perfectly happy here until *you* returned and began to change everything!"

"What in bloody hell do you mean?"

"No one asked you to come home," Joshua said acidly.

Will blinked with shock. "Is *that* what bothers you? You resent that I've come home?"

"I resent *you*, yes," Joshua said. "You've no right to come home after all this time and push us aside as if we are nothing."

"I've not pushed anyone aside—"

"I was the eldest here!" Joshua exploded. "I was the one who looked after our siblings and our father!"

"The place was a shambles when I returned!" Will bellowed. "Is that your idea of looking after things?"

"I did the best I could under the circumstances! The funds were tied up in *your* name, but you were off to God knows where while we languished! And when you came back, you never showed me even the slightest courtesy! You never inquired as to what we had done to survive! You dismissed me the moment you walked through the door!"

It was suddenly becoming clear to Will; the mistake he'd made began to seep into his brain. He'd come home assuming Joshua was still a boy. Will could hardly be faulted for his perception—the place had been in terrible disarray, and Joshua had already earned a black reputation for gambling and whoring. Worse, he was dragging Roger down the path of debauchery along with him, and Alice and Jane had been terribly neglected.

No, Will had seen nothing but disaster all around when he'd come home. He never really saw Joshua at all. He suddenly understood what a grave mistake that had been. "Perhaps you are right," he said, trying to smooth it over. "Perhaps I did not give you your due—"

"Don't speak to me of *due*," Joshua said sourly. "I do not answer to you, Summerfield! I am the son of the Earl of Bedford in my own right, and I do not need, nor will I seek, your permission to live!"

"Mind you have a care when you speak, Joshua," Will said low. "You may be his son, but I am his heir. Not you. Your livelihood will one day depend on me."

Joshua's gaze darkened. "Are you *threatening* me?"

"I am warning you. Behave like a gentleman, and there will be no issue between us. Continue down this path of thievery and whoring, and you will find yourself cut off and displaced from here, *heed* me. I cannot change what has happened to Papa or what happened here before I came home. But I can do everything within my power to ensure you do not bring another mark against this family."

If looks could kill, Will would be lying dead. "Have I your permission to leave, my lord?" Joshua asked, his voice dripping with rancor. "To sleep? To piss in a pot?"

He whirled about in disgust, stalking from the room before Will could answer.

When he'd gone, Will was suddenly spent and sank onto the settee, covering his face with his hands. He was not prepared for this—a little less than three months ago, he'd come home to an ailing father, but he'd never in his wildest dreams thought he'd have to step into his father's shoes.

He didn't know *how* to step into his father's shoes. Things that seemed obvious to him were lost on his siblings. He could hardly pretend to be a parent or a guardian to them—he was *appalled* by them. He had absolutely no idea how to change their behavior, and it seemed as though every time he tried he was met with resistance and resentment.

Joshua, of all of them, stretched Will's reason and comprehension to the breaking point. It was almost as if he *wanted* to hang, and damn if Will knew how to stop him. Joshua and Roger were both aimless, and Will had done his best to steer both brothers toward suitable oc-cupations—a naval officer's commission for Joshua and a chance to see the world. Perhaps the clergy for Roger and a parish he might call his own. Both brothers had scoffed at his suggestions.

Will sighed wearily and slowly leaned back, staring up at the elaborately plastered ceiling. *What he wouldn't give for his father's counsel.* Unfortunately, the most he could hope for was a flicker of agreement in the old man's eyes when Will told him what Joshua had done, and even then, Will could never be entirely certain of his father's agreement.

How odd it was, Will thought, to be in the bosom of his family and feel so terribly alone. It was that strange feeling of being shipwrecked again, and he wished only for comfort, a kind word, a soothing caress. When an image of Phoebe Dupree's lovely face appeared in his mind's eye, he didn't so much as blink.

The image of her naked and moving beneath him was not exactly the sort of comfort he needed, but it was certainly the sort of comfort his body craved. He closed his eyes and imagined Phoebe Dupree dancing the dance of the veils, just like the one he'd seen in the Levant. He imagined her hips swaying, her eyes blazing with desire for him as she removed the veils, one by one, dropping them at his feet and slowly revealing her body to him.

Just thinking of it made his cock hard. He fished the scarab out from beneath his collar and rubbed it between his thumb and finger. But it was useless—nothing would rid him of the image until he took himself in hand and banished it in the most primitive manner.

Unfortunately, that did not ease his restiveness, either. Later that afternoon, Will gave in to his body's demands and sent a maid to Phoebe's workroom with a message that he required her in the east salon. He had no idea what he thought to do once she arrived; he just wanted to see her.

His mood changed the moment she glided into the room—he felt much lighter in being. Phoebe was wearing a gown of blue trimmed in white that made her eyes all but leap from her face. And with those eyes, she gave him a wary look. "My lord? You sent for me?"

"I did," he said, and sauntered to the middle of the room. He looked around at the gray walls, the dark red drapes. "What do you think of this room?"

"I beg your pardon?"

"This room, Madame Dupree. How do you find it?"

She looked around; as she studied the walls, the drapes, the ceiling, her brow furrowed in concentration, Will contemplated the curve of her slender neck. "I find it . . . quite nice," she said, and looked at him sidelong.

"Madame Dupree," he said with a wry smile, "you've not been reticent about your opinions ere now. I assure you, my feelings will not be harmed. I need your help."

She considered that for a moment, then sighed. "In truth?"

"In truth."

"It feels like a mausoleum."

He nodded. He could not take his eyes from her succulent mouth. Her cheeks flushed. "The gray paint makes the room feel rather cold," she said, and began to walk the length of the room, telling him what she found offensive. Will scarcely heard her. He followed her, breathing in the scent of lavender, admiring the way her hips moved beneath her gown. He longed to touch those hips, to sink his fingers into them and hold them as he thrust into her—

"This wooden settee, for example," she said, twirling about and almost colliding with him. "Some upholstery would make it more inviting. And the carpet—a lighter shade would warm the room considerably."

"Ah."

She turned again and pointed to something—a painting, a piece of porcelain, he had no idea—as he admired the tiny wisps of curls at her nape, and the thickness of her pale blond hair, bound up in some artful twist. She moved on to the drapery as Will appreciated the flawless, smooth skin of her décolletage.

She suddenly turned toward him. "Perhaps something a bit more . . ." Phoebe paused. Her eyes narrowed. "I beg your pardon, sir, but are you listening?"

He blinked. "Yes, of course."

"Oh?" She folded her arms. "Then you agree with my opinions of the drapes."

"Naturally."

"Splendid! I thought perhaps you might be against bamboo."

"Bamboo?" he echoed, startled.

"You weren't listening at all," she said, her eyes shining with the triumph of having caught him.

"I—"

"It will do you no good to deny it," she said primly.

Will supposed that was true and smiled. He impetuously lifted his hand to her earlobe, caressing it with his thumb. "You are quite right, Madame Dupree. I confess that I find it very difficult to think of drapery when a sublimely elegant woman is standing so near to me."

Phoebe's eyes widened slightly. There was suddenly a current running between them—he could feel its powerful pull.

"What are you about?" she asked softly.

Will couldn't help himself. He touched his finger to her lips. Phoebe reacted by jerking backward; but she touched the tip of her tongue to her lip. The effect was incredibly arousing.

"You remind me of someone," he said. "An American in India."

"An *American*?"

"Her husband died while they were traveling through India, and she decided to remain there instead of facing the long voyage home alone. She was a woman of certain experience, one might say."

Phoebe caught a breath; her chest lifted with it, then slowly fell. "And what has that to do with me?" she asked suspiciously.

He shrugged a little. It had nothing to do with her,

other than serving as a means to prolong their meeting. "She was lonely."

"I am not lonely."

"She wore a sari—"

"A what?"

"A sari," he repeated. "It is a long piece of fabric that drapes here," he said, using his finger to trace a line over her shoulder and between her breasts, causing Phoebe to gasp softly. "And here," he added as he traced a line down her rib cage to her waist, and around her abdomen. Phoebe's eyes never left his, but he could feel how quickly her breath filled her body, how quickly she released it.

"She'd sit just so," he said, "so that the fabric would gape here." With his gaze fixed on hers, he drew a long, slow line down the center of her abdomen to the top of her pubis. "And here," he muttered, touching her breast again.

Phoebe's lips parted; she drew an unsteady breath. "And how," she managed to say, "could that *possibly* remind you of me?"

Will looked at her mouth, the little slope of her nose, the smooth column of her neck. He put his palm to her neck; her skin was warm to the touch, and he instinctively knew that he'd aroused her. "I suppose only in that I have imagined that sari on you."

Phoebe suddenly moved to the side, away from his hand. "Did you also learn in India to take delight in your attempts to seduce your staff?" she snapped as she moved behind a chair, putting it between them.

"No. But my delight would be greater if the desire for seduction was mutual."

Her cheeks reddened; her fingers fluttered along the back of the chair. "It is not a mutual desire. If you would like my opinion of this room, I am happy to give it. But I will remind you that I've quite a lot of work to do," she said pertly, as she studied the upholstery of the chair rather intently.

"Of course. Thank you for your help, Madame Dupree."

At last she risked a look at him. "If there is nothing else?" Her focus was on his mouth, and her hand, he noticed, had now curled tightly over the back of the chair.

He smiled a little and clasped his hands behind his back. "For the time being."

She said nothing else, but fairly flew from the salon. Will watched her go, and as he heard her move quickly down the corridor, he realized the only thing he'd accomplished was to increase his longing for her.

Eleven

———

Alice tried very hard to appear nonchalant about the supper party, but it was quite evident to Phoebe she was as excited as Jane, who Phoebe feared might burst out of the gown she had fitted so perfectly to her.

Phoebe was proud of her creations. She hadn't had time to adorn them properly—particularly not with all the nonsense in the salon that had resulted in her complete inability to do anything but stare out the window for another wasted hour—but the crowning glory of Jane's pale green gown was a silky rose sash.

Handmade rosettes adorned Alice's lavender satin gown. Alice looked attractive and softly feminine in it, which Phoebe would have thought impossible on their first meeting.

Jane looked rather sweet and twirled about during her last fitting, watching the train move behind her as she chattered incessantly about the Remington family. She knew precious little about them, really—if one took the time to actually listen to what Jane was nattering on about—other than what was said about them in Greenhill, and what the local gentry were certain to think if the Remingtons were to dine at Wentworth Hall. The last bit sparked an argument with Alice, who insisted no one would care a whit if they dined at Wentworth Hall or at a pig's trough, and even if they did, Jane should be the last in all of Bedfordshire to know it.

"You are mistaken," Jane said haughtily. "I've heard it mentioned that it is quite an important event for the Remingtons."

"*Where* have you heard it mentioned?" Alice asked, her eyes narrowed suspiciously.

Jane turned away from her and pretended to study the gown in the mirror. "I don't have to tell you where."

Alice snorted.

If Alice was pleased with her gown, Phoebe would be the last to hear it, but she rather suspected she was, given how she turned left and then right, admiring herself in it. For a young woman who could not feign interest in the supper party, Alice was awfully keen to ensure her gown fit perfectly and was worried that they would not find ribbons for her hair in Greenhill to match the fabric's hue.

Phoebe assured her they would. As they were departing for Greenhill that afternoon, Addison gave Phoebe a small purse. "His lordship sends this with you to purchase whatever his sisters may need," he said. He paused and glanced at the two young women in the drive. "And he asks that you keep a watchful eye on them."

"*Me?* I am not a nursemaid, sir!" she said, disgruntled, as she pocketed the purse.

Addison smiled thinly. "It shall be over and done before you know it."

She didn't believe that for a moment and rather imagined Addison didn't, either.

The first shop they visited in Greenhill sold undergarments. Alice and Jane tittered like girls as they held up delicate chemises and corsets, admiring the embroidery and fine cotton fabric. When they'd made their purchases, they moved on to a dress shop, where they bought several hair ribbons in various colors while Frieda stood outside, yawning and scraping the bottom of her boots against the edge of the walkway.

The last shop was the cobbler, where elegant slippers and sturdy boots were displayed in the window. With a squeal of delight, Jane went in, pulling Frieda along with her.

"I'll wait here," Alice said to Phoebe.

Phoebe looked at her with surprise. "Wouldn't you like to look at shoes?"

Alice looked longingly at a pair of blue silk slippers in the window—the same blue slippers Phoebe had admired—and shook her head. "I've plenty of shoes."

Frankly, Phoebe had only ever seen her wear one pair of boots and thought Alice was daft to turn down the opportunity. Certainly *she* had no intention of standing outside when a room full of shoes beckoned, so she smiled cheerfully, said, "All right," and went in after Jane to have a look. But a few moments later, as she perused the slippers in the shop window while Jane examined several pairs with the cobbler with Frieda's enthusiastic help, Phoebe noticed that Alice was no longer standing just outside. An alarm sounded within her—she was supposed to keep her eye on them.

As Jane was suitably occupied, Phoebe stepped outside. She looked up and down the street, but Alice was nowhere to be seen. Now her heart skipped a beat. She feared what Alice might do—she had hardly presented herself as a young lady of good breeding thus far. Phoebe looked anxiously about and noticed the smithy just down the road. "Oh *no*," she groaned. How had she missed the smithy? Surely Alice hadn't been so bold as to go there!

Of *course* she had. And had Phoebe been in Alice's position, she probably would have done the same thing. She instantly started striding in that direction.

Except for the covering of a thatched roof, the smithy's work area stood open to the elements. A fire was burning, but there was no one about. The open area was attached to a wooden barn, where Phoebe assumed the blacksmith's implements and horses awaiting new shoes were kept. She walked around the structure, and as she turned the corner, she spied a narrow space between the barn and the building behind it.

She did not want to look in that opening, but her feet were already moving. As she stepped in front of the narrow alley, she managed to refrain from gasping in shock. Just as she suspected, Alice was there, locked in an embrace with a man Phoebe presumed was Mr. Hughes. They were kissing with great passion; his hands were on her breasts, and her hands were in his hair.

In a moment of panic—and, all right, titillation—Phoebe called out, "Lady Alice!"

Her voice startled Alice almost as badly as it startled Mr. Hughes, who half jumped, half fell a good foot away from her. Alice jerked her head toward Phoebe. She didn't speak, didn't seem to even breathe—for a moment.

But when she realized who had discovered her, Alice's face mottled with her anger. "How *dare* you!" she cried. "You will be dealt with for spying, Madame Dupree, and the penalty will be quite harsh!"

"Perhaps you should go," Mr. Hughes said hastily, and pushed Alice toward Phoebe as he eyed her warily.

"Don't mind her, Roland!" Alice said, her voice soft and pleading now. "She's just a servant. I will deal with her—"

"I think it best you go," he said again, and backed away from her.

Alice realized he meant to abandon her there and she seemed frantic. "Roland! Please don't be angry! I had no idea the chit would follow me. She's a stupid seamstress, and I *swear* to you, I will beat her if she so much as *whispers* this to another living soul!"

"*Go,* Alice," he said, his expression dark. "Don't you see that you make it worse by lingering?" He abruptly turned and disappeared deeper into the narrow alley.

"Roland!" Alice called after him. "*Roland!*"

But he'd gone. When it dawned on Alice that he had left her there, she whirled around with such venom in her eyes that Phoebe actually feared her. And well she should have, for Alice was suddenly marching toward her. Phoebe didn't know what Alice meant to do, but she never expected the girl would raise her hand and slap her across the face.

Phoebe cried out with the blow and staggered backward, instantly putting her gloved hand to her face. Never in her life had she been struck. *Never!* She was shocked into speechlessness, stunned to paralysis. Had it not been for Frieda happening upon them at that precise moment, Phoebe was certain Alice would have struck her again.

"Lady Alice!" Frieda cried as she rushed to Phoebe's side.

For a brief moment, Alice looked confused. But the anger suddenly swept over her again, and she sailed past them both. "We are leaving!" she announced, and marched toward the carriage.

"God *blind* me!" Frieda whispered frantically as Alice put more distance between them. She pulled Phoebe's hand away from her cheek and winced. "Oh heavens— what will ye do?"

"Did she leave a mark?" Phoebe asked numbly.

Frowning, Frieda nodded. "You'll tell his lordship, aye? She ought not to get away with it," she said angrily, glancing over her shoulder as if she suspected Alice to come running back to attack them. "I can't abide those that hits," she said. "That's why I'll always be thankful to Mrs. Turner for giving me a place, I will. My last mistress hit us every time we came 'round."

Phoebe glanced at Frieda. "A *lady* hit you?"

"Aye, whenever she was of a mind," Frieda said as she linked her arm through Phoebe's. "Once she beat Nanny Bentley so badly that Nanny couldn't work for two days."

Good God—what more were servants forced to endure at the hands of their employers? Most immediately, Phoebe would be forced to endure a carriage ride with Alice.

"Come on, then," Frieda said soothingly. "Mrs. Turner will know what's to be done."

Phoebe had a very good idea what needed to be done, all right—Alice was in desperate need of discipline, and she was in desperate need of passage home.

As the two of them walked out from behind the smithy, Phoebe saw Jane standing outside the cobbler, a package under her arm, her bonnet hanging carelessly from her hand.

"There you are!" she shouted irritably, drawing the notice of more than one person on the street. "I have looked all over for you!" she called as she strode toward them. "What are you doing there? Why did you leave me?"

"Just taking a bit of air," Frieda said with false cheer.

"What were you doing by the smithy?" Jane demanded, eyeing Phoebe suspiciously. Her gaze flicked to the blacksmith's shop and her eyes lit with delight. "Is *Alice* there as well?"

"No," Phoebe said. "She is in the carriage. If you have made your purchases, Lady Jane, we really should—"

"What's this?" Jane interrupted, peering at Phoebe closely now. "It looks as if someone hit you." When neither Frieda nor Phoebe spoke, Jane gasped. "Dear *God*. Alice *hit* you, didn't she?" she exclaimed, seeming almost excited by the prospect. "Oh, my Lord! That *horrible girl*! She can't go around hitting people!"

The girl had no concept of discretion. "Come along, Lady Jane, *please*," Phoebe said, putting her hand on her elbow, trying to force her along before the entire village of Greenhill knew Alice had struck her.

"She's awful, and I don't care if she is my sister!"

Jane declared loudly, but at least she was moving. "She'll never receive an offer, for she has such a *wretched* disposition!"

Phoebe fairly shoved Jane toward the carriage. The waiting footman, Billy, quickly opened the door; when he did, Phoebe could hear Alice's sobbing.

Jane gleefully went in first with a cheery "Serves you right, you awful brat!" Behind Jane, Frieda rolled her eyes before climbing in.

But Billy put his hand on Phoebe's arm, slowing her. When she glanced up at him his gaze fell to the mark on her face, and he angrily shook his head. "Bloody awful," he whispered. "Are you all right?"

"I'm fine." She smiled reassuringly and allowed him to help her into the carriage. But she wasn't fine at all. She was shocked and confused and felt as if her little make-believe world was crumbling. The blow had put her on unfamiliar ground, and she felt incapable of living a moment longer in Madame Dupree's imaginary shoes.

In the carriage, Phoebe took a seat directly across from Alice, who refused to look at her. That infused Phoebe with indignation—the woman had struck her like an animal, and now she would cower? Phoebe kept her eyes steady on Alice on the long ride back to the hall while Jane chattered on about how she felt certain her brother would lock Alice away in a madhouse, and Frieda looked anxiously from one to the other, worrying the frayed edge of her sleeve.

And Alice—Alice never lifted her eyes, but sat slumped against the squabs, her bottom lip trembling. It wasn't until they had pulled into the drive at the hall that she looked tearfully at Jane. "Jane . . . give me your word you won't tell him," she begged meekly.

"Why shouldn't I?" Jane asked haughtily. "You're

hopelessly awful, Alice. You *deserve* to be put on the shelf."

"*Please* don't tell him!" Alice whimpered.

"I don't know if I shall or not," Jane responded imperiously, and crawled over Alice to get out, leaving her threat hanging in the confines of the coach.

Alice glanced at Phoebe from the corner of her eye. "*You* won't tell him." It was more of a question than a statement, a child's attempt at concealing her actions.

"Won't I?" Phoebe softly demanded.

Alice suddenly sat up and said beseechingly, "I am so *very* sorry, Madame Dupree! I don't know what possessed me! I was so angry and . . . and I did not *mean* to strike you, I swear I did not! Will you forgive me? Please say you forgive me!"

Phoebe could hardly forgive her with the sting of Alice's hand still in her flesh.

She glanced at Frieda, who was watching the two of them with the same sort of rapt attention she might watch a puppet play in Covent Garden. "Frieda, will you wait outside?"

Frieda blinked. "Yes, mu'um," she said reluctantly, and gave Alice a long look as she slowly exited.

When Frieda had gone out, Alice started to move, too, but Phoebe threw up her arm, blocking her exit. "One moment, if you please, Lady Alice."

Alice shrank against the squabs. "What?" she asked tearfully.

Phoebe leaned forward and said low, "If you *ever* raise your hand to me, I will strike back, so help me. Do not think I value my employment here so much that I will stand for such abuse."

Alice's eyes widened. "I am truly sorry," she said as a tear slipped from her eye. "I've never struck a servant in my life before this," she added as she shakily swiped the tear from her face. "I can offer no excuse other than to say I was alarmed. You cannot imagine how deeply my brother dislikes Roland."

Phoebe could very well imagine. When she was twelve years old, she had fallen in love with Brian, a footman. He was dashing and handsome and he smiled when she flirted with him and laughed at her silly jests. Her mother had been so fearful of Phoebe's infatuation that she sent Brian away. "It is no excuse," Phoebe said quietly.

"Yes, yes, I know," Alice said, swiping at more tears. "I assure you, I am not so hard that I do not understand. Yet I cannot convey my feelings for Roland."

Phoebe sighed. "Have a care with him, Alice."

Alice dropped her eyes to her lap and nodded.

Phoebe put her hand to Alice's knee, ignoring her flinch. "You must know that if you are compromised in *any* way, his lordship will be forced to take action. You risk too much."

Alice sniffed. Scratched her ear. "A perfectly fine thing for *you* to say. You're beautiful," she muttered petulantly. "I've seen the way men look at you, and be assured they do not look at *me* in such a manner. Before long, I shall be bartered away to a man who will smile at my purse and frown at my face." She glanced up at Phoebe, her eyes beseeching her. "So why shouldn't I be allowed to experience love at least once?"

"Your future husband may love you very well," Phoebe argued, but Alice was hardly convinced.

"I don't know how things are done at your station in life, Madame Dupree, but in mine *love* rarely has anything to do with the joining of fortunes. Roland was the only one to dance with me at the harvest ball last autumn. He was the only one to show me any kindness when others laughed at me and Jane and made awful remarks about our clothing . . ."

She paused, looked out the window. "And then Will came home and ruined everything! I love Mr. Hughes, and he loves me, and it may be the only time in my life I am free to experience it." She suddenly moved forward, stepping out of the coach almost before Phoebe could open her mouth.

Phoebe reluctantly climbed down after Alice and walked inside, looking neither left nor right, moving up the stairs until she reached her two small rooms on the top floor. When she'd shut the door soundly behind her, and slid the bolt into place, she threw her hat across the room, and pressing a hand to her mouth, she slid down her back to her haunches, squeezing her eyes shut to keep tears of humiliation from falling.

Twelve

Jane usually delighted in telling Will every little thing her siblings did that might cause them trouble, and that evening was no exception. Over supper, she gleefully told Will everything that had happened in Greenhill, beginning with the ribbons and shoes she'd bought to Alice's encounter with the smithy's apprentice, and moving right along to Alice's striking Phoebe.

Will could scarcely believe what he was hearing.

He could scarcely believe that the people seated at his father's table carried the same blood as he.

He stared at Alice as he tried to comprehend how she could defy him so openly and behave so abominably. He tried to fathom how she could strike *anyone*, much less a *servant*, who was, by virtue of her class, deserving of Alice's example and protection. That appalled him far more than if she'd struck *him*.

He was so distraught that he could not finish his meal. He looked down the table at four of the most misguided, ill-behaved young men and women in all of England and felt a roiling sensation in his belly. In the last thirty-six hours, Joshua had cheated at a gentleman's game, Alice had been found embracing the smithy's apprentice in an alley and had struck Madame Dupree, Jane was gloating with the delight in telling him, and Roger was still pouting for having lost their race the other morning. All in all, a spectacularly bad patch at Wentworth Hall.

Will threw his linen napkin on the table in disgust, shoved his plate away, and abruptly stood. "I cannot begin to imagine what has happened here in the last few years to make the four of you the most appallingly ill-behaved people in all of Bedfordshire," he said. "Nor can I imagine how your reputations and your futures might *ever* be repaired," he said, and stormed from the room, leaving his siblings gaping after him.

He strode to the green salon, slammed the door behind him, and poured a generous helping of whiskey. He removed his coat and yanked at the knot in his neckcloth, loosening his collar so that he might breathe. His anger and disappointment and disgust made his pulse race, and after downing the tot of whiskey, he stood gripping the edges of the sideboard, trying to calm himself, his mind racing with all the ways he had failed to affect the behavior of his siblings and all the ways he seemed inadequate to the job.

Phoebe Dupree was a beautiful woman who had been forced to endure the barbaric ways of his sister. He could not fathom how anyone might raise a hand to her, much less his own *sister*.

He feared the worst, if Jane was to be believed. A blackened eye. Or perhaps she'd already fled Wentworth Hall in terror. Who could blame her?

He could not bear it a moment longer and put aside the whiskey glass and strode from the room. He took the stairs two at a time, rounding each turn until he reached the top floor. He did not stop until he had reached her door.

He rapped firmly.

"Thank you, Farley, but please leave the tray outside," she said on the other side of the door.

"It is not Farley, it is Summerfield. Please open the door."

There was a long pause. "I am not well, my lord. Please forgive me."

He braced his hands on the door frame. "Open the door, Phoebe. I know what Alice has done. Just . . . just open the door."

Several moments passed—he believed she would refuse him. But then the lock turned and the door was opened a crack.

Will pushed it open. Phoebe hadn't been to bed at all—her hair was still put up in a bandeau, and wisps of ringlets brushed her neck. Her gown—a beautiful, shimmering pink—was suitable for supper. She did not look at him directly but kept her face turned slightly to one side, her eyes on the floor.

Will's gut sank—he could scarcely bear to look.

"Phoebe . . ." he started, but words failed him. He could think of nothing he might say that would ever atone for the indignity his sister had caused her.

Phoebe folded her arms defensively across her middle and turned away from him, walking deeper into the room. Will followed her to where she stood, but she turned her head again. He caught her chin in his hand and forced her to turn her head so that he could see.

The sight of the bruised skin over her cheekbone caused him to draw a sharp breath; Phoebe flinched and moved back, out of his grasp.

"Dear God," he uttered, completely at a loss for words. But he instantly thought of the obsidian stone in his suite. It was a stone he'd picked up on the Isle of Crete that held healing powers. He knew it did—he'd used it on himself more than once. "Stay here," he said shortly, and strode out of her room.

He returned a quarter of an hour later. She was seated at the window, staring into the black of the night. She turned her head slightly when he entered. "You're back," she said listlessly.

"Of course I am." He went to the window and sat on the sash before her. "Why did you not come to me?"

"I don't know," she said with a halfhearted shrug. "I feared what you might do to Alice."

"*Alice?*" he echoed in disbelief. "I swear to you, whatever I do to her will not be enough—"

"Please," she said, shaking her head. "Alice deserves your pity, not your disdain."

Will was so astounded, he could scarcely speak. He wondered wildly what twist of fate had given a mere seamstress more grace and elegance than he feared Alice might ever hope to own. And when he looked into those pale blue-green eyes, he tried to fathom how this woman could possibly believe that Alice deserved as much as an ounce of his pity.

She must have understood his confusion because she said earnestly, "Alice is . . . she is *lost,* sir. This man she holds in such great esteem—"

"A *smithy,*" he said disapprovingly.

"A smithy, but a man nonetheless," Phoebe quickly added. "A man who has shown a preference for her and her alone, however ill-advised, and at a point in time when Alice obviously needs it most."

Will reared back in astonishment. "How do you know this? Has she told you so?"

"No! Of course not," Phoebe said, shaking her head. "She can scarcely bear my presence at all. Yet . . . yet I understood her fear—I know as well as she that at some point in the very near future, a match will be made for her that has more to do with her heritage and her fortune than it does with love or compatibility. It is no wonder she seeks some affirmation of herself as a woman—"

"*Affirmation*?" he echoed incredulously, trying to make sense of what Phoebe was saying.

She looked very fatigued all at once and abruptly stood, walking away from him. "Yes, affirmation. Alice is not like other young women in similar positions in society—she is not certain that a man would find her desirable without the trappings of her family and her fortune."

Will gaped at her; such talk of affirmations and desirability was foreign to him, and when such notions were applied to Alice, it made him rather uncomfortable.

Phoebe glanced over her shoulder at him; he must have shown his disbelief, for she said evenly, "The situation is rather different for men—men are free to explore the bounds of propriety in ways women cannot."

"Is Alice 'exploring the bounds of propriety' by compromising her virtue with a mere smithy? Or by striking you?" he asked impatiently, gaining his feet. "For I confess, I am at a loss to understand."

"I am . . ." Phoebe paused and looked heavenward a moment. "I am *astounded* that she struck me," she said softly. "I am appalled and shocked and hurt by it. Nevertheless, I understand her. Your sister and I are close in age, my lord—she is not so different from me, really."

Will shook his head. "That is where you are wrong," he said sternly, and he meant it. "You are *vastly* different from Alice." Frankly, he thought she might be very different from any woman he had ever known. He certainly couldn't imagine another Englishwoman forgiving Alice as graciously as she had just done. He couldn't imagine another woman as delicate, but incredibly strong, as Phoebe seemed to be.

He looked at the mark Alice had left on Phoebe's face. She tried to turn her face from him again, but he stopped her by carefully touching two fingers to the bruise.

She winced slightly, but she did not look away; she held his gaze as he trailed his fingers down her cheek, to her jaw, and slipped them beneath her chin, lifting her face higher. With his free hand, he withdrew the stone from his pocket. "Here we are, an ancient remedy for your injury."

Phoebe glanced at the rock he held up. "It is a *rock*."

"The ancient Greeks believed it had healing powers. It will remove the bruise from your skin. May I?"

"Do you believe in such things?" she asked, but angled her face to him.

"I believe there are many mysteries in our universe."

He touched the stone to her bruised cheek; she did not flinch.

"How did you learn of this stone?" she asked him.

He snorted. "I gained it from a thief," he said casually as he rubbed the stone lightly on her bruise. "I was on the Isle of Crete when I caught a man attempting to steal my horse. I threatened to hang him."

Phoebe flinched at that.

Will smiled. "It was just a threat, madam. Even if I had been so inclined, I didn't have a rope. But he believed me, and in exchange for his life, he gave me back my horse and a few things he considered valuable. This was one of them."

"I suppose I should be grateful he didn't offer coin for his life."

Will chuckled and smiled into her eyes. She was beautiful. He moved the stone again, but he could feel that familiar heat rising in him again. The scarab he wore around his neck was worthless, and he had paid good money for that.

"May I ask . . . what is the mark on your wrist?"

He paused in his ministration and looked at it. He folded his cuff back so that she could see the entire mark, the serpent twining around the ancient symbol. "It is an old Hindu symbol for peace and prosperity."

Phoebe drew a breath and bent her head over his arm. "May I touch it?"

"Of course," he said, holding his arm closer to her.

Her fingers were very light on his skin and sent a peculiar shiver through him. She traced the symbol with two fingers, going around one curving end and up again, to the other. Will thought he might very well explode—the light touch was making him mad with the desire to touch her. "It's beautiful," she said softly.

That surprised him. He expected her to be appalled

like everyone else in Bedfordshire. "You . . . you like it?" he asked uncertainly.

"Oh, yes," she said, and glanced up at him. "I adore art." She looked at his arm again, retracing the lines. "See how it curves so elegantly here? That must have been very difficult to do on the canvas of your skin."

"Yes," he said low.

"I wish I could see more of this sort of art. It is lovely." She withdrew her fingers and looked up at him again. Her gaze was glittering; she held him mesmerized, enchanted, entranced. Rational thought deserted him. He slipped his hand to her neck, splayed his fingers across her bare shoulder as he sank deeper into his feelings of desire for her.

"You are extraordinary," he said softly. "I beg your pardon, Phoebe. For my sister, I beg your pardon." He leaned forward and touched his lips to the cheek he'd rubbed with the obsidian stone. Phoebe drew a shallow breath, but she did not move. "And for me, I beg your forgiveness," he said, touching his lips to the other cheek. Her skin was warm and smooth; he detected the scent of lilac and felt himself shift closer.

It was amazing to him that as a man, he was capable of deflecting most physical threats to his person, but the power of a woman's beauty could defeat him every time. He was a slave to it, could not resist the allure, and Will impulsively touched his lips to hers. She scarcely moved, but he could feel her come closer. He caressed her neck and shoulder as he kissed her, fighting the urge to grab her up in his arms and make love to her.

Her hand came up between them, and she pressed lightly against his chest. When he lifted his head, Phoebe stared up at him with those glittering eyes and asked quietly, "Would you now use this detestable occasion to seduce me?"

"Are you seduced by an honest apology?" he responded with another caress of her shoulder.

"No. I am fatigued by it."

He should have been put off, but he was, inexplicably, spurred on. "I can put it to rights," he said earnestly as his eyes moved over her face and he grasped her shoulders with his hands. "Allow me to put it to rights."

"Allow me to go to bed. I want to sleep and forget what happened. I want to finish my work here as quickly as possible and return to London."

The thought of her leaving for London jolted something deep inside Will. He was only now beginning to appreciate the treasure under his roof, each moment with her another revelation. Who *was* this seamstress? How had she, in such short order, captured his attention so completely? Was it merely a man's base desire that held him by the bollocks, the need to bed a woman?

Whatever it was, it was driving him mad with desire at the moment. He wanted to kiss this woman fully, wanted to feel her slender body in his arms. He was painfully aware that such thoughts conflicted with his responsibilities and principles. He had his siblings and his father and the search for his bride to occupy his thoughts—he'd vowed to himself and his father to set everything to rights as soon as was possible.

Yet somewhere in the last week, he'd left his desire unattended, unchecked, and it had sprouted like weeds, choking the life from his good intentions and convictions. He hardly needed the complication of an affair with a servant, no matter how much he wanted it.

Phoebe was right—the sooner she finished her work and returned to London, the better for them both.

She must have read his thoughts—she reached up

and curled delicate fingers around his wrist and pulled his hand off her shoulder. "Good night, my lord."

Will reluctantly stepped back. "Good night, Phoebe," he uttered. With one last look at the bruise on her face, he made himself shove his hands into his pockets to keep from touching her again. "Keep the stone," he said. "Rub it on your cheek in the morning. The bruise will disappear." And with that, he walked out of that room before he did something he would very much regret.

Will went directly to his father's bedchamber as he did every night.

At the advice of doctors, the Earl of Bedford followed a strict routine every day. He was awakened at dawn, dressed, and, weather permitting, taken into the gardens for the morning sun. After breakfast, he was wheeled into the green salon, where he was situated before the windows and a book was placed in his lap.

After luncheon, his father had another turn about the gardens, and was then put in the orangery, which received a good bit of afternoon sun and was very cheerful and warm, what with the various plants and orange trees kept within. Will usually joined his father for tea at five o'clock and reviewed the day's events with him. The physician did not believe that the earl understood him, but Will knew that he did. They had a method of communicating—his father lifted one finger for yes, and two fingers for no.

Moreover, the earl's red-rimmed eyes followed Will's every gesture. He understood Will.

At night, Will would look in on his father before he retired. Tonight, his father was seated before the hearth; Jacobs, the footman who attended him around the clock, was readying his bed.

"Good evening, Father," Will said, and bent to

kiss the pink top of his bald head before taking a seat across from him in one of the wingback chairs situated before the hearth. He followed his father's gaze to the ends of the neckcloth that trailed carelessly down his chest. Will smiled and pulled the neckcloth free of the collar. "It's been rather a trying evening."

The earl lifted his eyes to Will's face, and Will suddenly stood and moved to the mantel, avoiding his father's curious look. "I've had a rough patch," he said, and looked at the palm of his hand a moment. "On my honor, I don't know how to reach my siblings," he blurted, and looked helplessly at his father. "They seem intent on scandal and personal ruin."

The old man's eyes were on him, staring intently.

"I wish I knew how you managed with me, my lord. I know I must have been rather difficult—I wanted so badly to experience life, did I not? Had it not been for your wisdom and patience . . ."

That gave Will pause. He'd never thought of it quite like that. He suddenly realized his father had recognized the chafing at the constraints of his position when Will was a young man and had given him the outlet he needed. He would never forget what the earl had said the day he'd proposed the Grand Tour to Will: "Years of responsibility lie ahead, son. Take the opportunity while you have it." Will had done precisely that, and when he'd returned to England, he'd been ready to assume the responsibilities of his title and his role as his father's heir.

Perhaps his siblings experienced the same sort of chafing. Until he'd returned, they had been virtual prisoners at Wentworth Hall, with no one to guide them or put them out in the world. With no legal access to the family coffers, they'd rotted in their peculiar prison. When Will had returned, he'd certainly given them no relief. If anything, he had reined them in to the point they now seemed to be champing at the bit.

Will suddenly turned and smiled at his father. "You have convinced me that my idea of a house party is an excellent one," he said. "Indeed, the best way to put them into society is to personally introduce them." He would bring society to them for a fortnight and conclude the affair with a grand ball. He could keep a close watch on them, could help them mingle properly with the local aristocrats and gentry. He glanced at his father again. "I know for sure now what I must do."

His father blinked.

The door opened; Jacobs entered. "Shall I help the earl to bed, milord?"

"Yes," Will said, and moved to put his hand on his father's shoulder. He squeezed fondly, feeling some relief after the horrendous events of the day. "I shall see you on the morrow, my lord, and tell you what I have planned. Good night."

Thirteen

The first time Caroline Fitzherbert laid eyes on Lord Summerfield, he'd just returned from Egypt. She knew at the first meeting that he was the man she would marry. He was handsome and wildly virile, and, if her mother's reconnaissance was to be believed, quite wealthy. Rumors of the demise of the Darby family were just that—empty rumors. It seemed that a legal complexity had kept the younger Darbys from the family money. Their wealth, thank heavens, was intact.

Summerfield had led an exciting life thus far—far more exciting than that of any other gentleman in Bedfordshire, Caroline was quite certain.

But Caroline was shrewd—she knew very well that *all* the unmarried ladies in Bedfordshire were vying for the viscount's attention much like swine vied for truffles. They made complete cakes of themselves as they tripped over one another to put themselves in his path.

Caroline, on the other hand, was playing her hand carefully.

When her father happily presented an opportunity for an introduction to the viscount, Caroline declined, clearly flustering her father. Shortly thereafter, her mother pleaded with her to be presented to Summerfield, laying out all the reasons he would be a perfect match for her—as if Caroline needed to have that explained. Still, she refused. She reasoned that if she were introduced to the viscount too early, she would be but another female face, another sow in search of a truffle.

Her introduction had to be timed just right—after Summerfield believed he'd seen all there was to see in Bedfordshire.

When Caroline was convinced there were no birds left to twitter about him, she conceded to being introduced. Her father gleefully made the obligatory call on Lord Summerfield. Lord Summerfield and his brother Joshua, the one with the brooding brown eyes, returned the call, inviting the family to luncheon. And today, at long last, Caroline and her parents were guests at Wentworth Hall.

Unfortunately, she had not counted on all of Summerfield's awful siblings being present. She had insisted her parents leave her two young brothers at home, as they could be nothing but a distraction. She had rather hoped Alice and Jane had been dispatched to a convent to live out their miserable lives, but alas, they were seated politely on the settee, their hands in their laps, their gowns apparently new, as they were much more stylish than anything she had ever seen them wear. She was, remarkably, a bit covetous of Alice's gown in particular.

Jane, Caroline could not help notice, was unabashedly loud and talkative. Alice was subdued, but then again, the whole county knew of her utterly inconceivable infatuation with Roland Hughes—not to mention her indecorous meetings with him before Summerfield came home and put a stop to it. Alice Darby was little more than a trollop. The brothers, Joshua and Roger, looked rather bored by the polite company. The only exception to that was when Caroline caught Joshua looking at her—so intently that it rather startled her.

Nevertheless, Caroline suppressed a sigh of tedium before luncheon and focused on her parents.

Caroline's father prided himself on his ability to converse with people from all walks of life, and he held the entire Summerfield family captive with his tale of a boar he'd chased for two years before shooting him last hunting season. While he spoke, Caroline contented herself with looking about the room and imagining the changes she would make when she was mistress here.

In Greenhill, everyone knew Summerfield was in the process of completely renovating the hall. Carpenters, painters, and craftsmen had been hired. This room had obviously benefited from his efforts—the carpet was new and thick, the drapes clean and pressed. The chair on which she sat felt as if it had been restuffed and the windows were so clean and clear that it almost seemed as if the glass was missing.

But the room was too dreary. There were too many dark colors and not enough floral prints. Furthermore, a peculiar little marble statue of an elephant being ridden by a woman who was nearly naked marred the entire room. In fact, when luncheon was called, Caroline took the opportunity to have a closer look.

She hadn't realized Summerfield was near until he spoke. "You are admiring one of my favorite pieces. I had it sent from India."

"It's really rather indecent, my lord," Caroline said.

Summerfield smiled down at her in a way that made her blood run hot. "Do you find the female body indecent?" he asked quietly. "I think she is beautiful."

Caroline swallowed. "You must find English dress rather dull," she said, arching her back a little to present her bosom.

Summerfield laughed and held out his arm. "Not at all, Miss Fitzherbert. I am a great admirer of anything that displays the feminine form. Shall we dine?"

He led her into the dining room, where her father's long-winded tales—now featuring a horse race at some place or other—continued over a lunch of roasted quail and garden vegetables. While Summerfield asked pertinent questions and seemed attentive, it seemed to Caroline that Mr. Joshua Darby was in danger of falling asleep and landing, face-first, in his bowl of butternut soup, and that Alice felt the need to correct Jane's use of a fork, to Jane's great offense.

Caroline could not abide it another moment, and when her father paused to draw breath, she blurted, "Is it true you saved a ship's crew from drowning, my lord?"

The question seemed to startle Summerfield. Across from her, Joshua rolled his eyes.

"Oh yes, do tell them, Will!" Jane cried. "I love the part where the swells are over your head."

Caroline was appalled—Jane actually looked rather happy about a tragic shipwreck.

"Jane," he said calmly, and to Caroline, "No, it is not true."

"Oh." She was, she realized, rather sorely disappointed.

"I managed to save only three men," he said. "Regrettably, many, many more were lost."

"Indeed?" her father said. "What happened?"

Summerfield shrugged uncomfortably. "A rather violent storm in the Straits of Gibraltar. The ship was run up against a reef and the hull cracked in two. Fortunately for me, there were several barrels of wine aboard that had been lashed together. I can credit my survival to a stroke of luck, for somehow I managed to get on top of the barrels. I used some flotsam to help the three sailors onto the barrels with me. We tried desperately to reach others, but the seas were quite violent and they were lost."

"But . . . but how were you saved?" Caroline asked breathlessly.

"A companion ship," Summerfield said. "My manservant, Addison, was on that one. They found us the next morning. It was a tragic accident." He smiled. "How do you find the quail?" he asked, politely changing the subject.

But Caroline had lost her appetite. She kept looking at him, imagining him in a violent storm at sea, saving the lives of those poor sailors. It was terribly exciting.

When they finished luncheon and retired to the

sunlight on the terrace, the two younger Darbys made their excuses—Jane loud and boisterous, of course—and disappeared inside. With her parents suitably engaged with Lady Alice and Joshua Darby, Caroline had the opportunity to speak with Lord Summerfield alone. They stood at the edge of the terrace. He asked her if she enjoyed the summer weather. She said that she did. She remarked that the long summer days suited horse enthusiasts, and wondered if he enjoyed riding as much as her father did.

"Very much," he said. "And you?"

"I like horses . . . but I am a poor rider." She looked up at him. "I need someone to teach me to ride properly."

Summerfield cocked a brow at her suggestion. "A poor rider . . . that *is* a pity, for I had hoped to entice you to see the wild horses that come around."

Caroline wanted to kick herself, but she smiled as saucily as she might and said, "You tease me, my lord. I have heard of the wild horses. They are an elusive herd, are they not? I understand there are now two foals, yet no one has been able to get near them."

"No one?"

He smiled in a way that made Caroline feel as if she were a child when it came to clever repartee. "My father's friend, Mr. Higgins, is an experienced horseman and he vowed that no man has come within one hundred yards of them," she said, challenging him.

Summerfield laughed and leaned slightly closer to her. His eyes were shining, and Caroline felt a funny little tickle in her groin. "Would you believe me if I told you that I have gotten close enough to touch them?"

"I don't know," she said with a pert smile. "I must see it to believe it."

"A challenge, eh?" His gaze swept over her. "I rather like that. I never shy from a challenge."

She smiled demurely, but inside her heart was pounding with the triumph of having said the right thing. "So I gathered. Where do you see the horses?"

"They come to the lake," he said, and looked across the gardens, pointing. But something caught his eye, and he faltered.

Caroline followed his gaze and saw a woman in the gardens below. She was squatting next to a rosebush, making cuttings. Her hat had slipped from her head and hung on her back. Her hair, Caroline noted, was so blond it was almost white. She was not dressed in a servant's uniform, but in a pretty rose-colored day gown. "Who is she?" she asked.

"I beg your pardon?" Summerfield asked, startled.

"The woman," Caroline said, nodding in her direction. "Is she a relative?"

"Ah, no . . . she is the seamstress," Summerfield said, and looked past her to the lake. "There—do you see the gazebo?" he asked, pointing. "The horses go there to drink and graze in the early morning."

"I see," Caroline said, but she was looking at the woman in the garden, who had stood up and was examining the contents of her basket, holding up each rose and perusing it. "That must be the seamstress responsible for the beautiful gowns Lady Alice and Lady Jane are wearing."

"She is indeed," Summerfield said, turning around and putting his back to the vista and the woman.

"The gowns are exquisite, my lord. Your sisters are very fortunate. The seamstress in Greenhill is not as gifted."

"Here is one fortunate sister now," Summerfield said,

and held out his hand. Caroline suppressed a groan as she turned and smiled prettily at Lady Alice.

"I was just speaking of your gown," she said sweetly. "It is beautiful."

Alice, the silly chit, blushed furiously and looked down. "Thank you."

"I have begged Father to take me to London, where I might avail myself of an experienced seamstress, but alas, he is quite content to stay in Bedfordshire."

"We have an experienced seamstress," Alice said. "Perhaps you would like to meet her? She is just there, in the garden."

"Oh, I shouldn't like to impose." *Hurry up and go then, silly girl!*

"It is no imposition, I assure you. I will send a footman," Alice offered, and hurried off to do just that.

Caroline smiled again at Summerfield. "I hope you don't mind, sir."

"Not at all," he said. But it seemed to Caroline that he did mind, very much indeed.

Phoebe hadn't even noticed the family had come out onto the terrace, so engrossed was she in finding the perfect rose specimen for a gown she had in mind, one that mimicked the shape of a rose. In the last few days, she had buried herself in her work, trying to drive recent events from her mind. Alice seemed to have completely forgotten striking her. She'd been sheepish for all of a day, but quickly resumed her ways when it seemed Phoebe would not hold a grudge. She and Jane were still frequent visitors to her workroom, speculating as to who would marry Summerfield while Phoebe and Frieda tried to work.

But Alice and Jane were like children playing in the distance, bringing Phoebe's head up only occasionally.

What clouded her thoughts and vision was the smooth touch of the stone on her skin—which had indeed erased the bruise somehow—and Summerfield's careful attention to her. It was his soft but aggressive mouth, the feel of his lips on her skin and her mouth. It was a touch, nothing more than a touch, yet it had haunted her since that night. The feel of his lips never left her, nor the unbearable pressure she felt somewhere at the core of her when he was near. She couldn't keep from imagining his mouth on all of her body.

Since that night, she had counted the moments until she might see him—if only a glimpse of him, so that she might remind herself it was real, that *he* was real. The days seemed endless; she felt restless, unable to sit still for very long.

To keep from thinking—or longing—she'd worked nearly around the clock, had poured herself into sketching and designing the gowns she would make. This afternoon, she'd left Frieda to some routine sewing and was lost in imagining the gown she would create when Billy nudged her with his toe.

Phoebe started and glanced up.

Billy grinned. "Pretty as a rose ye are."

Billy had a habit of admiring her. Phoebe had made it quite clear she was flattered, but that there was no reciprocal feeling, yet it had not deterred Billy in the least. "Good afternoon, Billy. Shouldn't you be attending someone somewhere?" she asked as she bent down to snip another rose from the bush.

"I am attending, love," he said. "Haven't you seen me on the terrace with them?"

Phoebe glanced up again, this time shading her eyes with her hand. Good Lord, she hadn't noticed them, and she straightened up, taking note of Summerfield, Joshua, and Alice, and their guests. She unthinkingly put a hand to her unruly hair, then quickly brushed the wrinkles from her skirt.

"His lordship wants ye now."

"*What*? What should he want with me?"

"How should I know, sweetheart?" Billy asked, taking her in with a deepening smile. "Ah, now, why won't ye favor a lad with a walkabout on Sunday?"

"*Billy*," Phoebe said with exasperation, and thrust the basket of fresh-cut flowers at him, hitting him in the abdomen. She was irritated to be called, even more irritated that the hem of her gown was wet from wandering about the garden.

"Ye best go on," Billy said. "Never good to keep them waiting."

Phoebe sighed, removed one glove, and tossed it in the basket Billy held. She'd almost succeeded in tamping down her thoughts of Summerfield, but they were rushing up again, filling her cheeks with heat. Now she felt surprisingly vulnerable, particularly when she saw him standing up there on the terrace, looking down at her.

"Don't they know that there is work to be done?" she asked petulantly as she removed her second glove and tossed it into the basket after the first.

"Ah, lass, surely ye've worked for the Quality long enough to know they don't care a whit," Billy said congenially, and gestured for her to precede him down the walk.

Phoebe took a deep breath and walked through the parterres and up the terrace steps. When she reached the terrace landing, she saw Alice. With the proper clothing, she didn't look quite as gangly or awkward as she normally did, but rather regal in bearing.

"Lady Alice, how lovely you look," Phoebe said, meaning it.

Alice blushed and looked down. "Thank you," she said. "It is a beautiful gown." She even smiled a little.

They walked across the terrace to Summerfield and his guests, who were standing about as if they were waiting for something or someone. Joshua sat on a stone bench apart from the others, his eyes dark and steady on the young woman with honey-blond hair and soft brown eyes who stood next to Summerfield. Her parents—the resemblance was obvious—stood beside her, smiling as if they had already arranged a match with Summerfield for their daughter.

The young woman gave Phoebe a thin smile of tolerance. Phoebe curtsied. "You sent for me, my lord?"

"Actually . . . I did," Alice said. "Miss Fitzherbert was admiring my gown. May I introduce the Fitzherberts to you?" she asked, and introduced Mr. and Mrs. Fitzherbert, and Miss Fitzherbert.

As Phoebe greeted them, she noticed Miss Fitzherbert shifted closer to Summerfield so that her arm was touching his sleeve. "How do you do?" she asked as she boldly took in Phoebe's clothing.

"Very well, thank you." Their casual examination of her made her feel exposed; the kernel of doubt that perhaps these people knew or suspected who she was crept into her mind.

"I did indeed compliment Lady Alice on her lovely gown," Miss Fitzherbert said at last, drawing Phoebe's attention. "You do excellent work, madam."

"Thank you." Summerfield was infuriatingly expressionless, his hands clasped behind his back, his impassive gaze on Phoebe. It was a far cry from the man who had looked at her with such longing only days ago.

Miss Fitzherbert looked at her coldly. "What do you think, Father?" she asked. "Mrs. Dupree is a seamstress.

Perhaps we might retain her when Summerfield is through with her."

There was something in the way she said it, as if Phoebe were a milk cow to be traded, that made Phoebe bristle. "I beg your pardon, Miss Fitzherbert," Phoebe said, "but unfortunately, when I have completed my work here at Wentworth Hall, I must return to London."

"Oh? Surely there is something we can do to persuade you to stay."

"No, I am afraid I cannot be persuaded." With the possible exception of Miss Fitzherbert's head on a platter.

"We will pay you a good wage with room and board, Madame Dupree," her father helpfully offered.

Phoebe smiled at him. "Thank you, sir, but I have other obligations."

"Are you certain your obligations are unbreakable?" he persisted. "Perhaps if you tell us who has retained you, we might determine if an arrangement can be made."

"They are very firm obligations," Phoebe assured him. "It is a family matter," she said, trying very hard to look as if the family matter were very dire.

"Oh. Well," Miss Fitzherbert said with a bit of an insouciant shrug. Her eyes unabashedly wandered over Phoebe's form, lingering on the hem of her gown. She frowned a little, then lifted her gaze again. "Then perhaps you can see your way to providing me with a riding habit while you are here. Lord Summerfield has invited me to ride, and I daresay I've not the proper attire," she said, turning a coy smile up to him. "If Lord Summerfield will allow it, perhaps you will help me out of my predicament."

"Naturally," Summerfield said.

Naturally? What did he think, she pulled riding habits out of the clouds? Miss Fitzherbert's smile deepened with her pleasure, and she glanced at Phoebe as if she'd just bested her somehow.

Jealousy pricked at Phoebe. All right, they were to ride. What more did the woman want?

"Riding, eh?" Mr. Fitzherbert said, rolling up to the tips of his toes and down again. "Caroline is not one for riding. She prefers a bench and driver." He chuckled, and seemed oblivious to Miss Fitzherbert's murderous expression.

"I have offered to show Miss Fitzherbert the wild horses," Summerfield explained.

The pinprick of jealousy was now a cold stab to Phoebe's belly. She had no claim to Summerfield and the horses, but she felt suddenly and wildly possessive of them. Would he take Miss Fitzherbert in his arms and help her try to touch the horses as he had done with her? Phoebe couldn't help herself; she looked directly at Summerfield.

He returned her challenging look by raising a brow slightly. "Are you still walking in the mornings, Madame Dupree?" he asked, his look unwavering, his thoughts clearly on that morning, as were Phoebe's.

"When I am able. My work keeps me very well occupied, as you know."

"Have you seen the horses?" Miss Fitzherbert inquired.

Phoebe looked at her. "Many times. They are magnificent."

"Truly magnificent," Summerfield agreed, still watching Phoebe.

"Then you must convince Madame Dupree that, at the very least, a riding habit is necessary, my lord," Miss Fitzherbert purred, nudging him with her arm.

His smile was slow and deep and directed at Phoebe. "I beg your pardon, Miss Fitzherbert, but I have not yet mastered the art of convincing a woman to do anything," he said, to which Mr. Fitzherbert laughed appreciatively. "Nevertheless, I shall confer with Madame Dupree and see if she can't accommodate your riding habit in her busy schedule." And with that, he shifted a smile so charming to Miss Fitzherbert that it was all Phoebe could do to keep from groaning.

Certainly it made no difference to Phoebe whom he esteemed, whom he thought to marry, whom he would bring to his bed. It was his affair if he wanted to court such a plain, provincial woman. Why should Phoebe care in the least? She was the daughter of an earl, the sister of a marchioness, and the cousin of a princess. *Her* prospects were greater than those of a mere viscount. Stanhope was an earl! She had no call to be jealous of this tepid, rustic, backwoods society chit and her bloody riding habit!

Frankly, she could not bear to watch them smiling at one another like simpletons. If they wanted to ogle one another, let them at least do it without imposing on her—she already had too much work to do. She said, a little too imperiously, "If there is nothing else, my lord, I have quite a lot that must be done."

Miss Fitzherbert looked surprised by that, but her father smiled. "*That's* what I like in a servant," he said agreeably. "An eagerness to be about one's duties."

Phoebe looked impatiently at Summerfield.

Damn him if the corner of his mouth didn't tip up in the barest hint of a smile. "There is nothing else, Madame Dupree. If you are so eager to be about your work, you have my leave."

God in heaven, how did true servants *bear* such superiority? She nodded curtly to Miss Fitzherbert, who smiled at her in a way that made Phoebe's skin crawl, then curtsied to Summerfield as she ought. Without a word, she turned and walked from the terrace, remembering her mother's advice to always walk with her chin held high, for every woman was a queen in her own right.

Oh yes, she was the Queen of Seams.

Fourteen

⟨⟨⟨⟨⟩⟩⟩⟩

Will did not call on Phoebe to convince her to make Miss Fitzherbert a riding habit as he'd threatened—he scarcely had time to breathe in the course of the next two days as they finished preparations for the supper party he'd intended to host for the Remingtons. Henry suggested that it was a perfect opportunity to test society's waters. "Might as well give it a go," he'd said one afternoon. "There isn't much else to occupy the denizens of Bedfordshire."

So Will's idea of a small, intimate supper party with the Remingtons had grown into a full soiree. Now, in addition to the Remingtons, the Fitzherberts and the Fortenberrys—including Mr. Fortenberry's elderly parents—Vicar MacDonald and his young family would be in attendance. All told, including the Summerfield brood, there were twenty-six souls.

One would think the Darbys had never entertained in their collective lives—they were all of them on tenterhooks and cross with one another. But then again, society in Bedfordshire was bucolic. Most gatherings were around afternoon tea, and the highlight of the social season was a harvest dance in the autumn. There was really very little high society, and to pretend there was seemed to bring out the worst in the Darby family.

Will scarcely saw Phoebe, but he certainly wondered about her. He had the impression from their last meeting that Phoebe wanted to be left alone. That was just as well—he did not allow himself to dwell on how much he wanted to see her. He convinced himself that he merely missed a woman's touch—nothing more. He lectured himself on his duty to his family and his title. Taking up with a servant was hardly respectable.

So he kept his distance and didn't see her at all, really, except early in the morning, when he might spy her through the window of his study as she walked in the gardens, her sketchbook under her arm. Once, he'd seen her standing a little to one side at the window of her workroom on the top floor, watching as he accepted his mount to ride into Greenhill. He had touched his hand to his hat in greeting, and she had responded by ducking into the shadows.

Will had ridden hard that day, feeling absurdly unsettled by the sight of the seamstress. But he quickly pushed her out of his mind, as he had gone to pay a call on Caroline Fitzherbert.

Miss Fitzherbert was the only unmarried woman—among what seemed like a bumper crop of them in Bedfordshire—that he'd met since his return who had sparked his interest. He wasn't precisely sure what made her stand out. She was pretty, had a pleasant mien, as all of them seemed to possess. Her family was gentry, and her bearing and rearing seemed suitable for the wife of an earl. He enjoyed her conversation, he supposed, even as politely stupefying and superficial as it tended to be in the company of her ever-present parents. Yet he detected a certain intelligence behind her lovely brown eyes that intrigued him.

Moreover, when he'd told his father about her, the earl had raised a finger, leading Will to believe that he approved of the match. His father had not reacted when Will had mentioned one or two other debutantes.

He supposed Caroline Fitzherbert was perfectly suited to be his wife, but he was also keenly aware that she did not stoke any fires of passion in him. He was disappointed by that, but he believed—or rather, he hoped, and rather desperately so—that passion would come with time. He could not imagine being married to a woman he did not desire completely.

Frankly, he feared it.

But Will had not felt intense passion for a woman since leaving Rania, the dark-eyed beauty, in Egypt. Then again, Rania had been trained from an early age to entice a man and call forth his most passionate response. He doubted, however, that she would be much use as a wife in any other sense of the word.

Miss Fitzherbert, on the other hand, might not feed his physical desire in the marriage bed, but she would be a good wife in other ways. She would be a great help with Alice and Jane—she could teach them the proper behaviors that he could not seem to inculcate in them. Perhaps she would even be helpful in nudging Joshua and Roger into suitable occupations. Joshua, in particular, seemed calmer in her presence. Surely all that counted for something—or did it?

He'd not mentioned his thoughts about Miss Fitzherbert to anyone but his father; it was too soon. He was hardly certain she was the one to be mistress of Wentworth Hall. Nevertheless, the pressure to marry weighed on him, accompanying his every waking moment. It seemed hypocritical to lecture his brothers and sisters about their responsibilities if he didn't assume his own.

The pressure was exacerbated by his doubts about how much longer his father had on this earth. His father's desire to see Will married was one of the last things he'd been able to communicate to him. *It is time to come home,* he'd written Will. *It is time to marry. Nothing would give me greater peace.* He could not fail to give his ailing father peace.

So he made his call on Miss Fitzherbert. He asked after the painting she'd done, which seemed rudimentary at best, and listened attentively as Mrs. Fitzherbert praised her daughter's charitable work for the parish. He walked with her in the garden of her family's home, Floddington, and even picked a rose for her. She promised to press it between the pages of the family Bible. She spoke of the picnic the parish church was planning and said that she hoped he would be there. Will had smiled and thereby managed to suppress the yawn of tedium that was building in him, while privately wondering if there was anything more insipid than sitting around on a hot afternoon listening to Vicar MacDonald's thoughts on various scripture.

Even Henry dreaded such events. "They are so awfully *dull,*" he'd said. "I much prefer London. Come to London with me, Summerfield—we'll make a jolly time of it."

"You know I cannot," Will said. "I have responsibilities here."

"Your dedication is either inspiring or madness—I've yet to determine which," Henry said petulantly.

Neither had Will. He felt nothing inside, really. Just the wasteland into which he'd been shipwrecked, the desolation of it spreading a little farther each day.

When he took his leave of Miss Fitzherbert, he rode the long way home—through the forests and into the valley at the far end of the family estate—where he was certain the wild horses would be.

The big red one, which Will had named Apollo, had grown accustomed to Will's frequent visits, and slowly, steadily, Will was cultivating the horse's trust. On days when his family posed no end of problems, and Will felt completely at sea, visiting the herd of wild horses was the bright spot of his day, the time he felt most like himself, and not the useless, gentrified country lord he was becoming.

Apollo had come to accept Will's hands on his body, allowed him to stroke his coat from shoulder to hindquarters. Will had even placed a saddle blanket on Apollo so that he would begin to feel weight on his back and withers, preparing him for a saddle. Today, Will had brought a training bit they used at the hall to train colts. He had no idea how he would get Apollo to take the bit, but he had a sack of apples and he was determined.

The herd was precisely where Will thought they would be, in a small clearing where they had taken to grazing. They were down another horse, he noticed. One mare and her foal had disappeared last week; a colt was missing today. Fergus snorted and whinnied, heralding their arrival. The other horses started; some of them shied away into the woods, but Apollo slowly lifted his head and looked at Will. His nostrils flared as he took in the scent of Will and Fergus.

"Steady, old boy," Will said, patting Fergus's neck. He dismounted, tethered Fergus to a tree, and reached for the saddlebag that held the apples and the bit. He slung it over his shoulder and began to walk across the meadow to him.

Apollo tossed his head back and pawed the ground,

earning a high-pitched cry from Fergus in response. As Will neared him, Apollo neighed loudly and pawed the ground again before making a sudden move toward Will, as if to startle him.

"There now, Apollo," he said quietly, his voice flattening the horse's ears. "There now." Apollo lowered his head and made a threatening move. For a moment, Will expected to be butted across the clearing and he braced himself, expecting it. But Apollo did not hit him. Apollo lifted his head and touched Will's hand to see what he'd brought him.

An hour later, Will rode out of the clearing with a broad smile. Apollo had not liked the bit, as Will expected, but in the end he had taken it. Will believed he would be riding the spirited stallion in a fortnight.

He led Fergus onto an old, rarely used wooded path, a shortcut to the hall he'd often used as a boy. As he neared the edge of the woods and a path that cut across the hills, he was surprised to see a rider approaching him, coming from the direction of the hall. He recognized the rider as a slow-witted lad from Greenhill who often worked in the smithy. When the lad saw *him*, his eyes widened with surprise, and he pulled the cap down low over his eyes.

It was too late, of course. No one outside the estate ever used this path, and Will had already seen him. "Good day, sir," Will said, reining up.

"G'day, milord," the young man said, looking rather uncomfortable.

"Frederick, isn't it?" Will asked, looking at him curiously.

"Aye. Frederick Mayhew, milord."

Will glanced at the path the lad had just come up and then at Frederick again. "What brings you to Wentworth?"

Frederick shifted in his saddle and scratched his nose.

"Did you come to see me?" Will asked, knowing full well the lad had not.

"No, milord," the young man admitted with a wince.

"Then on whom have you called at the hall?"

Frederick frowned in thought a moment, and then suddenly smiled, his eyes bright with an idea. "'Twas a message, milord. I was paid to bring a message. Not a call, no."

"A message for whom?" Will pressed.

The lad was stumped by the question. He lifted a meaty hand and scratched the back of his neck for a moment. "The thing is, milord, I'm not to say."

Something clicked in Will's mind. He suddenly sat forward, pinning the young man with a hard look that caused him to rear back as if Will had physically struck him. "Did you deliver the message to Lady Alice Darby, perchance?"

Frederick did not need to respond—his look of panic was Will's answer. Fury raced through him as he fished in the pocket of his waistcoat. "How much did the man pay you?"

"A tuppence, milord."

Will withdrew several coins and selected one, which he held up between two fingers. "I will pay you this shilling to tell me how often you have delivered letters to Lady Alice."

Now the color seeped from the young man's ruddy face. He swallowed hard as he stared at the shilling Will held up.

"*How often?*"

"Hardly ever, milord, I swear it! A dozen times, no more, and sometimes only to fetch a letter from Lady Alice!"

Good God, it was just as he feared. He tossed the coin to Frederick, who caught it deftly in his paw and squinted down at it. "I've a message for the smithy's apprentice," Will said evenly. "Tell him if I should discover he has sent another letter to Wentworth Hall, I will personally see to it that the smithy's business is ended in Greenhill. Can you remember that, Frederick?"

"Aye, milord," Frederick said, and pocketed the coin.

"Go on, then. Tell him straightaway," Will said.

Frederick did not hesitate. He spurred his old horse forward, cantering past Will and Fergus.

Will did not move immediately. He stared down the path, to the point where it widened and a corner of Wentworth Hall could be seen. His pulse was pounding in his ears, his jaw was clenched tightly shut. He abruptly put his spurs in Fergus's flanks and sent the horse flying toward the house.

Fifteen

The shrieking Phoebe heard below brought her head up so quickly that she stabbed her finger with the needle. "*Ouch,*" she muttered, and put the injured finger in her mouth.

The shrieking was followed by a clattering of feet on the stairs. "Good heavens, not again," she muttered. Frieda was absent today; Phoebe had worked all morning on a seam only to find a mistake that forced her to take it out and start again. Her vision was blurry, her fingers ached from holding the brocade fabric of the ball gown, and she was in no mood to mediate another quarrel between Alice and Jane. The two young women were absolutely panicked by the evening's supper party.

With a sigh, Phoebe stood up, stretched her fingers long and wide to help the ache, and realized that she was hearing the sound of heavy boots as well as a lighter footfall racing up the stairs. The shrieking—which, Phoebe determined, was actually cries of *"I hate you!"*—was coming from Alice. She guessed the girl was yelling at Roger, as Roger seemed to delight in torturing his sisters.

Phoebe marched to the door of the workroom, prepared to greet the two hellions and send them right back down, but before she could reach the door, it banged open and she was nearly shoved against the wall as a sobbing Alice ran inside. She rushed to the corner of the room to hide behind the dress form on which Jane's ball gown hung.

Summerfield exploded into the room behind Alice, stopping just across the threshold, his expression dark, his eyes burning with anger, and his broad chest rising with the exertion of the chase.

"Give it over, Alice," he said sharply, holding out his hand. "I will not abide your disobedience a moment longer!"

"I *won't!*" Alice shouted as she clutched something to her chest. "If you want it, you must kill me and pry it from my hand!"

"Oh, for the love of Christ!" Summerfield strode forward. But Alice used the dress form like a shield, keeping it between her and Summerfield.

"No!" Phoebe cried out, and lunged to grab the dress form around the waist.

Summerfield tried to move around Phoebe, but Alice was too quick on her feet, her every move matching his. In a fit of frustration, Summerfield suddenly grabbed Phoebe and the dress form in one arm and moved them to the side while he thrust his hand out toward Alice, palm up. *"Give it to me!"*

Alice dissolved into wrenching sobs and sank down, turning her face in to the wall.

"Stop that!" Summerfield roared.

"Stop *that!*" Phoebe cried, shoving him.

Startled, he looked at Phoebe.

"Whatever your quarrel, I will not allow you to bully her!"

Alice's sobbing only intensified, but Summerfield turned his large, rage-filled body around to Phoebe. "*You* will not allow *me*?" he roared.

She wisely put the dress form between herself and Summerfield. "I will not be subjected to such awful behavior from either one of you! You are not barbarians!"

He was so stunned, he could not speak. Phoebe ignored him; she squatted next to Alice and put a comforting hand on her back. "What is it?" she asked as Alice sobbed. "What is wrong?"

"I will tell you what is wrong," Summerfield bit out. "Alice has defied me *again*. She and that bloody smithy are exchanging secret messages!"

Alice's wailing only increased. Phoebe could see now that what she held so tightly against her breast was a crumpled piece of vellum. "Oh, Lady Alice," she sighed sympathetically.

Alice lifted her head. Her skin was splotchy red from crying, her cheeks wet. "I *won't* give it to him!" she insisted. "He may beat me, and still I won't give it to him! It is *mine!*"

"Of course you won't give it to him," Phoebe said soothingly.

"*Madame Dupree!*" Summerfield bellowed. "This is hardly your concern! Kindly step aside so that I may address my sister!"

With another ear-piercing shriek, Alice suddenly clambered to her feet. In her haste to escape her brother, she shoved the dress form and toppled it over onto Phoebe, who was still crouched on the floor. Phoebe flung her arm up to save her head, heard the sound of several of her things clattering to the floor as Alice brushed by the worktable.

"*Alice!*" Summerfield bellowed.

"*Ouch!*" Phoebe cried out as the dress form hit her.

Summerfield quickly righted the dress form, grabbed Phoebe's arms, and hauled her to her feet. "Are you all right?" he asked, his eyes darting over her for any sign of harm.

"I'm fine," she said, pushing his hands from her. He moved as if he intended to go after Alice, but Phoebe caught his arm. "My lord! Have you no heart? You *cannot* take her letter!"

Summerfield stopped midstride and stared heatedly at her. "You are astoundingly bold, madam! Have a care how you speak to me—I will dismiss you for your foolishness!"

"*My* foolishness?" Phoebe shot back, fury filling her. "You burst in here like a rampaging bull and declare *I* am foolish?"

He blinked in disbelief. "Madame Dupree, have you *any* idea whom you are addressing?"

"Oh, I am well aware of whom I am addressing, but I rather think you have forgotten that you are also Alice's brother!"

He opened his mouth to speak and quickly shut it

again. He turned around and glared down at her. He was standing so close that she could almost feel the anger emanating from his body as he punched his fists to his waist. "I cannot imagine what possesses you to wag your tongue so carelessly! Have you no care for your position here? Your *livelihood*? Do you realize that I have the power to make certain you can't hire out as much as a *stitch* in this county again?"

"Have you never been in love, Summerfield?"

The question clearly stunned him; he reared back. *"What?"*

"Haven't you *ever* been in love?" she asked again, incredulous, but he looked as if words had deserted him. "You *haven't*," she said, fascinated that this man, this beautiful man, had never been in love.

"What possible bearing could that have on anything to do with your behavior?"

"It has nothing to do with my behavior, but clearly it has everything to do with yours." With that said, she moved out of the corner, brushing carelessly against him. She walked around to the front of the dress form to examine Jane's gown for any damage. So help them, if she had to redo as much as a stitch—

"And pray tell, what do you believe you have divined, madam? For I assure you, such maidenly notions have no place in a man's thinking," he said gruffly.

"Oh my, now it is painfully obvious that you have never felt love." She gave him a look of sympathy. "That is really very distressing."

"Love," he repeated stubbornly.

"Love," Phoebe insisted. "That exquisite feeling of pressure on your entire being when the one person you hold so dear walks into the room," she said, turning toward him. "The fever that courses through your body with just a *touch*. The sensation of gulping for air and

being quite unable to breathe," she said, pressing her hands to her heart. "When that person smiles, you feel as if you are breathing underwater. You can't possibly get enough of her smile and you feel that desperate, instinctive *mad* rush to breathe. *Love!*" she said, throwing her arms wide.

Summerfield blinked.

Phoebe lowered her arms. "There, you see? You've never felt it, for surely if you had, you would have some compassion for your sister."

He stared at her as if he were trying to work out the need for compassion in his head.

It suddenly dawned on Phoebe. "Oh dear Lord, you don't understand, do you?" she asked with shocking delight. "Alice is in *love* with Mr. Hughes."

His lovely hazel eyes widened with horror.

"And Mr. Hughes is in love with Alice! Clearly, he has written her a love letter that is intensely private and tender. It is not for *your* eyes, and really, why should you see it? You know he wrote it, you know she received it and defied your wishes. You need not take what little dignity and privacy she has left by *reading* that very personal letter."

"Have you encouraged her in any way?" he asked sharply. "Have you urged her toward Mr. Hughes?"

"Of course not," Phoebe said, folding her arms. "You will recall that she *struck* me when I encouraged her in exactly the opposite way."

His gaze, full of suspicion, raked over her. "Well, now that you have reprimanded me for my decided lack of sentiment and advised me as to how to address the situation, allow me to educate *you*, Madame Dupree. Alice should be married, and marriage is about more important matters than *love*."

That pronouncement unexpectedly infuriated Phoebe,

surprising her with the strength of it. She glared right back at him. "Oh, please *do* enlighten me, sir! What important matters is marriage about?"

"Compatibility of circumstances and the suitability of partners. A secure future, security for one's children's futures."

"Oh yes, of *course*," Phoebe said, twirling away from him. "The fortunes must be compatible, and the lineage suitable for proper heirs. And if love develops among the two people who are now shackled for life, how lovely! You do not need to explain the laws of society to me—my own mother taught me in the cradle that I was to expect no more than what you describe," she snapped, and straightened the dress form with so much force that it toppled backward.

He looked at her curiously as she righted it, and Phoebe realized, belatedly, what she'd said. "That is, were my family ever to *possess* a fortune."

"I do not know your particular circumstances, but you must at least allow that Alice's position is far different from yours. Marriages among our class take on more importance precisely because of the matching of fortunes and political alliances. It is not, nor has it ever been, about *love*. And those who fancy it *is* about love are destined for great disappointment."

It was so callous, so calculating that astoundingly, Phoebe teared up. "How very lamentable, then, for your *class*," she said, and quickly turned away before he could see the tears that had come to her eyes. "How tragic that you actually seem to *believe* it."

"And how earnestly you seem to believe love is something to die for," he said disgustedly. "What's this?" He stepped forward, bending his head to look at her face. She turned away from him again, but Summerfield caught her by the shoulder and turned her around.

"Why these tears?" he asked disconcertedly. "What I said does not affect you in the least. I should think you are free to marry or die for love, whatever you wish."

Phoebe swiped at the single tear that fell from her face. "None of us is ever really *free*, are we?" she asked angrily.

He considered that a moment. "No," he said, and caught a tear that spilled onto her cheek with the pad of his thumb. "I suppose none of us is ever really free, for if we were, there would be no cause to long for those we cannot have."

She wasn't certain if he was referring to himself or to her. "Longing for the ones we cannot have is futile," Phoebe said morosely. "That is why some grasp the chance for happiness where they can."

"Do you?" he asked, his eyes glistening, her desire reflected back at her.

Her tongue felt thick in her head, her throat closed.

"Have you ever?" he asked her again.

Phoebe shook her head. "I don't know."

"Perhaps the question is too personal. Perhaps one's grasp for happiness seems larger in a faded memory. Perhaps your late husband is only a faded memory—"

"That is not fair!"

"Then tell me of your happiness," he said, catching her by the waist. "Regale me, entice me, persuade me to let Alice have hers."

"Why?" she demanded. "Because you have so little heart you cannot imagine it?"

"Oh," he said, as his eyes slipped to her lips, "I can very well imagine it." He lowered his head and kissed her. His breath was warm, his mouth soft. He nipped lightly at her bottom lip, then touched the tip of his tongue to hers as his arms encircled her.

And in that moment, Phoebe felt as if she were breathing underwater.

He had submerged her in a pool of desire. A million things darted through her brain as his tongue tangled with hers. She was sinking; she could feel herself being dragged below the surface. Fighting for air, she suddenly shoved as hard as she could against his chest. "I am not your property," she said roughly. "Imagine your so-called happiness with someone else." She shoved him again.

Summerfield took one step back. "I would ... if I could possibly erase the image of you from my mind." The lids of his autumn-colored eyes were heavy, his lips dark. His gaze swept over her, but it was not the look of lust she associated with so many men. No, that was a fever in his eyes—a fever she felt inside herself.

Phoebe would never be certain what possessed her. Perhaps it was Madame Dupree who seized the moment; perhaps it was just the years she had spent craving this very thing. Or perhaps it was simply her opportunity to grasp happiness. But somehow she understood that he was not drowning her, he was actually saving her from drowning. She suddenly grabbed the lapels of his coat to keep from fading away from him and yanked him to her, rising up on her tiptoes to kiss him.

He made a sound of surprise, but one arm went around her waist, drawing her into his warmth and anchoring her firmly against him. With the other, he caressed her neck and cheek as his lips artfully softened hers. A strong tide of pleasure began to flow through her—she could feel his arousal, could feel the beat of his heart where she was pressed against him. He slipped his tongue into her mouth, swirling it around hers.

Phoebe responded with all the pent-up desire she had been harboring for years. Whatever she did seemed to entice him; his grip of her waist suddenly tightened, his fingers splayed against the side of her head, and his tongue thrust against hers with an urgency that she felt with equal intensity. Somehow her hair came loose, tumbling down her shoulders in unruly curls, and Summerfield plunged his hand into them. "Now *this*, madam, will live in my imagination for many years," he said lustily.

Phoebe shamelessly pressed herself against him, amazed by the shocking sensuality of his hardness against her belly. When his hand slid down her neck to cup her breast, his thumb brushing across the hard peak, something in her womb fluttered, and a rush of breath escaped her. She felt outside of herself, almost as if someone else were experiencing the tender pressure of his mouth and tongue and hand.

When she groaned with pleasure in his mouth, Summerfield suddenly twirled her around, pushing her up against the worktable with such force that more of her things clattered to the floor. Phoebe didn't care; she cared for nothing but the way his hands cupped her face, for the thousands of little waves of pleasure rolling through her. He drew her lips between his teeth, tasting and shaping them, then probed deeply, while his hands trailed to her ears, her neck, and her shoulders.

"Is this the happiness you seek?" he whispered hoarsely. "Tell me now, and I will give it to you." He moved down her body, his mouth on her bosom, his breath hot on her skin, and his hand freeing her breast. Phoebe ran her fingers through his hair, thrusting her breast forward as he took the peak into his mouth.

This was insanity! "Only a profligate would confuse happiness with desire— *Oh!*" The swell of pleasure his mouth on her breast gave her was startling, and she cried out.

"And only a fool would try and separate the two," he responded hotly before he closed his mouth around her other breast.

Phoebe gasped and gripped his head tightly to her. "The pleasure of the flesh and eternal happiness are two distinctly different things."

"Good God, woman, you would argue the semantics of this *now*?" he said breathlessly, and suddenly rose up and toppled her onto her back on top of the worktable. He moved over her; one hand spanned the whole of her rib cage, moving upward, pressing against her bare breast while he filled his mouth with the other one. "I have something much more pleasurable in mind than a debate."

The prurient sensations unfurling within Phoebe numbed her mind to everything. Her hands tangled in his hair, fell to his shoulders and the corded muscles in his back. When he lightly bit the tip of her breast, a violent shudder rifled through her. "You *are* a profligate and a seducer."

Summerfield lifted his head. His breathing was ragged, his eyes full of the fever. "Every bit. But I defy you to show me a man who could be anything but that when presented with such incomparable beauty. I want to touch you, all of you, every inch of you. I want to be inside you." His lips skimmed the column of her neck as his hand cupped her breast, squeezing gently, fitting it to his palm. "And I daresay you want it, too."

She did want it, she wanted it desperately. Phoebe

allowed herself to drift down this course with him, knowing full well that she was close to passing the point where she could stop this passionate encounter. She didn't *want* to stop. Her desire had blossomed out of control, drawing from a well deep inside her and pulsing to the breast that he suckled. *Oh, dear God, such pleasure!* She raised her hands above her head, inadvertently knocking fabric and rulers and scissors to the wooden floor. The desire inside her was building toward a violent eruption.

But Summerfield suddenly stopped. Phoebe moaned and opened her eyes. He was looking at the door. It was then Phoebe heard the voices. Someone was coming up the stairs.

He quickly and silently pulled Phoebe to her feet, helped her rearrange her breasts into her bodice. She knotted her hair; Summerfield cupped her face and kissed her passionately once more before moving quietly through the door that led to her bedchamber.

Phoebe stood at the worktable, her chest heaving with the excitement and desire that was still crashing through her, the residual feelings of his kiss and his touch still pulsing deep and hot between her legs.

When Mrs. Turner appeared in the doorway, her eyes widened at the sight of Phoebe and her work scattered on the floor.

"Good Lord, Madame Dupree! What has happened?" she asked as Frieda eagerly pushed in behind her.

Phoebe glanced at her things on the floor, seeing the mess for the first time.

"I told you, Mrs. Turner, did I not?" Frieda asked triumphantly. "Lady Alice is in a mood today!"

Phoebe sighed and went down on her haunches, letting the two women think Alice had upset the workroom as she began to gather her things.

Sixteen

—⊶⊷—

*S*pellbound.

Will could not remember a time he had ever felt so completely enchanted. Not even Rania, with all her seductive charm, had affected him quite like Phoebe.

It was hours later, and his body was still reacting to the passion he had shared with Phoebe, his heart still pounding with the anticipation of sinking deep inside her. He continued to wear the scarab, however—he feared how his desire might rage without it.

His convictions, he was sorry to note, had rapidly deserted him. His determination to be a good and decent man had flitted out the window with a single warm look from the blue-eyed beauty. He was surprised and appalled by his weakness, but even more startled by how completely spellbound he felt.

Perhaps it was her poignant description of love. Or the fact that she'd never held him in any particular reverence. Whatever it was about her, he could not stop thinking about her now, could not shed the feel of her from his body.

He was so enthralled that he could scarcely dress for the supper party. He stood in the middle of his dressing room, hands on hips, thinking about what he would do.

Convictions be damned.

He was a man, and he was physically and emotionally drawn to Phoebe Dupree in a way he had not been attracted to a woman in a very long time, perhaps as long as his first infatuation. That she was beautiful only intensified his desire.

His preoccupation with her allowed him to forget about Alice for a time. He decided to heed Phoebe's advice and let his sister keep her blasted love letter, but he'd warned her through her locked door—as chambermaids hurried by him carrying table linens—that if she thought to see Mr. Hughes again, he would put an end to their infatuation in a manner she would most assuredly not like. He did not believe in their *love*. He really wasn't certain what love was, for Alice or anyone else, but it seemed ridiculous to apply that word to her admiration of the smithy's apprentice.

And as for himself? Will was incapable of naming the feelings that were gaining control over him. Desire? Obsession?

For all his staring into space, he'd forgotten about Addison, until the man gave him an appraising look. "What is it?" Will asked. "Have I forgotten something?"

"No, milord," he said, and brushed a hair from Will's shoulder. "But you do not seem at ease."

Will snorted. "As usual, Addison, your powers of understatement are impeccable. Are you not the least bit acquainted with my sister Alice? No, Addison, I am not at *ease*. My brother cheats at cards, my sister is far too free with her affections, and there is a bloody seamstress underfoot . . ." He caught himself before saying more.

"Milord?"

"Nothing," Will muttered.

Addison said nothing, but his ears began to redden. "Might I suggest a whiskey, milord, to ease the tension before you greet your guests?"

"A capital idea," Will said gruffly as he pushed Addison's hands away from his neckcloth. "Make it a double, will you?" he asked, and moved to straighten his blasted neckcloth himself.

"By the bye," Addison said casually as he poured the whiskey. "I have done a bit of discreet inquiring about Madame Dupree."

Will looked over his shoulder at Addison. "And?"

"And it seems that she has been rather involved in her work and has not spoken much about herself. Very little is known of her, really."

"No mention of family? Lovers?"

"Not that I could ascertain, milord."

He turned back to the mirror. "Then I shall have to ascertain it myself," he said low.

Addison handed Will the whiskey—he tossed it back with the vain hope it would ease his burn.

It did not.

He was still on fire when he greeted his guests later. Everyone seemed in good spirits, and his siblings were, surprisingly, on their best behavior. Alice and Jane were beautifully turned out, and he marveled at their transformation. Jane's dress, made of a soft green fabric, was simply adorned with a rose sash beneath the bodice. The skirt was covered in fine lace, which lent it an elegance that Jane carried well.

But it was Alice who seemed almost a different person. Her hair was swept up and tied with ribbons, and her lavender gown revealed a woman's figure Will had not realized his sister possessed. Her gown was beautiful—rings of delicate little flowers lined the hem and sleeves. She wore the amethyst jewelry that had belonged to his mother, the earrings sparkling in the soft candlelight. Perhaps even more surprising, Alice smiled prettily when Samuel Remington engaged her in conversation.

Will could not remember the last time he'd seen her smile; her laughter warmed his heart in a way he would not have thought possible.

Roger, Will discovered, had an engaging way of conversing and was a natural host. In contrast, Joshua was brooding, keeping to himself as he often did when Will was present. He supposed he ought to at least be grateful that Joshua had not challenged anyone to a card game or made any lewd remarks to the ladies.

He had worried about the supper service, but the newly renovated dining room was large enough to accommodate them all, particularly when the younger guests were put at smaller tables in the corners of the room. And his staff, most of them rather new to their jobs, performed admirably well.

The conversation at supper turned lively when Mr. Fortenberry reviewed news from the last Parliamentary session. He very adamantly opposed reforms that Lords Radnor and Middleton were trying to push through the House of Lords that would give poor, working women certain protections and, to Mr. Fortenberry's way of thinking, encourage them to pursue unnatural occupations.

"*Unnatural?*" Mrs. Remington sputtered, ignoring her husband's wince. "Do you suppose, then, Mr. Fortenberry, that men should pursue the *unnatural* occupation of shopkeeper or seamstress?"

"A woman should concentrate on being a mother and a wife. She may sew her family's clothes if she has an inclination for it, but to be a shopkeeper or a paid seamstress is unnatural," Mr. Fortenberry exclaimed, putting his fist to the table to emphasize it.

"But what of those women who are not inclined to sew? What are they to do for clothing?"

"A woman who does not know the art of needlework has been given a negligent education in my opinion."

"Oh, Mr. Fortenberry! That is preposterous!" Mrs. Remington snapped, and pressed two hands to her fleshy bosom as if she meant to prevent herself from leaping across the table and strangling him.

The table fell silent for a moment, but then Alice surprised Will by smiling and saying, "I am thankful there are seamstresses for hire, sir, for I cannot bear to think what I might be wearing tonight had *we* not brought in a seamstress."

That was met with polite laughter around the table, interrupted only when Mr. Fortenberry went on to espouse his views that once a woman was given protective rights that took jobs from men, then the right to vote could not be far behind. Mrs. Remington loudly disagreed, averring women generally had no particular interest in something as dreadfully tiresome as politics.

And as the conversation turned livelier, with everyone tossing in their opinions, Will caught Miss Fitzherbert's eye. She smiled at him from her seat halfway down the table. He smiled, too, but he found himself wondering if Miss Fitzherbert had ever felt as if she were breathing underwater.

After supper, the ladies retired to the game room while the men enjoyed a cigar and a round of port. "I tell you, it is trouble to allow women any rights or privileges under the law," Mr. Fortenberry continued, stabbing the air with his cigar for emphasis. "In the blink of an eye, a man will not even be master of his house. He will be *lawfully* forced to allow his wife a say in the management of the home."

"My wife has long demanded a say in the management of our home," Mr. Remington said cheerfully. The men laughed.

"What do you say, Summerfield?" Mr. Fortenberry asked, fixing his gaze on Will.

What Will thought was that all the sitting about was tiresome. He wanted to move, to ride, and to be left to his thoughts. He felt oddly disjointed; the air was cloying and he had an almost overwhelming urge to rip his collar open. "I have not yet met a woman I feared, sir."

The gentlemen laughed, but Henry eyed him playfully. "Come, now, Summerfield. Have you no opinion on the matter? Do you think yourself capable of tolerating a woman emboldened with civil rights?"

Will grinned at his old friend. "My tolerance of any woman, with or without civil rights, is strengthened only by her comely looks."

Once again, the gentlemen laughed roundly, but still Mr. Remington would not cease trying to persuade the others that women who worked were a danger to the realm.

When the men finally rejoined the women, card tables had been set up for whist, and the billiards table had been prepared for players. Will had promised Miss Fitzherbert that he would partner her for a round of whist, but as he approached her, Joshua suddenly stepped in front of him.

"Miss Fitzherbert," he said, bowing low. "Will you do me the honor of partnering me for whist?"

Miss Fitzherbert seemed as surprised by Joshua's invitation as Will and uncertain what to do. "Oh. Well," she said, glancing anxiously at Will.

Joshua ignored Will; he stood with his clasped hands behind his back and patiently awaited her answer.

"Yes . . . of course, Mr. Darby," Miss Fitzherbert said at last.

"Splendid. Thank you," he said, and put out his arm to her.

With another helpless look at Will, Miss Fitzherbert put her gloved hand on Joshua's arm and allowed him to lead her away.

Will was not, as he thought he should have been, particularly disturbed by Joshua's invitation to Miss Fitzherbert. But the vicar's lovely young wife was disturbed for him—she disengaged from her husband and requested that Will be her partner for billiards.

They played two rounds, losing both times to Henry and an exuberant Jane. It was Will's fault—he could not concentrate.

"What the devil is the matter with you?" Henry asked as a footman rearranged the billiards for another game. "Just last week you astonished me with superior skill. Tonight you can't seem to find a single billiard pocket."

"Too much wine," Will said. But in truth, he could not shake the thoughts of Phoebe from his mind. He could not seem to wash away the taste of her or stop reliving her impassioned plea for Alice.

He had abandoned every last conviction, apparently, for after losing another round, instead of moving to a whist table as he ought to have done, he handed Mrs. MacDonald to Henry, asked one of the Remington boys to be Jane's partner—which made poor Jane turn very pale—and announced to his guests that he must excuse himself for a time, as he would bid his father good night.

He walked to the door of the billiard room, instructed the two footmen there to ensure that no glass went empty, and quit the room. And as he moved up the stairs, he continued past the floor that housed the family quarters, including his father's, and kept going up, to the top floors, where servants and closed nurseries and storage rooms were housed.

He noticed Phoebe's workroom door was closed and

withdrew his pocket watch from his waistcoat. It was half past eleven. She was certainly sleeping. Will hesitated, standing there with one foot on the stairs, one on the landing, debating whether or not to wake her.

Then he heard her voice. It was faint, but he heard her singing. The sound buoyed him. He moved down the corridor, straining to hear her, then stood outside her door, listening to her soft, lilting voice, marveling that any human being could sing so horribly off-key.

Good Lord, he'd heard mewling cats that sounded better than Phoebe Dupree.

Alas, my love, ye do me wrong
To cast me off discourteously,
And I have loved you so long,
Delighting in your company.

As she began the second verse, Will rapped on the door to stop her.

It worked. A moment later, she opened the door, a curious smile on her face that rapidly faded when she saw him standing there. She was wearing a nightgown and a dressing gown over it, her blond hair loose and hanging over her shoulders and around her face, as if he'd interrupted her brushing it.

"Good evening," he said, and leaned against the doorjamb, taking her in.

"My lord!" She suddenly whirled around and picked up a Kashmir shawl from a chair, throwing it around her shoulders and holding it tightly to her. "What are you doing here? Has something happened?"

"Yes, something has happened. I am in desperate need of asylum."

"*Asylum?*"

"Unfortunately," he said, stepping inside her room, "I am hopeless in social situations. I find them tiresome and tedious. I'd much rather be in a Bedouin tent listening to the *masnawa*."

"I beg your pardon?"

"To tales told very poetically."

"But you should be with your guests," she said, hurrying to the door. She peeked out into the hallway and, apparently satisfied that no one was about, quickly shut the door and turned around to face him. "You are the *host*," she admonished him, as if he might possibly have forgotten.

"It is a deplorable lack of manners, I agree," he said jovially, and looked around the room and at the gowns in various stages of tailoring. "They will hardly note my absence, and I shall not leave them long." He glanced at Phoebe from the corner of his eye. "I heard you singing."

"Oh." A blush stained her cheeks and she suddenly laughed. "I regret that I am not particularly accomplished."

Not particularly? Not at *all.*

"Greer—my cousin—she is an accomplished musician. She possesses all of the family talent, it would seem."

"Ah. Is there more to your family besides the accomplished cousin?"

Phoebe looked startled by the question. "Family?" she echoed, as if she were having trouble recalling.

"Mother? Father? Sister or brother?"

"Ah . . ." She looked anxiously at her feet. "*Ahem.*" She pushed a hand through the wild curls of her hair. "Well . . . my cousin, of course"—she glanced up—"the, ah . . . the accomplished musician."

"I think we've established quite clearly that you have a cousin."

"Yes. Well. I . . . I have a sister."

He nodded.

She shrugged a little.

When it was clear to him she meant to say nothing else, he asked, "No mother or father?"

"Deceased," she said with a quick affirmative nod.

A young widow practically alone in the world, was she? Why that knowledge made him think of her body beneath the dressing gown was unfathomable. "How long have you been widowed?" he asked bluntly, taking a step toward her.

Phoebe frowned a little and folded her arms tightly across her chest. "Did you really come here to ask after my family?"

"No," he said honestly. "I can't rightly say why I came. Frankly, I am trying to work it out whilst I distract you with questions. Humor me, will you?"

He could see her silently debating it. After a moment, she said, "More than a year."

She seemed uncomfortable speaking of it, but Will, who had taken in the wild curl of her hair, the soft glow of her skin, and her very appealing state of undress, had crossed some invisible line. "Do you miss him?" he asked quietly, unsure of what answer he wanted.

She colored, glanced down at the floor. "I . . ." Her voice trailed and she did not finish her thought.

Obviously, she mourned him, of course she did, and he was being incredibly callous in asking her about her husband. Nevertheless, he took another step toward her. He was standing so close that he could smell the scent of her perfume. He put his hand on her arm. "More than a year is quite a long time to be without the company of another, is it not?"

She gave him a hard look. "I am not without company."

"Perhaps. But the company of a sister or cousin

is a poor substitute for the company of a lover. Then again . . . perhaps you mean to imply that you have a lover to warm your lonely bed."

The blush in her cheeks deepened. "That . . . that is a very *private* concern," she stammered.

No lover, then. Will was ridiculously pleased by the realization, as well as baffled by it. How was it that a widow as beautiful as Phoebe Dupree had not been lured into an affair or even marriage by a powerful, wealthy man? Didn't every man see the beauty he saw in her? How could they not?

"And what company do *you* keep, sir?" she asked, challenging him.

He smiled. "My own."

That earned him a ladylike snort and a pert toss of her head. Ah, but the woman intrigued him as he'd never been intrigued before. He felt an unrelenting need to know everything about her, to hear her speak and laugh, to see her smile and eat and ride and read—whatever she did in the course of her day, he wanted to see it.

He shifted closer once more, standing so close that she had to tilt her head back to see him. He took a strand of her loose hair in his hand and ran his thumb down it, feeling the silk of it. "Do you desire a man's touch?" he asked, using the end of her hair to trace a line from her shoulder to the open throat of her night-gown, and down to her breast. "Do you miss having a man in your bed?"

She gasped softly. "Good heavens, will you try and seduce me at *every* turn?"

"Come now, Phoebe," he said with a chuckle as he pushed the hair behind her shoulder and brushed his knuckles in the place her shoulder curved into her neck. "We are not innocents, you and I. We understand what pleasure can exist between a man and a woman, and as we are both without such pleasure at this time . . . perhaps we might agree to a mutually satisfying arrangement."

Her eyes widened with surprise; she drew a breath that lifted her chest. Will leaned forward, touched his lips to her temple. "If you miss a man in your bed . . . I am at your service."

He heard her breath catch; he slipped his hand under her chin, lifted her face, and kissed her deeply with the promise of what would come. When he lifted his head, Phoebe's eyes were glittering.

She took another, steadying breath and released it so quickly that a wisp of her hair lifted. "You are depraved," she said breathlessly, but her color was high, and her eyes full of desire. "What could you possibly mean to suggest? That I abandon my virtue for the sake of your pleasure?"

"No," he said, and kissed her other temple. "For the sake of *your* pleasure. Let there be no doubt, madam . . . if you desire it, I will give you more pleasure than you can possibly bear."

She did not breathe, she did not move, just held his gaze.

Will kissed her. She stood stiffly, her lips pressed together. Just when he thought it was apparent she was not going to fling herself in his arms and agree to his outrageous proposition, as he absurdly hoped, she opened her mouth beneath his.

Elation surged through him; he abruptly swept her up in his arms. She held her arms at her sides, not touching him, but she returned his kiss, her tongue touching his, her breasts pressed against him. He could feel himself growing hard, and he moved against her, letting her feel how his desire for her surged through his veins.

When he did, she made a whimpering sound in her throat. Her hands came up to his head, his shoulders, his arms, and she kissed him like a woman who had been stranded in the same wilderness he'd been in for months now.

He would have made love to her there had not the niggling thought of his guests downstairs invaded his brain. He slowly put her on her feet, touched his hand to her cheek, and lifted his head.

"I will never agree to such an immoral arrangement," she said breathlessly.

Will almost laughed. He gave her a wink that suggested he knew otherwise, and let go of her. He walked to the door, but paused there to look at her once more.

Phoebe was staring at him as if she couldn't determine if he was man or beast. She was hugging herself, a slight frown of confusion on her face. "I won't agree," she said again.

"I think you will," he said, and with one last look at her in that arousing state of dishabille, he added, "Or I shall die trying to change your mind." With that, he made himself walk from the room before he took complete leave of his senses.

Seventeen

It was madness. Insanity. Yet it was the most tantalizing offer Phoebe had ever received in her life.

She lay in her bed, staring at the window and watching the moon's light drift across the floor. She could not stop thinking of the way Summerfield had touched her, or the way he'd *looked* at her—the memory of it made her shiver.

Once, Phoebe had confided to her mother that the way some men looked at her made her feel uncomfortably exposed. She felt ashamed when they looked at her in such a manner, as if she were somehow inviting their lust.

"Oh, darling," her mother had said sympathetically, "you are a beautiful girl. I daresay no woman in the *ton* is more beautiful than you."

"Really, Mamma," Phoebe had said, feeling herself blush.

"It is true. And men are creatures of the flesh—nothing pleases them more than looking upon a beautiful woman. But one day, a man will look at you not with lust in his eyes, but with fever."

"Fever!" Phoebe had echoed, pausing in her painting to look at her mother. "He will be *ill*?"

"Not at all! What I mean is that a man's lust is a hunger for the flesh, a burning for carnal pleasure, which, when pursued in the right circumstance, is quite nice," she'd added with a mysterious smile. "But a *fever*, Phoebe," she said, sinking down on the ottoman and taking Phoebe's hand in hers, "a fever is a different sort of hunger altogether. When a man looks at you with fever in his eyes, he is burning with a thirst that consumes *all* of him, not merely a single part. His hunger is not just for your flesh, but for your heart and soul. When you see it, you will know it—because you will feel that fever in you."

"Mam*ma*," Phoebe had groaned. Her mother was quite enamored with the world of ladies and gentlemen and the coquettish sport between them. She often waxed lyrical about the affairs of the heart. Phoebe had assumed her mother was crafting her poetry again and was refusing to understand her particular dilemma.

But last night, she believed she had seen a hint of the fever her mother had described in Summerfield's eyes. Moreover, she'd felt the fever in herself.

Nevertheless, how could she possibly consider his offer? She would be ruined if she agreed—or would she?

Elizabeth Montague had once boasted to Phoebe and Ava that she'd had a lover long before she was married, and when she did marry, there was not a breath of scandal. Elizabeth may very well have been untruthful with them—Phoebe and Ava had debated the possibility more than once. But Phoebe had seen Elizabeth in the company of Mr. Grant on several occasions and had believed they truly were lovers—there was an intimacy about them that she perceived was more than friendship.

And then again, Miss Beverly Randall had engaged in an affair with a notorious rake, and the ensuing scandal was quite severe. Her family sent her to Cornwall, where, as far as Phoebe knew, she remained to this day.

There had certainly been consequences for Miss Randall, and Phoebe was a fool to think she would suffer any less.

Except for one small thing—Phoebe had something neither Miss Randall nor Elizabeth had had in the course of her affair: anonymity. As far as anyone in Bedfordshire knew, she was the widow of a Frenchman and indentured to Wentworth Hall for a time. She could, were she to completely abandon her morals, engage in an affair with a man and no one would be the wiser . . .

Save a future husband.

Assuming there *was* a future husband. And if there was, Phoebe was old enough to have heard more than one way to explain a lack of virginal purity on one's wedding night. Not every woman found it to be messy and distasteful. Ava had said there was a bit of a sting, but nothing quite as dramatic as they'd heard from others. In fact, Phoebe knew of one woman who adamantly avowed that strenuous exercise—horseback riding in particular—could take one's virginity just as easily as a man.

Dear God, was she actually *considering* his offer, then?

Of course she wasn't! It was ridiculous to pretend for even a moment that she was! Yes, but . . . but she really did desire him—oh God, how she desired him—more than any man she had ever known.

She had a fever.

The next morning, Will rode Fergus into the hills, where the remnants of the first Earl of Bedford's castle still stood. The wild horses had moved up the valley, to the ruins, where the grazing was still good this late in the summer. As usual, Fergus sensed the other horses first, snorting and lifting his head, flattening his ears as they neared them. They were feeding in what Will supposed was once a lawn, near a meandering stream. A little foal had ventured too far from his mother and galloped awkwardly back to her side when he saw Will ride into the dale.

Will swung down from Fergus, discarded his coat, then removed the saddle from Fergus and heaved it over his shoulder. With his free hand, he grabbed the extra saddlebag that held the bit, bridle, and reins.

He was feeling on top of the world, and smiled when

Apollo snorted at him as he calmly walked forward. "Good morning, you bloody beautiful beast," he said, and dropped the bag with the reins. He shifted the saddle from his shoulder and held it out, inviting Apollo to sniff it. Apollo was accustomed to seeing it now, had even felt it on his back. But today Will intended to cinch it. Tomorrow he would ride.

Apollo sniffed the saddle, then dropped his head to the saddlebag, looking for apples.

Will had those, too.

As he worked, he spoke softly to Apollo, teaching him the commands he would eventually learn in the course of being saddled, such as *Lift your head,* and *Steady now.* And as Will began the process of cinching the saddle at the underbelly of the horse, he said to Apollo, "You and I have come quite a long way, my friend. It has taken some coaxing, but I believe we will have a fast friendship and long acquaintance."

Apollo looked over his shoulder at Will, eyeing him dubiously with his enormous brown eye, then neighed and dropped his head to the grass once more as Will carefully tightened the cinch.

Jane was ecstatically happy that afternoon, twirling about in a half-finished ball gown, admiring her form and chattering on about having made the acquaintance of John Remington, whom she declared the most perfectly charming and handsome gentleman she'd ever met.

"And what of you, Alice?" Phoebe asked, squeezing in her question when Jane paused for a breath.

"She did not speak unless spoken to," Jane said.

"That is not true. I spoke at length with Samuel Remington, but you were smothering John Remington with all your silly chatter and did not take notice. I even spoke to Caroline Fitzherbert's younger brother."

"Oh, he's so tiresome!" Jane complained. "And I cannot imagine what you might have said to him, for he asked to partner with *me* for whist after having sat with you through two rounds."

"That is not the slightest bit true. Mr. Fitzherbert suggested we all change partners. So did you, Jane."

Jane shrugged and yanked the bodice of her gown lower.

Phoebe yanked it up again.

"I hope Mr. Remington will return for our country house party. Oh, how I love the very *idea* of a house party! It makes us rather like Quality, does it not? I've always longed for one."

"Please hold still, Jane," Phoebe pleaded with her. "It is impossible to pin with you moving about so."

"Alice doesn't want a country house party. She wants to go and live behind the blacksmith with Mr. Hughes."

"Why do you say such wretched things?" Alice asked wearily. "I am very much looking forward to the house party and the company of many families."

"And the Fitzherberts?" Jane asked, twisting around to see her sister.

"And the Fitzherberts, yes, of course. Why ever not?"

Jane squealed with delight, almost knocking Phoebe over in her zeal. "You *do* esteem Mr. Fitzherbert!"

"I don't *esteem* him, but it seems perfectly reasonable to assume he'll be our brother by marriage one day," Alice said.

"*Ouch!*" Jane cried dramatically when Phoebe accidentally stuck her with a pin.

Alice rolled her eyes and turned around to examine her ball gown, which was still on the dress form. "I think I should like beading on the gown, Madame

Dupree. I was impressed with Miss Fitzherbert's beading."

God save her if she would now have to fashion the two of them after *that* woman.

"Oh! And the slippers! I want beaded slippers," Jane added excitedly.

Phoebe was about to tell her that there was precious little time to bead slippers, but she was interrupted by the appearance of Addison. "I beg your pardon for the interruption, madam," he said with a bow, then looked at Alice and Jane. If the tips of his ears were any indication, he seemed a little disconcerted.

"Addison, is something wrong?" Phoebe asked.

"No, no, of course not . . . *ahem* . . . Lady Alice," he said, "a gift has come for you. It is in the main salon."

Alice instantly dropped the fabric she was studying. "A gift? For *me*? From whom?"

"I could not say, my lady. But . . . there is a note."

"What of me, Addison?" Jane asked, looking absolutely frantic. "Is there not a gift for me?"

"I regret there is not, Lady Jane."

"But . . ." Her voiced trailed off, and she looked at Alice.

Alice rushed from the room, Jane fast on her heels.

Phoebe shook her head after the two of them, then smiled at Addison. "Truly, you have no knowledge who sent the gift?"

"Oh, I know," Addison said with a wince. "No one. I fabricated it completely."

"Addison!" Phoebe cried with a laugh. "Whatever possessed you?"

He looked over his shoulder and stepped deeper into the room. "I have a message for you," he said, and thrust his hand into the interior pocket of his coat and withdrew a small folded vellum and held it out to her.

Phoebe stared at the vellum but made no move to take it.

"His lordship bid me bring this to you and await a reply," Addison said, closing the distance between them. "I beg you make haste, madam, for when Lady Alice discovers there is no gift . . ."

He had a point. Phoebe took the vellum and quickly unfolded it.

Madame Dupree . . .

His handwriting consisted of bold, long strokes.

Please accept my invitation to dine with me this evening. I should very much like to continue our discourse.

Phoebe could feel herself color, and with a quick glance at Addison, she turned slightly so that her face was away from him.

I have taken the liberty, on behalf of my brothers and sisters, of accepting an invitation from the vicar to dine with his family this evening. As a result, I shall be quite alone at the supper hour and would enjoy your company. If you will honor me by accepting my invitation, I should be pleased to meet you at the gazebo at half past seven o'clock.

The *gazebo*? Phoebe glanced at Addison again.

The poor man's face had turned as red as his ears. "If you would, please, Madame Dupree, write your reply on the back of his note and I shall personally put it in his hands."

She was too astounded to speak. She was embarrassed, she was intoxicated—dreaming of something and acting on it were two entirely different things. She did not want to cause a scandal in this house. Her mind racing, she whirled around in search of a pencil on her worktable. In her haste, she knocked a pair of scissors onto the floor. It landed with such a rattle that both she and Addison jumped.

"May I help?" Addison asked.

"No, please, do not trouble yourself," she said, and stooped to retrieve the scissors. She tossed them onto the table and picked up the pencil.

This was absurd. Phoebe understood very well why Summerfield was inviting her to dine with him, but she was not sure how to phrase her response. She was keenly aware that whatever she wrote could be interpreted in any number of ways. She wrote:

> *My Lord Summerfield,* her handwriting flowing and light, *Your invitation to dine is insupportable. I am at a loss to understand why you would ask me to risk my good reputation in such an infamous manner as dining <u>al fresco</u> in a dilapidated gazebo.*

She paused, bit her lower lip, and tapped the pencil against the tabletop. She could picture him standing in his study, awaiting her reply. She could see the long, lean line of him, could see the fever in his eyes, the sensual curve of his lips. She could almost *feel* those lips on hers, his hands on her body.

The weight of her response was growing heavier and heavier.

> *I am quite unaccustomed to dining on dirty stone benches, as I rather suspect are you, and I therefore*

can only conclude you mean to use the gazebo for something else entirely.

Mme. Dupree.

There, then. Phoebe hastily folded the vellum before she lost her resolve and added a note that she would indeed come. She whirled around, thrust it at Addison. "Please take that to his lordship."

Addison quickly stuffed the note into his breast pocket. He gave her a curt nod. "Good day, Madame Dupree."

"Good day, Addison," she chirped in return, and watched as he walked swiftly from the workroom. When he'd gone, Phoebe sank onto a chair and released the breath she hadn't even realized she was holding.

She was still sitting in the chair, staring out at the window, imagining all the many things that might have happened, when Addison returned. He walked in the open door, and without a word held up a vellum.

"*Again?*"

"Again."

With a sigh, Phoebe gained her feet and moved to fetch the vellum.

Mme. Dupree,

You do me a grave dishonor to suggest that I should "use" the gazebo to dine or to seduce. It is merely a familiar meeting point. I have in mind something far more appealing and chaste, something that should bring you out of your square little rooms and into the warm summer night's fragrant air. There are no "dirty stone benches." If you prefer to remain cooped up with your dress forms and needles and whatnot, then by all means, you must do so. However, I would very much enjoy your company, and if you think there is even the slightest chance you might enjoy mine, I will invite you once more to meet me at the gazebo at half past seven.

S.

A thousand things raced through Phoebe's mind at once—that she could think of nothing else that would delight her or ruin her more quickly than accepting his invitation, that there was an unspeakable danger in her deceit, that she was at least as foolish as Ava or Greer might ever have imagined, and that she had to find something suitable to wear.

But neither could she stop thinking that for the first time in her life—if not the last—she was free to feel the fever.

She picked up her pencil.

My lord,

> *You must believe I am terribly naïve if you think that I am the <u>least</u> swayed by your earnest declaration of chastity in thought. I find your game to be a very dangerous one. That being said, I cannot possibly meet you a moment before eight o'clock.*

Mme. D.

She quickly folded it and nervously handed it to Addison, unable to meet his eye. With a bow, Addison went out. The moment the door shut behind him, she whirled about and ran to her wardrobe in search of something suitable to wear.

Nothing. She had nothing.

But then she spied a blue silk with long sleeves she'd worn to her nephew Jonathan's baptism. An idea came to her. She fetched a pair of scissors from her workroom and cut the sleeve from the gown. When she held the gown out to examine it, she smiled. *Perfect.*

Eighteen

A t the end of that long summer day, the sun was just beginning its descent into night when Phoebe hurried through the parterres like a woman rushing to meet her lover. She could see him at the gazebo waiting for her, standing with one shoulder propped against the entrance, watching her walk across the grass.

He looked . . . magnificent. Virile in a way that made Phoebe's belly do a queer little flip.

She had lost her mind, had let it turn to cabbage. What in God's name was she doing? She was teasing a dragon, that was what, for this was no flight of fancy, no game of make-believe. He was stunningly real.

Summerfield was dressed in a black coat and gray trousers tucked into a pair of Wellington boots. The cut of his coat was exquisite, fitting his broad shoulders and trim waist like a second skin. His neckcloth was fashioned from white silk and was tied in an artful knot above the lapels of his black waistcoat. His hair curled in natural waves around his face, and as Phoebe walked across the grass to him—her heart beating wildly, her palms damp—his dark lips spread into a smile against his bronzed skin.

Heaven help her.

She worried about her gown, now indecently sleeve-less, but rather fetching to Phoebe's eye. She'd put her hair up as best she could, holding it in place with hairpins tipped in tiny crystals that matched those that

hung from her ears. When she'd finished dressing,
she'd stood gazing into the mirror in her workroom,
listening to the breeze rustle the leaves of the trees outside her window, imagining herself a woman of certain
experience.

But she was nothing of the sort. She was a woman
working very hard at playing a fool, each step carrying
her closer to madness. She could assume a false identity
and possess it, could play with a fire that could very
well engulf her, but she couldn't really change herself.
She was still Phoebe underneath the façade, and Phoebe
worried that she was an even bigger fool than she could
have imagined, for her heart leapt at the sight of Summerfield, and all thoughts of disastrous folly flew out
of her head.

Like magic, she was transformed into an actress on a
stage, and her heart thrilled with the possibility of shed-
ding the suffocating mantle of being a proper young
miss.

As she neared him, he stepped down the steps of the
gazebo. She came to a halt before him, smiling wryly.
He held out his hand, palm up. Phoebe looked at his
palm, the tantalizing bit of ink on his wrist, then at him.
"I have agreed only to dine," she said.

The corners of his mouth turned up. "You have my
word I will not seduce your hand."

She smiled with the devilish confidence of Madame
Dupree. "It is hardly my hand that concerns me," she
replied, and slipped her hand into his.

He instantly lifted it to his mouth, pressing his lips
against her knuckles. "How beautiful you are, Phoebe.
At every meeting, I find I am even more astonished
by it."

"Hence, the seduction begins."

He smiled fully and put her hand on his arm, covering it with his own. "Come, then, before I am accused of more."

"Where?" she asked, peering toward the lake.

"It is a surprise."

"A *surprise*?" She laughed. "I fear your surprises, my lord."

"You? A woman so fearless that not even wild horses or dancing Gypsies can sway her into alarm? No, I do not believe you fear my surprise. You fear your reaction to it."

Astoundingly true.

"Rest easy, madam," he said with a slow smile. "I shall surprise you gently."

That remark certainly caused a flutter deep inside her, but Summerfield was moving, guiding Phoebe down to the lake, then into the tall reeds. As he pushed a path through them, giant dragonflies swarmed around Phoebe's head.

"What are we doing, precisely?" Phoebe asked, swatting at one of the dragonflies.

"Looking for your chariot," he said enigmatically, and letting go her hand, disappeared into the reeds.

Phoebe waited, swatting at dragonflies, until she heard the sound of him splashing about in water. She paused in her swatting. "My lord?"

A moment later, Summerfield reappeared. "This way, if you please."

"Where?" she asked, trying to see through the reeds.

"Will you not trust me, if only a little? Come, Madame Dupree," he said, gesturing for her.

Phoebe stepped forward, lifting her skirts high above the ankles to move through the reeds, and saw that just below them an old rowboat was pulled up on shore.

Summerfield lunged forward on one leg to pull the boat up a little higher.

"I beg your pardon?" Phoebe exclaimed. "Do you mean for me to get *in* that?"

"On my life, I have never known a more obstinate woman," he said with a smile. "Look there," he said, pointing across the lake. "Do you see that island?"

She followed his gaze. In the middle of the lake was what looked like nothing more than a copse of trees, an island no bigger than an acre, perhaps two at most. She looked curiously at Summerfield.

"You like surprises, do you not?" he asked with a wink.

"Yes, but . . ." She looked down at her gown of beautiful blue china silk. Summerfield must have surmised what she was thinking, for he moved before she could voice her objection, sweeping her up in his arms as if she were a child.

Phoebe let out a shriek of surprised laughter as he spun around, splashed into the water, and deposited her effortlessly in the middle of the boat. Phoebe threw her arms wide for balance and froze. "Oh dear. Oh *dear*," she said again as the boat tilted.

"I'd sit, if I were you," Summerfield said cheerfully, and threw one leg over the edge of the boat and planted his foot at the stern.

Phoebe sat in a *whoosh* of blue silk and gripped the sides of the boat with all the strength she had. "I think I should warn you, sir, that I swim very poorly."

"No need to worry—I do not intend to let you swim." He gave the boat a mighty shove and clambered into the hull, taking the small bench at the stern as the boat rocked dangerously from side to side. Phoebe cried out with alarm as he grappled with the oars while the boat sailed out onto the pristine surface of the lake.

Summerfield actually laughed at her as he gained control of the oars and began to row. "You surprise me, Phoebe. One would think you'd never been on a boat ere now."

"A *boat*?" she exclaimed breathlessly. "That seems a rather generous word for a wash bucket!"

"Have you no sense of adventure?" he asked cheerfully. "I should think marriage to a Frenchman would necessitate a lot of sailing back and forth across the Channel in conditions far worse than this lovely summer's eve."

Her very real fear of drowning had caused her to momentarily forget her assumed identity. "Yes," she said, perhaps a little too quickly. "But that . . . that was much different from this." She glanced at the lake, lapping against the sides of the boat. "And not quite as close to the water as this."

"Unless you intend to stand up and dive over the edge, I do not think you are in danger of falling. And if you do find your way overboard, you have my word that I will fish you out and dry you off," he added with another, saltier smile.

"Can you swim?" she asked him.

He laughed. "I once swam in the middle of a high sea in a storm. I can certainly navigate a lake."

"In the middle of the *sea*?"

"It's rather a long and involved story. Look there," he said, nodding to something beyond them. "Have you ever seen such a sunset?"

Phoebe turned as much as her grip would allow her and looked at the sky. "Oh *my.*" It was breathtaking—it was as if someone had painted great swaths of pink and orange across the sky, then tossed purple puffs of cloud across them. Such vistas were not possible in

London, where crowded buildings and foul air rose above the city in the summer to hide the sunset. She wished she had her sketchbook so she could capture the look of the sky and paint it later. "It's *beautiful*," she said. "As lovely as I have ever seen."

She turned around again. Summerfield was not looking at the sky—he was looking at her. She could see the hall behind him, situated idyllically against the blue hills. The beauty of this estate took her breath away.

"What are you thinking?" Summerfield asked as he rowed them along.

"That the scenery at Wentworth Hall is glorious. You are very fortunate."

"Do you truly think so?" he asked, cocking his head charmingly to the side. "I find it confining at times."

"I can scarcely guess how one might find such an expanse of natural beauty confining."

"It is beautiful, I will grant you that," he agreed. "But it is rather sedate."

"Sedate in what way?" she wondered aloud.

"Sedate in that life moves very slowly here. I spent years exploring—every day was a new diversion. Here, every day is much the same."

"And where did your exploring take you?"

He shrugged a little. "Everywhere, really. The Continent. Then the Greek Isles and India. Africa and the Levant. Egypt and Morocco—"

"Everywhere," she said with a smile.

He grinned. "Wherever life took me. I was a fortunate man." He nodded at something over the top of Phoebe's head. "We're almost there."

Phoebe turned. At the end of the little wooded island, someone had lit a torch. Summerfield rowed the boat directly at the torch, driving the boat up onto the shore before leaping out into ankle-deep water and pushing the boat to higher ground. He walked to the end of the boat and held out his hand to Phoebe.

She stood carefully, but as the boat began to list to one side, she grabbed his hand with both of hers, leaping so anxiously to dry ground that Summerfield had to catch her by the waist. He laughed, his eyes glimmering with delight. "Have a care you do not leap over the island," he said. "It is not very large."

He did not immediately let her go; his eyes were so intent on hers that she felt a little weak at the knees. "You promised me a surprise," she finally reminded him before her knees buckled.

"That I did," he said, and took her hand in his, as if they were intimate acquaintances. He picked up the torch with the other hand. "It is just this way."

As they began to walk, Phoebe realized the island was larger than she had at first perceived. A well-worn path curved into the trees, disappearing into the greenery. The sun was sinking quickly now, and it was hard to see, but as they continued to follow the path around, Phoebe could see something other than the evening light filtering through the trees. When they reached another bend, Summerfield stepped back and gestured for her to precede him.

She felt almost like a child on the brink of a marvelous surprise. She eagerly gathered her skirts and walked down the path. It widened into a clearing that was breathtaking—whatever she might have imagined, it wasn't this.

In the clearing was a ruin. All that remained of the original structure was a marble floor and four columns that rose up, their majestic, fluted ends blackened by the fire that had apparently brought the structure down. It almost appeared as if the columns held up the gloaming sky.

In between the columns were torches similar to the one Summerfield was holding. And on the marble floor, there were dozens of beeswax candles—in votive holders, large crystal bowls, and on pieces of wood dragged in from the forest floor.

In the center of the marble floor was a circle of low cushions that surrounded a small brazier. In addition, there was a small table that stood only inches above the ground, upon which sat three silver domes on platters and two decanters of wine.

It was magical, taken right from the pages of a fairy tale. Phoebe walked up the steps to what surely had once been a grand entrance, pausing there to turn about in the midst of it all in order to take it in. She turned once more and faced Summerfield.

He'd put his torch aside, was standing with his hands clasped behind his back, his head lowered as he watched her, his eyes glowing with pleasure.

"What is this place?" she asked breathlessly.

"I'm not entirely certain," he said as he walked up the steps. "Probably a monastery or abbey at one time. My grandfather made it into a summerhouse, but as you can see, it burned down. He never rebuilt it. I suppose the lake became more of a hindrance than an asset to those seeking the solitude of this little island."

"It is a treasure," she said, twirling slowly, looking around. "And the *candles!*" she exclaimed. "I am . . . I am overwhelmed by the effort you have put forth on my behalf."

"I am happy you are pleased," he said.

A wave of delight spilled through Phoebe, erupting in an exuberant smile. She quickly turned from him and lifted her skirts, stepping carefully past the candles as she made her way to the cushions. "What an interesting arrangement—it's quite exotic."

"It is quite Egyptian," Summerfield said, gesturing for her to take a seat on one of the cushions. "I brought them back with me. I found Egypt to be inspiring—I never felt as free of the trappings of life as I did there." He cast a lazy smile at her. "I thought to give you a taste of that freedom."

The very idea of *Egypt* thrilled her—she was emboldened by the magical surroundings and lowered herself to one of the cushions. She could imagine herself in an Egyptian camp, dressed in silks that covered her face as well as her body, just like in the picture books she and Ava and Greer had pored over as children.

"It is the custom of the Bedouin nomads to take their supper in such a manner," Summerfield explained as he squatted down behind her and brushed a curl from her shoulder, his fingers grazing her bare skin. "They use their hands to eat bits of unleavened bread . . . but for your sake," he said softly, his fingers brushing so lightly against her neck that she shivered, "I have bowed to the English custom of fork and leavened bread."

"How *daring*," she teased him.

He grinned and rose to his full height, towering above Phoebe. "Do you enjoy wine?" he asked as he stepped over the cushions in one long stride and reached for the wine bottle. At her nod, he settled onto the cushions and poured wine into a goblet, and handed it to Phoebe. He poured a second goblet and smiled very charmingly when he touched his glass to hers in a toast.

He was making it difficult for her to remember she was a servant presumably in the throes of being seduced by her lord and master.

"How do you find the wine?" he asked after she had sipped. At her nod of approval, he said, "It is French. Smuggled across the Channel at great peril."

"You *smuggled* wine from France?"

"Me?" He chuckled. "No. But it was purchased from a smuggler. I have always maintained that if one cannot do one's own smuggling, one should at least know of a good smuggler."

Phoebe laughed, not believing him. "You think to fool me, my lord. But why should anyone smuggle wine from France?"

"Don't you know?"

Drat it all, she could not seem to remember who she supposedly was! She laughed and averted her eyes in response.

"Because the French are quite fond of their wine and exact a high price when it is taken abroad. And the English are quite fond of *their* wine and impose some rather stiff import duties for the privilege of drinking French wine. The resulting cost of French wine encourages some to seek their libations from less official channels. As it happens, I know one such fellow, and he impressed on me his firm belief that I should own several bottles of agreeably priced French wine."

Phoebe smiled and sipped.

"I thought you might be a connoisseur of French wine, given that you were married to a Frenchman," he said, and looked at her expectantly.

"Oh. Ah . . . not really," she said, and smiled.

He smiled, too, sipped from the wine, and nodded appreciatively. "Hungry?" he asked, and put aside his glass to remove the dome from one platter of food.

"Mmm," said Phoebe, realizing that she was ravenous.

Underneath the dome was a selection of cheeses and fruits: grapes, oranges, and cubed apples. He uncovered the second platter to reveal sliced meats and bread. He forked a sampling of the various foods onto a small plate for her, then prepared one for himself.

He watched her take a bite of orange. "English oranges don't compare to those I had in Paris," he said languidly, his gaze still on her mouth. "Paris is a city of many decadent delights, wouldn't you agree?"

Phoebe all but swallowed the orange slice whole.

"Whereabouts did you live?" he asked idly.

"Live?" she echoed stupidly.

"In Paris. The left bank, I'd presume."

The left bank of *what*? she wondered frantically. "Mmm," she said.

"We might have been neighbors, can you imagine it? I was in Paris only a few short months, but I took lease of a small town house just off Rue Monge. I am certain it is known to you."

The panic of her deceit was suddenly cloying. When she had imagined this night, she had not imagined a lot of chatting, for heaven's sake. "Yes, of course," she said thickly, hoping he would not press it further. "An excellent cheese, my lord. What is it?"

He glanced at the cheese on her plate and shrugged. "Cook's finest, I suppose." He looked at her again, assessing her. "There is really nothing lovelier than the Seine in springtime," he remarked. "Where did you say you resided in Paris?"

"Ah . . ." Phoebe took a large bite of chicken while she frantically thought, stealing more time by licking her fingers. Summerfield watched her with some amusement, waiting patiently for an answer. She smiled, sipped her wine, brushed a bit of chicken from her lap, and glanced at Summerfield again.

"Where again?" he asked.

Phoebe gave him a dismissive flick of her wrist and said, "*Where*? Oh, I can scarcely remember now. Rue . . . something or other." She smiled.

So did he.

"You left Paris," she said, desperate to leave it herself. "Where did you go then?"

"To Switzerland. Might I inquire—from where did your late husband hail?"

Oh bloody *hell*. Phoebe put down her plate, shifted off her knees and onto her hip, reached for her goblet, took another, fortifying sip of wine, and nervously cleared her throat. "He was from . . . from Rouen," she said, a little uncertainly.

"Ah," he said instantly, and nodded as if he knew it well. "Another fine city. The cathedral there is *recherché*, would you agree?"

Good *Lord*, was there no place he'd not seen? "I *would*," she said breezily. "But I must confess . . . since m-my husband . . ."—she made a gesture with her hand—"*passed*, I have tried to forget—"

"Dear God, of course," he said with a frown of worry. "Forgive me."

"No, I . . ." She smiled sheepishly. "It would seem *you* have traveled the world over, sir. You are quite the adventurer, are you not?"

He gave her a sensual smile. "I am an adventurer in every sense of the word." He put down his plate and leaned on his side, propping himself up on an elbow. "I thrive on it, actually." He sighed, took a long drink of wine, then looked in his cup. "That is why I find England and her bucolic countryside to be stifling. I fear I am no longer accustomed or suited to the life of the nobility."

That declaration surprised and intrigued Phoebe. "What does not suit you?" she asked curiously.

"I rather think a better question is what *does* suit me? My role as a country gentleman is tiresome beyond my endurance. Englishmen pride themselves on reaching that station in life where they are not pressed to actually work for their livelihood, but I should rather work than sit about remarking on the weather or the prospects for a good crop," he said with some disgust. "There are no diversions here, nothing to pique my interest. I feel as if I am a bird in a cage."

Phoebe couldn't help herself; she laughed.

He looked surprised, which only caused her to laugh more. "What?" he demanded.

"I beg your pardon, sir, but I cannot believe anyone would actually *want* to toil for their living," she said, and laughed again.

"If one is capable, one might," he said a little defensively.

Grinning, she shook her head. "If you think the life of a country viscount is tiresome, you must try rising at dawn and working until sundown."

Now Will laughed. "I've witnessed you working at dawn with your sketchbook, madam. That is hardly toiling."

"But I am toiling!" she insisted, and thrust out her hand. "Look at my fingers!"

He took her hand in his and made a show of examining it. "This tiny bit of a callus is a hazard of your trade."

"But I never had a callus until—" She caught herself before she said anything too revealing.

But not soon enough. "Until what?" he asked, looking at her curiously.

"Until you forced me to work so many of the day's hours," she said blithely. "If you find your life here so tedious, why do you not live in London?" she asked. "I am certain you would find many diversions there to suit your adventurous spirit."

"My father's illness makes that impossible, I'm afraid. Until I have seen my sisters married and my brothers engaged in proper occupations, and indeed, myself married and siring an heir, I am duty bound to Wentworth Hall."

He smiled wryly, missing Phoebe's look as he helped himself to more food.

"And what of you, Phoebe? What of your life's adventures?"

Her heart ratcheted up a beat or two and she shrugged a little. "My life has been rather plain. I grew up as most, I married, I was widowed. And now I am a *modiste*. Hardly an adventurous life."

"But you married a Frenchman," he pressed. "You learned your trade in France, did you not? Tell me of your life there."

"There is really very little of interest to tell," she insisted.

He snorted. "That's nonsense. I should think a woman as comely as you would have many invitations to adventure. Is love not an adventure?"

"*Love?*"

He laughed at her surprise. "I assumed, given your rather passionate speech to *me* on the virtues of love . . . that you found it to be quite an adventure."

"Well . . . I suppose it is," she said vaguely.

He popped a piece of chicken in his mouth and munched, watching her. "How did he die, if I may?"

"Who?" she asked.

"Your *husband*, madame."

"A fever," she said instantly, and imagined, had he really existed, it might have been the same sort of fever she was feeling at the moment, here in this private place with a man who made her heart take wing like no other ever had. She shook her head and glanced at her plate as if it pained her to speak of it.

"I beg your pardon. It is clear you mourn him still."

Phoebe didn't answer, but looked away, to the deepening shadows beyond the line of torches, counting all the moments since she had created this dead husband. "Why did you stay away so long?" she blurted, hoping desperately once more to change the subject.

"Do you know how long I was gone?" he asked, touching her knee, drawing her gaze back to him.

She nodded. "Mrs. Turner told me."

"Then she surely told you I stayed away *too* long." He casually reached up and stroked her hair.

"Why do you say that?"

"My father needed me, and I was not here."

"Then . . . why stay away so long?" she asked again, confused by his answer.

"Shall I show you why?" he asked as he traced a line from the back of her hand up her bare arm.

"Yes," she said. "Please."

He considered her a moment longer. Without a word, he shifted, reaching away from her, across the cushions, and withdrawing a worn leather book from beneath a cushion. He sat up, held it in his lap for a moment, studying the weathered cover. "I wanted to show you this after you admired my tattoo," he said, glancing at his wrist. He gave her a sheepish look, then handed her the book.

Phoebe had no idea what to expect. She turned a little, so that she could see better by the light of a torch, and opened the book to the first page.

June 12, 1816
   I departed this morning on a clipper bound for France. We set sail in a cold rain but with the trade winds at our back. . . .

Next to the entry was a picture of the ship, drawn in ink, the detail remarkable. It was his travel journal. A thrill of excitement ran through her, and she eagerly turned the pages, reading a sampling of the entries, looking at the pictures he'd drawn. He'd made entries almost every day for six years, had drawn pictures of his adventures between the journal entries.

> *... in an unkind manner, and with a gun pointed at my head, the bloody scoundrel urged me off the road and divested me of my horse. ...*

Next to the entry was a rendering of the bloody scoundrel, his face gaunt with several days' growth of a beard on his chin. And his eyes were so well done that Phoebe felt he was looking directly at her.

> *... houses reduced to ashes. In this general devastation were penned cattle. ...*

Small cattle were drawn within the confines of a wooden fence.

> *... the Raja's hospitality, for which he is celebrated throughout India. ...*

A man with a happy countenance, a gap-toothed smile, and clever eyes wore a large, tubular hat.

> *... natives drink a concoction of goat's milk and anise, which left me feeling rather numb in body. Every attention was shown me, and I shared in their meager bounty. ...*

A drawing of a small and strange-looking cottage, a family of six standing before it.

When she reached the end of the written entries, she found pages upon pages of drawings. Some were of scenery, others of people he'd met. But what intrigued her most were the drawings of women in various stages of dress and evocative postures. They were, she realized, erotic drawings of women he'd known.

"Oh my," she said, and looked up at him. "This . . . this is *extraordinary*." She quickly looked down again.

"You are not offended?"

Offended? She was aroused by it. She ran her hand over the drawing of one beauty. She had posed nude for Will. Her skin had been darkened with charcoal. She lay on her side, one leg bent at the knee. Her head was propped onto one hand, and the other lay carelessly on her breast. Phoebe wasn't offended, oh no.

She could picture him drawing this woman. She could picture him drawing *her*.

"I am not offended," she said softly. "I am enchanted."

"They are not as good as your sketches," he said, studying the drawings on the page.

"No, you are wrong. They are better," she said, and smiled up at him. "These drawings tell a story."

Will smiled a little crookedly and took her hand, turning it palm up. He pressed a kiss into her palm. "Thank you."

"Thank *me*?" she asked as he touched the tip of his tongue to her skin. Every touch was sending her closer to the brink of giving in to her desire.

"I've never shown it to anyone. Well, Addison, of course, but no one else."

"Why not?"

"I don't know, really."

His eyes were dark and unfathomable. Phoebe was tumbling down a slippery slope, sliding into trouble. The day's light had all but faded, and in the glow of the fire, his eyes seemed incomprehensibly bottomless. She watched the light flickering off the gold in his irises, saw a flash of deep light in them. The yearning for him swelled in her, filling every inch, every crevice, squeezing the breath from her. It felt as if another piece of desire that had lain dormant in her had broken off out of necessity and now floated free.

There it was again, that feeling of breathing underwater.

"Thank you for showing it to me," she said, and closed the book, pressed it to her chest. "It's beautiful."

He said nothing, just quietly contemplated her face, her neck, and bosom, while the light in his eyes turned feverish. "It is amazing how one may travel the world and find the greatest beauty at home," he said, and kissed the inside of her wrist. "An incomparable beauty," he muttered, and kissed the inside of her elbow. "A treasure, discovered under my very own roof."

Phoebe's breathing turned shallow; she clutched his journal to her breast.

Will shifted closer, and slipped his arm around her waist. "To think I have traveled far and wide, and here you are," he said, coaxing her down, onto her back. He kissed her neck, ran his hand up her rib cage to her breast, squeezing it, kneading it, as he nuzzled her neck.

The tension began to flow out of her body. Phoebe closed her eyes, allowed herself to enjoy his attention, and inadvertently dropped the journal. She was feeling the fever again, but it was more intent than ever before. She wanted Summerfield to have it all, all of the passionate feelings that were rising from deep within her, everything that made her who she was, that made her Phoebe.

"It was fate that brought me into service in your house," she whispered as his hands caressed her body.

It *was* fate—this was the man who could take her virginity and show her how to love, to live, to experience life.

But Summerfield did not take her. He swallowed hard and suddenly pushed up and away from her.

Nineteen

———⊗⊗⊗———

He wished for a rope, something to bind his hands to restrain him from touching her.

Will's desire for Phoebe was tremendous, but so was his respect for her, and when she reminded him that she was his servant, he was struck by what a cad he was and had acted reflexively.

He was no better than Mr. Hughes.

He pushed a hand through his hair as he sought to drag himself up from the depths of his physical desire. He fumbled for the scarab and angrily yanked it from his neck, tossing it on the ground. Phoebe pushed herself up and picked it up, staring at it. "Forgive me, Phoebe," he said, hearing the disgust in his voice. "I have failed you."

"No, I—"

"You cannot deny it. My intentions have been less than honorable," he said, meaning it, yet knowing that even as he spoke, he would give all of Wentworth Hall to taste her lips, to feel the softness of her body against his, to be inside her. "You are very beautiful, Phoebe, and I . . . I would have compromised you completely, given the opportunity."

"Completely?" she repeated softly, sounding, he thought, oddly hopeful and remorseful at once.

He suddenly shifted forward and cupped her face. "I have struggled with my duty and my true feelings, I cannot deny it. I find you . . ."—God save him, but he found her intoxicating, mesmerizing—"extraordinarily beautiful. And bright, and clever, and impossibly talented. And I thought, given that we are two adults with opportunity—and what I hoped was mutual desire—that we might find satisfaction in one another. But I did not think of the consequences. I have behaved badly, you must forgive me."

Phoebe blinked. Will frowned, feeling more despicable. He didn't know what, precisely, he expected her to say. He supposed it was the chaos that raged beneath his placid exterior that had caused him to offer something so vile to this woman. Even looking at her now—so guileless, so arousing—he thought she should loathe him.

He did not expect her to rise up on her knees and place her hands against his chest. He caught one hand and pressed it tightly to his heart, which had begun to beat with the strength of ten men. With his other hand he cupped her face, splayed his fingers against her cheek, drinking her in, suddenly fearful of losing her, of losing this moment.

Phoebe slowly leaned forward and touched her lips to his before sinking into him, toppling them back onto the cushions. Will caught her in his arms—she felt almost weightless on him, a mere wisp of the scintillation that singed him deep within.

He had not kissed a woman like this in some time—at least not with such ardent devotion, with such fire in his belly. He rolled them over, onto their sides, dimly aware of a wine goblet tumbling over in his carelessness. He stroked her face and her hair as he slipped his tongue into her mouth.

Phoebe moaned with a woman's pleasure and sent his blood racing through his veins. As he kissed her, the myriad things he'd been feeling about her suddenly consumed him. He lifted his head, looked down at her face in the soft glow of the candles. Her skin was luminous—*she* was luminous—her eyes were full of longing. Her chest rose and fell rapidly with her panting, the skin of her bosom was milky white, her body was swathed in the soft blue silk that made her eyes seem even larger.

"Dear God," he whispered in reverence, and lowered his head to the flesh above her bodice and kissed her, pressing his hand to her breast. He dipped his fingers into her gown, closing around the peak of her breast, and felt it swell in his hand. Phoebe gasped and arched into him, and his desire for her swelled monstrously, pushing inside his chest and his trousers.

"*I cannot resist you,*" he murmured against her skin. "I cannot bear to be near you and not touch you." Wildly, he kissed her neck, the hollow of her throat, and her lips, her luscious lips, before returning to her breast again.

Phoebe groaned and put her hands on his shoulders, kneading him through his coat. Desire roared like a violent river in his veins; he caught the edge of her gown and pushed it up, and slipped his hand around her ankle.

He moved up, his fingers whisper light on her skin, running over her knee, to the top of her stocking, and touching the bare flesh of her thigh. Phoebe gasped with titillation; her eyes flew open and she looked at him, wide-eyed. He should stop, he *wanted* to stop, but her flesh was too tempting, too soft, too warm, too fragrant.

"My lord—"

"*Will*," he answered breathlessly, suddenly needing to hear her say his name. "Call me Will, I am Will."

Phoebe rose up, caught his face in her hands. "*Will*." As her hands flitted across his temples, his shoulders, and his neck, he caressed the inside of her thigh, moving higher. She made little gasping sounds, as if every stroke of his finger inflamed her. Her lips parted; she closed her eyes and gripped his shoulders.

Will slipped his fingers in between the slit of her drawers and brushed against the curls that covered her sex, spurred by her whimper of pleasure.

He caught her in the crook of his arm, drew her close so that he could kiss her at the same moment he parted her flesh with his finger. She cried into his mouth as he began to stroke her, lifting her leg and bending it at the knee.

Now it was Will who groaned, finding his pleasure in giving her pleasure. He quickened his stroke, swirling up and around, then sliding into the wet depths of her. She began to gasp for air; her grip of his shoulders tightened. "Oh Lord," she whispered. "I shouldn't, I should . . . *God in heaven* . . ."

She climaxed quickly with a spasm that Will felt reverberate throughout his body and into his cock. She sobbed with pleasure as she sagged against him, her forehead pressed against his, her breathing ragged, and her grip so tight that he wondered if she could move her fingers at all.

When she at last opened her eyes, she looked at him with such wonder and fulfillment in her eyes that Will felt an unusual tug at his heartstrings. He believed he could die a very happy man if he could give her such pleasure every day of her life. His body ached with desire, his heart pounded with exhilaration, but he felt remarkably—and uncharacteristically—satisfied by her pleasure alone.

"*Will*," she whispered in amazement.

He folded her in his embrace, kissing her forehead as he leaned back against the cushions, Phoebe nestled into his side.

They lay that way for a time, staring at a fire that had begun to die. They talked about fanciful things, about dreams and hopes and pleasures. About Egypt, India, and Greece.

When she talked, Will smiled in the dark at the way her hands moved so expressively. He admired the way the light brought out the gold in her pale blond hair.

She was indescribably lovely.

But when the moon had moved across the sky, and most of the candles had burned out, it was time to return to the hall. He doused the last of the torches and led her back to the boat, his arm around her waist, clutching his very private journal.

Their trip across the lake was undertaken in silence; Phoebe still gripped the sides of the little boat, but her face was turned up to the night sky, her eyes closed as she basked in the moist, warm night air. There was no sound but the slice of his oars in the water and the creak of the old boat as it was propelled across the lake's surface.

When they had made their way to the gazebo, Will paused. This was where they would part ways, where they would each slip back into their roles of master and servant. He looked down at Phoebe. The moonlight reflected the crystal pins in her hair, making them look like little stars. It was appropriate, he thought—he felt as if he'd moved among the stars this night. He gathered her in his arms, kissed her once more, then reluctantly let her go.

Phoebe's smile faded; she drifted out of his arms until the only part of her that touched him, the only spot of warmth he could feel at all, was her fingers, which she entwined with his. "Thank you," she said. "It was . . ." She glanced up at the night sky and sighed, smiling. "It was magical."

His chest swelled with her words, and he felt the great satisfaction of having gone to quite a lot of trouble for the favor of such a smile.

Phoebe rose up on her toes, kissed his lips, then stepped away. Her fingers floated away from his, and still smiling, she turned and hurried toward the house.

He stood rooted to the ground, watching as she moved through the parterres like a ghost in her luminescent blue gown.

It was magical.

What had happened to him? How had he reached the precipice from which he had fallen this night? It felt almost as if he'd been building a ladder to it these last few weeks, building it higher and higher to a perch so small and so high that his only option was to fly or to fall.

Which had he done—fly or fall?

The question plagued him into the night as he lay sleeplessly in bed. He imagined Phoebe on the other side of the house, in her little bed next to her workroom. He imagined her in the most private of fantasies, lying with him, both of them naked, or holding herself above him as he moved deliberately within her. That image, the memory of those blissful hours on the island, and the knowledge that she was a servant, a seamstress, under his protection, kept him tossing and turning most of the night.

She was still very much on his mind the next morning when Farley informed him there were three gentlemen who wished to see him.

"Tenants?"

"No, my lord," Farley said. "They've come from Greenhill."

Will felt his gut sink. Intuition told him it was about Joshua.

His intuition was keen, as it turned out. The three gentlemen in question were horse traders, and had struck a deal with Joshua for horseflesh he did not own—the horses belonged to his father. Yet Joshua had deliberately given the men the impression that he, and he alone, owned them.

As usual, Will promised to make amends for Joshua's careless and mendacious behavior. He walked the three men out into the drive, stood in the bright sunlight, and vowed to them: "You may trust the matter will be satisfactorily resolved, good sirs. I cannot abide even the slightest dash of dishonesty or deception. One who has chosen to deceive has lost my good opinion and support forever."

"Thank you, my lord," said Mr. Broadwick, the one who had done the most talking on behalf of the three. He extended his hand. "I trust you will retrieve the money we laid in good faith and set this matter to rights."

"You may be assured of it," Will said through gritted teeth. Part of him wanted to let Joshua answer for his lies—let him see a jail, if that is what he deserved. But he thought of his father and knew that once again, he would buy Joshua's honor.

He waited until the gentlemen had mounted their horses and ridden away from Wentworth Hall before turning on his heel and striding into the house, intent on seeing his father, and then strangling Joshua, before he was due to call on Miss Fitzherbert and her family.

He did not see the open window above him, or Phoebe sitting on the sill just inside, fingering the scarab he'd discarded last night, which she now kept in her pocket.

Twenty

Caroline Fitzherbert dressed for tea in a new gown that she had commissioned a local seamstress to embroider in precisely the way Madame Dupree's gown had been embroidered along the hem and the sleeves.

The seamstress had done a passable job, she supposed, but Caroline was not satisfied, and she would not *be* satisfied until she was Countess of Bedford and ruled over the London seamstress Lord Summerfield seemed to regard so highly.

As to becoming the countess, it was only a matter of time, Caroline felt certain. Summerfield seemed taken with her, and her mother had heard in the village that he'd mentioned casually to a friend he ought to be married before the end of the year.

Caroline looked in the mirror and smiled at herself. She would be a gracious and generous countess. She would not be the least surprised if Summerfield made his offer at the house party he intended to host the last fortnight of the month, where he could announce it to one and all. The country bumpkins adored such events.

Later, when the family butler informed her Darby was calling, she thought it strange that her butler would refer to the viscount by his family name, and noted that he had the wrong day. He was expected on the morrow, and she took his mistake as a sign of his eagerness.

But it was not William Darby who had come calling, it was his brother, Mr. Joshua Darby.

Joshua Darby walked into the salon with both hands clasped behind his back, smiling enigmatically. He was as tall as his brother, but not as broad. His eyes, a deep, rich brown, were much darker than Summerfield's. He was wearing a dark coat and a striped waistcoat that made him look very lean. In a strange way, Caroline mused, he looked more civilized than Summerfield, which she thought odd, given this one's reputation.

She was taken aback that he had called at all, and was confused as to why. "Mr. Darby," she said uncertainly. "How . . . how kind of you to call."

He said not a word, merely bowed his head, then dropped one hand that he had held behind his back, holding out a single rose to her.

Caroline looked at the rose, then at him. "I don't understand."

"Don't you?" he asked, his voice smooth and deep. "I should think there are only two viable explanations why a gentleman would bring a handsome woman a single red rose."

"Oh? And what are they?" Caroline asked suspiciously.

"One, that he offers his condolences."

Caroline raised a brow. "Are you offering your condolences, sir?"

"Certainly not."

"Then what is the second explanation?"

"That the gentleman greatly esteems the lady."

She made a sound of surprise. "I beg your pardon, sir, but there seems to be a bit of a misunderstanding. I am being courted by your brother, the viscount."

Joshua Darby smiled devilishly. "I assure you, Miss Fitzherbert, there is no misunderstanding. You may now consider yourself being courted by two Darby men."

His conduct was shocking . . . yet oddly fascinating. Caroline cocked her head to one side, assessing him. He was handsome, but there was the matter of his reputation. Moreover, he would never be the earl unless some awful tragedy made it possible.

He smiled at her, and Caroline was mildly surprised by her body's reaction to it. Nevertheless, she had set the course of her destiny and would not deviate from it now. "I fear, Mr. Darby, that you have made an error in judgment," she said coolly. "Nothing can entice me to be courted by two brothers. I cannot accept your calling, for I have an understanding with Lord Summerfield."

He laughed a little and walked forward, halting just before her and touching the rose to the tip of her nose. "Don't be so very certain of that," he said, and smiled again.

A lack of the appropriate number of beads for Alice's gown sent Phoebe to Greenhill that morning in the company of Frieda. When she returned to Wentworth Hall and her workroom, she put on her work apron, then put the beads into one of the boxes of thread and beads she now kept in her bedchamber, as the gowns and fabrics and dress forms had taken up all the space in the workroom.

She paused there to look again at the strange charm stone Will had pulled from his neck and tossed aside. It was green, flat, rectangular in shape, and polished to a shine. But several little figures had been carved into it. They were curious, a mystery . . . just like him.

When she walked back into the overflowing workroom, she realized that something seemed different. Or out of place. But as she glanced at the dresses in various stages of construct, the bolts of fabric stacked in one corner, the baskets that held needles and scissors and ribbons scattered about the floor, she could not put her finger on it.

Then she saw it—the dress form that had held Jane's ball gown was bare. Phoebe gasped with shock—the gown was not yet finished, was still basted in some places and lacking the proper cover in others—how could anyone *possibly* have taken it? "Oh *no,*" she moaned. "Oh no-no-no! She wouldn't *dare!*"

But apparently she had.

Destined for Jane's room in the family suite in the east wing, Phoebe ran out of the room, flew down the steps to the first floor, traversed the corridor that connected the two main halls, and arrived at the first door of the family suite where she rapped loudly. "Lady Jane! Please do open the door!"

No one answered. Phoebe rapped hard again. One of the chambermaids poked her head out of a room across the hall. "What's all the trouble?" she demanded crossly.

"Lady Jane," Phoebe said breathlessly. "Have you seen her?"

"In the ballroom, with the dance instructor."

Phoebe whirled about and hurried to the main staircase.

In the foyer, she looked right and marched down the

refurbished corridor, stopping at each console to arrange the flowers. Who *was* it in this house that believed flowers could merely be tossed into a vase and left to arrange themselves?

She had no idea which was the ballroom, and paused and knocked on each door, winding her way to the back of the hall, pausing once more to rearrange a trio of porcelain figurines on a console that had been lined up like an invading army.

But then she heard music coming a little farther down the hall, and strode in that direction. Outside the door, she heard not only the music, but the sound of girlish laughter. She rapped on the door, did not wait for an answer, threw open the door, and marched inside, startling the inhabitants of the room out of their wits.

Jane was there, all right, wearing the gown Phoebe had not yet finished. Alice was also in the room, sitting on a window seat and looking rather cross. The dance instructor, a tall, reed-thin man with a bony nose, looked at Phoebe as if he expected her to announce the sky was falling, and just behind him was a young woman at the pianoforte.

"What are *you* doing here?" Alice demanded as Phoebe swept into the room. "Shouldn't you be off sewing?"

"As a matter of fact, I should be . . ." Phoebe said breathlessly as she shot a dark look at Jane, "sewing *that* gown. It is not yet finished, Lady Jane. You must return it at once."

"I *told* you it was not allowed," Alice said triumphantly. "Now take it off before you send Madame Dupree into an apoplectic fit."

Not surprisingly, Jane refused. "I will return it later, but I should like to see how the gown fits when I am dancing," she said, and held out her arms to the dance instructor, her fingers daintily parted like those of a ballerina.

"Take it *off*, Jane," Alice said. "You're not allowed."

"You are not the one to tell me what to do," Jane shot back.

"Lady Jane, *please*," Phoebe said as the instructor looked nervously from Jane to Alice and slowly took one long step back, out from between the two. "If you have ripped a basted seam it should be quite a lot of work to repair it, and there is very little time."

"I don't see the harm in wearing it for one afternoon," Jane said airily, and like a spoiled child, she swished the train around in front, then back again.

Phoebe winced. The train was only basted on the back of the gown.

"If you don't take it off, I shall tell Will," Alice said.

"I don't care if you do," Jane said petulantly.

Alice instantly began moving. Jane was quickly behind her, carelessly reaching for her sister, but Alice easily shrugged her off.

"Lady Jane!" Phoebe cried. "Do *please* have a care!"

The two young women ran from the ballroom, Phoebe following them quickly. She could hear the young woman at the pianoforte exclaim as she did so, but Phoebe had worked too hard to let Jane destroy the gown in a petulant snit.

However, years of proper breeding would not allow her to run like a hoyden, so she walked briskly after them, watching the two of them disappear into a room at the end of the corridor, their voices raised.

When Phoebe reached the door, she was surprised to find the entire family within and quickly drew up. "Oh my," she said hastily. "I beg your pardon," she said, her eyes on Will. The heat she felt in her neck was not due to the exertion of chasing Jane, she knew.

"Madame Dupree?" he asked coolly, as if they were mere acquaintances, as if they had never shared an extraordinarily intimate evening on a magical island.

"I . . ." She looked at Jane, who glared at her with disdain. Roger, sitting indolently in a chair, was smirking. Alice was standing near the door, her lips pressed in a thin line, and Joshua—Joshua was looking at Will, his gaze blistering. "I beg your pardon. Please forgive my intrusion," she said, looking around at the lot of them. "I meant only to speak to Jane before she began her dance instruction."

Jane snorted at that and picked absently at her sleeve. "*I* do not require dance instruction. I was merely dancing. *Alice* is the clumsy one."

"Will!" Alice cried.

"Jane, please," Will said, sounding weary.

"It is her gown," Phoebe explained quickly, suddenly conscious that she was wearing an apron with pins stuck in it. "It is not yet finished—indeed, it is merely basted in some places. She took the dress from the form and I really *must* have her remove it at once."

"Dear God, please don't suggest such a thing," Roger drawled.

"Hush, Roger!" Jane cried.

"Or what? You will dance me unto death?"

"That is enough!" Will said sternly, and turned a dark frown on his youngest sister. "Is this true? You have taken the dress before it is finished?"

"It is *my* dress."

"Go upstairs and remove it," he snapped.

"I told you so," Alice quipped snidely.

"Alice, I do not need your assistance."

No, Phoebe thought, he needed the assistance of a warden and a sheriff.

"And there he is, the mighty viscount, seeing to the important estate matter of who shall wear the gown," Joshua said with a sneer.

Their lack of manners and regard for one another was stunning. Phoebe could not help but gape at the insolent bunch.

"*Jane*," Will said, a bit more forcefully. "Go at once and change out of the gown. And do *not* take anything from the sewing room unless Madame Dupree has given her explicit permission."

"I am to take my orders from a *servant*?" Jane groused, but with a sniff, she shrugged and quit the room, brushing carelessly past Phoebe on her way out.

Across the room, Joshua chuckled. "There you have it, Madame Dupree. My brother has just done what Parliament cannot do and granted you, a tradeswoman, certain rights. You must be overcome with elation."

She was overcome, all right; she glanced at Will. "Thank you."

"You are welcome," he said shortly. "If there is nothing else, you have my leave."

The perfunctory dismissal stunned her. She curtsied awkwardly and went out, taking care to shut the door behind her. But in the privacy of the corridor, she paused, braced one hand against the wall, and pressed the other tightly to her abdomen.

Whatever had flowed between them last night, whatever the emotions she had been feeling, the real situation was quite plain—she was nothing more to him than an illicit affair, someone with whom to pass the time until he was married. It was an arrangement she had, in essence, invited.

It did not feel liberating.

She thought she understood the weight of her actions—the words she used in her note, a look, a seduction. But she had not realized how heavy were the consequences of them.

Her heart felt like it was twisting in her chest.

After taking a moment or two to compose herself, she followed Jane to the workroom and retrieve the ball gown. Jane dressed quickly, refusing to speak to Phoebe, and flounced out when she had finished dressing.

Phoebe had redressed the dress form by the time Frieda reappeared. But when Frieda opened the door, a draft from the open window sent scraps of fabric on the table scudding across the surface. Phoebe and Frieda both lunged at the same time, trying to catch as many of them as they could before they hit the floor.

"Oh, it's so bloody *hot!*" Frieda complained as she set the fabrics on the table again. "What I'd not give for a spot of rain—that would bring a bit of cool air to us, eh?"

Another strong gust tipped one of the dress forms, which Frieda caught, while Phoebe hurried to shut the window. As she pushed the two halves of the window together, she glanced down at the drive and recalled seeing Will down there this very morning, vowing that he would not tolerate dishonesty or deception of any kind.

That, coupled with the cool reception in his study, made her feel extraordinarily weak. She was too naïve for this sort of game, too unschooled in the art of deception or seduction.

Yet she could not stop thinking of last night. She couldn't keep from thinking of the candles, the wine, or his book, the precious journal of his life abroad that he'd shared with her. She could not stop thinking about the way his hands and mouth felt on her body.

She wanted more of that. However ill-advised or

truly mad it was, she could not help but want more.

"You are flushed!" Frieda declared with a frown. "The heat is too great for you, I think."

"No, it's not the heat," Phoebe said with a wan smile. "I'm feeling a bit under the weather, I suppose."

"You're not carrying a child, are you?"

Phoebe gasped at the question and stared in alarm at Frieda, who laughed with delight. "It's naught but a jest! Why, it's hardly possible, is it, without having had a poke or two while you've been at Wentworth Hall? Aye," she said with a cheerful shake of her head, "you've worked harder and longer than even his lordship, that much I know. I suppose I am the one who must worry over it now."

"W-what?" Phoebe exclaimed. "Frieda, are you—"

"No, no," Frieda said with an airy wave or her hand, and she laughed. "Of course not. I'm not a *doxy*," she said with a playful frown. But her smile faded, and she glanced up at Phoebe. "I'm naught but two days late."

Phoebe saw the worry in Frieda's brown eyes, and instantly put down the scraps she held and went to her, putting her arm around her, hugging her close.

"There now, you mustn't be concerned," Frieda said, patting Phoebe's hand. "It will be a lot of fretting for naught, I am certain of it. I was right careful, I was. I kept a sponge and vinegar inside me like I ought to have done."

It was a common way to prevent pregnancy that many women used. But Frieda didn't sound certain— she sounded completely *un*certain. She patted Phoebe's hand again, then shifted forward, forcing Phoebe's arm from her thin shoulders, and bent over the piece of beading on which she'd been working. "I'm quite all right, truly I am."

"Frieda—"

"We need more thread, do we not?" Frieda said, and suddenly stood up, walking into the bedroom to rummage through the boxes there.

Phoebe slowly resumed her seat and her work, her mind whirling. How close she had come to giving herself to Will last night. How easily, thoughtlessly, she would have done it.

Long after Frieda had gone, Phoebe continued to work, sewing precise little stitches to keep the train firmly attached to the back of Jane's gown, her mind roaring with so many emotions. When the light began to fade, she stopped long enough to light a pair of candles. The tinderbox was in the bedchamber, however, and when she went to retrieve it, she heard the muffled sounds of raised voices coming up through the flue.

She sewed well into the night, her mind working against her, her thoughts on Will. She was so preoccupied that she did not hear anyone at the door until he had come almost to the table.

"Farley!" she gasped when she saw him standing there.

"We missed you at supper tonight, Madame Dupree."

"Thank you for sending a tray up again, Farley. But with the house party only days away, I really must work."

He nodded, and glanced around uncomfortably. "Unfortunately, there has been a bit of a quarrel between Lord Summerfield and his brother Joshua. His lordship asks that you come straightaway to his father's sitting room."

Her heart surged. "His father's sitting room?" she asked, taking care to show no emotion.

"On the first floor, madam, in the master suite of rooms."

"Now? It must be nearly eight o'clock!" she said as she absently put a hand to her hair.

"I beg your pardon again, but his lordship's precise words were, 'as soon as she is able.' "

Phoebe blinked.

Farley winced a little and took a step closer to the table. He leaned over it and whispered, "There is trouble with Joshua."

"*Oh.*" She nodded. "I shall be along directly," she said, and stood up, removing her apron.

When Farley had gone, Phoebe whirled around to the mirror. She looked fatigued and unkempt. Wisps of her hair were uncurling from the prim bun she wore at her nape, and her plain day gown was wrinkled from sitting all day.

She tried to soothe the loose ends of her hair, but to no avail. She pinched her cheeks to bring a little color to them, smoothed her skirt as best she could, took the charm stone and slipped it into her pocket, then picked up the candelabra to make her way to the master suite.

Twenty-one

Will ignored the leap his heart took when he heard the knock on the door. He quickly took the candelabra from her, put it aside, and ushered Phoebe into the sitting room. "I've no one to turn to, Phoebe," he said, keenly aware that in this house the walls heard all. He could not risk treating her as anything but a servant. "My brother is in need of assistance," he said quietly, omitting the part that Henry had sent his gardener to tell Will that Joshua had fallen so far in his cups at a pub in Greenhill that he feared he might drown—or be shot. Apparently, Joshua was saying things he ought not to say.

"Oh," she said, looking confused as Will hurried her into the interior rooms.

"Jacobs, the man who usually tends my father, was called away to see his ailing mother. Jane and Alice have gone to dine at the vicar's, and Roger . . ." He paused. Shook his head. "I have no idea where Roger is off to, in truth. I should not like to impose, but I really must have you tend my father," he said.

"I—I beg your pardon?"

"Come," he said, and gestured to the bedchamber where his father was seated before the fire.

Her eyes fixed on his father, widening as she understood what he wanted her to do. "Oh no," she whispered. "I can't possibly be trusted—"

"Of course you can. You need only sit with him and read aloud, if you'd please."

"Surely Mrs. Turner—"

"Mrs. Turner has her family," he said as he picked up a cloak and tossed it around his shoulders. "And truthfully, Phoebe, if I bring anyone else here, I cannot trust that the news of Joshua's behavior will not be known to all." He strode to where his father sat and leaned down. "Father, you remember Madame Dupree, do you not?"

Phoebe eyed the old man as if she expected him to answer, which of course he would not. But the earl lifted his index finger. Will looked again at Phoebe. "You know that he cannot speak," he said. "But he is aware of us and his surroundings."

She hesitated a moment before moving forward and placing her small hand on his father's arm. "It is a pleasure to make your acquaintance again, my lord," she said, and curtsied as gracefully and surely as any lady-in-waiting, and Will's heart stopped. The world had cast his father aside, yet this seamstress treated his father as the earl.

Her gracious greeting stood in stark contrast to the ugly row he'd had with Joshua in this very room about the horses, only an hour or so ago.

"Why shouldn't I sell them?" Joshua had asked. "Those horses belong to me every bit as much as they belong to you. They are the property of the estate, and I have every bit as much of a right to them as do you."

Will had been astounded by his reasoning. "They don't belong to either of us, Joshua. They are Father's property. He would never consent to you selling them to feed your gambling habits."

"Indeed?" Joshua had asked coldly, then looked at his father and drawled, "Have you *asked* him?"

Truly, he could not fathom what demon possessed his brother—but he had realized that the man standing before him this afternoon was not the same boy who had once followed Will about the house, pestering him to distraction with such questions as how the moon stayed in the sky when the sun was shining or where the rabbits went when they ran away.

"How *dare* you dishonor our father in such a manner?" Will had demanded with soaring anger.

Joshua had snorted disdainfully. "Our *father* knows neither honor nor dishonor! He is merely a shell of the man that once lived. Do you really think there is any intelligence within? Do you think that this . . . this *being* knows who any of us are?"

"*Yes*," Will had said sharply, horrified by his brother's words. "And he knows precisely what you are saying now, Joshua. He can *hear* you and he can understand you very plainly!"

For a moment, a single sliver of a moment, Will saw pain glance Joshua's features. But his brother quickly pressed his lips tightly together and looked at his father. "No," he said low, with a firm shake of his head. "He is nothing but the living corpse of the man that he was."

Will had felt the insult reverberate through his father's body. He had not prolonged the interview but had, in no uncertain terms, warned Joshua that if he could not be depended upon to be a gentleman and a loyal son, he would have the family solicitors to answer to, for Will would take all necessary measures to protect the earl's estate.

Joshua had responded with his own threat to Will's person as he'd quit the room.

The moment the door shut behind Joshua, Will had gone down on his haunches next to his father and implored him, "He does not mean what he says, Papa. He is troubled and afraid and he . . ." *He is lost.* "He does not mean what he says. You must believe me."

His father's eyes showed him nothing but pain.

And now Joshua was trying to get himself killed for reasons that Will could not fathom.

Looking at Phoebe, he felt ashamed of his family. "Thank you for coming," he said sincerely. "I won't be long."

He turned, began to stride from the bedchamber.

"No, wait!" Phoebe cried. "Is there nothing more you would tell me?"

He took a quick look around. "There are some books on the table there," he said. "Find one you would like to read. Good night, Phoebe. I shall return as soon as I am able."

And with that, he rushed out the door, the sense of foreboding in him growing the longer he tarried.

Phoebe flinched at the sound the door made when it swung shut behind Will. He'd left so quickly she hadn't yet moved an inch.

She looked down at her charge; she could see the pink of his scalp through the shock of white hair.

She saw the earl's crooked index finger move and believed that was meant for her. "I beg your pardon, my lord, I am being rude," she said.

He lifted the finger again.

"I . . . Would you like me to read to you?" she asked, and glanced around the room. Two chairs were pushed up against the wall farthest from the hearth. A round table was at the opposite end of the room and was stacked with a collection of books. She walked to the stack of books and selected one that didn't seem as dry as the others: *The Cremona Violin* by Ernst Theodor Amadeus Hoffmann.

She returned to the earl's side and looked about for a place to bring the candle closer. There was only a single chair, pushed away from the hearth.

"This will never do, I'm afraid," she said, and glanced again at her ward. "I rather imagine the furniture has been placed to allow you to move about freely, my lord, but I would suggest—*gently*, I beg you—that it makes for a rather unwelcoming room. If you will bear with me, I can make a few slight changes and then read to you for a time in a more comfortable setting."

She waited for some sign that he heard her. A moment passed; he turned his head slightly, his gaze moving as high as it might—to her belly. And he lifted the index finger.

Phoebe grinned. "Marvelous. You will be very pleased when I am done, I am certain."

Will eventually did return to the hall with Joshua, both of them covered with dirt, and Will's knuckles bleeding from having fought off the two ruffians who were trying to rob his very drunken brother when Will found him.

But the fight had roused Joshua, and for the space of a quarter of an hour, the two brothers had fought side by side while Henry had gone for help.

When Henry returned with two friends, the ruffians took flight, Joshua slipped back into his inebriation, and it had taken all of Will and Henry and his friends to seat him on his horse. By the time he and Farley had put Joshua to bed, it was half past eleven o'clock. Cursing under his breath, Will strode to his father's suite of rooms.

When he opened the door to the outer room, he was surprised by the sound of laughter and paused to listen.

"Oh, it was *wretched* of them!" she said, her voice lilting. "Can you imagine? The whole of London saw them! I thought my mother would faint with despair, but she *laughed*."

Will tried his best to comb his hair with his fingers—his hat had been lost in the fight, unfortunately—and walked to the door of the sitting room. He could not say what surprised him more—that the furniture in the room had been rearranged or that Phoebe was sitting on the edge of her chair, animatedly relating some tale to his father.

"Well, my lord, I can assure you she was the *only* one who laughed. I firmly believed Miss Chadwick— *Oh!*" she said, noticing him standing in the door. "I didn't hear you come in."

"Please do go on with your tale—I am certain Papa would like to hear the end of it."

"Oh," she said, glancing nervously at the earl, "it was nothing more than a diversion, really, and I . . ." She stopped and squinted at Will. "I beg your pardon, but are you *bleeding*?"

"Am I?" he asked, and touched his face. His finger came away with blood on it. "I hadn't realized."

Phoebe was already on her feet, marching toward him. "You hadn't *realized*? My lord, you are . . . you are *covered* in dirt, and . . . and look at your hands!" she exclaimed, taking one in her hand and lifting it.

"Ah," he said, wincing when she touched the knuckle. It felt broken.

She frowned at him with the full weight of feminine disapproval. "Have you engaged in a *fight*, sir?"

"Unfortunately, yes."

"Your poor brother," she said, looking at his knuckles again.

"No, no—my poor brother is asleep in his bed. This was done in defense of him."

"These wounds should be cleaned," she said sternly. "Is there a basin nearby?"

"My father's bedchamber. I will go—"

"You can't do it alone, not with both hands cut so badly," she said, and gestured like a quartermaster toward the door that led into the bedchamber.

Will was not a fool—nor was he opposed to a little tender attention after what he'd endured this evening. "All right," he conceded. "How is the earl?" he asked.

"Weary, I think," Phoebe said, and as they passed

him, she laid a hand comfortingly on his shoulder. It seemed to Will to be as natural an act of comfort toward his father as he'd ever seen.

He paused and put his hand on his father's shoulder, too, in a much more feeble attempt to comfort him.

Phoebe was already at the basin when he entered the chamber, dipping a handkerchief in the water and wringing the excess from it.

He joined her and held out his right hand. She carefully began to clean the cuts and scrapes, her touch gentle, her head bent over his hand. "It must have been quite a fight."

"Ouch!" He winced when she touched a particularly deep gash. "They were thieves, intent on divesting Joshua of his money . . . if not his life."

"How terrible! Did they know him?"

"I don't know. My friend seems to think that they did." Personally, Will could think of any number of scenarios. Just thinking of his brother's attempt to sell the horseflesh right out from under Wentworth Hall caused anger to surge through him all over again, and in a moment of weakness, he said, "I cannot fathom what makes him say or do the things he does. He knows very well that I cannot abide deceit in any form, for any reason."

Phoebe suddenly dropped his hand and dipped the handkerchief in the soapy water.

"I cannot fathom *any* of my siblings, in truth," he admitted further, and sighed heavenward. "I can't seem to set it all to rights. I feel as if we are pieces of broken china—the large pieces have been put back together and sealed with the glue of a family . . . but there are little pieces chipped away from the whole, and I cannot seem to patch it together."

Phoebe smiled thinly.

"Is something wrong?" he asked.

"Not at all," she said. "I suppose I am a bit tired, that's all."

"Of course you are. I have kept you too long. I can't offer you enough of an apology—"

"Please, you mustn't," she said, looking up at him with eyes that looked like twin summer skies. "Your father and I have become friends. And I rather think he likes the room's new arrangement."

"Yes," Will said, smiling, too. "I noticed."

She laughed low, the sound of it almost a whisper as she gestured for his other hand. He dutifully brought that one up and looked at his cleaned fist as Phoebe ministered to the other. He watched the way her fingers moved on his. She was elegant in everything she did.

"Good Lord," he said as a thought occurred to him. "The first guests for the house party will be arriving on Tuesday. To think I will be presenting my siblings to proper society!" The thought was almost overwhelming. "May I assume that the girls will be properly outfitted over the fortnight?"

"Of course," she said. She was no longer looking at his hand as she cleaned his wounds, but at his face. "Frieda and I are putting the finishing touches on the ball gowns, which I hope to have finished by week's end. We have completed the day dresses and morning gowns."

He didn't respond—he was looking at the way the candlelight played over her blond hair, making it shimmer in places. Her cleaning of his hand came to a stop. They stood looking at one another. She smiled; she was heart-stoppingly beautiful to him, and her smile warmed his heart.

"Well," she said softly.

Will swallowed. "I must put my father to bed," he forced himself to say.

She nodded. "There is one thing." She reached into the pocket of her dress and withdrew the scarab, which she held up to him. "You left this behind . . . what is it?"

He smiled. "A scarab." When Phoebe looked at him, he continued, "An amulet. The bloody merchant who took two pounds for it promised it was a charm to keep my physical desires at bay." He smiled wryly, his gaze sweeping over her. "It is obviously worthless," he murmured.

"But it is lovely. It is very unusual."

"Then you must keep it," he said, and folded her fingers over it. She opened her mouth to protest, but he shook his head. "I want you to have it," he said, and squeezed her hand. "That is a decree."

"Thank you."

"Thank you for tending to my wounds." Yet he did not remove his hand or otherwise move.

She smiled as if she knew what she was doing to him. "Your father," she reminded him.

"Yes." He had to hold her in his arms again, to kiss the lips that smiled so enticingly at him now. But he only brought her hand to his mouth and kissed her knuckles before returning to the sitting room, to his father.

"I owe Madame Dupree a debt of thanks," he said to his father. "She has been very kind to sit with you this evening."

His father lifted his finger.

Phoebe came around on the other side of his chair and knelt down. "Good night, my lord. I promise to finish *The Cremona Violin* on my next visit." She stood again and looked across the earl to Will. Her eyes were glistening in the candlelight, and Will could see the longing there, as deep as he felt it inside himself.

"Good night, my lord."

"Sleep well, Madame Dupree. And thank you again."

With another soft smile, she glided across the floor and disappeared through the door.

Will stood a moment, listening to the sound of her footfall. When he could no longer hear her, he looked at his father's eyes. He could see the fatigue there, the worry for Joshua. "He's all right, Papa," he said. "He's sleeping."

He did not imagine the look of relief that filled his father's eyes.

"Come on, then," he said, rising up. "Let's get you to bed. I will tell you of it all on the morrow."

Twenty-two

The next morning, Will had a row with Alice, who was determined to go into Greenhill, even though there was no one to take her. He was expecting some tradesmen about some repairs that needed to be done to the house, Joshua was hardly in a condition to take her, and while Roger had offered, Will did not trust him in the least, because his youngest brother favored Alice over Jane.

Alice was furious with him for keeping her from town, but he had seen the way she had looked at the smithy last Sunday at church. "It is no use," he told her. "I know what you want in Greenhill."

That is when Alice began to sob and accused him of ruining her life. Will was not as hard-hearted as that—frankly, it was almost more than he could bear to see her so unhappy. But he also knew what was said about the young smithy, and he took his sobbing sister in his arms and said, "Whatever he has told you, darling, it is your fortune he courts. He is not an honorable man."

With a shriek, Alice pushed against him. "You will say *anything* to keep me from him!" she cried, and fled the room.

He had listened to her slam the door, had heard her slippers against the marble foyer as she ran up to her rooms, and then sank onto a chair. He felt ridiculous in this role of father and brother and mother all tied up in one. He was hardly equipped for it—he had spent the last years of his life doing as he pleased, loving whom he pleased, consorting with whomever he pleased. He had been free.

Now, he felt like a prisoner in his own home. It was just as he'd blurted to Phoebe last night—he was hardly the person to guide them to any understanding of life. Yet he was all they had. What he wouldn't give for a mother, a father—*anyone*—who understood them better than he.

It had been a trying couple of days, and he was hardly in the mood to sit idly and chat about the heat, but he had promised to call on the Fitzherberts. He would never be able to convince his siblings to adhere to proper decorum if he himself did not adhere to it, would he?

He arrived shortly after four o'clock, determined to carry on the course that he must follow in spite of his weariness. Caroline Fitzherbert received him as she always did, with a demure smile and an invitation to sit. Her mother was in attendance as well, her spirits high—she prattled on about the efforts of the household to catch a snake that had been discovered in the kitchen garden, the details of which sent Will into a near fit of slumber. His mind wandered horribly, through a jumbled disarray of thoughts about Joshua, about Phoebe, about the look in his father's eyes when he had explained Joshua's attempt to sell some of the horses, followed by his drunken binge.

But as tea wore on—or droned on, as it were—Will began to notice that Miss Fitzherbert was not her usual, attentive self. She seemed distracted, and kept glancing at a single rose in a vase on the end table near her chair.

When he invited her for a turn about the gardens before he took his leave, it seemed to him that she came along almost reluctantly. "Thank you for calling, my lord," she said as they strolled past yellow daffodils and blue forget-me-nots. "We are always delighted with your company." She smiled again and looked away.

"Your delight cannot possibly compare with my joy," he said, the polite words coming to him from some place that was nowhere near his heart. He tried very hard to summon the same feelings of eager anticipation and warmth that he felt for Phoebe, but could not seem to find them. That made the situation even more preposterous, naturally, for Caroline Fitzherbert was a perfectly suitable candidate to be his wife. Phoebe was not.

Perhaps he was giving Miss Fitzherbert short shrift—he hadn't kissed her, hadn't attempted to find the same pleasure in her as he had found in Phoebe. So as they walked under the arbor, Will impulsively put his hand to her arm, stopping her.

"My lord?" she asked sweetly.

He said nothing, just slipped his fingers under her chin, lifted her face, and kissed her.

She froze, her body unyielding, her lips unmoving.

It was pointless. Will felt nothing but a faint stirring—nothing like the passion that had roared up in him when he'd kissed Phoebe the first time. He lifted his head and smiled.

Caroline blushed. "I . . . I . . ."

"Forgive me for being so bold," he said politely as his mind's eye envisioned Phoebe.

"Not at all," she said, and glanced at the ground as she timidly touched her hand to his.

Will caught her hand and lifted it to his mouth, kissing her knuckles. "I should be going," he said quietly, and released her hand. "I have quite a lot of business that requires my attention."

"Yes, of course." They continued walking, both of them with their hands clasped behind their backs. When they reached the drive, and a boy had been sent for his horse, Will smiled again and said, "It has been my pleasure, Miss Fitzherbert."

"Oh, you are too kind," she responded, and glanced at the door of the house. "I believe I was not very good company today," she added shyly. "I confess to having a bit of a headache."

"You should be resting," he said instantly. "I have kept you from it—"

"Oh no," she said quickly. "Were it not for your call, I should have been miserable, I assure you."

He bowed again and stepped back. "I wish you well, then, Miss Fitzherbert. Good afternoon."

She curtsied, then folded her arms tightly about her as Will swung up on Fergus. He lifted his hand to her as he rode out, but the moment he turned from Caroline she was forgotten. His mind was on Phoebe and the memory of her in his arms, the taste of her lips and skin. He wondered how he might ever balance his desire to be with someone like Phoebe and his duty to marry someone like Miss Fitzherbert.

It seemed impossible.

The day was so warm that all the windows were open, and as a result, Phoebe and Frieda could hear the notes rising from the pianoforte as Jane and Alice practiced their dancing.

Phoebe also heard the sound of a horse riding into the drive and could not help but peek out the window. It was Will, dressed in fine clothing, his hair combed back. He certainly was handsome, wasn't he? It was little wonder that so many people were coming to spend the fortnight—Mrs. Turner said they all had unmarried daughters and would give their right leg and a milk cow to make a match.

Phoebe understood why. Were she not in such a peculiar predicament . . .

"Three days late," Frieda said behind her. "It's not uncommon, is it?"

Phoebe reluctantly turned away from the window. "No," she said with a sympathetic smile. "My sister can scarcely guess when she will be indisposed, while I could set a clock by it."

Frieda's face fell. "I can generally set a clock by it, too." Her eyes were rimmed with worry.

Before Phoebe could respond, the door flew open and Jane burst in, pirouetting and stumbling into a shallow curtsy before bouncing back up with a laugh. Behind her, Alice slipped in, watching her sister.

"You should never curtsy before you are formally introduced, Jane—should she, Phoebe?"

"Ah . . . no," Phoebe said, and smiled at the two of them. "Shall I show you a proper court curtsy?"

"You *know* it?" Jane asked elatedly.

"I do."

"Yes, yes! Show us!" Jane exclaimed, clapping her hands together.

"All right." Phoebe laughed, and stepped into the middle of the room, moving a chair and a dress form. She extended her arms wide and said, "You must extend one leg very deeply, like this," Phoebe said. "Carriage erect, you descend as if you were suspended from the ceiling by a string to the top of your head," she said, gracefully moving down. "How do you do, my lord," she said, inclining her head just so.

She quickly came up. "Do you see?"

"Now me!" Jane cried, and stepped into the middle of the room to practice. They laughed at her awkward maneuvering, but after several attempts—and Phoebe's corrections—Jane did it well.

Alice needed far less help—she curtsied perfectly on the first attempt, earning applause from Frieda and Phoebe.

"There, you see?" Jane said as she twirled around and planted both hands on the table. "Alice believes she is better suited to country dances with blacksmiths and farmers than she is to society balls, but she is really quite good at curtsying."

Phoebe and Frieda exchanged a look as Jane smiled and twirled away again.

"Alas," she continued, "I rather imagine she will not be dancing with the smithy, either, for when I was walking with Miss Abernathy on the village green this morning, I saw him in the company of the girl who tends Mr. Reynolds's shop."

Alice colored. "Don't be ridiculous, Jane," she said as

she idly smoothed her hair. "I have done what Will asked. I am no longer in communication with Mr. Hughes."

"No?" Jane asked, clearly titillated by the news.

Alice turned and looked her directly in the eye. "*No,*" she said.

"It's just as well," Jane said as she moved to the dress form that held her ball gown and spread the skirt. "Is it finished?"

"Almost," Phoebe said, calmly removing Jane's hands from it. "We will finish the beading today, I should think."

A knock at the door caught their attention.

"I'll see who it is!" Jane said with some delight, and hurried forward to fling the door open and sink into a deep curtsy.

"My, my, Lady Jane!" Will praised her from the open door. "Allow me to help you up," he added, and extended his hand, palm up.

Jane slipped her hand in his, and with her head bowed, she rose up gracefully, then lifted her head and beamed at her brother. "What do you think?"

"I think it was the most majestic curtsy I have ever seen," he said indulgingly.

Delighted, Jane twirled around again.

Will looked across the room at Phoebe, his eyes quickly raking over her. "Please forgive the intrusion, Madame Dupree, but I should like to spirit Jane away for a time." He looked at Jane. "There seems to be a matter of a book that belongs to Roger."

"Goodness, is *that* all," Jane said with a sigh of impatience. "It wasn't as if he intended to actually *read* it."

"Come along, Jane. Alice, if you please. I am certain Madame Dupree and Frieda have quite a lot of work to do." He looked at Phoebe as Jane pirouetted and Alice walked out the door. "If you will excuse us," Will said.

But he did not move. He paused to look at a gown that hung from one of the many hooks Phoebe had asked Billy to put around the room.

Phoebe and Frieda waited. He glanced at Phoebe. "Who shall wear this?" he asked.

"Lady Jane, my lord."

He studied it again, then shook his head. "It will not do."

Frieda turned a look of pure shock to Phoebe. "I beg your pardon?" Phoebe asked as she looked at the rose-colored day gown. It was beautiful, cut to perfection and adorned with slender ribbons. She thought it one of her better day gowns.

"No," he said again, and glanced over his shoulder at Phoebe. "The décolletage, madam, is too low. I spoke to you about it once. Did you not heed my instruction?"

His *instruction*? "But it is *not* too low," Phoebe said adamantly. "It suits Lady Jane very well, my lord. It is styled in the latest fashion and—"

"It is cut too low," he said again, and turned to face her. "Do you argue with me?"

Phoebe blinked. She looked at Frieda. Then at Will. "I beg your pardon, my lord," she began. He nodded, and turned to examine the dress again. "But indeed, I do take issue."

Her response did not seem to surprise him. There was a strange look in his eyes, almost as if he invited her argument. He spared a glance for Frieda. "Frieda, would you be so good as to allow me a word with Madame Dupree?"

Frieda's eyes went wide—she looked fearfully at Phoebe, but quickly stood and curtsied as she hurried out.

Will waited until he heard her on the stairs, then looked at Phoebe.

"No," she said, shaking her head. "I cannot—I *will* not—alter that gown to suit some puritanical view of fashion, sir! You hired me to provide your sisters the latest styles and I will not be persuaded that the latest styles include some provincial notion of decency." She folded her arms defiantly. "I am quite resolved in this," she added, less confidently.

"The gown," he said low, "is beautiful. I merely wanted an excuse to speak to you privately, but it is near to impossible."

"Oh," she said, dropping her arms. "*Oh.*"

He moved closer. "I must see you," he said quietly. "Tomorrow is Sunday, the other servants will be away with their families."

"*Will!*"

It was Jane, coming up the stairs.

"Damnation," he muttered softly. "Tomorrow, one o'clock, behind the orangery. Can you meet me there?"

"Will! How long must I wait?" Jane called up.

"A moment, Jane!" he called back, and looked at Phoebe.

She nodded. He pivoted sharply about, striding across the crowded little workroom before Jane could come up.

Phoebe didn't even realize until he had gone how wildly her heart was beating.

It was still beating wildly when Frieda returned. "What came over you?" she cried. "Did you want to lose your position here?"

"No!" Phoebe insisted. "But I . . . I really admire the gown."

Frieda shook her head. "You might admire the roof over your head before you think to speak in such a manner again, Phoebe. I've seen dismissals for less than that. Indeed, I expected it."

"Yes," Phoebe uttered, looking at the gown. "That was foolish of me."

"Aye, it was foolish," Frieda said adamantly, and resumed her beadwork.

Phoebe glanced surreptitiously at Frieda. "Where did we put the gold thread?" she asked idly, and wandered into the adjoining bedroom under the guise of looking for thread, needing a moment to calm her wild heart.

On the morrow, behind the orangery, one o'clock. A slow smile spread her lips. She felt a lightness inside her that she had felt that night on the island, an indescribable freedom of spirit.

Twenty-three

He'd had a devil of a time getting away from his siblings. Alice and Jane had had a row over a pair of kidskin gloves, Roger refused to rise and greet the day, and Joshua had left at dawn for God only knew where. Will had been late to the stables and saddled Fergus himself, lest anyone inquire where he meant to ride.

And now, seated on Fergus's back, Will waited behind the orangery.

He withdrew the watch from his pocket and glanced at it again—a quarter past one.

She wasn't coming.

He couldn't deny his great disappointment—he had thought of little else yesterday and today, the anticipation of seeing her again filling his dreams in the night.

Perhaps Mrs. Turner had captured her. Will knew that the housekeeper was working through the weekend to make the house ready for the arrival of the first guests on Tuesday. But Mrs. Turner would never impose on Phoebe without first asking Will.

Where was she? Had she changed her mind about their arrangement? The thought sent a shudder of dread through him. He could not imagine seeing her in his house and not being able to be near her.

Will glanced at his pocket watch again. It was now seventeen past one o'clock.

She wasn't coming.

With a sigh, Will urged Fergus around and gently spurred him forward. The horse had only taken a step or two when he pricked his ears and lifted his head. Will looked up just in time to see Phoebe hurry around the corner of the orangery, coming to an abrupt halt directly before him.

She was panting, as if she had run. Her cheeks were flushed, the hem of her pale yellow and green gown rimmed with the faint trails of dirt and grass. But her eyes—her eyes were luminous, shining with anticipation. Neither of them spoke for a moment, just stared at one another as their tacit understanding, and mutual desire flowed between them.

Will remembered himself; he extended his hand, palm up. "Put your foot on mine."

She did not hesitate; she understood him completely and stepped around a restless Fergus, slipped her hand into his, and fit her foot on top of his for leverage. Will easily pulled her up, putting her directly before him on the saddle. With his arms wrapped securely around her, he spurred Fergus into the trees.

Once they were deep behind the veil of trees, he

released the breath he hadn't even realized he was holding, and bent his head next to hers. "I thought you wouldn't come."

"I thought I'd miss you," she said, still breathless. "Frieda came this morning instead of going to her mother's, as is her habit, and by the time I was able to shoo her away, I discovered I had no idea where the orangery stood! I was afraid to inquire of anyone lest I invite questions."

He hated the subterfuge that they had to engage in, but there was nothing that could be done for it. Anything less than the utmost discretion would be too scandalous for them both.

"Where are we going?"

"I have another surprise for you."

She twisted about so that she could smile up at him, her eyes glowing with pleasure. "*Another* surprise? You shall ruin me completely for ordinary days—I shall be cross if I don't have a surprise every time we meet."

If he could, he would surprise her every single day.

They turned onto a deer trail and moved deeper into the forest.

Phoebe leaned forward, peering at the shadowed trail ahead of them. "This path hardly appears to be used at all."

"Trust me," he said.

She did not respond, but she slowly leaned back, nestling her body against his. Trusting him. After a few moments, she said, "One might think we are leaving civilization, for it seems as if the forest goes on forever. But really, I should hardly mind if we did, for one always finds something new and exciting when one leaves the comfort of one's sitting room."

"Oh?" he asked idly as he slipped his arm around her waist, anchoring her to him. "And what new and exciting things have you found in leaving your sitting room?"

She laughed. "Frightfully little, really. I suppose I dream of something new and exciting more than I experience it."

"Indeed? A widow such as you has the freedom most women her age do not possess. I should think you'd go abroad or into society."

"And do what, pray tell?" she asked airily. "Perhaps I have the freedom, but there is little joy in such adventures when undertaken alone."

A forbidden thought occurred to him—if Phoebe were to stay in Bedfordshire after her work here was done, he would change that. He would take her places with him, he would show her all the excitement and adventure the world had to offer.

Perhaps it was not such a far-fetched idea. Perhaps he might find a permanent position for her here, at Wentworth Hall.

"Ooh, look!" Phoebe suddenly exclaimed as they crested a hill, catching his wrist to draw his attention. She pointed to the right and Fergus began to whinny. At the base of the hills where the stream widened was a small meadow and the castle ruins.

The horses were there, grazing where the grass always seemed lush and green. There were only four of them; the foal and its mother were missing now, their numbers culled by poachers. Soon there would be none left but Apollo.

"Now here is a bit of unexpected adventure," Will said, and urged Fergus into the meadow. As they rode into the clearing, Apollo lifted his head, glanced insouciantly in their direction, and resumed his grazing. He was very much accustomed to Will now—he hardly minded him at all, not even on his back. But only for a short time. Apollo was far too intelligent to allow his surrender completely.

Will dismounted, then helped Phoebe to the ground. He removed the saddlebag from Fergus's flanks, unfastened the cinch that held the saddle on Fergus, and pulled it off of him.

"What do you mean to do?" Phoebe whispered.

"You will see." With a wink, he slung the saddlebag over one shoulder, and the blanket and saddle in hand, he began to walk through grass and daisies not yet eaten by the feral horses.

Apollo eyed him with lazy curiosity as he approached, greeting him with a grunt and a jerk of his head.

"Good day to you, old friend," Will said, and stroked Apollo's nose. The horse instantly nudged his pocket, looking for the apple or carrots he knew would be forthcoming. Will did not disappoint him. From one half of the saddlebag, he withdrew an apple. The other horses were quickly at his side—they, too, had become accustomed to his frequent visits and apples. But only Apollo had agreed to be ridden; the others had merely accepted his presence in exchange for the apples.

He reached into the saddlebag and withdrew one apple after another, feeding them to the attentive horses. He glanced over his shoulder, to Phoebe. Fergus had wandered off to graze and Phoebe stood in the middle of the meadow, frozen with wonder, her gaze fixed on him and the horses. He smiled and held out his hand to her.

She did not hesitate—she gathered her skirts in one hand and moved quickly through the daisies to reach him. He handed her two apples, one for each hand; one of the horses attempted to take it from her hand before she had even closed her fingers around it, and

Phoebe laughed, the rich sound of it sending a shock of delight through Will.

The look of genuine pleasure on her face was enough to make a man want to move mountains, or, at the very least, tame wild horses.

"It's *remarkable*, Will," she exclaimed breathlessly.

"There's more," he said, and handed her the nearly empty saddlebag. "Keep feeding them," he advised her, and quickly put the blanket on Apollo's back.

Phoebe watched him with an expression that suggested she thought he was mad, but Will stroked Apollo's neck, then slid the bit in between his monstrous teeth. In a few moments, he had fastened the bridle as well. He rubbed his neck and withers for a few minutes, then lifted the saddle to shoulder level and carefully placed it on Apollo's back. The last time he'd ridden him, Apollo had objected to the saddle, even though he had taken it thrice before.

But Apollo must have sensed this was important to Will, for today he remained quite calm, even as the other horses began to move away. The only outward indication the horse gave that he even noticed the saddle at all was the sudden switch of his tail. Will bent down, reached under Apollo for the girth, and brought it up, cinching it as tight as he dared.

Apollo continued to stand calmly, his tail switching.

Phoebe watched him intently, holding the saddlebag in both hands before her.

"Good lad," Will said soothingly to Apollo. "Just as we've done before, slow and easy."

Apollo turned his head slightly, fixed his eye on Will.

"Slow and easy," Will said again, and tested his weight in the stirrup before pulling himself up and onto the saddle.

Phoebe gasped softly and pressed a hand to her mouth as Will gently spurred Apollo forward. He received a snort and a toss of Apollo's massive head for it, but the horse allowed Will to jog him in a circle around Phoebe.

She turned slowly, following his progress with bright blue eyes as big as moons.

When he came full circle, he reined Apollo to a stop. "Do you know how to ride?" he asked.

She looked at Apollo and nodded solemnly.

"Then allow me to invite you to a bit of adventure outside your little workroom."

Phoebe shifted her gaze to him and beamed. "Truly?"

He smiled and gestured toward the horse.

"*Thank* you!"

From the tips of her stylish boots, to the row of tiny buttons that fastened her gown at her side, to the small cross that hung around her neck, she was perfect. She was beautiful.

He spurred Apollo into trotting a tight circle around her. "Take down your hair."

"Why?"

Because he would have a bit of his fantasy, too. "Please," he said.

She looked at him with a curious smile, but withdrew a pin from the back of her head. One tress of hair as thick as his arm uncurled down her back. She withdrew two more pins, and the rest of it fell.

He drew Apollo to a halt and dismounted. "Ride astride," he said, and helped her up to the saddle. It took a moment of maneuvering in her gown, but she managed it. Her legs were bared from the knee down, ending in boots that were hardly suitable for riding.

Will caressed her knee. "Are you afraid?"

Phoebe leaned over to rub Apollo's neck. "No," she

said at last. "I am exhilarated beyond compare. I rather feel like the warrior queen."

He smiled at that—he knew precisely how she felt. "Shall I lead you?"

"No," she said instantly, and picked up the reins.

Still, Will held the bridle. She beamed at him—he did not believe a smile could be so broad, or that eyes could shine with such delight.

"You do not trust my abilities," she said with a playful frown.

"I do not trust Apollo," he said, and looked at the horse, which appeared to be resigned to his fate for the afternoon.

"Apollo! A splendid name," she said approvingly, and stroked the stallion's neck again. "Will . . . I would have never believed a horse as magnificent as this could be tamed."

He grinned proudly. "It's really not so hard to believe—horses are meant to be ridden. It is in their nature. One must merely coax it out of them."

"Ah," she said, petting Apollo's neck. "If horses were meant to be ridden . . . then perhaps you might allow me?"

He gave her a dubious look.

"Please," she said with a purely feminine smile.

She looked so earnest that it was impossible for Will to object. Frankly, something deep inside him wondered if he could deny that beautiful face a bloody thing when pressed. He certainly couldn't find it within himself to deny her this, and he reluctantly let go the bridle.

With a cry of delight, Phoebe picked up the reins and put the heel of her boot in Apollo's side. The horse started, but then began to trot.

"A circle, Phoebe!" Will called out to her. "He's just been broken."

"Yes, of course," she called back to him.

She did ride expertly, he noted, moving in rhythm with Apollo's gait. Her hair glistened behind her like a silken banner as she led the horse to trot around the meadow in a circle.

The other horses, Will noted, had begun to move away, toward better grazing. As Phoebe came around, he extended his hand. "There you are. Let me help you down."

But Phoebe laughed and spurred Apollo a little harder into picking up his pace.

"All right, then," Will said, smiling, his arm still extended. "Come down now."

Phoebe clearly had no intention of it. Apollo began to canter in a circle.

"You have bested me," Will called up to her, bowing low. "But you really must come down now."

"This is marvelous!" she exclaimed. "I feel so free! I believe I could ride to London and back before he'd even as much as—"

She never completed her sentence, for Apollo grew weary of the game and suddenly bolted after his herd, startling Phoebe. She lost her balance, and with a shriek, she went tumbling off the side, heels over head, as Apollo raced to the edge of the meadow.

She landed flat on her back in a cloud of yellow and green muslin.

"Phoebe!" Will cried, racing to her side.

Wide-eyed, she blinked up at the clear blue sky. There was an ugly gash across her leg where she must have caught the cinch.

"Dear God," Will said, as he gingerly ran his hands over her arms and legs, looking for any breaks. "Are you hurt? Speak to me!"

She didn't answer; she just gaped at the sky, her mouth open.

He realized the breath had been knocked clean from her lungs, and he instantly bent over her, pressed his mouth to hers, and breathed into her.

A moment later, Phoebe drew a hard, rasping breath.

"Are you hurt? Does anything feel broken?" he pressed her.

"Nothing," she said hoarsely, "but my awful pride." She pushed herself up. "What *happened*?"

He put his arm around her back and helped her to her feet. "He's not entirely tamed," he said. "It is my fault—I should never have allowed it."

"Don't be silly. It was *my* fault. I would not come down when you said. Oh dear," she said, hissing in pain as she raised her right foot from the ground. "I think I have sprained my ankle."

"It must have been caught in the stirrup," Will opined, and realized how lucky they were she hadn't been dragged, or caught under Apollo's hooves.

"I do not think I can put my weight on it," she said, gripping his arm.

He quickly swept her up into his arms and carried her across the meadow, to the old ruins and a wall covered in moss. He removed his coat and laid it down for her to sit on.

"I am so very sorry," Phoebe said as she put her hands to her ankle, wincing. "How foolish of me."

"Allow me," Will said, removing her boot and feeling her ankle. "May I move it?" At her nod, he moved it one direction. She did not flinch. When he moved it again, she moaned in pain.

"Never fear, madam. I am quite prepared in all manner of aid." He rose to his feet, uncoiled his neckcloth. "Stay exactly where you are, and whatever you do—no riding."

She gave him a petulant smile.

Will strode across the meadow to the stream. He dipped his neckcloth into it—it was ice cold, exactly as he'd hoped—and then returned to Phoebe. He squatted down, put her bare foot on his thigh, and cleaned the cut. When he'd finished, he took a knife from his boot, cut the neckcloth into pieces, and carefully wrapped the cloth around the cut, and then her ankle, inwardly wincing each time she exclaimed in pain.

"But it's so cold!" she complained when he'd finished.

"The cold will reduce the swelling," he said. "Now, then, you must remain where you are while I fetch my saddle. I will return as soon as I can."

She nodded, examining her ankle.

He leaned over and kissed the top of her head, and carried on with the strength of her smile to propel him.

Twenty-four

While Phoebe waited for Will to return, she worked herself into a panic and even attempted to repair her ankle by walking on it. She had to try something— the gash she could hide, but she couldn't return to the hall with a sprained ankle! How on earth would she explain it? What would everyone think?

Will and Fergus trotted up from the stream at last, the saddle hanging off Fergus's rump. Will paused in the middle of the meadow to retrieve the forgotten saddlebag.

Phoebe was holding onto the moss-covered wall as Will rode to her. A strong and hot afternoon breeze lifted her hair around her face, but provided little relief from the heat. Will reined Fergus to a halt, dismounted, put a hand on his hip, and looked at her ankle. "I know you pride yourself on being fearless, Phoebe . . . but I did not think you were foolish as well."

"I *must* walk on it," she said irritably. "How will I return to Wentworth Hall in such a state?"

"On horseback," he said calmly.

"Which will not invite any speculation whatsoever."

Will gave her sarcasm a wry smile. "I hardly care—I care only that you not harm yourself further by standing or walking."

"I beg your pardon, but *I* care very much what will be said at Wentworth Hall."

"Phoebe," he said, and smiled so warmly that Phoebe felt her heart break a little, "you have nothing to fear, sweetheart. I would be less than a gentleman if I allowed one untoward thing to be said of you."

"How do you propose to stop it?" she asked, alarmed by her sudden and passionate anger. "Even *you* cannot stop tongues from wagging!"

Will touched her face with the tips of his fingers and looked deeply into her eyes. "I have not forced you here against your will," he said calmly. "I believe we had an understanding . . . did we not?"

"Yes, but . . ." She glanced at her foot, suddenly confused. "But I did not expect to . . . to . . ." *To what?* she shouted in her mind. *To feel so deeply?* "To injure my ankle," she said weakly.

He sighed. His fingers drifted to her neck. "All right, I will admit that this does present us with something of a problem."

"It very much does," Phoebe said flatly.

He squatted down on his haunches to examine her foot. "Perhaps we can ease your pain. I know an old Indian cure," he said thoughtfully as he touched her toes.

"I do not think a shiny rock will heal my ankle," she said petulantly.

He cocked a brow. "You must believe, Phoebe, for the cure involves a bit of Hindu mysticism," he said, and took her hand in his, turning it palm up. With his finger, he traced a line from the edge of her index finger to the bottom of her palm, then lifted her hand and kissed it.

That tiny, tender little kiss sent a thrill through her. He lowered her hand; she stared at it. "Is that the cure?"

He shook his head, and still holding her hand, he stepped closer, so that he could reach around her. He traced a long, slow line down her spine, sending a most remarkable shiver that spread little fingers of a tingling sensation to her limbs. "Do you feel your ankle?"

Phoebe shook her head.

He moved her hair over her shoulder, exposing her neck. "Tell me what you feel." He bent his head and kissed her neck, his breath hot, his lips warm on her skin.

She felt . . . a torrential downpour of desire. She felt weak, washed away by it. He lifted his head. "How is your ankle now?"

"Have I an ankle?" she whispered.

He chuckled softly, cupped her face, and kissed her on the lips, detonating something deep inside Phoebe that pushed her into a pool of desire and uncertainty. She needed to feel the comfort of his arms again. She could not fathom his hold on her when no other man had come so close to making her lose herself so completely. She actually felt like another woman, desperate for his touch and his attention and desperate to return it.

Her ankle was truly forgotten—she knew nothing but his fierce embrace, his urgent kiss. He raked his hands through her hair and kissed her deeply. She grasped his wrist with one hand, his lapel with her other, anchoring herself to him.

He slipped one arm around her waist and picked her up, so that her feet were dangling above his, her body held firmly and effortlessly against his. He moved them up against the wall of the ruin, shifted from her mouth to her neck, then slid down her body, to her bodice, his fingers curling into her flesh.

He moved feverishly against her, stroking every curve of her body, seeking every patch of exposed flesh. Phoebe closed her eyes and tossed her head back. Her body was thrumming; every bit of flesh his lips touched flared with heat. She felt hot; she needed to feel his flesh, too, and grappled with the buttons of his waistcoat before pushing the fabric aside. She could feel his hard, lean body through the lawn fabric of his shirt, and pulled the shirt from the waist of his trousers.

He suddenly stepped back, shrugged out of the waistcoat, and hastily pulled the shirt over his head.

Phoebe managed to suppress a maidenly gasp at the sight of his naked torso, but he was heart-achingly beautiful. He looked like the Greek sculptures that graced the terrace at Middleton House in London. She had never seen a man's naked chest so very close, and she could not help but touch it in wonder. Her fingers fluttered over the slight indentation between the muscles that ran from his sternum and disappeared into the top of his trousers. She grazed his hardened nipples, ran her hand over the thick expanse of his shoulder.

Will's breathing was shallow, his jaw clenched as if he strained to keep himself still as she touched him. But when she touched his chin, he grabbed her hand, kissed her palm, and said roughly, "I cannot bear to be near you. When I see you in your rooms, or in the dining room with Farley and the others, or walking near the gazebo, I cannot . . . I *cannot* bear to be set away from you. Nor can I be near you and not touch you."

His eyes were blazing with a man's fever, his jaw taut. "I cannot bear it," he said again through clenched teeth, and suddenly grabbed her up in his arms and sank to his knees with her, pulling her down onto the coat, which he'd tossed on the soft, moss-covered ground.

He could not have aroused her more. Phoebe's hands were everywhere then, running over his body, feeling every sinewy inch of him, caressing him, gliding over him, stroking the soft down of hair from his chest to his groin.

Will caught a breath in his throat when her tongue flicked across his nipple as her hands fumbled clumsily with his trousers to free his erection. They were engaged in a sensual melee, and it made Will impossibly mad with desire. He frantically sought the fastenings of her gown and released two succulent breasts from the confines of the fabric. He caressed them, took them in his mouth, sucking the hardened peaks with his tongue.

Phoebe's hand surrounded his erection, moving so lightly, almost too lightly—it was driving him mad. The conflagration in him was beginning to roar out of control. She covered the top of his head with kisses, kneaded his shoulder. When he lifted his face to kiss her, she smiled with pleasure and kissed his face, pressed her lips to his eyes, to his nose, to his lips, and trailed a river of simmering kisses to his chest. And down again, *Lord God*, down his torso, her lips, soft and moist, searing him with each touch.

Every fiber of his body burned. He'd been without a woman too long; it seemed almost as if he'd never felt a woman in his life. It startled him, aroused him, and frightened him on a very deep level.

When her lips touched the head of his shaft, Will lurched violently. She shied away when he did, but he put his hand on her mass of blond curls and gently led her to return.

She bent over him and traced her tongue along the length of him, her touch excruciatingly sensual, incredibly carnal, and Will gasped as he tried to keep from writhing and bucking beneath her. But it was no use; his self-control was hanging by a thread. This woman, this widow, was pushing him beyond the limits of yearning.

Her lips surrounded him once more, but it was unbearable. As fantastically pleasurable as it was, he needed to be inside her. He groped blindly for her, lifting her and yanking her up to him like a rag doll, then encircling her tightly in his arms. Her lips landed softly on his as he twisted about to put her on her back.

He moved over her, pushing her skirts up until they were hiked above her hips, then slipped his hand between her legs, into the opening of her undergarment. She was hot and slick, and her moan against his mouth came close to undoing him completely. His fingers slipped inside her heat; his thumb stroked her mindlessly until she made a little cry and shifted against him.

He could endure it not a moment longer. He caught the waist of her undergarment and yanked it down. As he covered her mouth with his, he moved between her thighs, nudging them farther apart with his knee.

"You have put me at the end of my endurance. I *need* you," he said roughly, and slid into her on a swell of raging desire.

She was so *tight*—almost impossibly so, and she let out a small yelp. Will froze, paralyzed with confusion, and looked down at her.

Phoebe's eyes were closed, her brow creased with pain.

"Dear God," he muttered. He tried to withdraw, but her clarion blue eyes fluttered open, and she lifted up to him and kissed him, then threaded her fingers through his hair and pressed her head to his. "*Stay,*" she whispered. "Make love to me. I'm fine."

Will could not fathom what had happened, but his body was seething with the need to be in her. He began to move—slowly and reluctantly, afraid of hurting her—but Phoebe kissed him, drawing him back into the pool of desire and submerging him completely in it with her body and her tender response.

He buried his face in her hair as her body drew him in. He moved deeply inside her, his heart growing with each stroke, with the primal claiming of her. With every stroke he came closer to claiming her completely and reached between them to stroke her, intent on bringing her with him. She whimpered with pleasure at his touch, tightened hard around him, and softly cried out, biting into his shoulder as she shuddered and contracted around him.

Her climax drew his more powerful one—with a strangled sob of ecstasy, he released into her. He gasped for air, unable to catch his breath, in awe of what had happened between them, and confusingly, as moved by it as he was horrified.

Somberly, he gathered Phoebe in his arms and rolled to his side. She nuzzled her face into his neck. They were covered with a sheen of perspiration, and they lay there until the heat had ebbed from their skin.

Still, Will did not let her go. He tried to make sense of it all, to understand how it was that he, a man of certain experience, had never felt as intensely alive as he did. He'd never experienced such deeply heartfelt yet foreign emotions.

The sensation, he quietly realized, was not unlike breathing underwater.

Phoebe sat up, used the bottom of her chemise to quickly clean herself. He silently watched her, noting her lips, red and swollen from their lovemaking, her cheeks flushed with the exertion of it.

And her eyes, filled with disquiet.

He could scarcely look at her without wanting to kiss her or to hold her, yet it alarmed him to be so wholly consumed as this. He had no notion of what would come of it, if the feelings would hold or fade away over the course of the night.

The jingle of Fergus's bridle brought him back to reality, and Will realized the hour was growing late. He stroked Phoebe's hair. "We must go."

She nodded.

Dozens of questions coursed through his brain as he stood up and donned his shirt. Phoebe was looking at him, her expression a little disconcerted. "How is your ankle?"

"I . . . I don't know."

"Let's give it a go." Will helped Phoebe up, helped her to put her gown in order. She put a little weight on her ankle, found it more bearable than she had even an hour ago. "I think I can walk."

Will nodded and stepped away. "I'll just fetch Fergus," he said, and took one step toward the horse. But he froze, staring at the horse for a long moment before wheeling around. "Are you all right?" he asked.

She looked confused. "It's better—"

"Not your ankle," he said, and watched the color begin to fade from her face.

Phoebe bit her lower lip. "I'm fine."

"Yes, but you seemed . . ." He couldn't bring himself to ask. He didn't know what *to* ask.

"Will . . ." Her voice was so soft, he could scarcely hear her. "It's been . . . it's been a very long time since . . . since . . ."

"Ah," he said, and lifted a hand to stop her from saying more. He walked back to where she stood, embraced her, cupped the back of her head and held her against his shoulder. He wanted to ask how long it had been since she'd lain with a man, if she'd loved her husband, if her marital lovemaking was as powerful as what they'd just shared. But he felt her sigh, and realized that regardless of her past, something extraordinary had happened between them. "Come, then," he said gently. "We must return to the hall before it grows too late."

He kissed the top of her head, and with his arm around her shoulders, he helped her to walk to Fergus.

Addison happened to be standing in the foyer speaking with Farley when his lordship and Madame Dupree arrived on horseback, her in front of him, her hair undone and falling wildly about her shoulders in a way that made Addison swallow hard, and Lord Summerfield holding her in a firm and familiar grip.

Addison glanced at Farley, whose face darkened as he, too, spied them. "Well, well," the butler muttered, and turned to a footman who happened to be passing through. "Billy, a hand for his lordship," he said.

Billy instantly glanced at the drive. His young eyes widened with surprise, but then narrowed with an innate understanding. "By the *saints*."

"Billy!" Farley snapped.

"Aye, sir," Billy said, and moved swiftly out the door and into the drive.

"Billy!" Addison heard his lordship call. "You've come just in time, sir. Madame Dupree has suffered an accident."

" 'Twas no accident, I'll grant you that," Farley murmured as he, too, went out.

Addison sighed as he watched Billy help the seamstress down. He rather liked Madame Dupree, and hated to see her harmed in any way.

Of course she would be harmed—they always were. The moment his lordship offered for Miss Fitzherbert—which of course he would do, as it was his duty—poor Madame Dupree would be harmed.

Twenty-five

It should have been something marvelous, a moment to remember always—but it had filled Phoebe with as much heartache as it had wonder.

God help her, she'd never meant it to go so far, never meant to lose herself to him so completely. But she'd been entirely seduced by the magic of the moment, by the feelings of lust and . . . and *love*—it was love, wasn't it?—that had filled her as she lay on his coat in that old ruin. She'd been powerless—unwilling, really—to stop him from giving her the most sublime pleasure she'd ever known.

She hated the fact that she'd deceived him so utterly. She had tried to think, had debated telling him the truth then and there, but he had so readily accepted her fragile explanation, and she was incapable of finding the courage to correct him. And now, she was torn between her respect for herself, which was miserably low, and what she was certain was love for him.

How had she *ever* believed she could assume the identity of someone she was not? If Ava and Greer were here, they would lambaste her for her foolishness and her silly fantasies. She remembered the day she'd left London on this ridiculous and badly conceived trip, and what Ava had said to her then: "*You mustn't be too dreamy, Phoebe. You know how bird-witted you can be with your head in the clouds.*"

What she wouldn't give to see her sister's face now! How she longed to feel her arms around her, to be able to tell her what a horrible, wretched, wonderful thing she had done!

She scarcely slept at all—her violently perplexed, disconcerted thoughts kept her awake. Phoebe hugged her pillow tightly to her and kept her face buried in it, hoping for some sort of divine clarity, something that would show her the right path.

The clock on the mantel had just struck two when she heard the creak of floorboard. She came up with a gasp and start, her eyes focusing on the dark figure at the foot of her bed. *Will.* She knew without asking—she could sense him, could feel his strength and energy in a way she would not have believed possible before today.

He moved around to the side of her bed and sat on the edge. He didn't speak, but entwined his fingers in hers. In the eerie light of the moon, she could see his handsome face, could see the troubled look in his eyes. "If I had known," he spoke hoarsely, "had I understood, I should have done it all differently."

Phoebe instinctively, impulsively pressed her fingers to his lips to keep him from saying more.

But Will pulled them away and drew her to him, as if he'd done it one hundred times before. "Had I understood, Phoebe, I would have loved you carefully," he whispered, and kissed her temple. "Like this," he said, and moved to kiss her other temple. "And this," he murmured as he kissed the bridge of her nose. "And this . . ." He pressed his lips to hers, kissing her tenderly as his hand slipped to her breast, and he quietly pushed her back, into her bed.

He made love to her with great deliberation this time, taking the time to touch every part of her with his hands and mouth, his manner as gentle as a summer rain. Where he stroked her, her skin tingled. Where he tasted her flesh, she felt heat rising up and pushing through her skin. And when he moved between her legs, stroking and tasting there, too, she felt herself being lifted to another plane, floating away from earth, unbound from all her chains.

His tongue and lips were everywhere, on her body, even inside her. A white-hot heat began to build in her belly as he laved her, pulsing toward a violent finish as his tongue flicked in and out of her before taking the most sensitive part of her in his mouth. He buried his face in the valley, drawing from her the intense pressure reverberating in her body. When she thought she could not bear it another moment, he rose up and carefully entered her, moving tenderly inside her as he kissed her. Smoothly, gently, he provoked her with his rhythm, pausing when she was on the brink of losing herself, then starting the whole, extraordinary experience again, all the while touching her in the most intimate way imaginable.

When she finally whimpered for mercy, he took her to the pinnacle of fulfillment, whispering her name again and again as the pressure flowed out of her, groaning low when he found his own release.

Phoebe didn't remember when she drifted off to sleep, but when she awoke the next morning, he was gone, and Frieda was bustling about in the workroom.

For a moment she thought she had dreamt it. But the indentation of his head in the second pillow of her bed told her she hadn't dreamt it at all.

Yes, she thought as she rose and felt the soreness between her legs. *Yes, this was love.*

The following day flew—the entire house was in a frenzy as everyone worked on final preparations in advance of the houseguests. Rooms needed to be aired and dusted, linens ironed and laid out, floors swept and carpets cleaned.

There was a final fitting for the ball gowns, too, as well as a fitting for the morning gowns.

Phoebe realized, as she measured the arms of Jane's morning gown once more and Jane's complaints were drowned out by Phoebe's own private thoughts, that when she finished the morning gowns, her work here would be done.

She couldn't think of it. She *wouldn't* think of it.

Phoebe kept working, drawing from a surprisingly deep well of determination *not* to think. In those moments when she wasn't sewing, she was reviewing the performance of a proper curtsy with Alice and Jane, reminding them of the proper etiquette for tea, and in those moments she could, she stole away with Will.

They met in the gazebo after luncheon. Will brought her a bouquet of flowers taken from the gardens on his way through, and whispered a few words of esteem before continuing on to the stables and his horse so that he might attend a meeting in the village with his father's secretary. Phoebe saw him again before supper, when she contrived to go out for a bit of air, knowing full well he'd be wheeling his father out onto the lawn.

She saw him again after supper, when he assembled the entire staff and family to review the plans for the fortnight. Phoebe stood in the back, in the shadows, aware that her expression might reveal her true feelings for Lord Summerfield. But Will caught her eye and smiled in her direction on more than one occasion.

And that night, Will came to her again, slipping into her bed after the clock chimed two, and lifting her to sensual heights she had never imagined possible.

Yet the next morning, she awoke alone.

By the time Frieda appeared for work, Phoebe was dressed and standing at the open window, hoping for a glimpse of him. With an ebullient smile, she turned toward the door at the sound of Frieda entering—but her smile quickly faded when she saw that Frieda was crying.

"Frieda!" Phoebe exclaimed, hurrying through the debris in the room to Frieda's side. "What on earth has you so wrought?"

"It's been almost a week," Frieda said tearfully. "I can no longer deny what must be true—I am with child."

"Oh *no*," Phoebe whispered, and embraced her friend. She was at a loss as to what to say or do other than to hold Frieda while she cried and blathered about how she'd be dismissed and tossed out into the world with no one to turn to.

"I can't even turn to me own mother," she sobbed, pausing occasionally to blow her nose. "She'll not have me, not with my younger sisters still in the house. I've got no place to go."

"Summerfield won't toss you out," Phoebe said adamantly. "I don't believe it for a moment. He is a good man."

"Aye, but he will! He told us all when we was brought on that he'd not tolerate any tomfoolery or indecency under his roof."

"But what of Charles? Surely he will be held to the same standard. Surely he will do the right thing by you, Frieda."

"Aye, he should, shouldn't he? But he accused me of trickery and claims I could be carrying the babe of any number of men," she added solemnly as she wiped her eyes with the hem of her work apron. "He will not lose his position or risk a brat clinging to his boots. But I cannot hide, can I?" She looked at herself in the full-length mirror, and her bottom lip began to tremble. "No one will give me work with a belly the size of a melon and no husband to support it!"

"You mustn't think that way—"

"You don't understand at all!" Frieda snapped, and pushed away from Phoebe. "And why should you, really? You're as fair as any I've ever seen. Were it *you* Charles had put his seed into, he would have offered for you then and there."

Phoebe shuddered and refused to think of her own situation.

"Not me," Frieda continued. "I'm a doxy, a mere portal for his putrid flesh."

"*Frieda!*" Phoebe exclaimed. She tried very hard to think of an argument, but nothing came to mind. Frieda was right. Poor girls who became servants and had nothing to recommend them—not even good looks—had a much harder life than most.

For the first time since she'd begun this charade, Phoebe prayed her brothers-in-law would be successful in enacting reforms for women in Parliament.

Ashamed that she could think of nothing that would soothe Frieda, Phoebe asked timidly, "What do you intend to do?"

With a shrug and a rough wipe of her nose, Frieda said morosely, "Can't rightly say." And that was the last she would say. She took her seat at the table and said little else for the remainder of the day, her thoughts obviously in faraway places, her dark head bent over her work, her jaw tightly clenched.

They both worked through the afternoon, until they were startled by Jane and Alice's abrupt and loud arrival into the workroom, clad in day gowns Phoebe had made, their faces uncharacteristically bright with big smiles.

"They've come!" Jane exclaimed excitedly as she sailed to the open window and leaned out.

"Who has come?" Phoebe asked.

"The first guests to arrive—Lord and Lady Fremont and their sons," Alice said breathlessly as she joined Jane at the window. Both of them leaned forward so far that Phoebe could see the hems of their chemises. Alice turned around to Phoebe and gestured impatiently for her to join them. "Come, come!"

Phoebe smiled at their exuberance, remembering a time when she would have been just as excited by the prospect of houseguests, and joined them at the window.

She squeezed in beside Alice and Jane and leaned forward to look out. Below them, a sleek black traveling chaise pulled by four grays had arrived, boasting fluted gold finials at each corner and an embossed crest on the lacquered door of the coach. Three Summerfield footmen, dressed in formal livery, were helping a woman from the interior. Just behind the footmen, Will was flanked by Farley and another footman.

As Alice and Jane giggled about one of the Fremonts, Phoebe looked at Will. His darkly golden hair was combed and trimmed, his collar flawless and his neckcloth perfectly knotted and matching his brown and gold striped waistcoat. He greeted the woman warmly, bending low over her hand, graciously helping her up from her curtsy, and smiling so beautifully that Phoebe could feel her insides fluttering.

"Oh—there he is!" Jane whispered frantically, nudging Alice so hard that she bumped into Phoebe.

"Is that him?" Alice asked, frowning. "I thought he'd be . . . *bigger* somehow."

"Who is he?" Phoebe asked, looking at a young, spindly man who had come out after the woman. His coat dwarfed him, and his collar made his neck look even thinner than it was.

"Lord *Canham*," Jane said with a sigh of longing. "I grant you, he is young yet—but he will one day be the Earl of Fremont and inhabit a fabulously large estate and have fifty thousand a year."

"Aha," Phoebe said. "I see his attraction quite plainly now."

That elicited giggles from both of the young women.

Will bowed to the young Lord Canham, who returned it with an awkward bob of his head. But then Lord Canham happened to look up. The three women gasped at once and surged backward, out of sight.

"Good Lord, did he see us?" Jane asked frantically.

"*Look*, Phoebe," Alice hissed, pushing her forward.

Phoebe carefully leaned forward. Another young man—a boy, really—had come out of the coach, and they were all engaged in conversation. "No," she said, shaking her head. "I am certain they did not see us."

That prompted Alice and Jane to surge forward again.

"That's his younger brother, Master Paul," Jane said. "Pity that he's not a bit older, Alice—perhaps he might offer for you."

"Don't be silly," Alice said. But she was smiling.

The three of them watched until the full party—including Lord Fremont, the last to step out of the coach—had entered the house, then turned as one away from the window.

"I can scarcely *wait* to be properly introduced," Jane said gleefully, and stepped away from the window before sinking into a very deep and proper curtsy.

"Very good!" Phoebe praised her. "And when shall you be introduced?"

"Not until supper is announced," Alice said. "We're to remain quite out of sight until then like poor relations."

"I cannot *bear* such a long wait," Jane complained.

"You may not be able to bear it today, but come the end of a fortnight, you will be very glad to see them all gone, I assure you," Alice said with a snort as she picked up a reticule Phoebe had made. "May I have it?" she asked Phoebe.

"I will not!" Jane vowed as Phoebe nodded at Alice. Jane danced her way to the door. "I adore house parties, and particularly those that end in grand balls, and I will not be the least bit glad to see them gone."

"You will!" Alice argued as she followed Jane out, the reticule in her hand. "Mark me, you will!"

It wasn't until they'd quit the room that Phoebe realized Frieda was gone.

Twenty-six

A fortnight of guests, of hunting and games and dining and dancing until the early hours of the morning, had seemed like a grand idea weeks ago. Now the idea seemed unbearable to Will.

His idea to see his siblings properly introduced into society and to acquaint himself with all the eligible young misses in Bedfordshire could not possibly have come at a worse time. Will's mind was filled with Phoebe. He could think of scarcely anything else but seeing her again, but unfortunately, Lords Fremont and Daughtry and their respective broods had arrived, and he was now fully immersed in his role as host.

Not to mention that Lord Daughtry's daughter, Lady Candace, was quite keen to engage him in conversation.

They dined as three families that first night. But the night was hot, and the formal dining room was stifling. He suggested they take their evening entertainment on the terrace, a suggestion that seemed to come as a relief to almost all of them.

On the terrace, Will was pleased to see that Alice and Jane were behaving perfectly, and even Roger and

Joshua—engaged in a game of billiards just inside from the terrace—had managed to pass the evening without causing offense to anyone.

He was perfectly content to admire his siblings for once, but Lord Daughtry suggested Will show his daughter the parterres for which Wentworth Hall was renowned. The shrubbery was whimsical, cut and pruned in figure eights, curlicues, and various animal shapes.

But as Will led Lady Candace through the parterres in that time where day meets night and the day's last rosy gasp of light was cast across the earth, he saw Phoebe walking at the far end of the gardens. Her shawl had slipped from her shoulders and was draped loosely over her forearms. Her hair, a ghostly white in the waning light, was gathered carelessly and held in place with one long pin. Wisps of long curls had worked themselves free and fell down her back. She carried her sketchbook and moved purposefully forward.

As Lady Candace talked about her family's trip from the village of Keysoe, Will watched Phoebe move deeper into the shadows. When Lady Candace mentioned the lack of rain the last weeks, a pair of footmen moved into the gardens and began to light the rush torches. Phoebe appeared in the midst of them, walking up from the end of the gardens, and paused to speak to both of them, her smile brilliant. He noticed the way both men looked at her, and felt his blood rush hot in his veins. Of course they would look at her as they did—she was a beautiful woman, and they were men. He had no right to feelings of jealousy.

"Have you been to London recently, my lord?" Lady Candace asked, forcing his attention away from Phoebe.

"No," he said with a smile, and offered his arm, ready

to deposit Lady Candace with her family. "Have you?"

"For the Season, of course."

"Of course."

"I should like to return for the Little Season. It will be upon us soon."

"Indeed it shall," he said, and began to lead her back to the group. He glanced over his shoulder—the footmen were at work lighting the torches, but Phoebe had disappeared.

The next day dawned hot and dry. The dust of a dozen or more carriages seemed to choke the air from the sky as the rest of the guests arrived. Most seemed oblivious to the stifling heat, however, and swarmed around the hall and the grounds.

And again today, Will's siblings were on their best behavior. He wondered—hoped—that they'd turned some sort of invisible corner, that they had, after four months under his watch, become good, upstanding citizens worthy of their august name.

He was so pleased, in fact, that he made a special trip to see his father that afternoon, speaking in glowing terms of their accomplishments in the midst of so many guests.

There was only one thing that marred an otherwise perfect day for him—Farley told him that Frieda, the young woman who had helped Phoebe create such beautiful clothing for his sisters, had run away.

"Run away?" he asked, confused. He rather thought that the terms of employment he offered were very generous.

"It would seem she has found herself in a delicate situation, my lord," Farley said.

At Will's look of confusion, he leaned in and whispered, "*With child.*"

"Who?" Will asked instantly.

"We cannot say for certain, my lord. It would seem that Frieda was rather free with her charms."

"Are you certain? There is no man to be held responsible?"

"Not that I can determine, my lord."

"Then good riddance," Will said gruffly. He wondered where Frieda might have gone—and assumed she'd gone to her family. It was just as well, for he would have been forced to dismiss her. He could not have her working under his roof—society could be very hard about such matters.

There was only a tiny recognition in the back of his mind that Frieda's situation was rather uncomfortably close to Phoebe's.

Phoebe learned of Frieda's disappearance from Mrs. Turner. "Carrying a bairn, she is," Mrs. Turner said, her disgust evident. "I warned her to mind herself, but she paid me no heed."

"Where could she have gone?" Phoebe asked, horrified to think of a distraught Frieda out there in the world with nowhere to go.

"Who can say? Out of Bedfordshire and to London if she knows what's best. At least there she might find herself a position before her condition is obvious." With a cluck of her tongue, Mrs. Turner shook her head. "Serves her right, it does, for being so careless with her virtue."

Phoebe's belly did a queer flip; she looked at the tiny scrolls she was embroidering on the bodice of a morning gown that matched the scrolls carved into the shrubbery in the gardens. She wondered if Mrs. Turner suspected anything about her own wretched behavior. She couldn't help herself—she stole a glimpse at the housekeeper.

If Mrs. Turner suspected anything, she did not show it. She was examining a pair of day gowns that hung from hooks on the wall. "Such lovely work," Mrs. Turner said admiringly. "I hope you'll be able to finish without Frieda."

"Yes," Phoebe said. "We were almost finished."

"Well, then!" Mrs. Turner said, and moved toward the door. "I've quite a lot to do, what with all the guests."

"I will miss Frieda," Phoebe blurted. "She has been my friend."

Mrs. Turner paused and looked at Phoebe, her mouth set in an unforgiving line. "Then I am glad she is gone, Madame Dupree. It would not do to have a respectable missus like you lie about with pigs." With that, she walked out.

Phoebe sank onto her seat, her heart pounding. *Frieda. Dear, poor Frieda.* It infuriated her that the man who had put the child in her belly would not be made to suffer as much as Frieda. Phoebe truly appreciated what her brothers-in-law were trying to accomplish, how important their success was for women like Frieda, who had made the mistake of falling in love with a rogue. Of course Phoebe had known of other women who had fallen, too—but all of them had the protection and resources of a powerful name behind them. Their mistake was hidden from the world, and they certainly weren't made to seek refuge in some awful employment.

Frieda, however, would never be able to hide.

Without the distractions of Jane and Alice, and in spite of her worry about Frieda, Phoebe completed Alice's morning gown that day. She worked well into the evening, until her fingers were aching.

She paused in her work to open all the windows—

the late afternoon had made the room stifling. As she opened them, she guessed all the windows in the house were open, for she could hear laughter filtering up through the chimney and the windows open below her. She was reminded of the first day she had come here, when she had heard nothing but arguing.

How gay this house sounded with laughter. How happy Will must be at this moment.

Will. She missed him terribly. If she were in London, if she'd met Lord Summerfield there, she would be seated across from him at some supper party. Everything would have been so very different—he might have actually courted her, and she . . .

Phoebe suddenly tossed aside her work apron. "It is far too hot," she muttered to herself, and tossed her napkin aside. As everyone would be engaged in supper, perhaps it was a good time to take some air. She'd walk on the east side of the house, near the stables, so as not to disturb anyone.

When she'd made her way out of the house and onto the drive, Phoebe paused to toss her head back, close her eyes, and breathe deeply. Even in the heat, the air here was so much fresher than that in London—it enlivened her.

Phoebe continued on, her arms swinging. She was walking so quickly up the path to the stables that she scarcely heard the girlish laughter at first. She paused and cocked her head—there it was again. Phoebe turned toward the shrubbery that lined the path to the stables, trying to determine precisely where the voice was coming from. When she heard it again, she also heard the low voice of a man.

Clearly, the antics of the country house party had begun already, and most of the guests had only arrived today. She intended to creep quietly away, to go back the way she had come and try a different path—but then she recognized the woman's voice.

"You must go now," Alice said in a husky voice. "My brother cannot possibly dine forever."

"He's got enough to keep him occupied for a time," the young man said. "Come on, then, Alice . . . come with me. I know a place on Tanner's Hill."

"No," she said pertly. Her refusal was followed by silence—and then the rustling sound of shrubbery being pushed aside.

Stunned, Phoebe twisted about, frantically looking for a place to hide. She ducked behind the shrubbery just as Alice and Mr. Hughes emerged from the other side. They were whispering together, and from where Phoebe hid, she could see the shine in Alice's smile. The two lovers paused once to embrace; Mr. Hughes kissed her passionately until Alice bent away from him with a laugh. Then, with hands clasped, they hurried in the direction of the stables.

Stunned, Phoebe stood rooted to her spot, her breath coming in rapid gasps of surprise and alarm. Alice had sworn she no longer saw him. Alice was deceiving them all.

The irony was clear—Phoebe could hardly fault Alice when she was in the throes of deceit, too. Her whole existence was a lie!

She stumbled from behind the shrubs and turned back, moving in the opposite direction of Alice. Her thoughts were raging—everything she thought she understood about herself was suddenly suspect. She was so lost in thought that she took a familiar path without thinking, and ended up in the parterres. It was of little consequence—she could still go in the servants' entrance and avoid the guests.

As she walked through the parterres, she saw two footmen ahead of her, lighting the rush torches that would illuminate the gardens. They hadn't seen her yet, she realized as she neared them, and one of them laughingly made a rather crude remark about a haystack and a pair of stockings. They were speaking of Frieda, Phoebe knew.

The other footman laughed low at the crude joke and glanced at the house. "Truth is, I'd have had her, if I'd wanted."

"What?" the other scoffed. "And you didn't want to have her, is that it?"

The second footman made a remark Phoebe did not quite hear, but that had both of them snickering.

"I beg your pardon," Phoebe said coolly, startling both men.

"Madame Dupree," said the second footman, whom she recognized as Edward. "We did not see you standing there."

The first footman, Beck, looked especially chagrined. "You ought not to have heard us," he said sheepishly.

"But I did. And I wonder if either of you have thought about a young woman who is now lost in this world while her friend continues his employment unscathed?" she demanded, surprised by her anger.

"Come now," Edward scoffed. "He might have shot the fateful bullet, aye, but Frieda should not have lifted her skirts, eh?"

Phoebe's face flamed. "Nevertheless, it is hardly fair. There were *two* people involved in the tragedy, not just Frieda."

Edward snorted. "Why would a proper missus defend her?" he asked, his tone challenging. "Perhaps the rumors are true then, eh, Beck? Perhaps Frieda is not the only one who's lifting her skirts."

Phoebe gasped with shock. Edward laughed at her reaction, but Beck seemed as startled as she. Phoebe gathered up her skirts and marched away, cringing at Edward's laughter, which floated after her.

Mortified, she ran up the steps to the terrace, turning the corner in the staircase just below the terrace, where she inadvertently almost collided with one of the guests.

It was then she noticed all the guests were assembled on the terrace, and Will, *her* Will, was standing by the balustrade with Miss Fitzherbert's hand clinging possessively to his arm.

Twenty-seven

Lord Duckworth was a man who enjoyed his vices—cigars, whiskey, and women. It was common knowledge that his wife and pastor threatened him with hell frequently, but it did not deter Lord Duckworth in the least, and when he saw Phoebe, his eyes lit up like a man who had just found a diamond amid a cart full of coal.

Will watched him twirl around and catch Phoebe by the arm, clamping his beefy hand down on her. At almost the same moment, Caroline clamped her hand down on *his* arm.

"Ho, there, who have we here?" Duckworth asked gleefully as he peered at Phoebe, all the while chewing on the end of his cigar.

"I do beg your pardon," Phoebe said, politely removing her arm from his grasp. "I didn't realize anyone would be about—"

"Madame Dupree?" Will called down to her. "How good of you to join us." She looked up at him with an expression full of dismay. "Madam, are you all right?"

"Yes, of course," she said, mustering the thinnest of smiles. "I beg your pardon, my lord, I didn't realize . . . I . . . I thought you were all to supper," she stammered.

"It's much too hot to eat just yet. Thank goodness for it, too, or we might not have found you," Duckworth said, and smiled at Phoebe's décolletage as he grabbed her hand and clasped it tightly. "Allow me to help you to the house."

"No, really, you mustn't trouble yourself—"

"I *insist*," he said, looking at her mouth. He even withdrew the sodden cigar from his mouth and carelessly tossed it into the pot of a plant before turning a tobacco-stained grin to Will. "Who are you hiding from us, Summerfield?" he called up. "I don't recall being introduced to this exceedingly lovely young woman."

"Of course you've not been introduced, my lord, as you are not in need of a gown," Caroline said silkily.

Will had almost forgotten she was standing beside him.

"The lady's hand you hold so dear belongs to a seamstress," she added.

"Ah, the *seamstress*," Duckworth said as if that pleased him. He smiled broadly at Phoebe's bosom. "What a treasure you are—"

"For God's sake, Duckworth, if you are going to bring her up, kindly do so," Will said sternly.

"Oh no, I really should not," Phoebe tried.

"You heard our host," Duckworth said cheerfully, and proceeded to lead a reluctant Phoebe up the stairs.

She gave Will a doleful look when they reached the terrace—he had the impression she would rather be anywhere but here at the moment.

"Come now, Summerfield, why have you been hiding your seamstress?" Duckworth asked jovially. "Had I known you had one under your roof, I would certainly have sought clothing for Lady Duckworth."

"Allow me to make a proper introduction," Will said coolly, looking pointedly at his hand on Phoebe's. "Madame Dupree, may I present Lord Duckworth?"

"How do you do."

Duckworth's arm fell away from Phoebe, but he could hardly tear his eyes from her. Of course he couldn't—she was a beautiful woman, and uncommonly so in the evening light.

"And from where do you hail, Madame Dupree?" Duckworth asked, clasping his hands behind his back. "I should like to commission a new wardrobe for my wife."

"Unfortunately," Will cut in, "Madame is rather exclusively engaged at the moment."

"Oh?" Duckworth asked, his disappointment evident.

"Indeed, my lord. When I have finished here, I am committed to an engagement elsewhere." She did not look at Will, did not see how her words sliced across him.

"London, you've said, no?" Caroline asked coolly.

"Yes. London," Phoebe confirmed with a glance at Caroline.

Will hardly wanted to be reminded. "Madame Dupree, we do not mean to keep you."

"Thank you," she said quickly. "I will leave you to your guests." She backed away, curtsying politely.

But Duckworth would have none of it. "Nonsense, Madame Dupree," he instantly interjected. "You *must* join us." He shifted his gaze to Will. "She is the perfect companion to Miss Dumbarton, our governess. She would delight in Madame Dupree's company, I am certain of it."

Phoebe seemed frantic to be gone. "My lord, I can*not* impose."

"It is no imposition," Will assured her.

"Yes, do, please, Madame Dupree. Your presence would make Lord Duckworth and Miss Dumbarton incandescently happy," Caroline said wryly.

Duckworth alone laughed at that.

"Where is Miss Dumbarton?" Caroline asked Duckworth. "Perhaps we might introduce them straightaway."

"In the green salon," Duckworth said.

Phoebe's eyes went wide. "My lord, I *should* not—"

"Nonsense," Will said, and gestured toward the door. "Duckworth is quite right. Miss Dumbarton will enjoy your company, as shall we all," he said briskly, and dropped his arm from beneath Caroline's hand. "Duckworth, you'll look after Miss Fitzherbert, won't you, while I make the introductions?"

"I'd be delighted," Duckworth said, but Will could see from Caroline's expression that she was less than pleased to have been put in his charge.

He would smooth it over later. At the moment, he cupped Phoebe's elbow firmly and led her inside.

They moved into an empty corridor. "Have a care you don't slip and turn your ankle in your haste to return to your rooms," Will said low.

"What do you think you are doing, may I ask?" Phoebe whispered hotly. "I cannot *join* you!"

"Why not?"

"Why *not*?" she repeated, stopping midstride to face him and almost levitating with ire. "*Why not?* It is highly improper! There will be more than one who speculates as to *why* I am included, and given the events of this day, I think they will draw the most wretched conclusions if they haven't already!"

"Why should anyone imagine this is anything other than it is? It is not as if you will join me at the dining table—you will join Miss Dumbarton. Asking you to keep a governess company hardly seems sinister to me," he said, just as hotly. "Are you so jaded?" he asked, and grabbed her by the elbow again, steering her forward.

"Yes! *Yes!* I am so jaded! Recent events at Wentworth Hall have made me so!" she cried, and looked at him as if she didn't know him. "Frieda is *gone,* sir! She has run away because of her shame and everyone is speaking of it! What do you suppose all your guests might think if your *seamstress* is suddenly granted a position in your salon—"

"They will think you are gentry, Phoebe," he said as he opened a door onto a small secretarial office. "They will think you are being a companion to a young woman in a similar position. They will think nothing ill, I assure you." He quickly ushered her inside, leaving the door open a crack for the little bit of light the wall sconces in the corridor afforded.

"What will Farley say? Or Mrs. Turner?" she continued, and began to pace as much as the tiny office would allow her. "They will suspect something, and they will compare me to Frieda—"

"I scarcely think anyone would ever compare you to Frieda."

"Oh, but they will," she said. "And I am hardly *dressed* for the evening," she said, looking down at her gown before taking two steps to her right, then two to her left. "I have *nothing* in common with these people, I don't care for society, and I . . . I . . ."

Will silenced her nerves by catching her and kissing her, hot, hard, and with all the longing he'd felt since he'd last held her.

At first, Phoebe pushed against him, but Will would not let go of her—he *could* not let go of her. The moment his lips touched hers, he was lost. A moment after that, Phoebe sagged against him, giving in. He pushed her against the wall, ran his hands down her body. "I have missed you," he whispered. "I have thought of little else but you."

"I don't know what has happened to me," she said weakly. "When we are apart, I think I never have you enough, but the moment we are together, I think I can scarcely bear it—"

He kissed her passionately again, his feelings for her as raw as they had ever been. "Join us tonight," he said low, and pressed his forehead to hers. "Give me that one small pleasure."

She sighed longingly as he moved down to kiss the swell of her breasts; she put her hands on his head and groaned with indecision. "All right," she whispered at last. "All right."

Will kissed her breast once more, rose up, and kissed her mouth. He caressed her cheek with his hand, then stepped outside to ensure there was no one about. When he was certain there was not, he gestured for Phoebe to join him. Together they walked into the green salon, Phoebe's head down, Will's heart pounding.

Miss Dumbarton, who was as dark as Phoebe was fair, was very happy to make Phoebe's acquaintance. She was very personable, and when Will left them alone, she fairly collapsed on the settee. "You cannot imagine how unruly the Duckworth children are!" she said cheerfully.

Phoebe learned she had two small children in her charge, who were, at last, in bed. Miss Dumbarton—or Susan, as she insisted Phoebe call her—was in the salon, reading and waiting until the formal supper had been served before joining the other guests. She drew Phoebe into a gay conversation, and Phoebe quickly realized she liked Susan Dumbarton from Manchester very much—she was the youngest daughter of a solicitor who yearned to live in London.

When Farley came for them later and asked them to join the others, Susan linked her arm in Phoebe's, and together they faced the crowd of Quality.

Yet surprisingly, Phoebe did not see the looks of disdain she expected, the envious looks from women and the leering looks from men. With the exception of Duckworth and Miss Fitzherbert, the people she met that evening were delightful.

The evening was very gay. There was none of the artifice one would find at a similar gathering in Mayfair, no maneuvering to see and be seen by the most important peers in the room. There were no whispered asides, no smirks over the tops of wineglasses. These people genuinely seemed to enjoy one another's company—and they didn't seem to care a whit about who was who in the pecking order.

Even the younger Darbys seemed quite at ease. Alice—in spite of her assignation—was charmingly polite, even when she discovered Phoebe's presence. Jane was her usual giddy self, but with a degree of restraint, which Phoebe believed was due to two handsome young gentlemen seated on either side of her. Joshua had engaged Miss Fitzherbert in conversation at the end of the room, and Roger led a boisterous round of whist.

Susan was quite funny, Phoebe discovered. She remarked that Lord Duckworth was aptly named, given his mouth's unfortunate resemblance to a duck's bill. And she complained that she was a wretched dancer, with the feet of a bovine. Phoebe laughed openly. Had she been in London, she would have been quite reserved, taking care not to speak to any one gentleman overlong, taking even more care to speak to their female companions.

She also noticed that Will's attention was in great demand. But he looked quite at ease and was solicitous of his family. Just looking at them here, one would never suspect the troubles that plagued the Darby family. Will was, Phoebe understood, a revered member of the community. He had established himself as a lord in this county, and in spite of the problems his family had suffered, he was respected.

More than one young lady who hoped to someday inhabit Wentworth Hall as its mistress looked at Will with bright eyes, blushing when he smiled at them, tittering when he spoke. And Will . . . Will beamed at them all.

But his gaze would inevitably fall on Phoebe, and a look would pass between them, and Phoebe's heart soared. More than once she joined the ranks of the hopeful young misses in this room and imagined herself on his arm, imagined the two of them hosting this lovely summer evening.

"What on earth are you thinking?" Susan asked, nudging her.

Phoebe smiled. "How good my bed shall feel this night. The hour is late and I have much work to do. I'd best retire."

Susan's chagrin was obvious. "You will come tomorrow, won't you?" she insisted, and leaned in to whisper, "I must have someone to whisper to as we watch the parade of eligible debutantes march past Lord Summerfield."

Phoebe laughed.

"You think I am jesting," she said, nudging Phoebe again. "I assure you that I am not. Summerfield told Lady Duckworth that he will make his offer before the fortnight is through—although one cannot imagine how he might *choose*. There are so many of them, are there not?"

Phoebe's smile faded. "Surely he cannot determine who he might spend the rest of his life with in one fortnight," she said, forcing a small laugh.

"Oh, but surely he can," Susan said with a snort. "It hardly takes a fortnight to add one fortune to the other and derive the sum." She laughed at her own jest. "You will come again tomorrow, won't you?"

"If I am permitted."

"Of course!" Susan exclaimed happily. "I will see to it!" Phoebe could not possibly imagine how she might, but Susan winked at her nonetheless.

Phoebe laughed. "On the morrow, then, if you are so bold."

"I certainly am," Susan said. "Good night."

"Good night," Phoebe said, and walked from the room, catching Will's eye as she went. Something flowed between them, something feverish.

Caroline watched Madame Dupree glide out of the room, watched her turn and catch Summerfield's eye. She did not miss how they looked at each other. She did not misunderstand it.

A million thoughts began to swim in her mind. She told herself she should not be alarmed—she should not infer more from that look than there could possibly be. He was lord of this estate, if not in name, in deed. He was well respected in the county, something that seemed rather miraculous given the reputation his awful siblings had managed to create for themselves in his absence.

He was determined to marry. Everyone knew it. Everyone was talking about it.

And Madame Dupree, like every other woman presently at Wentworth Hall, had fallen in love with the dashing Lord Summerfield. But what disturbed Caroline was that Summerfield had returned that look—or had she imagined it?

She turned away from the door, deep in thought. But when she lifted her eyes, they landed squarely on Mr. Joshua Darby. He arched a brow and smiled knowingly.

Caroline instantly turned away, but it was too late. The smile had given her a shiver.

Twenty-eight

———∞———

When the first week of the fortnight-long house party drew to a close, Will told his father it had been a grand success. "My brothers and sisters have been on their best behavior," he said as he stood at the window of his father's suite, looking out over the green where a game of lawn bowling was in progress. "I've been amazed, frankly."

He cast a smile over his shoulder at his father. "Joshua has been attentive to the females, of course. Alice is shier than I expected and often does not join us in the evenings. Roger and Jane," he said, watching Jane bowl on the lawn, "have been full of vigor and, I am pleased to report, surprisingly good manners." He laughed.

His father's eyes crinkled slightly in what Will knew was a smile. His father turned his head a bit and focused his eyes on Will.

"Aha," Will said with a nod. "You would know about your eldest son." He glanced at the group on the lawn again and sighed. "I have spent almost an entire week riding with all the eligible young women of Bedfordshire, I have escorted every one of them on a private walk in the parterres, I have even deigned to play croquet," he said with a wink. "I have dined, I have chatted, I have smiled and listened and . . ." And he was exhausted. He'd been inundated with the attentions of eight young women. It was all a bit too much for a man who, just a year ago, had been living in a Bedouin tent in the Egyptian desert.

He'd tried—he'd tried very hard to find the distinctive virtues in each of the young women. But all he could think of was Phoebe. He had watched her in this past week, had admired her grace and beauty, her ability to fit in so well among her superiors. He loved the sound of her laugh when she was in the cheerful company of Miss Dumbarton, the brightness of her smile, and the way she blushed when a gentleman would pay her a compliment.

"I have given them all my due consideration," he

continued thoughtfully. He recalled the one night his guests had retired early; he'd hied himself up to Phoebe's rooms in the middle of the night. In a room full of gowns and fabrics and dress forms, he'd touched her shoulder. She had awakened and squealed with delight, pulling him down onto her bed, and pouncing on him. He had shushed her—the windows were open—but he had quickly succumbed to her fervent greeting, the warmth of her body, the sweet smell of her skin.

The next morning, when he had crept into his suite of rooms, Addison had been within, laying out his clothing for the day. The tips of his ears had burned red. The awkwardness was nothing new for them, but that morning, Will had felt a wave of disapproval from his steadfast companion. He had felt reproof from a man who had never shown him anything but a happy, agreeable face. He knew why—Addison esteemed Phoebe. She was different from the others.

Will swallowed and glanced at his father. "It would seem," he said reluctantly, the words forming in his mind but his tongue loath to say them, "that Miss Caroline Fitzherbert is the most suited to me in personality and situation."

The skin around his father's eyes crinkled slightly. He lifted his index finger, indicating his pleasure with that choice.

"I suppose I shall offer at the end of the fortnight," Will said. But as the words he believed were expected of him fell from his lips, he felt a painful clench in his gut. He could not imagine how he might possibly offer for Caroline Fitzherbert's hand—not while his heart and mind were fixated on Phoebe.

After Will left his father to return to his guests, he walked the long corridor, debating his intentions, debating whether or not he should follow his true desire for Phoebe. He could not imagine how he might. There were certain expectations placed on his shoulders as the heir. He had a responsibility to the family's name and the continuing legacy.

But what of *his* happiness? Was he expected to subjugate it completely to the family's honor? Was that the price he must pay to keep his family's reputation impeccable and their situation in Bedfordshire and London immutable? He didn't know the answer to those questions, but he had realized something: He loved Phoebe. He loved her as he'd never loved before. He could not believe he would give that up so easily, not even for duty or family honor.

He had to think of something.

But for the moment, he had guests to attend to, and as he walked into the grand salon where they gathered every evening before supper, and made his way around the room, asking after their day, his eyes found Phoebe's, who, from across the room where she stood with Miss Dumbarton, smiled at him in that way she had of making his heart take wing.

The winged flight was short-lived, however, because Mrs. Fitzherbert and Caroline intercepted him.

"Lord Summerfield, I simply must thank you for the lovely drive into the country this afternoon. I do think taking the air is so important to one's health," Mrs. Fitzherbert said.

"It was my pleasure," Will said, and over Mrs. Fitzherbert's shoulder, he caught sight of Phoebe again. She had turned away, was listening to Miss Dumbarton.

"The air did Caroline much good. She is looking quite refreshed, is she not?"

Will looked at Caroline. She smiled prettily. He tried again to summon those feelings a man ought to have for a woman he was contemplating spending the rest of his life with, but he could feel nothing.

For some reason, he thought of himself as a boy. He'd never feared the world or the people and places in it. He had been filled with wanderlust and love of adventure as far back as he could remember. He'd wanted to see everything, to do everything. He'd had an atlas as a boy, and would make meticulous notes about all the places he intended to see. What he'd feared, even then, was ennui, of being caught at a standstill. Looking at Caroline now, he felt he'd already been caught, had walked the plank into a cold sea of ennui. He was floating along precisely in the place he'd never wanted to be.

"She looks very well indeed," he said politely.

Caroline blushed and gave him a meaningful smile. "Thank you, my lord," she said, curtsying. "How very kind of you to remark."

"But then again," another male voice said, "Miss Fitzherbert always looks very well, whether or not she has had her airing."

Surprised, Will turned to find Joshua standing next to him, smiling politely at Caroline.

"Very well put, Joshua," Will said, nodding in agreement.

Joshua did not spare Will a glance. "Perhaps Miss Fitzherbert would like a turn about the terrace. The sunset is beautiful this evening." And he offered his arm.

It was a stunning affront to Will. It was obviously done, too. Mrs. Fitzherbert fidgeted like a mother hen, and Caroline's blush suddenly deepened. She looked at Will as if she expected him to stop her from going, but Will could hardly do so without cutting his brother, and stepped aside. "By all means," he said, looking curiously at Joshua. "Miss Fitzherbert should not be denied the pleasure."

Caroline's eyes widened slightly. She glanced at Joshua, then at her mother, and reluctantly put her hand on Joshua's arm. Will could scarcely blame her; given Joshua's reputation she likely feared for her virtue. But Joshua was, nevertheless, Will's brother, and Caroline apparently remembered that as she allowed Joshua to lead her out onto the terrace.

"Well!" Mrs. Fitzherbert said as the two of them walked out onto the terrace. "Well!"

"Shall I fetch you a wine, Mrs. Fitzherbert?" Will asked.

"Thank you, but no, my lord. I find wine does not agree with my constitution." She excused herself, wandering off to a pair of ladies who were having tea.

With a sigh, Will glanced around the room. Phoebe and Miss Dumbarton had left the room. Roger was in the company of the Remington sons, as was Jane. Will glanced around again, looking for Alice, and noticed that she was missing once again.

Where was Alice?

On the terrace, Susan and Phoebe were watching Joshua and Miss Fitzherbert as they strolled across the flagstones. Miss Fitzherbert was looking away from Joshua, but Joshua never looked away from her.

"*Interesting,*" Susan drawled. "It is a foregone conclusion that Summerfield will offer for her. One would think his brother would leave well enough alone."

Susan did not know Joshua Darby—and had it been another moment, Phoebe might have said so, but the words "foregone conclusion" had tied her tongue.

"Is it . . . is it indeed a foregone conclusion?" she asked as lightly as she could.

Susan looked at her with surprise. "What? No gossip belowstairs?" she teased. "No speculation among the servants? How very well behaved you are here. At Merryton, it would be *all* the talk. Why, his lordship's mistresses invite talk."

Phoebe blushed; Susan laughed. "You are really very sweet," she said to Phoebe. "You must live very quietly in London."

Sequestered from society was more the thing. "I suppose I do," Phoebe said.

Susan looked again at Joshua and Miss Fitzherbert, who had paused at the edge of the terrace to look out over the gardens. "Then I shall tell you all, Phoebe Dupree. Yes, dearest, it *is* a foregone conclusion that he will offer, and, I think, it will happen sooner rather than later." She smiled at Phoebe. "No point in keeping the hopes of dozens dangling, is there?"

Phoebe could feel the blood drain from her face, her limbs. "But . . . but there are so many debutantes here. What of Miss Williams?"

"Her father is in debt," Susan said instantly, and shook her head, as if the very notion of marrying debt was distasteful.

"Lady Elizabeth Frederick?"

"Her family is more than suitable, naturally. But she is as timid as a church mouse. A man as handsome and"— Susan paused to draw a breath—"*lusty* as Summerfield needs a strong woman, wouldn't you agree?"

"Yes," Phoebe said sullenly.

"There *is* Miss Pratt," Susan added thoughtfully. "Personally, I am very keen on Miss Pratt. But I understand her fortune is not up to snuff."

"What of Miss Fitzherbert?" Phoebe asked.

"Her fortune is certainly up to snuff," Susan said. "But she is hardly an Original, is she? Ah, but that hardly matters in these matrimonial arrangements, I fear."

It felt as if all her blood were seeping out of her—Phoebe's legs felt weak, and she put her hand out to the stone wall to steady herself.

Susan glanced curiously at Phoebe—and a knowing look came over her. She put her arm around Phoebe's shoulders. "He is *quite* handsome," she said soothingly. "Good looks and adventurous spirit spark the most ardent of fantasies in women." She winked at Phoebe and turned them away from Joshua and Miss Fitzherbert. "And what is your desire, Phoebe? You are young and widowed—surely you hope to marry again?"

Phoebe blinked. "I hope to, yes," she said. "I would like to have children. Scores of them, actually."

Susan laughed. "The Duckworth children haven't put you off the idea?"

With a smile, Phoebe shook her head.

"Well . . ." Susan touched her hand to Phoebe's arm. "Have you any prospects?"

She thought of Will again, and the question made her feel ill. She shook her head and averted her gaze. "Not . . . not really," she said. She could feel tears building behind her eyes and bit them back. "What of you?" she asked Susan in as cheerful a voice as she could muster.

Susan snorted. "Lord Duckworth has his eye on his good friend Mr. Winston, a dull old bachelor who reads dull old books, who is old enough to be my father and large enough to smother me."

Phoebe laughed.

"I'm very serious, Phoebe! I shall have to seek other employment when I refuse, for his lordship is *quite* keen on the idea."

Phoebe smiled, but she couldn't help looking at Joshua and Miss Fitzherbert again.

"I must tell you that Lady Jane's gown last night was

the most exquisite thing I have ever seen on a woman," Susan said, politely changing the subject.

And while Phoebe managed to make light conversation, she felt as if her heart were suspended by a mere thread in her chest. Her fantasy, her adventure was coming to an end. She had finished the last of the commissioned gowns just this afternoon.

There was no reason for her to remain.

Will would soon offer for Caroline Fitzherbert, and Madame Dupree would return to London, where she would be tucked away and buried, along with Phoebe's memories of this extraordinary summer.

A different outcome was not really possible.

Unless she confessed her deceit. . . .

Phoebe was up with the birds the next morning, packing her sewing things away, when Addison appeared.

"Good morning, Addison," she said with a smile. "You are about very early this morning."

"I am indeed," he said, and reached into his coat pocket, withdrawing a folded vellum.

Phoebe looked at him, then the note. "Am I to reply?" she asked quickly, taking it from him.

"No, madam." He bowed and went out. Phoebe hurried to the window and opened the vellum.

Sunday at dawn, behind the stables.

That was it, the sum of his note. Phoebe stared at it, tracing her finger over each bold stroke of the pen. It was only hours. She had only to endure two days before she could be in his arms again.

Voices in the corridor brought her up from her ruminations; she quickly put the note in her pocket.

"I assure you, Mr. Farley, I know precisely which room."

Phoebe gasped just as Mrs. Ramsey sailed into her workroom ahead of Farley, who gave her a sympathetic shrug.

"Madame Dupree!" Mrs. Ramsey said as she tossed her bonnet aside. "How good it is to see you! I trust that as you are not busily sewing at the moment you must be quite finished with the commissioned work. I look forward to seeing it."

"Mrs. Ramsey! What are you doing here?" Phoebe exclaimed.

"What do you think? I have come to see that his lord-ship is well satisfied with you, of course."

Behind Mrs. Ramsey, Farley blushed and backed out of the room, leaving Phoebe to face her nightmare alone.

Twenty-nine

———— ∞ ————

Will was surprised to hear from Farley that Mrs. Ramsey had come without invitation—and with one large portmanteau. She'd requested an audience, and Will had begrudgingly bowed out of a round of grouse hunting after luncheon.

When he entered the library, Mrs. Ramsey and Phoebe were already waiting within. Mrs. Ramsey exclaimed with delight and sank into a curtsy so deep that Will had to help her up from it. "Mrs. Ramsey, good afternoon. I beg you forgive me for keeping you waiting, but I had not expected you," he said, and glanced at Phoebe.

She lifted her shoulders almost imperceptibly, as if to suggest she was at least as surprised as he.

"I daresay I'd hardly expected to come myself, my lord! But things in town are awfully quiet given the heat, and it seemed a prudent time to see after my charge and her work," she said, and smiled rather coldly at Phoebe.

The woman ought to get on her knees and kiss Phoebe's hem, thought Will. "And how did you find your charge and her work?" he asked coolly.

"Oh, very well indeed! And her work!" Mrs. Ramsey sighed with pleasure. "It is exceedingly good. Why, your youngest sister appears to be quite a different woman altogether, my lord. It's as if the clothes have given a sense of self-worth that was sorely lacking when we first met."

Behind her Phoebe gaped in horror, then glanced heavenward and shook her head.

Will was taken aback by her remark as well, but Mrs. Ramsey didn't seem to even notice her gaffe. "I rather think Lady Alice was helped by it, too," she continued blithely. "But she has not been about this morning. I trust you are satisfied?"

He glanced at Phoebe. "Beyond my expectations."

"Splendid!" Mrs. Ramsey exclaimed happily as Phoebe rolled her eyes. "Now then," she said, drawing Will's attention back to her. "I counted the articles of clothing Madame Dupree has finished and I believe your original commission to be complete."

That was news to Will. He looked at Phoebe again, but she had averted her eyes. She had not mentioned she was finished. Then again, there hadn't been a moment to speak of such matters.

"However, Madame Dupree informs me you have added a riding habit for the young lady who will soon be your fiancée," Mrs. Ramsey said cheerfully.

Phoebe turned away, to the window.

"That I did," Will said, watching Phoebe from the corner of his eye.

"Naturally, you may trust in my utmost discretion," Mrs. Ramsey added.

"Naturally."

"Furthermore, I am pleased to extend the same offer of services for the riding habit as the original commission," she continued with a gracious bow of her head.

"How very good of you."

"And of course, if your affianced requires a trousseau, you may count on my conservative pricing."

"Thank you," he said.

That caught Phoebe's attention—she looked at him over her shoulder.

Mrs. Ramsey coyly smoothed the lap of her gown. "I had intended to have Madame Dupree return to London with me on the morrow," she said, "but as you have added the riding habit, I suggested that perhaps I might remain on until Monday or Tuesday, so that Madame Dupree would have sufficient time to complete that work as well."

The woman was canny. Not only had she finagled an addition to his rather generous order, she had also determined how she might have a country house holiday, all under the guise of providing service.

Moreover, she had effectively taken Phoebe from him in these last few days of her employment. He felt a surge of angry frustration and turned slightly from Mrs. Ramsey.

But instead of asking after rooms as he fully expected the brazen Mrs. Ramsey to do, she sighed and said, "Unfortunately, I had not realized you had also asked Madame Dupree to fashion your family's dominoes. That will take quite a lot more time."

Will blinked. A hint of a smile appeared on Phoebe's face as she turned away, toward a bookcase, and pretended to examine the titles there.

"I beg your pardon?"

"Your dominoes," Mrs. Ramsey said, and made a motion around her head. "The masks. You will need masks for the masquerade ball."

Will blinked again. Phoebe cleared her throat. With her hands clasped behind her back, she rose up on her toes and down again.

Before her, Mrs. Ramsey looked at Will curiously. "You did request dominoes, my lord?"

"Yes, of course," he said instantly. The very suggestion of a masquerade ball would give Farley fits—but he would not let on to this woman that there was the slightest thing amiss.

"An excellent idea, my lord. Masques are all the rage in London. All the best shops are keeping masks now. You are quite right to introduce it to the country people," Mrs. Ramsey said with an exuberant smile. "Given these additional pieces, I believe Madame Dupree will need one more week to complete her work. Unfortunately, I cannot remain away from London for that long."

Thank God. "That would be too long away from your shop, naturally," Will averred.

"Oh, indeed it would. I expect there will be a rush from the country in a fortnight, in preparation for the Little Season. Therefore, I shall be on Monday's public coach to London. Until then, I will share Madame Dupree's very spacious lodgings. That is, if you approve."

Bloody hell. Will tried to smile. "You must join us for supper, Mrs. Ramsey," he said begrudgingly.

"Oh!" she said, her face lighting with pleasure. "I should be delighted! Thank you!"

He glanced at Phoebe; she was looking at him again, her expression full of helplessness. "If there is nothing else, you will excuse me?" he asked.

"There is . . ." Mrs. Ramsey said quickly. "There is one last, tiny little matter," she said. "I have taken the liberty of preparing a bill of sale for the gowns and whatnot. I thought as long as I was here . . ." She withdrew a vellum from her reticule and held it out to him.

The wench was shrewd. "Yes, thank you." Will took the vellum and opened it, his brows rising only slightly at the exorbitant price she had added for the making of the dominoes and riding habit he didn't know he'd commissioned. He folded it and put it in his coat pocket, smiled at Mrs. Ramsey, and said, "If there is nothing else?"

"I wouldn't dream of keeping you from your guests a moment longer," Mrs. Ramsey said, and extended her hand. "A bank draft will be sufficient as payment."

"Very well," Will said, and shook her hand. "Good afternoon." He glanced at Phoebe and went out.

When this fortnight of frolicking was over and done, Will intended to write Lord Middleton and voice his opinion that there were *some* women, such as the venerable Mrs. Ramsey, who did not need the protection of Parliament in the pursuit of their trade. That woman was very adept at taking care of herself.

Phoebe's unwelcome bedmate snored as loudly as a bull—therefore, Phoebe was up very early Saturday morning.

In truth, she probably would not have slept much had Mrs. Ramsey been in London where she belonged. She had much on her mind, obviously—most notably, the letter she'd received from Ava, courtesy of Mrs. Ramsey, who'd almost forgotten to give it to Phoebe.

That letter forced Phoebe into a moment of frantic indecision. The very same moment she had concocted the masquerade ball.

In her letter, Ava had urged Phoebe to come home as soon as possible, for the most extraordinary thing had happened: Lady Purnam was, apparently, bound for Wentworth Hall and the Summerfield ball in the company of Lady Holland.

Lady Purnam had been their mother's dearest friend, and after their mother's unfortunate death, Lady Purnam had taken it upon herself to continue motherly instructions for Ava, Greer, and Phoebe. It hardly mattered that the three women neither sought nor particularly heeded Lady Purnam's instructions; Lady Purnam was intent on giving them.

There was another thing they had learned about Lady Purnam in the years since their mother's death—in addition to her good and determined intentions, Lady Purnam was completely lacking in social discretion. Were she to find Phoebe here, it was not possible even to guess what she might do, but one could trust it would hardly be handled discreetly.

That was why Ava had written in very firm and hurried strokes:

Come away from Wentworth Hall __at once__! If Lady P discovers you there one can only imagine the delirium that will follow! She will cause no end of grief, which is why I was quite adamant that you should not go through with your ridiculous plan! You must come away, darling! You must put an end to this fantasy once and for all!

Phoebe was as mortified by the news that Lady Purnam was coming as was Ava, but she could not think what to do, not with Mrs. Ramsey staring at her. It felt as if everything was spiraling out of control. If she left now with Mrs. Ramsey, she'd never have the chance to even speak with him. She couldn't bring herself to leave Will—not like this, not so soon!

She'd made a quick excuse with the masquerade ball in spite of her fear of being discovered by Lady Purnam. But she was at terrible odds with herself and her blasted identity, all of which led to a single conclusion: She had to tell him the truth before Lady Purnam arrived.

But when? And *how*?

If that wasn't enough to keep her awake, she surely would have been awakened by the voices raised in argument floating up from the flue last night.

She needed some tea, and made her way to the kitchen. She was surprised to find Mrs. Turner there, still wearing her nightcap.

"Mrs. Turner?"

"Can't sleep either, can you?" Mrs. Turner said as she methodically sliced bread. "It's a wonder anyone could sleep with all that shouting," she said, and when Phoebe admitted she didn't know what had happened, Mrs. Turner told her in a hushed voice that Alice had been discovered in the gazebo with the young smithy late yesterday afternoon, and Will had all but turned her out for it.

"I cannot imagine what the child was thinking," Mrs. Turner said despairingly, shaking her head and dislodging wisps of dark hair from her cap. "Apparently they've been going on about it for a time, even though she *swore* she'd not see him."

Phoebe said nothing, but felt the guilt rise up in her.

"His lordship has locked her away in her rooms until he can think what is to be done about it," Mrs. Turner continued cheerfully as she munched on a piece of bread. "Imagine! And what will happen with all these guests underfoot?" she said, gesturing fitfully to the ceiling.

"What will he tell them?" Phoebe asked.

"That Alice has taken ill and is indisposed for a time. We're all to say it."

"Poor Alice," Phoebe sighed.

"Poor Alice!" Mrs. Turner scoffed. "He's only doing what's right for her, he is. Why, just last week, I saw that bloody chap in Greenhill chatting it up with Molly Fabian."

"Who?"

"A serving girl at the Horse and Feather," Mrs. Turner said. "Everyone knows that she and Mr. Hughes are bedmates. Oh, he's a bloody rooster! He'll peck every hen he can catch and then crow about it."

Phoebe swallowed hard at that unappealing description. "I honestly believed . . . I thought Mr. Hughes loved Alice," Phoebe said thoughtfully.

"*Loved* her?" Mrs. Turner snorted into her tea. "You've quite a fanciful notion of love, Madame Dupree."

That was an understatement. The good Lord knew the concept had filled her thoughts and dreams of late. Still, Phoebe had great empathy for Alice—she understood what it was to be a woman in love with a man she could not have.

She felt so deeply for Alice that in the evening, when Mrs. Ramsey went down for supper, Phoebe sought Alice out.

She knocked lightly on Alice's door; Alice called out a terse "Come."

She peeked around the edge of the door and saw

Alice seated at her desk, writing furiously. She scarcely glanced at Phoebe. "Aha. Even the great London seamstress has come to gawk at the inmate," she said sourly.

"I have not come to gawk," Phoebe said. "I have come to offer you my . . . my . . ."

When she could not think of the proper word, Alice looked up with a bit of a sneer. "Condolences? Advice? What could you possibly have to offer?"

"Sympathy," Phoebe said, ignoring her bitterness. "My deepest sympathy."

"Why should I want your sympathy, Phoebe?"

"Because I understand your feelings for Mr. Hughes. Because I know what it is to love someone you cannot have."

"Oh, do you indeed?" Alice sniffed and turned back to her writing. "And who have *you* loved that you cannot have—my brother?"

Phoebe gasped.

Alice snorted. "Don't look so gobsmacked. Everyone knows it."

"Lady Alice, I assure you—"

"Oh, please do not attempt to dissuade me," she said with a flick of her wrist. "I hardly care."

For a moment, Phoebe couldn't breathe; she sank onto the edge of Alice's bed and braced her hands against her knees.

"Honestly, Phoebe," Alice said with a cold laugh, "you must be very naïve to think you could keep company with my brother and escape the slightest detection. You must know that his every move is watched."

Apparently, Phoebe was more naïve than she had ever realized. Ava and Greer were right—they'd certainly warned her of it often enough. They would be beside themselves if they knew how Phoebe had compromised herself so completely.

"Don't look so glum," Alice said as she dipped her pen in the inkwell. "At least you'll be leaving soon."

"Yes," Phoebe said, surprised by how weak her voice sounded.

"I, on the other hand, must suffer in agony at this wretched place for the rest of my life."

"It is a cruel fact," Phoebe said unevenly, "that among the *haute ton* such things as pedigree and fortune have more bearing on a match than compatibility and emotion. And I . . . I know how deeply you feel for Mr. Hughes, Alice. I thought only to offer you my friendship."

"There, then, you have offered it," Alice said, bent over her letter. "So now you may toddle off to your needles and thread, for I have a number of letters I should like to write."

"Alice—"

"No," Alice said, with a glare for Phoebe. "I will not hear words of advice from you, of all people."

Phoebe swallowed a bitter lump of exasperation and regret. She forced herself to stand. "One day, you will regret your demeanor," she said quietly. "One day, you will need a true friend."

"If I am ever in need of a friend, it will not be you," Alice muttered indifferently.

Nevertheless, Phoebe could see the high color in Alice's cheek and neck, the telltale puffiness around her eyes that indicated she'd been crying. Instead of walking out of the room as she should have done, she walked to where Alice sat and put her hand on her shoulder.

Alice did not shrug her off; Phoebe squeezed her shoulder affectionately and went out, leaving Alice to her private demons.

Thirty

———— ⦿⦿ ————

At dawn Sunday morning, Will was waiting impatiently for Phoebe at the stables. He'd saddled Fergus and another horse and was anxious to be away before the stable hands arrived for their morning chores. He was acutely aware that any more scandal might irreparably harm the Darby family's reputation.

He could scarcely believe what Alice had done—just thinking about it made him ill. He closed his eyes and leaned his head against Fergus's neck. What had possessed her? What inferior logic or intellect had allowed her to believe she could deceive him so blatantly and avoid discovery?

To be discovered in the gazebo with the smithy's apprentice while more than two dozen guests were under his roof was unfathomable. He supposed he ought to thank God she hadn't been discovered *in flagrante delicto,* but merely engaged in something of a chaste kiss. Or so he'd heard from Roger—he'd missed the tumult when several of the guests had wandered down to the lake to race small boats in the late afternoon. He'd been escorting Miss Franklin through the portrait gallery, nodding and smiling as she gamely and subtly tried to present her accomplishments for his consideration. He'd been thinking that try as she might, the poor girl could not seem to distinguish herself in a favorable way from Caroline Fitzherbert, when Henry had joined them and asked if he might have a word.

Will had been very glad to see Henry. He'd arrived the day before from business in London—a euphemism for his affair with a married woman. Upon arrival, Henry had quickly taken stock of the many unmarried ladies and grinned. "Allow me to cull the herd," he'd said playfully, and had sauntered off, heading right for Phoebe and Miss Dumbarton.

Will had intercepted him, had pointed him in the opposite direction.

"But I find her quite comely," Henry had protested, nodding toward Miss Dumbarton.

"She's a governess. Your mother will never approve."

Henry had looked at Miss Dumbarton and winced. "Bloody hell," he'd muttered as he'd gone off in the direction in which Will had pointed him, where other, equally delightful women would welcome his attentions.

But Will's delight in Henry's interrupting his walk with Miss Franklin in the portrait gallery was short-lived. When they'd made their excuses and Miss Franklin had left them, Will sighed. "Thank you," he said. "You have saved me once more."

"Unfortunately, I have not," Henry said. "I've some wretched news." And he'd told Will about Alice.

Will had paled as Henry talked, could feel his gut sink with despair. When Henry finished, he put a comforting hand on Will's shoulder. "I am sorry, Will," he'd said sincerely. "I wish that I could help you."

But nothing could help Will—it was the social ruination of his sister.

Now Will raised his head from his horse's neck because he heard Phoebe before he saw her. She came striding around the corner of the stables, her arms swinging. She looked quite determined about something. He'd never seen a more welcome sight.

How odd it was that Phoebe was the only person who made sense to him at the moment. The only person he felt he could trust completely. Having been so gravely deceived by his sister, that trust was very important to him.

"I worried you'd not get away," he said when she reached him. "I am thankful you have, for the last couple of days have been very trying," he said, and cupped her chin, lifting her face to kiss her.

"Yes," she said quietly, "I have heard."

Of course she had—the entire county had heard of it by now. Will gestured impatiently to the horses. "We must be gone before we are seen," he said, and took her by the waist, lifting her up and setting her on the little roan mare he'd saddled for her. He fairly leapt onto Fergus's back and paused just to let his eyes run over her before spurring Fergus forward.

As they moved deeply and quickly into the woods, Will realized that his pulse was pounding—not with the anxiety of being discovered, but with disgust. He despised the situation he'd created with Phoebe. What had started out as an opportunity for physical release had developed into something much greater, much deeper, and to treat it as anything less seemed tawdry.

His feelings for her were anything but tawdry.

But Alice's indiscretion had made it near to impossible for him to even see Phoebe. Alicia's scandal had tainted the entire family, and for him to add to it would only make the situation worse for all of them, Alice and Jane in particular.

It wasn't until they had reached the meadow where the horses usually grazed that Will finally allowed himself to relax a little. Up here, they were away from everyone. Up here, they were merely a man and a woman.

There were no titles, no families, no social mores, no families to interfere.

He reined Fergus to a halt and swung off, then helped Phoebe down and instantly wrapped her in a strong embrace, his crop dangling from his fingers. He kissed her face, her lips. He caressed the crown of her head and smiled into her eyes. "You cannot imagine how I have longed to see you."

Her smile widened. "I beg to differ, sir—I can very well imagine."

With a laugh, he kissed her again, then reared back, frowning playfully. "A *masquerade* ball?"

"Ah yes . . . *that*," she said with a wince. "I scarcely knew what to do," she admitted. "Mrs. Ramsey would have had me on the first coach to London had I not thought of something."

"Then I will thank the good Lord for masquerade balls," he said, wrapping her in his arms once more. "I could not bear it if you left so soon."

He felt her go still, then pull away. Will dropped his arms as she backed away from him and turned around to look out over the meadow. "Where are the horses?" she asked, shading her eyes with her hand as she looked to the east.

"I imagine they have gone to higher ground for bet-ter grazing. We shall look for them if you'd like."

She shrugged a little, then glanced at him over her shoulder. "You seem distressed."

He smiled wryly. "I suppose I am. I have wanted very much for things to go well for my brothers and sisters."

She gave him a sympathetic smile and folded her arms as she cast her gaze to the ground.

"I don't know what more I might have done to prevent it. I cannot seem to impress on Alice the need for circumspection and careful thought. Nor can I seem to contain my anger with her," he said, slapping his crop against his open palm. "She has put *so* much at risk, has brought such shame to our family when we have worked so hard to rebuild our good name. To think how I forbade her, threatened her—and still she would deceive me."

"Love has a rather strange way of making one do things one would never even contemplate doing," Phoebe suggested softly.

He scoffed at that. "Do you mean to imply that love would give one license to deceive?" he asked harshly, and shook his head. "No. I would have better understood and better respected her had she told me she could not honor my wishes. But Alice knows that if there is one thing I cannot and *will* not tolerate, it is deceit."

"Indeed?" Phoebe asked, frowning a little.

He understood what she was thinking and adamantly shook his head. "Ours is not the same situation at all, Phoebe. Alice is a young, unmarried woman with a reputation to protect."

Phoebe cocked her head to one side.

"You know very well what I mean by that," he said brusquely, and tapped Fergus on the rump with the crop, sending him to trot a few feet away. The little mare followed. "It is quite a different matter for us than it is for Alice. She will be forever marked by her indiscretion."

"As was Frieda."

"*Frieda!*" he said irritably. "Frieda's indiscretions were far greater than Alice's."

"Were they?" Phoebe countered coolly. "I had not realized there were degrees of wantonness."

"Of course there are! Alice has not, insofar as I know, lifted her skirts to a man who is not her husband."

Phoebe paled; Will instantly realized what he'd said. "Good God, Phoebe," he said wearily. "It is *different* for you. You are a widow. Your chastity is not an issue—the horse is out of the barn, as it were."

That remark caused her jaw to drop open.

"Damnation," he said irritably, slapping his crop against his leg. "I did not mean—"

"I know very well what you meant, Will," she said low. "You speak very plainly."

He felt frustrated with everything—his family, his life, his love. "I do not mean to argue this with you. Do forgive my bad humor—I am cross, for Alice's deceit has put a wall between me and my sister that cannot be overcome. I cannot abide such deceit. I think I might bear anything—*anything*—but that," he said, slapping the crop against his leg again.

Phoebe dropped her arms and whirled around, in a full circle, and faced him again. Her expression was a mix of hurtful regret and anger. "Are you so callous?" she asked hotly.

His gaze narrowed. "You would *defend* Alice?" he demanded incredulously. "What do you think will become of Alice if her virtue is lost? What other virtue has she when honesty is so lacking in her?"

"Can you not understand that her love for that man is blinding her to all she knows?"

"No," he said, shaking his head. "You will not sway me with poetic talk of love again on her behalf, Phoebe."

"Then what of our situation?"

"What of it?" he asked angrily as his frustration with his position and his desires, and the feeling of being caught in the vise of some notion of duty, overwhelmed him. "Do you honestly believe we'd be standing in a bloody meadow miles from the hall just so that no other soul will see us if I had the *slightest* choice? And if I did believe for one insane moment that I *might* have a choice, can you not see that Alice has effectively ruined any chance of it? How can I possibly own up to my feelings for you and bring even more shame to my family than she already has done?"

He didn't realize what he'd said—what he apparently *believed*—until it was too late. The color had drained from Phoebe's lovely face, and she covered her gaping mouth with her hand.

"Phoebe—"

"No!" she said, holding out her hand to stop him as she backed away. "Please do not say more!" She turned partially from him and pressed her hands to her abdomen.

Her reaction alarmed Will. "Phoebe!" he blustered. "You knew as well as I did that this was all we might expect!"

"A meadow? A few hours here and there? And what will it be after you have married Caroline Fitzherbert? What will we share once you have lain with *her*? I suppose you think all will be right and you may come to my bed, for the horse is out of the barn and that is the way among gentlemen of Quality!"

"Did I ever give you cause to expect more?" he snapped angrily.

A sob caught in her throat and she looked heavenward. "No," she said softly. "Never. It seems Alice is not the only one who has been blinded by love."

Will sighed wearily. He shoved his hands through his hair. "I want to make love to you, Phoebe. Not argue. I never . . . I *never* expected to love you," he said, feeling the words twist around his heart as he spoke. "I never considered even the possibility when I offered an arrangement for us. I never expected or knew myself capable of falling so hard or deep . . . but now I have, and I am forced by my position and my responsibilities to face the reality of it."

She turned her head to look at him. Tears filled her pale blue eyes. She looked as if she wanted to speak, but she swallowed and bowed her head.

"Phoebe," he uttered, and quietly closed the distance between them, putting his arms around her.

She felt stiff in his arms, her body trembling, but she turned and pressed her face to his shoulder.

Will cupped her head, held her tight. He couldn't think clearly, not in the wake of Alice's scandal. He did not *want* to think of it now. He had only a few hours with Phoebe, and he didn't want to mar them with unanswerable questions about the future. He slipped a finger beneath her chin and lifted her face to his. Her eyes said everything—he could see the hurt and confusion there, and would have given the earth to remove the sadness from her eyes.

"I have to go back," she said tearfully. "I have to go now."

He nodded and let her go. She walked away from him, toward the mare. Will watched her a moment, wondering where this had left them, and reached no conclusion.

He followed after her to help her mount the mare.

Caroline Fitzherbert was up very early Sunday morning. At the advice of her father, she and her mother had accepted Summerfield's invitation to stay at Wentworth Hall for the fortnight instead of traveling seven miles each way every day.

Caroline had argued with her father, fearing that she

would lose her advantage of being separate and apart from the other unmarried girls. "There are too many people and therefore too great an opportunity for talk," she'd argued.

"But talk is what you want, darling," her mother had said as she'd stirred her tea. "You want everyone in attendance to whisper in Summerfield's ear that there is only one possible match for him, and that is Miss Caroline Fitzherbert."

She was, therefore, ensconced in a lovely suite with her mother, with a view of the lake and gazebo.

Unfortunately, Caroline had not been sitting in the window seat yesterday and had missed the scandalous discovery of Alice and the smithy in the gazebo. The very thought of it caused her to smirk a little to herself. *Alice*. What a tragedy she was! Entirely lacking in fine looks and social graces, the poor thing would have had a difficult time gaining an offer under the best of circumstances. It would be near to impossible now.

But Caroline had hardly thought of Alice since. She found it difficult to think of anything but her own particular situation, and privately bemoaned that there was nowhere to go to be alone at Wentworth Hall and think things through. So many things had happened that Caroline felt like a sieve with a steady stream of emotions rushing through her. She wanted nothing more than to walk in the gardens, alone, to think.

At last, she had her opportunity Sunday morning. Caroline was blissfully alone in the parterres while the other guests slept late. She moved languidly, soaking up the sun's morning light before it became too warm. She paused to take a deep breath of air and turn her face up to the sky—until she heard the sound of someone running.

Good *Lord*. She was not in the mood to converse, so

she quickly ducked behind a topiary tree and hoped whoever it was would pass by quickly.

But when Madame Dupree scurried past, Caroline was very intrigued. Madame Dupree was walking fast, her head down, obviously lost in thought. She was wearing a plain morning gown, and her hair was fixed in a braid down her back. She was quite unlike the lovely, perfectly-put-together woman who presented herself every night. This morning she resembled the servant she decidedly was as she hurried up the path.

Now wherever could the seamstress have gone?

A few moments later, she had her answer. The distinct sound of a man's stride startled her. She knew who it was instantly. She gathered her shawl around her shoulders and boldly stepped onto the path. Summerfield came to something of an abrupt halt when he saw her.

He was obviously surprised; for the briefest of moments, his eyes darted to the terrace before returning to Caroline. "Miss Fitzherbert, how good to see you this morning. I trust you slept well?"

Caroline smiled. She could not yet bring herself to speak.

He seemed a little perplexed by her reticence. "It is a lovely day for walking," he remarked.

"It is," she said, and glanced down at his boots. They were covered in dust. "It would seem that you have walked quite a long way already, my lord."

His hand clenched as he smiled. "As a matter of fact, I took the opportunity to ride up into the hills to see after the wild horses."

"Did you find them?" Caroline asked, watching him closely.

"No. I think they have moved higher into the hills where the grass is still green."

Caroline moved closer to him. "That is quite a long ride, my lord. I should think you would have wanted some company."

Summerfield steadily held her gaze but did not respond.

Caroline smiled again. "You once promised to show me the wild horses."

His eyes drifted to her lips. "I did indeed. I have been woefully remiss. We must ride out today and see if we can find them." He looked her in the eye. "If you'd like."

"It won't be a great burden to you to go up twice in one day?" she asked sweetly.

"Not in the least. Shall we ride after luncheon?"

"Yes, thank you." She smiled. "That would be lovely."

"Would you care for breakfast?" he asked, offering his arm.

Caroline glanced at his proffered arm and with another sweet smile laid her hand firmly on it.

Thirty-one

"Why so sullen, Lady Phoebe?" Mrs. Ramsey asked. Phoebe sucked in a breath and quickly looked over her shoulder—Mrs. Ramsey had insisted Phoebe join her on a walkabout of the magnificent grounds. Apparently, several of the guests thought it was a splendid time to walk, too, and Mrs. Ramsey's voice had a tendency to carry. "Do have a care, Mrs. Ramsey," she cautioned her.

"Don't be so fussy," Mrs. Ramsey said. "There is no one even near." She opened the gate that led from the parterres out onto the lawn. "This is glorious, is it not?" Mrs. Ramsey asked, and strolled on.

Phoebe reluctantly followed her. Her deceit was hanging over her head like an ax. She hardly knew who she was any longer—she wasn't really Madame Dupree, but neither was she Phoebe. There was only one thing that seemed even remotely true: Had she been honest with Will from the beginning, she might very well be on the verge of securing a happy future for herself. But her deceit and her lies had created the need for more lies, which had made that impossible.

As they moved toward the lake with Mrs. Ramsey nattering on about another grand house she had visited, they saw a pair of riders.

"Oh! I do believe it is Summerfield!" Mrs. Ramsey said.

It was indeed Summerfield. He was riding with Miss Fitzherbert, and it left a surprisingly deep gash across Phoebe's heart to see Miss Fitzherbert laughing so gaily and Will smiling so steadily at the young woman.

Will never saw Phoebe.

But Mrs. Ramsey did. "I'd shut my mouth if I were you," she said snidely, jerking Phoebe's attention back to her. The woman watched as the riders disappeared over a hill. "I daresay you've ruined any opportunity for that one, eh?"

Phoebe looked at Mrs. Ramsey incredulously.

"You need not be so high and mighty with me." Mrs. Ramsey sniffed. "You are quite fortunate that you've not been made to suffer more for your folly."

"And what folly is that, Mrs. Ramsey? That I made a few gowns for you to sell?"

Her flippancy surprised and angered Mrs. Ramsey.

She suddenly turned around, pinning Phoebe with a glare. "Do you think I could not ruin you yet, Lady Phoebe?"

"I beg your *pardon*?"

"You seem to forget that you have undertaken a deceit that could tarnish your reputation and that of your family. Do you think even a country lord such as Summerfield would have you if he knew you had lowered yourself to engage in a common trade and in such a *deceitful* manner?"

Phoebe flinched. "You make it sound as if I am a *thief*."

Mrs. Ramsey gave her a bitter smile. "Your crime is far worse," she said harshly. "You will wish you'd merely stolen a bauble or a crown. But you stole the trust and good opinion of those around you, and that, madam, is not so easily replaced."

The words felt like a kick square in the belly; Phoebe abruptly turned away. With her hand on her abdomen, she walked down to the water's edge and stared at the ducks so she wouldn't have to see Mrs. Ramsey's face.

The supper hour stretched interminably for Will. The gentlemen were quite excited about the prospect of more hunting on the morrow, and several of the ladies had determined they would go to Greenhill in search of masks for Thursday night's fortnight-ending ball.

It was a fortunate thing, given Phoebe's hasty decision to turn the ball into a masquerade, that Will's parents had kept various costumes and masks for guests in a room belowstairs for occasions such as this. After a reckoning of what they had and what the house-guests were seeking in the village—some of them had their own ideas for masks—it seemed everyone would be suitably attired, except the family and Henry, and Phoebe was to make those masks. In addition, messengers had been sent to two hundred fifty invited guests to inform them of the masquerade.

Will's guests were in high spirits tonight, as were his siblings.

Jane had flowered into a lively young woman and Will expected, given the looks of the young men gathered around her, that he would receive an offer for her hand—perhaps not as soon as he'd hoped, given Alice's scandal—but eventually, in spite of Alice.

Roger likewise seemed to have made new friends. Just before supper, Lord Montgomery had remarked that he would like to have Roger up to Scotland to shoot, that he was an excellent marksman and a congenial fellow at the card table.

Will was pleased that his two younger siblings seemed to be adapting to society. But Alice and Joshua were quite another story. Alice remained in her room, her defiance growing. She was not missed at the supper table.

Joshua rarely engaged anyone other than Caroline. He lurked on the fringes of the activity, watching everyone behind a glass of whiskey or port. Will sensed that something was eating at Joshua, and whatever it was had him firmly in its grip. Will had tried to speak to Joshua about it, but Joshua had brushed him off, insisting it was nothing, that he did not care for society. There was nothing Will could do—and he had his hands full with his own dilemma.

But at the very least, as Will told Henry that night, his reason for hosting such a prolonged event had been to introduce his siblings into society, and on that front, he had been successful. It had not gone as well as he might have hoped, but if two of them found their way to proper living, he supposed it was well worth the effort and expense.

"Of course," Henry agreed. "Jane shall eventually receive an offer," he said, agreeing with Will's thinking. "But what everyone wants to know is . . . what about Summerfield?" He winked at Will.

Will gave him an enigmatic smile. "I think the answer to that is obvious, is it not?"

Just as he guessed, Henry misunderstood him. He grinned, touched his glass to Will's. "The Fitzherberts will be apoplectic with joy."

But with his father, Will was honest. When he'd reported the day's events, the earl lifted a finger, then bent his head at an odd angle and looked up at Will.

"You wonder if I shall make an offer," Will said, and glanced at his hands. He imagined them on Phoebe's body. "Truthfully, my lord, I want to make an offer to Miss Fitzherbert to please you," Will admitted. "But it is just as true that I do not believe I can, for that place in my heart where feelings for one's wife ought to reside are filled with constant thoughts of another."

He looked at his father and was not surprised to see him looking somewhat confused. "Madame Dupree," he said, "has bewitched me completely." He stood up, walked to the window, and propped his arm against the wall as he stared out in the dark. "You might well imagine how it happened," he said, aware that after his mother's death, his father had carried on a rather torrid affair with a young chambermaid. "And I never intended it to become more. God help me, Papa, it has. I can think of no one but her, I can *see* no one but her, and when I imagine myself married and raising a family, I imagine it with Phoebe Dupree."

He could only imagine how his father must be receiving this news—unable to speak or cry out, unable to voice the frustration that filled him. He restlessly pushed a hand through his hair and squatted next to his father. "I beg your forgiveness, my lord," he quietly beseeched him. "I should rather die than disappoint or dishonor you. But I fear that I would be cheating Miss Fitzherbert of her true happiness were I to offer for her."

Will bowed his head, trying to think of the right words. "Perhaps, in time, I shall rid myself of this desire," he said. "Madame Dupree will be gone from Wentworth Hall in a matter of days as it is. I pray you will forgive me. I pray you will understand, Papa." He looked up and tried to read something in his father's wet eyes.

But if the earl understood him, if he agreed, if he was horrified, Will could not tell. The earl lifted a finger once—maybe twice. Will wished for all the world that his father could speak. If he ever needed his counsel, it was now.

But the old man couldn't speak, and Will smiled sadly, put his hand on his father's bony knee. "You must be fatigued after such a long day. I shall leave you to Jacobs." He rose, leaned over and kissed the crown of his father's head, and quit the room to tell Jacobs his father needed him.

Phoebe thought Mrs. Ramsey would never leave. She fussed about the room, insisting she'd left a glove. Phoebe quickly found the glove—in the woman's portmanteau—and sent her on her way before she was in danger of missing the public coach.

She had just seen her off when Addison found Phoebe and informed her she was to accompany several ladies into Greenhill who wanted to purchase masks. "Your services are required."

"My services?"

"They would have you assist them," he said.

"How exciting," Phoebe muttered irritably.

"There is one more thing," Addison said. "His lordship requests that you keep Lady Alice company today, as she has requested to go into the village."

"Addison, please, *no!*" Phoebe cried. "I cannot stop her if she is determined to see Mr. Hughes!"

"And you mustn't trouble yourself to do so," Addison said quickly. "His lordship is sending two footmen to ensure that she does not."

She could only imagine the spectacle that would make. "Oh *Lord*," she sighed.

"His lordship also advises that you should avail yourself of one of the masks available at Wentworth Hall, or purchase one," he said, his ears going red. "He will purchase what you need to dress appropriately for the ball."

Phoebe's eyes narrowed. "Please tell his lordship that I cannot possibly attend."

"I rather think you must," Addison said politely. "Lady Duckworth has threatened to make quite a scene if you are not . . . 'let out of your prison,'" he said, repeating words he obviously found distasteful, "to keep Miss Dumbarton company."

"Shall the entire *house* determine what I am to do from one hour to the next?"

"It would seem so," Addison said, his thin face as red as his ears now.

The ladies arrived in Greenhill in a train of carriages at two o'clock. The minute the carriages rumbled onto High Street, the doors of the best establishments were flung open.

The women—twelve in all—as well as two unruly children, marched along in search of masks. There were so many questions put to Phoebe that she could scarcely see Alice most of the time, much less watch her like a child. But the two footmen kept her in their sights, and she moped about each shop, scarcely speaking.

Fortunately for Phoebe, one shop had several lovely masks, just arrived from London. The proprietor, seeing so many rich women gathered in one place, was bargaining enthusiastically.

Jane eagerly led the ladies; each one stepped to the counter to choose her perfect mask for the ball. Susan took that opportunity to pull Phoebe aside.

"I've missed you terribly!" she exclaimed. "Mrs. Ramsey was quite miserly in sharing your company." She twirled Phoebe around and away from the others as she deftly pulled Master David's hand from a pair of ladies' slippers. "It is all but assured Summerfield will offer for Miss Fitzherbert—everyone expects it to happen at the masquerade ball."

"Indeed? Miss Fitzherbert must be very happy."

"Really, who would know if she is or is not?" Susan said with a flick of her wrist, and leaned to her right, to glance around Phoebe. "Master David, do not touch the linens, if you please." She looked at Phoebe again. "She's rather phlegmatic, isn't she?"

Phoebe glanced at Miss Fitzherbert, who, with her mother, was examining a feathered mask.

"One would think Summerfield would want someone with a little more élan, wouldn't one?"

One would think, Phoebe thought morosely.

"And Lady Jane!" Susan whispered excitedly. "It is likewise assumed that Lord Tankersly will make an offer for her hand, and in spite of her sister's terrible lack of judgment, and Lady Jane only seventeen! She has quite a lot of Summerfield's *joie de vivre* in her. *Quite* unlike her sister, mmm?"

"Mmm," Phoebe agreed wearily.

"Would that you had been nearby when Lady Alice was discovered in the gazebo with the awful smithy!" Susan whispered, her voice even softer as she took up the tiny hand of her charge, Lady Elizabeth. "If the party had not happened upon them at the *precise* moment that it did, they might have found the pair in *far* worse circumstances."

Phoebe knew the circumstances and how easily one could get swept up in her feelings, how quickly the strictures a woman had been taught to uphold melted away with a man's touch, a kiss. She glanced at Alice across the shop, quietly examining a pair of gloves. Phoebe's heart went out to her.

When the ladies had finally settled on their masks, they proceeded out of the shop, flowing like a river to the next shop. Alice was the last to leave; Phoebe followed her, and almost collided with Alice's back when she stepped outside. Alice had come to a dead halt. The footmen, Phoebe noticed, were watching the ladies. Phoebe glanced at Alice again and noticed she was staring at something across the street.

Phoebe stepped up beside her and followed her gaze. She saw Mr. Hughes then, on the village green. He was leaning over a woman whose back was against a tree. She was smiling up at him, and he at her. There was no mistaking the look between them—to an innocent bystander, they looked like a young couple in love.

Phoebe didn't speak. She didn't even look at Alice. But she slipped her hand into Alice's.

Alice never spoke, never so much as looked at Phoebe. But she closed her fingers tightly around Phoebe's and clung to her.

Thirty-two

—⦿—

With only a few days of the fortnight remaining, Will was caught up in the hunting, the lawn games, and because of the unusual heat, blanket parties at night, as they were being called.

He saw Phoebe only twice during that time. Once, when Miss Dumbarton brought her down from her workroom and out onto the lawn. He was alarmed at how fatigued Phoebe looked.

While most of the group chased a ball across the lawn during a disorderly game of lawn bowling, Will found a moment to speak to her. His eyes searched her face. "Are you all right?" he asked as she wiped her forehead. "You seem fatigued."

"Oh, no," she said. "I am presented with difficulties when it comes to making a few masks," she said, and gave him a weary smile before watching the game again. "I've never made them—but I am learning."

"I have regretted our last conversation," he said quietly.

Her sigh lifted her shoulders. She glanced at him sidelong and smiled a little lopsidedly. "We've made quite a mess of things, haven't we?" she said sadly. "If I had it to do all over again, I would—"

"Please," he said quickly, fearing she would say she would never have come to him in the gazebo that night, and realizing that hearing it would wound him deeply. "Do not say it."

Her lips parted; her brow furrowed with confusion.

Will felt his heart twist in his chest. He'd never meant this, he'd never meant to harm her—he would sooner die than know he'd harmed her. "Phoebe," he said, a bit desperately, "there is something I feel I *must* say—"

"Summerfield!"

The voice of Fremont startled them both; they turned toward him as he hurried to Will's side. "Come down, then, you must see what Mr. Ellison found at the edge of the gardens!" he called eagerly.

"I beg your pardon?" Will asked, trying to get his bearings.

"A *snake*, Summerfield! Ellison found a remarkable specimen!" Fremont exclaimed happily. "He saved Miss Waters from certain harm!"

"I am certain he did," Will drawled, and glanced at Phoebe, but she'd already moved away.

He did not see her again until Wednesday afternoon, and even then, in the company of Miss Dumbarton and the two Duckworth children. Miss Dumbarton chatted so much that Will thought he would go mad. He wanted only to speak to Phoebe, not listen to some tale of two ill-behaved children.

"They have permission to attend the ball for one hour," Miss Dumbarton informed Will as the children kicked a ball along the edge of the terrace. "It seems as if everyone shall be there but Madame Dupree. Can you imagine it, my lord? That after all her effort to make the family masks, adjust the masks, *adorn* the masks—she will not attend?"

Will looked at Phoebe. She smiled a little self-consciously. "I hardly have the proper attire, Miss Dumbarton. I am not a guest here."

"The honor would be ours, Madame Dupree, if you would attend the ball," Will said. "I would escort you myself—"

"My lord, you will have quite enough to keep you occupied," she interjected, and glanced at the children. "I will keep company with Mr. and Mrs. Turner. They've invited me to dine."

"Are you certain?" he asked, feeling hopeless. "Miss Dumbarton and I will be inconsolable if you do not attend."

"Yes, we will!" Miss Dumbarton chimed in. "I have come to rely on her friendship."

Phoebe laughed. "You will hardly be inconsolable! There will be much to divert you!"

"Master David! Please do not put dirt in your sister's hair!" Miss Dumbarton called. "Excuse me," she said, hurrying off to tend the children.

Will looked at Phoebe. He felt remarkably chaotic inside—he needed a moment alone with her, just a moment.

"Oh, Madame Dupree, will you lend a hand?" Miss Dumbarton called. The children's hands were both covered in mud.

"Yes, of course," Phoebe said, and left Will standing there wearing his heart on his sleeve.

No matter how much Susan begged her, Phoebe declined to attend the ball. She couldn't tell Susan that Lady Purnam might see her—or worse, Will might offer for Miss Fitzherbert and shatter her heart to pieces. She could not attend. She was really quite adamant about it.

But the night of the ball, there was a knock at her door that she was certain must be Susan. Phoebe stopped her packing—she'd been slowly and methodically packing her things these last two days—and opened the door.

"You seem surprised," Alice drawled as she swept

inside, wearing a gold ball gown Phoebe had made her. She looked resplendent. Regal.

"Come to the ball," Alice said, dispensing with any small talk.

"What?" Phoebe said, certain she'd not heard her correctly.

Alice touched a gloved hand to her forehead. "Please, Phoebe," she said softly. "I cannot face them alone. I've been such a fool."

"You won't be alone—"

"Yes, of course I will. Who will be by my side? Jane? My brothers?" She laughed sardonically. "Please. I . . . I need a friend just now."

Phoebe sighed. They had clearly crossed some line. "But I have nothing to wear," she said low.

Alice smiled and held up a silky blue mask she had kept hidden in the folds of her gown. "I found it among all the other masks in the room downstairs. There is a hood to go with it. It would go well with your eyes . . . and the silver gown."

"The silver gown?" Phoebe asked her suspiciously. The silver gown was the one she'd worn to her court presentation. "How do you know about the silver gown?"

Lady Alice chuckled. "Really, Madame Dupree—do you think Jane and I haven't had a look through your wardrobe? The silver gown with the lovely embroidery and beading is beautiful and would go well with this mask," she said, thrusting it forward.

Phoebe looked at the mask and smiled a little. "It would indeed."

Will stood at the door to receive the guests arriving at Wentworth Hall, feeling a bit ridiculous in his mask. He stood a head taller than most men—it was hardly a disguise.

He'd heard enough talk to know that all of Bedford-shire had looked forward to this event. When he was a boy, his parents were renowned for their beautiful balls, which were still remembered with reverence. There were many in the county, he gathered, who hoped there would be a return to those idyllic days at Wentworth Hall when he married.

His guests were in high spirits. Someone thrust a tot of whiskey in Will's hand, and Jane, wearing plumes of feathers, trilled with excitement when he pretended not to know her.

Will moved through the crowd, playing at the game of masquerade, but inside, he was counting the moments until he might slip away to Phoebe. He had realized these last two days how excruciatingly empty the week had been without her. He didn't want to be host to more than two hundred souls without her. He didn't want to dine at his table if she were not seated there. He could no longer deny what was in his heart—Phoebe was the one woman he would love all his life. Now that he'd tasted that sort of love, he was afraid of losing it.

But the end was in sight. On the morrow, his guests would begin to take their leave. He had only to endure a day, two at most, and then he might chart a course with Phoebe, the two of them thinking and planning together. He had only to make it through this night.

Intent on making the best of it, Will tried to enjoy the event. He'd attended two masquerade balls in his life—one in Paris, one in Barcelona—and both had led to rapacious behavior on the part of most everyone in attendance. A simple mask seemed to release the most basic inhibitions in the meekest of people.

Tonight was no exception. Henry was in high spir-its, dancing with all the young women. Will looked for Caroline, but could not make her out in the sea of young women with plumes and masks who were dressed in various shades of white. He danced with a woman in black who brushed her fingers suggestively high across his thigh and said, "What a pleasure it is to dance, my lord. Would that we might enjoy a more intimate dance."

Another time, another version of himself, and Will would have enjoyed her offer of an intimate dance. But he handed her off when the music ended and sipped another tot of whiskey as he moved below the glittering light of the candles in three massive chandeliers.

He was surprised to see Alice standing to one side. He'd not seen her enter the ballroom. She looked, he thought, very lovely. Her mask was simple and gold to match her gown, her smile beneath it pretty. It was amazing, he thought, how her countenance was so transformed with her smile—he'd never really noticed that before because she smiled so seldom.

Was Alice truly so unhappy? He questioned his wisdom in keeping her from Hughes. But, no, he assured himself. Hughes was not only from the wrong rung of the social ladder, he was a rogue and a bounder. His sister deserved much better than that.

He turned away from admiring Alice and inadvertently collided with a woman whose jeweled mask could not have come from Bedfordshire. It was so exquisite and expensive it could only have come from London.

"Lord *Summerfield*," she purred. "How lovely of you to have such a delicious gathering so far from London."

Will leaned forward and peered at the sparkling, wide brown eyes behind the mask. "Lady Holland?"

"You have discovered me," she said smoothly, sinking into a curtsy.

"How good of you to come all this way," he said, taking up her hand and bowing over it. "I regret that I did not receive you when you arrived."

"You were dutifully occupied when I arrived, my lord. But of course I came! The notion of a country ball was simply too grand to be missed. My good friend Lady Purnam from London has never attended a country masquerade, can you imagine? I assured her she would be suitably diverted. The poor woman has not stopped dancing since the orchestra began playing, and she has not once complained of her poor ankles! Have you any idea how remarkable that is?"

"I do not," he said, smiling. "You must point her out so that I might make her acquaintance," he said.

"She is just there!" Lady Holland said, and pointed across the room. He followed the line of her fan and spied a slightly rotund woman with a similarly elaborate mask, dancing the quadrille. And about ten feet behind her was Alice, speaking with a woman who stood partially in the shadows. The woman put her hand to her throat and Will started.

Phoebe.

His entire body reacted, filling with heat. She was speaking with Alice, her conversation animated. Dear God, had he noticed how gracefully she moved before this moment? The regal carriage? The beauty in her when even her face was covered? She wore a silver gown embroidered and beaded with tiny crystals, and a pale blue hood that covered her lustrous pale blond hair. Beneath it, she wore a matching blue silk mask shaped like cat's eyes.

He could hardly carry on the conversation with Lady

Holland. His whole body felt as if it were reverberating with his heartbeat. He managed to nod and smile at Lady Holland as she spoke, and finally extracted himself.

He headed directly for Phoebe, pushing through the crowd, ignoring any greeting put to him as the quadrille ended and the dancers moved into the crowd, making the navigation across the room even more difficult.

When he reached them, he spoke to his sister first. "Alice," he said, leaning in to kiss her cheek. "How lovely you are."

"Thank you," Alice said with a surprised smile.

Standing beside her, something flickered across Phoebe's blue eyes.

Will turned to her and inclined his head. "Madam."

A smile curved her rouged lips. "Sir, I believe I know your identity."

"I am certain I know yours, and if my sister will be kind enough to excuse us, I should like to invite you to dance."

Alice looked at him, then at Phoebe, and nodded politely. Will offered his arm; Phoebe glanced around the room as if she were looking for someone before hesitantly laying her hand on his arm. He covered it quickly, lest she take it away, and led her to the dance floor.

"You came," he said, feeling ridiculously pleased as they faced each other on the dance floor.

"How did you know me? My hair is covered," she said, sounding disappointed.

He couldn't help but smile. "It is impossible to explain how the heart knows what it knows. I would know you if you were covered in muck."

She laughed softly. "Let us hope you will never know me in that state."

"I am surprised you have come," he said softly. "You seemed determined to avoid this masque."

She smiled again and glanced anxiously about. "I came for Alice," she said, and glanced up at him. The music was beginning; Will took her in hand and stepped into the dance. Phoebe's eyes were glittering behind the mask, and for Will, the effect was astonishingly arousing.

"Alice is . . . she is uncertain of herself," she added.

"That is very kind of you. Phoebe . . . I must speak with you privately," he said. "Before the night is done."

"No," she said instantly. "There are too many people here."

He twirled her and pulled her close. "I hardly care if anyone should notice."

"*Will—*"

"Meet me on the side terrace."

"What you are suggesting is careless," she said, and gripped his hand tightly as he twirled her again.

"I've scarcely seen you this week," he said earnestly. "I *must* see you. I must speak to you privately."

Phoebe blinked. He was reminded of other times he'd looked into those pale blue eyes, when he'd been on top of her, loving her. He realized his breathing was shallow, as if he could not catch his breath as he waited for her answer. *He was breathing underwater.* He was gasping for breath.

"All right," she whispered, giving him the breath he needed. "But only a moment—"

"The side terrace, outside the breakfast room," he said before she could change her mind. "Do you know it?"

She nodded.

"It is dark there—you will not be noticed."

"Are you certain? It's so warm that there seemed to be dozens milling about outside."

"There is a full moon and a torchlit path that leads to the lake. Most of the guests are walking there."

She nodded, and glanced around again, shifting slightly so that she did not stand so close. "When?" she whispered.

"One hour. Midnight. Most will go up for supper then."

Phoebe's gaze was filled with longing, Will thought, and another emotion that eluded him. "Midnight," she whispered.

Will smiled and spun her into the stream of dancers.

Thirty-three

⎯⎯⎯∞∞⎯⎯⎯

The minutes until midnight seemed the longest of Phoebe's life.

People were going out of the house in groups and returning with their masks askew. Women were brazenly flirting with men, and men were actively pursuing women, and not always their wives.

The only bright spot in the night was that Phoebe was certain Lady Purnam had not come. She hadn't seen her familiar rotund figure walking among the more than two hundred guests.

She thought she'd never endure the waiting, but when the clock struck twelve—the witching hour, she wryly noted—she walked through the terrace doors and took several deep breaths.

The night was cloyingly warm, a sign of changes to come. Everyone seemed to feel it—there were people everywhere in various stages of unmasking, laughing together, and roaming about the parterres. Beyond the gardens, beneath a full moon, were more guests. They were not, as Will had suggested, going up to supper.

Phoebe moved around the edge of the terrace, glancing over her shoulder before she stepped through the large planters that separated the main terrace from the narrow one that ran along the east wing of the house.

But before she could slip through, she caught sight of something in the full moon's light that arrested her. Just below the parterres, near the gazebo, stood Apollo. She would recognize that majestic beast anywhere.

For a moment she thought she had imagined it, for the horse moved into a shadow. Phoebe hurried to the edge of the terrace, leaning forward, straining to see in the dark. The horse moved back into view beneath the full moon. He seemed to be alone, and she wondered if his herd had been completely decimated by poachers. It seemed as if no one could see him but Phoebe—no one turned in his direction. The people by the lake were diverted by something else, all of them gathered around someone or something near the water's edge. She could hear the raised voices, the deep tones of the men, and the ladies exclaiming.

Phoebe removed her mask and watched Apollo paw the ground. He seemed anxious, as if the people made him skittish. And then, just as he had appeared, Apollo wheeled about and cantered into the woods.

"Lady Phoebe? As I breathe! It *is* you!"

Phoebe gasped and whirled about, her eyes wide and her heart already in her throat.

Lady Purnam pushed up her mask and squinted at Phoebe. "What on *earth* are you doing here?" she demanded, clearly confused.

"Ah . . ." Whatever excuse Phoebe might have made was lost, for that was the moment Will walked out onto the terrace. He saw her immediately, and as he began striding toward her, Phoebe's heart began to race painfully.

"I was quite certain Ava told me you were at Broderick Abbey," Lady Purnam said as Will reached them. "When did you come back from Broderick Abbey? I was not informed."

Will glanced at Lady Purnam, who had yet to see him on her right.

"I, ah . . . well, no, actually, I was not at Broderick Abbey. I've been *here*. I have been, ah . . . *retained* here."

"*Retained?*" Lady Purnam all but shouted. "Whatever do you mean, *retained*? Lady Phoebe, is the marchioness aware that you are even here?"

"The marchioness?" Will repeated, startling Lady Purnam.

"I beg *your* pardon?" Lady Purnam asked, tilting her head back to look at Will.

"I beg *your* pardon," he said, taking off his mask, too. "I am Lord Summerfield. I don't believe I've had the pleasure."

"Oh!" Lady Purnam said, sinking into a curtsy. "My lord, Lady Agatha Purnam at your service." She rose up and smiled brightly. "I was just asking Lady Phoebe what on *earth* she is doing here instead of at Broderick Abbey."

"Broderick Abbey . . ." he said, looking curiously at Phoebe. "Do you have a commission there as well?"

"A commission?" Lady Purnam repeated, then

snorted. "I can't imagine what sort of *commission* her sister, the marchioness, might have arranged."

Will blinked. He looked at Lady Purnam, his gaze intent. Phoebe could feel the life draining out of her.

"The marchioness," he repeated.

"Lady Purnam, please—allow me to explain—"

"—The *Marchioness* of Middleton, my lord," Lady Purnam said proudly. "Lady Phoebe's sister. Oh, the two of them and their cousin, Lady Radnor, are thick as thieves. I was assured by the marchioness not two days ago that Phoebe was summering at Broderick Abbey but would return to town before the start of the Little Season."

Phoebe groaned; Will's gaze went from hard to confused. He gaped at Lady Purnam as if she were a lunatic. "I beg your pardon—am I given to understand that this . . . this *woman* is—"

"Lady Phoebe Fairchild," Lady Purnam offered proudly as two men raced up onto the terrace and looked wildly about. "The daughter of the late Earl of Bingley and Lady Downey, may God rest her soul."

Will turned his head and looked at Phoebe. His eyes raked over her so hard that she could almost feel it slicing through her skin. It took a moment to find her voice. "I can explain everything, if you will—"

"Are you not acquainted with Lady Phoebe?" Lady Purnam interrupted, and just as abruptly, she suddenly giggled. "Oh *dear*, I had not realized! Lady Phoebe does usually care for parlor games, you may ask anyone in Mayfair—I hadn't realized she was partaking in the games of the masque."

Phoebe had never seen such a look as she saw in Will's eyes in the moment he comprehended she had lied to him, that she had deceived him. It felt as if her heart had been pierced and all the blood had been let out of it. "I can explain—"

But she was interrupted again by the two men who raced to Will's side. One of them caught him by the arm in what seemed like a dream. Will turned slowly, the light of the torch catching his golden hair.

"My lord, forgive us," the man said. "You must come!"

"Not now," he said gruffly, and shrugged off the man's hand, stepping forward and grasping Phoebe by the elbow.

"My lord!" the man cried with alarm.

"Not *now!*" he snapped—he only had eyes for Phoebe. "If I may, *Lady Phoebe*, I should like a word," he said, and began steering her past the potted plants onto the small side terrace. Once they were out of sight and earshot of the others, he pushed her away from him with disgust. "*Lady* Phoebe?" he said acidly. "What sort of cruel game are you playing?"

"It's not a game! I can explain if you will just listen," she said desperately. "I don't . . . I never meant to deceive you."

"Oh no? So by presenting yourself as some seamstress and assuming a different name you did not mean to *deceive,* you meant to . . . to *what*, Phoebe? What did you mean to do?" He was furious; his hand clenched and unclenched at his side, and his eyes were blazing with anger.

"I did *not* . . ." She closed her eyes a moment, sought her breath. "It is so complicated, Will," she said, opening her eyes. "I was forced into this. Mrs. Ramsey blackmailed me into this work—"

"Blackmail!" he scoffed.

"Yes, blackmail! If you would just *listen* to me! She blackmailed me and threatened me with scandal and said she would derail the reforms my brothers-in-

law would see through Parliament, and I thought . . .
I thought there would be no harm in doing what she
asked because I was not acquainted with anyone in
Bedfordshire."

"Would you now have me believe that you just *happen* to have the skills of a trained seamstress and then
fabricated your entire *life*?" he said, incredulous.

It sounded ridiculous, even to her. "It is complicated," she said again. "There were other people who
had to be considered, and if you . . . just *please* try and
understand me—"

"How many lies did you tell me?" he asked flatly.

"I—how many? I don't know," she said as her belly
began to churn. "My life—but not about us. *Never* about
us!" she cried, seeing the look of disbelief in his eyes.
"Will, you must believe that I never meant to hurt you. I
was going to tell you everything! *Tonight!* Tonight I was
going to tell you everything!"

"Yes, well, that seems too little, and far too late,
madam. You must think me a bloody fool."

He said it with such disgust that Phoebe bristled.
He looked at her as if she were some sort of villain, as
if she'd concocted some elaborate plan expressly to deceive him. Her fear mixed with a sudden surge of anger.
"I wouldn't have lied to you at all, I would not have
spoken to you, had you not persisted in seducing me!"
she said sharply.

Will's eyes widened with surprise. "I beg your *pardon!*"

"You cannot deny it!" she said heatedly. "You pushed
and *pushed* me, even while you were planning to marry
someone else!"

"How ironic it is that the thing I had to tell *you* tonight, the thing that could not wait another moment,
was that I was *not* going to marry anyone else, for I

love you, Phoebe. I . . ." He drew a quick breath as if he'd just been struck. "I *love* you!"

"Dear God, Will . . . you *must* know that I love you, too."

"I don't know what I know, Phoebe, except this: The difference between us is that I will never be certain you love me because I can never be certain of you again. But you can always be certain I loved you because I was never anything but completely honest with you!"

"What do you want from me?" she cried, throwing her arms wide. "What do you want me to say? I am sorry I deceived you. It was never my intent! But once it started it mushroomed out of control and I am trying desperately to explain it to you! But it doesn't change the fact that I love you!"

"Do you?" he sneered. "Or is that yet another of your damnable lies?"

Phoebe gasped; the venom in his voice made her physically ill.

At the same moment, a gentleman stepped around one of the potted plants and clamped a hand down hard on Will's shoulder. "*Will*," he said sternly.

Will hardly spared him a glance. "Henry, please. I—"

"Joshua has been called out."

Will dropped his mask. Phoebe gasped and covered her heart with her hand; everything around her seemed to stop. The wind, the flickering of the torches—everything.

"By whom?"

"Mr. Fitzherbert."

Will blinked. "*Where?*" he asked simply.

The gentleman pointed toward the lake, and Will was suddenly striding away from Phoebe.

The air seemed to thicken, but Phoebe shivered. She felt suddenly cold on the inside and out, and folded her arms tightly around her, trying to stop the shivering as she followed the two men past the potted plants.

Lady Purnam was still there, up on her tiptoes, trying to see over the crowd that had gathered on the terrace. "Have you heard? I cannot imagine such ill behavior!" Lady Purnam declared when Phoebe touched her arm. "But I've heard woeful tales of this family. You'd do well to keep your distance." She glanced at Phoebe and frowned. "What on *earth* were you doing with him?"

"Lady Purnam, I must return to London straight-away," Phoebe choked out. "At morning's first light."

"What? You cannot mean it, darling. We're to stay until Sunday. And besides, I came in the company of Lady Holland—"

"*No,*" Phoebe said, and suddenly gripped Lady Purnam's arm. "I *must* go as soon as possible, and you have to help me! Have a carriage brought around at dawn, *please!*"

Lady Purnam gasped. "Good Lord, child, are you ill?"

"Yes," Phoebe said as tears filled her eyes. "I am on death's door. I have to leave here."

"Oh my dear, I think with a bit of rest—"

"Madam, will you please just *once* do as you are asked and not debate it?" Phoebe cried, earning a look or two from those around them.

Lady Purnam reared back. "Very well. I will speak to Lady Holland and see if we can't borrow her coach to take you home."

"*Thank* you," Phoebe said. She glanced down to the lake's edge, where dozens of people had gathered. She could see Will's golden head at the center. She could not see his face or his eyes, but God help her, she could feel them. They were still burning through her, still slicing her open.

She abruptly turned and ran into the ballroom, leaving her battered and bleeding heart on the terrace.

The house erupted into chaos when Mr. Fitzherbert, who'd had very high hopes of marrying his only daughter to Viscount Summerfield, stumbled upon her in a compromising position. Not with the viscount, unfortunately, which, some would argue later, might have sped along a happy ending for the Fitzherberts. But with the viscount's brother, Mr. Joshua Darby.

That could not be a happy ending for either family.

A debate would rage for several months in Greenhill as to whether Miss Fitzherbert had welcomed the young man's advances and had, indeed, loved him, or if she had been caught completely unawares, having mistaken Mr. Joshua Darby for Lord Summerfield on that dark and hot, sultry night of the masquerade ball.

Whatever had happened, by the following day, it was all over the county. Mr. Fitzherbert had called out Joshua Darby, intent on avenging his daughter's honor. It was a fabulous scandal, one that rocked the household staff and titillated the many guests. Fortunately, a duel was averted by Summerfield's quick thinking and actions. He extracted an agreement from Joshua and Caroline that they would marry straightaway, thereby making it impossible for Mr. Fitzherbert to risk killing his future son-in-law in a duel. The agreement was sweetened by a favorable negotiation for the Fitzherberts regarding a dowry.

The crisis was averted, but nevertheless, everyone remarked on the stunning deceit between the brothers, and in that furor Phoebe had slipped back to London.

No one seemed to notice she'd gone—except Billy,

who'd helped her load her things on the carriage. And Addison, whom Phoebe begged to deliver a letter over which she had labored all night. It was for Will. In it she tried—admittedly, very badly—to explain everything.

Only Phoebe knew the extent of the deceit Will had suffered that night: His sister, his brother, and his lover had all managed to deceive him in the space of one week.

Thirty-four

―❧❧❧―

LONDON
ONE MONTH LATER

At Middleton House, where Phoebe had taken refuge after she'd fled Wentworth Hall, Ava tried daily, and vainly, to bring Phoebe back into the fold of proper society, particularly with the Little Season upon them—but Phoebe would not have it. She could not face Lord Stanhope's attentions or any other attempt at matchmaking.

Ava persevered as only Ava could. Everyone was coming back from the country, and Ava finally managed to extract from Phoebe a promise to attend a soiree one evening. It was to be held at the home of the venerable Lord Murdoch, but the numbers would be small, as debutantes had not yet been presented to court, and gentlemen had not yet begun to trawl the ballrooms of Mayfair in search of potential matches.

But as Phoebe seemed resigned at best, Ava took it upon herself to review Phoebe's trunk full of gowns and select one that would present her sister in her best light. She was digging through the many gowns when she suddenly whirled around and said, "I forgot to tell you what news I have had from Lady Purnam!"

"I can scarcely wait," Phoebe drawled. She had her nephew, Jonathan, on her hip and was trying to rearrange the tresses of hair he had managed to work free from her coif.

"Lady Purnam tells me that the ladies of the *haute ton* are *quite* displeased with wretched Mrs. Ramsey for having lost Madame Dupree," Ava said gleefully as she pulled the pale green silk and chiffon gown Phoebe had made and held it up to herself in the mirror. "It seems there is no suitable substitute for her exquisite gowns, and ladies across Mayfair are taking their commissions away from Mrs. Ramsey. More threaten to do so if she does not produce a suitable *modiste* before the start of the Season next year."

"Oh?" Phoebe asked, perking up a bit as she put Jonathan down on his wobbly legs. She never tired of hearing how well her gowns were received. Or how far Mrs. Ramsey might fall.

"I, for one, am surprised the slatternly woman hasn't come around to convince you to continue," Ava said pertly.

"Ava!" Phoebe cried with a laugh, and turned around, to where Jonathan had fallen onto his bottom and was crawling toward a skein of yarn from which Phoebe was attempting to knit a cap for him. "You shouldn't speak so carelessly in front of my nephew!"

Ava flicked her wrist at Phoebe before holding the

gown up to her. "He doesn't understand me, and besides, she *is* slatternly. Oh, this is *wonderful*, Phoebe! It is the perfect gown for you!"

"I do not believe she has the courage to even speak to me," Phoebe said, trading Jonathan for the gown and walking to the full-length mirror to have a look herself. "And besides," she added absently, "on the day I went to her shop to demand that she *never* speak of Madame Dupree again, she had a bank note from Lord Summerfield and seemed to be quite done with the whole ruse."

"I wonder if you will ever speak of it," Ava muttered.

Phoebe sighed. "What is there to say, Ava? I told you everything. I loved him, and he will never speak to me again."

"Yes, you told *me* everything. But did you tell *him*?"

"You know I did. I wrote it all in the letter that I left for him. I told him about the blackmail and the reforms and how I believed I had no choice but to do what I did. I told him *everything*," she said adamantly. How much she loved him, how desperately sorry she was for what had happened.

"If he can't accept it, then there is nothing to be done for it. I just think . . ." Ava's voice trailed off.

Phoebe turned and looked at her sister. "What? You think what?"

Ava shrugged a little. "That if he loved you, he'd forgive you."

Phoebe had thought the same thing, and she turned abruptly, swallowing down the tears that were building. "Stop, Ava, stop right there. There is no point in such speculation. I haven't heard a word from him because he *can't* forgive me." When Ava didn't speak, Phoebe looked at her in the reflection in the mirror.

Ava shrugged again. "He wasn't exactly innocent, was he?" she asked quietly.

"Ava, *please*," Phoebe said wearily.

"You know what else I think?" Ava asked, eyeing Phoebe in the mirror. "*That* is the one gown you must wear, darling. Look how it enhances the color of your eyes. You are so beautiful, Phoebe."

Phoebe didn't feel beautiful. She felt ugly. And when she looked in the mirror, she saw a very sad woman full of regret.

The Murdoch soirée was not Will's first foray into London society, but it was certainly the most august. He'd been surprised by the number of invitations that had been extended him, particularly given the reputation of his family and what had come to be known as the Summer Scandals in and around Bedfordshire.

But it would appear that Will's reputation for being unmarried, titled, and in possession of a fortune was enough for any number of mothers and fathers in the *haute ton* to turn the other cheek. Will was beginning to believe he was the last bachelor in all of England.

He might very well be the last bachelor in England, for he could hardly bear the thought of a courtship now. The loneliness inside him had only intensified since that black night he'd been sent reeling. Joshua's betrayal of him was enough to drive a man mad, but Phoebe's deception had been . . . devastating.

Lady Phoebe Fairchild, the sister-in-law of the Marquis of Middleton and the Earl of Radnor. Not a seamstress. Not a servant. A woman from the highest circles of the aristocracy, playing at some game and using his heart as her pawn.

Once he'd realized her chicanery, he'd suddenly recognized the signs of it that he'd missed. She hadn't remembered where she'd lived in Paris because she had never been to Paris. She was reluctant to speak of a husband she never knew. She claimed to be from the moors, but then cited Berwick-upon-Tweed as the village where she was raised. He'd thought her too refined for her position, and worst of all, he realized, he had taken her virginity that afternoon at the ruins.

What a bloody fool he'd been. A bloody, naïve, ignorant fool.

To make matters worse, he'd discovered how very painful love could be. He'd never imagined such pain, but it woke him in the middle of the night and kept him from sleep, for he had loved Phoebe. He had *loved* her.

He'd still not recovered. But he had forgiven her.

He'd read the letter she'd left him after the debacle with Joshua had been repaired and the guests had all left. He'd understood the words that explained what had happened to make her do such an extraordinary thing—the death of her mother, her attempt to help her sister and cousin. How she had been caught up in a lie that had continued to build. And Will couldn't help but admit to himself that part of him was relieved she was not a seamstress, and therefore unattainable for him in some respects. She was in truth someone he could love openly, could marry without censure.

But part of him could not help but ache at her betrayal. He relived every moment they had shared, wondering why she hadn't told him at one point or another. He wondered what was a lie about her and what was real, and made himself mad trying to guess.

He did not respond to her letter. He couldn't. He was still reeling from all the events of that night, of the betrayals he had suffered between Joshua, Alice, and Phoebe. He had spent a fortnight moping about, cleaning up Joshua's mess, and wishing he were in a desert, or on a mountain—anywhere but in England.

Yet he continued to make his way—numbly—through supper parties and soirées, still intent on his duty. Tonight, he would force himself to dance with the debutantes, to remark on the weather and the cuisine, and to try once more to find a woman with whom he might spend his life.

But he had not counted on the breath being knocked clean from his lungs, for the very ground on which he was standing to begin to roll, making him feel ill. Perhaps it was a bit myopic of him, but Will had not counted on Lady Phoebe Fairchild attending the soirée.

Truthfully, the Murdoch soirée was not as bad as Phoebe had feared. She danced once with Lord Harrison, another of Middleton's bachelor friends, and rather enjoyed speaking with an old friend, Emily Rothschild, who titillated her with the scandal of one Grace Holcomb, who had defied her father's wishes and married a sheep merchant. But it seemed a rather romantic story and Emily assured Phoebe that Grace's husband, Mr. Barrett Adlaine, was very handsome and prosperous.

"I wish someone like that would take a liking to me," Emily said wistfully.

"They will, Emily!" Phoebe said, laughing. "In just a matter of a few months, we will embark on another Season full of dashing gentlemen."

"But they are all taken!" Emily pouted. "All but *him*, and the queue has already begun."

"Who?" Phoebe asked, and turned to look where Emily nodded.

She looked right into Will's hazel green eyes. His hands were clasped behind his back, his expression cold. She froze—her body simply froze. She was incapable of moving. But oh, how her heart started in leaps and fits.

His golden hair brushed his collar, his sideburns were long and trimmed against his cheek. He was wearing a black suit, impeccably tailored. He was beautiful, impossibly handsome.

"Do you know him?" Emily asked excitedly, nudging Phoebe with her shoulder. "He's only just arrived from the country, you know—my father called on him yesterday. He's terribly handsome, is he not?" Emily sighed.

"I, ah . . . yes, he's . . . he is handsome," Phoebe stammered. She couldn't speak properly. Her limbs suddenly felt like lead, her feet mired in quicksand.

"Quite handsome," Emily said again, very wistfully. When Phoebe did not answer, Emily gave her a sidelong glance. "Well, for God's sake, don't *stare* at him," she whispered, turning away.

But Phoebe couldn't help staring. Her heart was floundering, her palms growing damp. She had dreamt of him so often, and here he was, not ten feet from her.

"*Phoebe!*" Emily hissed.

Still, Phoebe did not move. She smiled. Briefly, tremulously, but she smiled. At the very same moment, some people stepped between them. When they moved again, Will's back was to her. He may as well have cut her heart from her chest and ground it into the carpet. It hurt no less than that.

How Phoebe managed to endure the rest of that night, she would never know—he was everywhere she turned, laughing with friends, dancing with ladies, and looking so beautiful that she wanted to cry. Yet every time his gaze landed on her, a hard look would shutter his eyes, and he would turn away.

He reviled her. He despised her. And Phoebe thought she would perish from shame and hurt and the most intense longing she had ever felt in her life.

She just wanted to be gone, to hide until this interminable, wretched night was over. She was so caught up in Will that she did not see Alice until she appeared at her side. "*Alice!*" she exclaimed, startled.

"Good evening, Phoebe," Alice said smoothly. She was wearing one of Phoebe's creations and looked very well. "How do you do?" Her decorum was as stunning as her sudden appearance.

"I . . . I am well, thank you."

"I am surprised to see you," Alice said. "But I had hoped that I would."

Phoebe nodded and swallowed hard. Whatever Alice had come to say, she deserved it, and she steeled herself, waiting. "You look very well," she remarked.

"Thank you," Alice said, with a bob of her head. "I am to be married."

Phoebe blinked.

"Surprised, are you? I have accepted a match with Mr. Samuel Remington. You remember him, do you not? He was the only gentleman not put off by my scandal," she said with a hint of a smile.

The news was startling. "Are you . . . are you happy?" Phoebe asked curiously.

"As happy as one can be about these things, I suppose." She shrugged insouciantly. "It might interest you to know that Joshua and Caroline Fitzherbert married just a fortnight after you left. Naturally, given the scandal, it was prudent that they marry straightaway."

Another stunning piece of news. Phoebe wanted badly to ask after Will, but did not dare speak his name aloud.

"Jane and I are to be presented to London society

with the hopes that Jane will secure a match. Unfortunately, after my scandal, Jane's prospects dimmed . . . and everyone was so certain she'd be the one to emerge from it all unscathed. She swore she'd never forgive me . . . but then, she had not yet seen London." Alice smiled a little. "Roger has purchased a commission in the Royal Navy. He'll be joining them after Christmas."

Phoebe's thoughts were tumbling over themselves—she was too unhinged to respond.

"What do you think of our news, Lady Phoebe?" Alice asked.

"I think it is splendid," Phoebe said. Her mouth was dry; it felt as if her throat was closing. "How does . . . how is . . . ?"

"Will?"

Phoebe shook her head and cleared her throat. "Your father."

"The same," Alice said evenly. "The doctors have said he might remain in his state for years before succumbing."

Phoebe nodded. An uncomfortable silence spread like water between them.

"Won't you ask about him?" Alice asked quietly.

She meant Will. Phoebe wanted to ask, God knew how she wanted to ask.

"He is sullen still," Alice offered without waiting for Phoebe to find the courage to ask. "But I think he'd be cheered to speak to you."

"What?" Phoebe exclaimed, and quickly shook her head. "No, Alice. I cannot. I *dare* not—surely you must know what a complete disaster I have made of things."

"Surely I do," she said matter-of-factly. "But you once showed me friendship at a time I desperately needed it. Now I have the opportunity to return the kindness."

Phoebe eyed her warily. "He hates me."

"Well, he cannot hate you here without risking another scandal, can he? And who is to say what he thinks? He certainly hasn't said. Perhaps he does not hate you at all."

"You do not understand what you are asking of me!"

"Oh, but I do," Alice said quietly. "I *do* know. I may perhaps understand better than anyone."

God help her, but Alice looked so earnest. So determined. And when she linked her arm through Phoebe's and gave her a little tug, Phoebe did not resist. She felt her feet moving. She was moving, walking, on Alice's arm, to Will.

She thought she might faint from trepidation.

Will's back was to them. He was talking to a pair, men or women, Phoebe could hardly guess—she couldn't take her eyes from his back. When they reached him, Alice tapped Will on his shoulder. He instantly turned, his smile warm and loving for Alice—and then he saw Phoebe.

The moment he saw her his smile faded and the expression in his eyes turned cold. He said something to the people he was talking to and then turned slowly to face her.

"You remember Lady Phoebe, do you not?" Alice asked slyly.

He looked at her eyes, then at her mouth. "Of course." He politely inclined his head. "How do you do?"

"M-my lord," Phoebe managed, and curtsied.

"Phoebe, won't you introduce me?"

Thank God, it was Ava, appearing from nowhere at Phoebe's side. She put her arm around Phoebe's waist and smiled at Will. "I don't believe I've had the pleasure."

"May I introduce Lady Middleton," Phoebe said. "My sister. Ava, this is . . ." *This is him, he who is every-*

thing. "Lord Summerfield of Bedfordshire, a-and his sister, Lady Alice."

"A pleasure to meet you both," Ava said cheerfully, and beamed at Alice, then at Will. "From Bedfordshire, are you? Are you in London long, then, my lord?"

No, Ava, no, Phoebe silently pleaded with her sister. She knew her too well, knew that she would extract any information she could glean.

"Only a month," Will said. "We should like to be in the country before the weather turns too cold."

"Wentworth Hall, I presume? I have heard it is beautiful," Ava continued. Alice snorted a little, but Will looked at Phoebe again. She could read nothing in his eyes—he was carefully expressionless, she thought.

"I think it is," he said, and clenched his jaw tightly. His eyes flicked to Phoebe's throat and for the first time since seeing him again, she saw a hint of emotion. It was just a flicker, so brief that she couldn't be certain. Her hand fluttered to her throat and necklace. She'd forgotten—she was wearing the scarab. She wore it every day—it was the only thing she had of him.

"We have renovated the hall completely and it is quite improved," he said, his gaze flicking to her décolletage and to her eyes again for a breath of a moment.

"Oh, it must be divine. What do you think, Phoebe?" Ava asked, surreptitiously pinching her at the waist.

"I think . . . I *know* it is divine. I am certain of it," she said softly.

"Lady Alice, may I compliment you on your gown," Ava blithely continued. "It is *beautiful.*" She dropped her hand from Phoebe's waist, moving to Alice's side.

"Thank you," Alice said, giving Phoebe a curious look. She was wearing a gown Phoebe had made.

"I've rarely seen such careful needlework," Ava said,

putting her hand on Alice's back and forcing her to turn away from Phoebe and Will. "It is very elegant. One cannot find such elegant gowns in London any longer. One must send to Paris," she said, moving Alice away from Phoebe and Will. "But I know of a *modiste* who can be persuaded, from time to time, to make such elegant gowns as yours."

Behind them, Will and Phoebe stood not a foot apart, regarding one another. The silence between them was heartbreaking. A million things she might have said blazed through Phoebe's mind, but she rejected them all as too trite, too cavalier, and too empty. She looked at his eyes, remembered how they looked in the throes of passion. She looked at his mouth and recalled how tender and firm it was. She remembered every moment between them, every touch, every laugh, every caress. "You . . . you look well," she said softly.

He nodded curtly. His eyes flit over her face, over her eyes, her mouth. She wondered what he saw. A face that was once dear and now repugnant?

"Will, I . . . I am so happy to see you," she said.

"It has been a pleasure to see you again, Lady Phoebe," he said, as if he was speaking to a mere acquaintance. He looked into her eyes, then abruptly looked away. His expression, Phoebe thought, seemed almost helpless.

She realized then that he despised her that much—he despised her and he was helpless to escape her in this oppressive social setting. As if to prove it, he gestured to the crowd. "You must forgive me, but I promised Lord Chalmers . . ."

"Yes, yes, of course," she said, resisting the urge to weep. "You must go and . . ." *And leave me to crumble.* She couldn't bear to look at him again. She couldn't bear to see that helplessness. She glanced down and curtsied.

"Good evening," he said, and with a curt nod, he walked away.

That was it, then. She watched him walk away as her heart broke. He would never forgive her. All hope was gone.

Thirty-five

⸺⟨∞⟩⸺

Two days passed before Phoebe could speak of that awful night at all, much less face what it meant. She stayed in her suite of rooms, unable to rouse herself to do much more than sit at the hearth.

On the third day she refused to leave her suite of rooms, and she and Ava had quite a row about it. "You cannot continue to mope about!" Ava had snapped.

Phoebe collapsed onto the settee, her hands pressed against her burning cheeks, her head spinning. "I knew he would come to London eventually," she said morosely. "But I did not know it would hurt so, Ava. I cannot go out."

"Phoebe! I refuse to allow you to sit glumly in this room and waste away! You cannot possibly remain locked away from all of society!"

"I am quite content to paint," Phoebe said.

That earned a frown from Ava, who looked pointedly at the dozens of canvases scattered about Phoebe's sitting room, paintings in various stages of completion, of wild horses and country fields full of flowers, and of a grand old house with a stone gazebo. They were made from the dozens of scenes Phoebe had sketched during her days at Wentworth Hall.

There was one painting in particular—tucked behind several others—of a man holding out an apple to a magnificent horse.

"How many paintings will it take before you are able to face the world again?" Ava demanded crossly.

"I don't know," Phoebe said wearily. "Perhaps until . . ." *Until she stopped feeling so broken. Until she could look at herself in the mirror and not see the aching regret that ran so deep she could feel it in her marrow.*

When Phoebe didn't finish her sentence, Ava sighed heavily and sat on the edge of a chair across from her sister. "You are *impossible*," she said softly.

Phoebe blinked back tears. "I truly loved him, Ava."

"I know you did, darling." Ava put her arm around her.

"I shall never forget the look on his face when he realized how completely I had deceived him. Just thinking of it now brings these bloody tears to my eyes. And if you had seen the way he looked at me at the Murdoch soirée—Ava, he *loathes* me."

A moment of silence stretched between the sisters, Phoebe lost in her painful thoughts, and Ava having lost the ability to summon meaningless words to try to console her.

Ava did eventually coax Phoebe from her rooms, but she could not be convinced to go out into society—not while there was the slightest danger of encountering Will. But Ava soon let Phoebe be, as rumors suddenly began to swirl around Mayfair linking Phoebe to Madame Dupree.

Ava was very distressed that the rumors were impacting the work her husband was doing on the reforms—the battle in Parliament was becoming very intense. So intense that Greer and her husband, Rhodrick, returned from Wales earlier than they had planned.

Soon all of them were avoiding society, and the rumors of Phoebe's involvement in trade had reached an *on dit* in the morning *Times*.

> *The reforms some lords would see passed to benefit women engaged in occupations that, in effect, take a livelihood from a man, would seem to extend to ladies of leisure as well. A certain lady well connected to such reforms is thought to have engaged in a trade and profited from it. If ladies are now engaged in trade, will other privileges soon follow? Will dabbling in a man's occupation lead to suffrage? Will a woman's vote one day determine the men who will guide this country? Women are put on this earth to bear children and nurture their husbands, not determine the course of nations.*

It was a stinging rebuke, for the reforms and for Phoebe personally.

"I don't understand it!" Greer complained one afternoon as she held Jonathan on her lap. "Why should anyone want to deny poor women such basic rights?"

"Because women with rights are dangerous," Ava said snidely. "They might attempt to put food on their table instead of sitting about like frogs on their lily pads."

"It's ridiculous," Greer said. "There are times like this I should like to take certain thickheaded men onto a scaffold, explain the error in their thinking, and then hang the lot of them."

Ava laughed.

Greer did not. "What? What do you find so amusing?" she demanded. "There are some *very* thickheaded men in Parliament!"

As Ava and Greer debated the merits of the House of Lords, Phoebe thought of Frieda, and continued to paint. Her mind was a million miles from London.

But one rainy afternoon, a chambermaid informed them that Lucille Pennebacker, the spinster sister of their stepfather, Lord Downey, was calling for Phoebe. Ava and Greer both moaned, but Phoebe was glad for the respite.

"I'll see to it," she said, and left her sister and her cousin to debate to their hearts' content.

She made her way listlessly to the main hall and the receiving rooms there, smiling at one of the footmen, who opened the door to the small yellow salon. As she crossed the threshold, she smiled at Lucy. "How are you, Lucy?"

"Very well, thank you," Lucy said. She had been a rather strict minder when she'd come to supervise the three of them directly after their mother died, but since falling in love with Mr. Morris, the Downey butler, Lucy seemed to have adopted a different persona altogether. She was actually very pleasant at times.

"I hope you won't mind, but I escorted Lord Summerfield here myself, as he was given the wrong information as to your whereabouts."

Phoebe suddenly realized there was someone else in the room; she whirled about and saw Will standing at the front window. He steadily returned Phoebe's gaze.

"He called at Downey House in search of you, and as I was on my way out, I thought to escort him so he'd not get lost. The streets turn in such strange places."

"Oh. Yes. Thank you, Lucy," Phoebe muttered.

"Well, then, I have done my duty," Lucy said cheerfully. "I must continue on, for I am late to a meeting at the Ladies' Beneficent Society. We are gathering petitions to support Middleton's reforms."

"How very good of you," Phoebe said numbly. Her mouth was moving ahead of her brain; she could not take her eyes from Will.

"You really must call on your stepfather, if you don't mind me saying, dear. He's rather lonely since Violet returned to France. Well, then, until next we meet. My regards to your sister and cousin," Lucy said cheerfully, and with a nod of her head to Will, she quit the room.

Neither Phoebe nor Will spoke, but the tension between them was palpable, filling the room around them, swallowing them up. Oh, but Will looked magnificent—tall and strong and everything she recalled over and over again in her mind's eye. She longed to touch him, to lay her hand against his breast and feel his heart beating.

Will glanced at the door, and for a moment, Phoebe thought he would flee. How easily, she thought, love could shatter like a crystal snowflake. One touch, one ill wind, and its perfection was shattered.

How long had she felt shattered now, completely and irrevocably shattered?

He seemed to debate what he would do, but then slowly—excruciatingly, heartbreakingly slowly—he looked at her again. "You . . ." His voice was rough and caught on emotion. He pressed his lips together and nervously dragged a hand through his hair.

Phoebe caught a sob of despair in her throat. The sound of it caused Will to look at her, and his brow knit in a frown.

She felt the heft of this moment, knew that it would be her last and only opportunity to repair the rift between them. But it felt as if there was a bloody ocean between them—a cold, fathomless ocean that seemed too large to cross.

"You . . ." His eyes were intent on her. "You look beautiful," he said with great difficulty.

Phoebe gasped and covered her mouth. She had expected him to say something awful, something that would haunt her dreams. Not that she was *beautiful*.

He took a breath that filled his chest, and slowly released it. "I . . . I have been remiss," he said, sounding uncertain, looking at his hand as he stretched his fingers wide, "in not responding to your letter." He closed his hand again and looked up at her. "I did not know what to say."

"Will . . . please forgive me. What I did was . . . was—"

"Reprehensible?" he finished for her. He unclenched his fist and turned his head to look out the window.

Phoebe felt her knees give way a little and braced herself on the back of a chair. "I don't suppose it matters why I did what I did, but I . . . I never meant to fall in love with you, and I never meant to cause you any harm," she said.

He glanced at her sidelong, a slight frown on his face. "Phoebe—"

"I treated you ill," she said quickly. "I deceived you abominably." Tears filled her eyes as she remembered it all, as she'd remembered it all a thousand times since she'd left Wentworth Hall. "I never expected to *know* you, much less fall in love with you. But I did fall, headfirst and very deeply. Lord, how I wanted to tell you, but the lie . . . it started before I'd even met you, and then it got so deep and so wide so quickly that I did not know how to tell you. And when it was clear you would offer for Miss Fitzherbert, I allowed myself to believe there was no harm."

He suddenly threw up a hand. "No. No, Phoebe, I beg of you," he said, his voice raw, "you have apologized enough."

She gripped the back of the chair, uncertain if she could bear what he would say next.

"Phoebe . . . Lord God, you don't understand. It is *I* who have not apologized enough."

That stunned her.

"That night of the masque, I wanted to tell you that I would *not* offer for Miss Fitzherbert. I wanted to tell you that I loved *you*, and I hardly cared about your station in life." He took an unsteady step forward, his hand clenched at his side again. His gaze was so deep, so intent, she could see the raw hurt in him from a few steps away. "I would have told you that night that I would give up everything for you, Phoebe. I would give up all just to be with you."

"*Oh my God,*" she whispered. "*Oh my God.*" Her heart began to beat wildly.

"The discovery that you were not who you said you were was quite a blow, I admit," he said, wincing with the memory. "I was angry, and I suppose I reacted from shock and some odd notions of propriety that have been ingrained in me since birth—I hardly know. But you were right, Phoebe—I seduced you, I pushed our affair on you. You didn't want my attentions, but I pressed them home."

She was afraid to speak, afraid her emotions would collapse her.

"When I read your letter, I understood what you'd done—yet I still believed it was a wretched, inexcusable thing you had done. But in London . . . there have been so many things written that I appreciate now how impossible your situation must have seemed to you. I cannot fault you for what you did."

She gasped softly.

"There is one other thing I must concede to you," he said a little sheepishly. "I have come to realize, through some of the longest nights of my life, that love *does* matter when one is contemplating with whom one will spend the rest of one's natural life." He sighed wearily and opened his arms wide. "Phoebe, what I am attempting to say is that . . . I love you yet. I never knew how much until I saw you at the Murdoch assembly. When I saw you there, looking for all the world an angel, a bloody angel, I could scarcely speak. I could scarcely *breathe*."

Phoebe did not realize tears were sliding down her face until she tasted them on her lips. His words overwhelmed her, the realization that she had not lost him after all. She felt her knees giving away, felt herself sliding down to her knees, her hands still gripping the back of the chair, her forehead pressed against the fabric. "Dear God," she whispered. "I thought you hated me."

She closed her eyes as his words drifted through her. She couldn't seem to catch her breath; she was drawing big, thick gulps of air between sobs.

She started at the touch of his hand on her back. It felt so warm, so strong, just as she had remembered it day after day since she'd left. Phoebe wanted nothing more than to fling her arms around him, but she could not seem to let go of the chair. She could not seem to move.

"It is astonishing," Will said softly as he pried one of her hands from the back of the chair, "how a man can churn on the inside, yet give no hint of his true feelings on the outside." He pried her other hand free and caught her by the waist, pulling her up to her feet, and catching her when Phoebe sagged against him under the deluge of her relief.

Will took a handkerchief from his coat pocket and wiped the tears from her cheeks. "When I saw you at Murdoch's, all that I'd ever felt for you rose up like a storm in me, and I was perfectly incapable of speaking. I felt what someone once told me was a sign of true love—I felt as if I were breathing underwater."

Phoebe's heart soared. The hardness was gone from his eyes, replaced by a glimmer of the fever she'd come to know at Wentworth Hall.

"I did not," he said, dabbing the handkerchief beneath her nose, "reach the surface until the moment I laid eyes on you here, in this very room." He stopped dabbing her face and laid his palm against her cheek. "I love you, Phoebe—I never stopped loving you. And I will never stop loving you."

She tried to tell him she loved him, too, but her words erupted in one loud sob.

Will chuckled. "Marry me, Phoebe. Come back to Wentworth Hall. Travel with me, paint with me, have children with me. Just never leave my sight again."

"Yes," she said, grabbing the lapels of his coat. "Yes, yes, *yes* . . ."

He silenced her with a hard, passionate kiss full of longing and missed opportunities. Phoebe kissed him back with as much passion, with joy and hope and the promise of what was to come.

When he bent down and swept her up in his arms and carried her to the divan, she did not protest. She fumbled with the buttons of his waistcoat, eager to touch his flesh and feel his heart beat against her hand. He moved over her and looked down at her with eyes dark with passion. "I have missed you," he said. "God, how I have missed you."

"Show me," she said, and sighed with happiness when he put his hand on her ankle and began to slide it up her leg.

Will felt a little guilty a half hour later, when he and Phoebe emerged from the salon where they had engaged in rude, wretched, and thoroughly pleasurable behavior. He'd never met Middleton—it was hardly polite to take his sister-in-law on his divan. But what a taking it had been.

He knew a moment of panic when, hand in hand with Phoebe, they encountered Lady Middleton in the corridor. Lady Middleton gasped when she saw them. Her eyes raked over his disheveled state, then Phoebe's. With a cry of alarm, she slapped Phoebe on the forearm, and then just as abruptly threw her arms around Phoebe and squeezed her tight. "I am so *happy* for you!" she cried.

"Ava, I have something to tell you," Phoebe tried, but another woman appeared in the corridor, holding a baby boy.

"What has happened?" she demanded.

"Greer! Are you so lacking in perception?" Ava cried.

The other woman gasped. "*No!*" she cried, and hurried forward to hug Phoebe while Lady Middleton threw her arms around Will, surprising him. The three of them began to talk at once. One of them handed him the baby who instantly reached for his neckcloth and pulled one end free.

He couldn't help but laugh. He had a feeling he was about to embark on the greatest adventure of his life.

Epilogue

The charitable ball for the benefit of the works of the Ladies' Beneficent Society became the opening ball of the full Season, beginning in 1823, and for several years after, three couples hosted it—the Marquis and Marchioness of Middleton, the Earl and Countess of Radnor, and the Viscount and Viscountess Summerfield. They personally greeted the three hundred guests from the highest ranks of the Quality who attended, and graciously accepted donations throughout the night to help poor women and children.

The ball was begun as a consolation for the two lords who had fought so valiantly to see reforms benefiting poor women through Parliament. Unfortunately, their efforts had been derailed and no reforms were enacted—protections for working women would not begin to find widespread acceptance in Parliament until midcentury.

While not everyone agreed with their drive to protect poor women, donations to the Society grew nonetheless, and numerous poor women were helped into positions that paid a livable wage for them and their children.

And although Phoebe would never know it, even Frieda found a spot of happiness. After she had given birth to her first child, a young clergyman without a parish had taken pity on her, and the two of them eventually married and went to India to do missionary work.

The social furor over Summerfield's offering for Lady Phoebe Fairchild (several members of the *ton* felt they had not been given an adequate opportunity to present their unmarried daughters) died down over the course of that winter, and most people seemed to have forgotten the entire affair by the start of the Season the next spring.

It was also revealed that Lady Summerfield enjoyed designing and sewing gowns. While she did not accept commissions for them any longer—she could hardly do so while carrying her first child, after all—the women in her family were always thought to be clothed in the finest gowns in all of London.

The summer of 1824 would be known as the summer of the babies, as Ava, Greer, Phoebe, *and* Alice all gave birth. Jane, having only recently married Lord Richfield of Essex, was still touring Europe. Unfortunately, with birth there came death, and Will lost his father in the autumn of 1824. But the earl had lived long enough to hold his first grandchild in his lap.

Joshua and Caroline Darby inherited a small manor estate in the north of Bedfordshire and, against all betting odds, lived quite happily. Roger's natural charm quickly led to him being promoted to captain. He was rarely at Wentworth Hall, but he sent long letters home detailing his many adventures, just as Will had once done.

In the spring of 1825, Will Darby was happier than he'd ever been in his life, even during the years he'd spent exploring the far corners of the world. He and Phoebe had spent their honeymoon in Paris, but Will seemed to have lost his wanderlust. There were more important things to him now. His daughter, Cassandra, named after Phoebe's mother. And of course his darling wife, Phoebe, who delighted him every single day.

He realized, one afternoon when he was riding back from Greenhill on Apollo's back—the only horse he'd managed to salvage from the wild herd—that he had the life his father had always wanted for him. He was happy. He was content.

It was a beautiful day—the wildflowers were in full bloom, the air was crisp and clear, and Will wanted to share it with his family. He handed Apollo to the stable boy and strode inside Wentworth Hall. "Phoebe!" he shouted from the foyer.

Farley was there to greet him, bowing low before Will tossed his hat and gloves to him. "She is in the nursery, my lord, and begs you remember Lady Cassandra's nap time."

As if he could forget. Will grinned at Farley and took the stairs two at a time. When he opened the door of the nursery, he was instantly met with a strong *"Ssh"* issued by his wife.

"She's sleeping," she whispered. She kissed Will, then took him by the hand and led him to the cradle. They stood together, leaning over the rail and staring down at the angelic face of Cassandra Elaine Darby.

Phoebe pulled him away again, winking at the wet nurse who sat reading nearby, and drew Will along into the adjoining suite of rooms. When she had shut the door quietly behind him, Will grabbed her up and kissed her lustily, smothering her with kisses.

"Your daughter is beautiful," Phoebe said between kisses.

"So is her mother."

"She needs a brother and you need an heir."

Will reared back and looked into Phoebe's pale blue eyes. "Phoebe, darling, you needn't worry about that now," he said laughingly.

"Why not?" she asked, sliding her hand down from his waist. "Cassandra is ten months old," she said as she cupped him, squeezing him through his trousers.

Will sucked in a breath through his teeth. "What are you about, minx?"

"I want more," she said with a grin. "I want cherubs like Cassandra to fill our house. I want a house full of our children," she said, and slipped her hand into the waist of his trousers.

Will grit his teeth as she began to rub him.

"Give me babies, Will," she said with a lusty glimmer in her eye. "Give them to me right now."

He grinned. "Phoebe, love of my life, I will give you anything. Anything your heart desires." And true to his word, he took his wife to bed that beautiful spring afternoon and fulfilled her heart's desire.